GEOFFREY JENKINS

In Harm's Way

FONTANA/Collins

First published by William Collins Sons & Co. Ltd 1986
First issued in Fontana Paperbacks 1987

Made and printed in Great Britain by
William Collins Sons & Co. Ltd, Glasgow

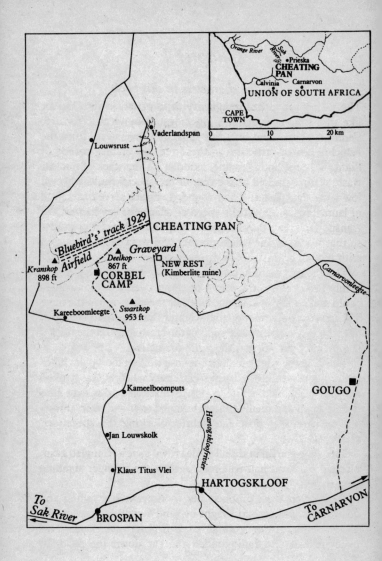

Chapter 1

The racing car jerked convulsively, leapt, arced into the air like the spine of a prisoner interrogated by electric torture. Fenders, bonnet and boot lids separated themselves from the vehicle's central structure and resorted to a clumsy parody of flight. Wheels, body, engine, skidded off the stack of nuclear waste drums stacked at the rear of the special multi-wheeled low-level transporter. Their rounded surface served as a kind of launching-ramp. At the speed at which the car had hit the transporter's rear, they acted as a catapult to project it upwards, so that it missed the cab altogether and went high. It carried with it a tail of dust, like a drunken comet.

The monitoring TV cameras held the cartwheeling object firmly dead-centre; the group of about twenty-five onlookers could make their own choice whether the close-up on the huge TV screens, only fractionally brighter than the hard sunlight, or their own long-distance sight of the crash itself on the track's shimmering surface was the more dramatic.

The airborne wreck made a one-in-a-million four-point landing on its wheels at the track's extremity where it was flanked by low black and white concrete markers. It sprang into the air again and finally thump-bumped over and over, throwing up clouds of dust and debris, blocking the spectators' view.

The only woman in the all-male crowd gave a strangled gasp, blacked out, and half-collapsed against the stranger standing next to her.

Dr Kepler West grabbed her to prevent her falling and missed the split-second sleight-of-hand switch of view on the TV monitors from ground to helicopter overhead. This machine had also radio-guided the car down the dead-flat track; it ran straight as an arrow and vanished into the mirage-blurred distance.

It was the first time the track had felt the bite of a racing car's wheels in nearly sixty years.

That occasion in the past had been to try to prove that the British racing ace, Sir Malcolm Campbell, was the fastest man in the world on wheels in his speedster *Bluebird*; the present was to prove that the transportation of nuclear waste by road was safe by surviving a high-speed crash with impunity. A section of *Bluebird*'s old track had been pressed into service for the demonstration.

The track was eighteen kilometres long on the billiard-table surface of a giant pan in semi-desert country some seven hundred and fifty kilometres north of Cape Town, South Africa. Known as Verneuk Pan – Cheating Pan – it had an iron-hard surface area of some five hundred square kilometres and was selected by Campbell as the best site in the world for his record attempt. It is situated at the northern extremity of a huge, almost level, almost waterless plain stretching northwards from the mountains of the Western Cape. The nearest town is two hundred and fifty kilometres away. The entire landscape is a complex of pans, big and small, of which Verneuk Pan is the largest. The name Verneuk means Cheating. It derives from the blinding heat mirages which have conned men to their deaths from thirst, even as close as half a kilometre from the edge of the Pan itself.

Campbell and *Bluebird* were also lesser victims of this cheating: he had to make his record attempt runs soon after daylight to try and avoid the mirages. In the event, he failed to break the record, which then stood at three hundred and seventy kilometres an hour.

Nearly sixty years ago, the eyes of the world were fixed on Cheating Pan through a corps of international pressmen housed in a camp near the Pan's edge. Today, after the intervening years had been swallowed without trace by the stark, savage, sparsely-populated countryside, treeless, its wind-and-sand-contorted black basalt outcrops testifying to still greater sterility below the surface, the world's attention was back on

Cheating Pan. Twenty-five members of the Vienna-based International Atomic Energy Agency and associated nuclear bodies – from France, Britain, the USA and China, but not the Soviet Union – were on an eight-day inspection tour of the area. Target of their visit was a nuclear waste repository – a 'nuclear dustbin' it had been dubbed by the media – in the process of being established by South Africa near the Pan. Approval by the international body was a prerequisite for going ahead with the project.

It was these delegates, plus the representatives of other expert bodies – the US Department of Energy, Radchem, a leading German nuclear waste company, British Nuclear Fuels, the China Nuclear Energy Industry Corporation, and South Africa's Nuclear Development Corporation, Nucor, who witnessed the crash demonstration. The international team was housed in the remains of Campbell's old camp, now renovated, and renamed Corbel Camp after a distinctive local stone 'beehive'-style architecture.

The young woman's eyes were open, staring. It was the look of horror in them, a window into some trauma or nightmare, which stopped Kepler West from calling immediately for help from the nearest bystanders. These were a little apart from them; their attention was still riveted on the crash. It was this gap in the crowd which had brought Kepler West to the spot in the first place; it was neither by desire nor design that he had positioned himself next to the only woman there. And a very attractive one at that, as one corner of his brain now registered – long auburn hair which targeted itself on her left breast, and wide, disturbing eyes whose greenness was now opaque and unseeing from the shock erupting in them. Due to his late arrival, at the first likely spot in the crowd he had simply jumped out of the car which had hurriedly collected him from the runway – instead of joining the President of the IAEA, Professor Louis Jaboulet of France, and other VIPs as he should have done. The whole show had been waiting for him: without him neither the international focus of attention nor crash demonstration would have been possible.

Thirty-five-year-old Dr Kepler West, an Australian geo-chemist, had made a top secret discovery which would revolutionize the disposal of nuclear waste – 'radwaste', as it is known scientifically. He had invented a man-made artificial rock matrix for the safe containment of radwaste. This was in contrast to the conventional methods employed of burying radwaste in metal, ceramic or glass containers. His discovery was named SYNROC-R – Synthetic Rock Radionuclide. It was a safe containment substance whose rate of decay was known and could be monitored. The lack of this in usual disposal methods for radwaste was a major hazard and disadvantage.

SYNROC-R was a manufactured substance; South Africa had established a pilot plant for its production adjacent to its first nuclear power station near Cape Town. Serious teething-troubles at the plant until that very morning had delayed Kepler West – at one stage it had seemed that the IAEA inspection might even be jeopardized – but he had succeeded in righting matters. Production was now running smoothly, and the first shipments were due to flow to the repository near Cheating Pan in two days' time. A special light aircraft had been standing by to fly him from Cape Town to the IAEA gathering; he had arrived as the crash demonstration had been about to begin; the controlling helicopter was already hovering in position.

As his machine had come in to land on a section of *Bluebird*'s track not occupied by the demonstration, he had seen the flatbed transporter standing forlornly among black and white concrete markers and empty radwaste drums like a bull awaiting the slaughterhouse. A hill blocked the far end of the track; there was another to one side about three kilometres away which was fronted by a stone wall and backed by a graveyard. Out of the scatter of headstones rose, incongruously, a beehive-domed stone building in the characteristic local corbelled style – a lying-in hut for bodies, presumably.

Kepler's aircraft had nudged underneath the helicopter; he had seen the upturned, expectant faces of the crowd; a car had whipped him away even as his pilot had pulled aside to allow the show to start.

Focus and sense started to flow back into the young woman's eyes and Kepler felt her muscles begin to come alive again under the loose, boldly-flowered patterned green jacket she wore to match olive-green slacks and a cream and brown blouse. She straightened from the position in which she had sagged against him.

She still seemed not to grasp that she was back in the present. 'Is he dead?' she whispered. 'He looks so . . . so crumpled . . .'

Kepler released her. 'No one is hurt,' he said quietly. The agony in her eyes was dimming. 'The crash was only play-play. No persons were involved. The car was remote-controlled from the air.'

She shook her head as if trying to clear away the cobwebs of nightmare from her brain. 'I'm sorry,' she said mechanically, 'I'm sorry – who are you?'

Kepler decided to pull her back to reality as speedily as he could: she seemed about to collapse.

He said, with a reassuring laugh, 'It was all a big shop-window – a very expensive piece of entertainment for the first day of the IAEA delegates' visit. I don't go along with it. It told them nothing about what they have come all this way to see. It's in the same category as that spectacular staged by the British power industry a couple of years back when they crashed a driverless train into a nuclear flask just to demonstrate to the public that it was safe. That exhibition cost over three million rand.'

The woman was very pale, and her eyes went round the crowd, to the transporter, and across the horizonless emptiness of the Pan as if to reassure herself.

'Please get me out of here,' she half-whispered. 'I am sorry to have embarrassed you. Take me home, please.'

'Home – where is home?' He made an all-embracing gesture to take in the great pan with *Bluebird*'s track stretching away into eternity.

'Corbel Camp.'

'Shall I find your husband?'

'I am not the wife of one of the delegates. I own Corbel Camp.'

'I see. My car's quite close – can you manage to walk?' He moved as if to take her arm.

She evaded the gesture. 'I'm okay.'

Because of his late arrival, Kepler's driver had left the car in which he had picked him up from the plane close by and not among the other official vehicles further off. He himself had joined the other drivers watching the show.

They turned to go.

'I'm Rencha Krummect,' she said, as if she grudged a necessary explanation.

'Kepler West,' he responded.

Her acute glance at the strong face, with its wirecut, somewhat untidy full black beard, black eyebrows and inscrutable eyes beneath, showed that she knew his importance.

'You can't leave. It's your big show.'

'I told you what I thought of it.'

'I can get someone else to take me.'

'Come.'

They walked towards the car.

The spectators had a new sight on the track to keep their attention off the departing pair. A radio-controlled drone 'crawler' started nosing about the wreck of the car and the transporter. It was based on the type of British Army bomb disposal robot used against suspected IRA targets in Northern Ireland and adapted to the examination of radwaste drums in the event of a real road accident.

One man in the crowd, however, had missed nothing of the minor drama of Rencha's collapse or their departure. He had, in fact, been keeping her under observation all morning, and when she had fallen sideways against Kepler West, he had given a cynical little smile to himself. He was a stocky little man with a neat oval face, short-cropped hair, and typical French moustache. He seemed as if he would look best in a black tie in a champagne advertisement. His grip on the bottle, however, with his muscular shoulders, might have revealed to a shrewd observer that he knew more about handling a rugby ball than a magnum – he had once played scrumhalf for France. And the way he hovered on the edge of the subsequent scene between Rencha and Kepler might have reminded the observer of a scrumhalf waiting for the ball from the ruck. Had he intervened, he might have put himself offside.

His name was Henri Bossiere. He was a colonel in French Intelligence.

Chapter 2

Bossiere watched Kepler West and Rencha Krummect walk towards Kepler's car. He was overcome by a sense of unreality. Not only to his outward vision – he found himself blinking repeatedly against the strange light which undulated off the Pan's surface with a superbright, unreal movement – but from an inner disbelief at the sight of Rencha Krummect. It dated from the moment late the previous afternoon after he and the other IAEA delegates had been ferried in from Cape Town in a big Hercules L100 aircraft. The machine's short take-off and ruggedness made it ideal for using *Bluebird*'s track on Cheating Pan as a makeshift runway. They had been driven to Corbel Camp, four kilometres away, and introduced to its owner and hostess for the IAEA gathering, Rencha Krummect.

Both her name and status were a fake.

The woman now getting into Kepler's car was the most wanted terrorist courier in Europe.

Her real name was Anna-Kai Cerny. She was a Czech-Hungarian who French Intelligence – the famous DST – had hunted for years. Bossiere had led the hunt. She was also a top priority suspect on Uclat's – French Anti-Terrorist Co-ordination Unit – list.

Involuntary shock had half-sent Bossiere's hand plunging into the inner pocket of his jacket – not for his gun, which lived there, as close as his shirt – but for the only positive clue to the identity of the mysterious terrorist courier the DST had. His wallet contained an indistinct photograph of the woman (Bossiere could not think of her as Rencha Krummect but only as Anna-Kai Cerny) taken years previously in half-darkness outside a Paris Metro station in the rain. The face, younger then and scared, but unmistakable because of its beauty and large slanting eyes, was half-turned from the camera and the lower part by the raincoat collar. A long sheaf of hair, from under a beret, had escaped and fallen down to her left breast. She wore it the same way still.

The DST's net had been closing on her, and Bossiere knew when he had been given the photograph that it was only a matter of time before he pulled her in.

But the net never closed. Anna-Kai Cerny vanished, as if she had never been.

Bossiere had anticipated her capture as the way in to France's most mysterious and dangerous terrorist group, the Bakunin Movement. This organization took its name from the nineteenth-century Russian anarchist Mikhil Akun. In one year alone it had been responsible for fourteen serious explosions in the Paris area, but the DST, Uclat and the French police had been completely baffled in trying to trace the bombers. From the nature of the blasts, the DST believed that the movement was composed of militant anarchists who had undergone special training in carrying out sophisticated explosives attacks.

Even as he had stumbled out a greeting to Rencha – he had spoken in French and she had replied in the same language – the Bakunin connection with South Africa had flashed through Bossiere's mind. Its hostility towards South Africa was well established. In 1982, Bossiere had recalled, the Bakunins had threatened the French government itself with retaliation if it dared to go ahead with plans to sell South Africa a second nuclear power station – the country's first, French-designed, power plant was in operation at Koeberg, near Cape Town. It was from Koeberg, with its satellite SYNROC-R pilot plant, that Kepler West had flown to Cheating Pan for the crash demonstration.

Now Bossiere's hand plucked unconsciously at an uneven patch of skin on his face where his razor always missed the bristles in shaving. It looked as if his jaw had once been broken and had mended askew. It had. A Bakunin booby-trap had gone off in his face. Bossiere's eyes were unsighted at the antics of the robot drone as it climbed up the back of the flatbed transporter and seemed to sniff among the nuclear waste drums like a dog, raising a laugh from the spectators. They did not even seem to wince from the iridescent light lancing back from millions of tiny stones – black, indigo, slate and coral – with which the surface of the Pan was covered.

They were blazing with an inner fire of their own, a kill-lust.

It was directed at a sandy-haired, tall, youngish man in a loose windcheater, cigarette in mouth, standing in a group with two Chinese whom Bossiere knew as Professor Chillun To and Dr Chang Nakanishi. They were Red China's representatives on the IAEA and members of the China Nuclear Energy Industry Corporation. With them was another man whose Fu Manchu-type beard and moustache might have passed him off as Chinese, except that Bossiere knew he was a German, forty-five-year-old Dr Erich Waldegg. Dr Waldegg, logged Bossiere's computer-like mind for facts and figures, was head of the giant nuclear chemical concern named Radchem, based in Dusseldorf. Radchem acted as agents in Europe for Chinese nuclear interests.

The man standing there had been Bossiere's second stunning shock of the previous evening after Rencha Krummect. When the man had come into dinner, late, with Dr Waldegg, Bossiere's gun-hand had leapt again to his inner pocket. This time it was not for his wallet. It was for his pistol. For one blinding, out-of-control flash his hand had been on the butt of the weapon in order to gun down the newcomer on the spot. The effort of getting control of himself had been so great that it had drained his face of colour and left his trigger-finger muscles twitching. Poison from a decade of revenge-lust against the latecomer had so infected the normally suave DST operative that he had almost triggered his pistol before he knew what he was doing.

Ten years before, Jean Ledoux had stopped at a pavement café in Paris and emptied the magazine of a UZI sub-machine-gun into the faces of three of Bossiere's unarmed DST colleagues as they had sat having an evening glass of wine on their way home from work. When, a little later, Bossiere had seen the mangled and bloodied remains of his friends, he had wept. He had also vowed that if it took him all his life, he would have his revenge against Ledoux.

The wallet containing Rencha's photograph also housed one of Ledoux. It was right that it should be there with hers. For Ledoux was now the leader of the Bakunin Movement. This photograph showed two men in Arab dress walking the deck of a ship. One of them was Ledoux. The other was the notorious international terrorist, Carlos the Jackal.

The photograph had been achieved by Israeli Intelligence, the Mossad, and passed on to Bossiere. The date was 1982, after members of the Palestine Liberation Organization pulled out of West Beirut. In all, thirty international terrorists had fled on that occasion.

The ship, Bossiere had established later, had conveyed the terrorists to South Yemen, and Carlos and Ledoux had spent some time in exile together on a small island off the Yemeni coast before Carlos went into permanent exile on the Soviet-controlled island of Socotra, off the Horn of Africa. Ledoux vanished.

Ledoux was a past master at disappearing. It was part of the man, as idiosyncratic as his bombing style, as distinctive (Bossiere had told himself) as fingerprints. His first vanishing act had been when he had, as a very young dropout, been wanted for killing a French policeman who had followed up a lead after a bank robbery. On that occasion Ledoux, whose mother was Spanish, had escaped to Spain with her help under the name of Ramon Ruiz. There he had joined the Basque terrorist guerrillas, called the ETA. From them, Ledoux learned the 'art' of interrogation, of twisting a prisoner's arm into confession.

Bossiere, in pursuing his vendetta against Ledoux, had gone into every aspect of the terrorist, including his psychological make-up. Ledoux had always been a natural rebel. But there was a certain mental quality about him which set him apart from the plain killer-thug which caused him to try and rationalize his own deep inner guilt feelings. He had always idolized anarchists, and somewhere along the line Mikhil Akun had swum into his ken. Ledoux had seized upon him as a rationale for his way of life.

Ledoux, alias Ramon Ruiz, had made Spain too hot for himself and, using his Spanish name and passport, had fled to the Argentine. Here he had come into his own with the infamous military regime which had been responsible for the undercover deaths of thousands of Argentinians before the Falklands War. The post-military regime had unearthed the remains of over six thousand unidentified bodies which had been tortured to death by special squads of 'interrogators'. Ledoux had been a leading member of one of these death squads and had brought torture to a fine art.

Before the Falklands War in 1982, Ledoux had been tipped off that he was due for elimination, and had fled one step ahead of retribution. He had amassed a fair amount of money from the assets of his victims. He had gravitated to West Beirut, hide-out of Yasser Arafat.

By this time, not only Bossiere but the Mossad wished to question Ledoux about his association with Carlos the Jackal. But, after South Yemen, Ledoux sank out of sight.

A year later, Bossiere knew his man was back in France. A bomb had exploded aboard the Paris–Toulouse express, killing five people. The explosion bore all the hallmarks of Ledoux's methods; that it was him was reinforced by a description from a passenger who had seen a man in heated discussion over a briefcase shortly before the blast. The Bakunin Movement, shadowy and elusive as ever, subsequently claimed responsibility for the attack.

At Corbel Camp the previous night, Bossiere's reaction had been so noticeable that Professor Jaboulet, the French President of IAEA, had asked him whether he was feeling ill. Professor Jaboulet was, of course, aware of the fact that Bossiere was a DST operative who had been insinuated into the team of three official French representatives for security purposes. Bossiere had excused himself from the table, gone outside and got a grip on himself, his mind in turmoil. Either he killed Ledoux there and then, or – his long training and background pulled him back on to the rails – he found out what he (and Rencha) were up to.

What could be the Bakunin target at Cheating Pan?

The annihilation of twenty-five of the world's top nuclear waste scientists? The radwaste repository which was situated not at Cheating Pan itself but fifty air-kilometres away at a place called Gougo?

Should he report Ledoux's presence to South African Security? What concrete evidence could be produced – if he did so – regarding Ledoux's true identity? He felt sure that Ledoux's credentials as a member of the Radchem team would be watertight. Ledoux's alias was Carl Lentz. There was no language problem – Ledoux spoke fluent French, German, English and Spanish.

Bossiere knew that South African Security had concentrated its men at the Gougo repository – the logical thing to do – and had left only a token force of several men at Corbel Camp. Besides, it was not Bossiere's way to run off to the nearest security outfit. He had paddled his own canoe and had been on Ledoux's trail for a long, long time. Overriding everything was his burning desire for personal revenge against Ledoux – how could strangers understand his inner motives? They had never seen his friends' mashed-in faces after the murder. A security alert at this stage might only put Ledoux and the Bakunin on their guard . . . how far, too, were Dr Waldegg and the German Radchem team implicated in what he felt sure was going on?

Bossiere made up his mind to go it alone. He went back to dinner.

Now, at the crash demonstration on *Bluebird*'s track, Bossiere kept his eyes on the Radchem-Chinese group. Apart from another German, Dr Günter Dieckmann, there was a man whose youth made him more Ledoux's companion than the others. He had been the third of the trio which had come in late to dinner when Bossiere had undergone his Ledoux shock. His name was Ernst Fichte. Bossiere had learned this when he had circulated briefly on a social get-together after the previous night's meal. He, Ledoux and Dr Waldegg had not been on the plane with the other IAEA delegates and himself from Cape Town. They had come by station wagon from up-country after a flying visit ahead of the rest of the IAEA to South Africa's famous game reserve, the Kruger National Park. Was that fact in itself suspicious? Bossiere had asked himself during a night in which he had slept fitfully.

During the demonstration, Bossiere had been on the lookout for any sign of collusion between Ledoux and Rencha as he had to learn to call her. There was none. But then, there wouldn't be, between such professional operators as Bakunins. He wondered how Rencha had engineered it to be alone and just at the right spot to put on her passing-out act for Kepler West's benefit. He had to admit, it had been very smartly done. It had paid off, too. She was now on her way – alone – to Corbel Camp with the most distinguished scientist in the gathering.

Was he the Bakunin target? Bossiere found himself sweating for a moment and then dismissed his hypersensitive fears. Not even a Bakunin would stick a gun into a VIP's side and pull the trigger on a public road which a score of people would travel shortly on their way back to the camp from the demonstration.

Besides, Bossiere argued intuitively, it wouldn't be Rencha but Ledoux who would do the dirty work. He looked across again at the relaxed figure with the Radchem men. He couldn't see Ledoux's eyes at the distance and behind dark glasses as he had done when he had met him the previous evening – eyes almost devoid of all pigmentation under pale eyebrows, so light that you lost yourself and were swindled by their amorphous depths – like Cheating Pan itself, Bossiere told himself fancifully. With his longish, hooked nose, he might have got away with posing as an Arab under traditional headdress in the Mossad photograph of himself and Carlos aboard ship. Bossiere wondered where Ledoux kept his gun in that loose windcheater, worn with casual blue pants and an open shirt. There would be one, for sure. Ledoux, he reminded himself over and over, would be a tough nut to crack.

Rencha was his soft option. Bossiere resolved to go for Rencha.

Chapter 3

'It's the biggest bastard piece of outback this side of the black stump that I've ever seen.'

Kepler let go of the steering wheel with one hand and gestured. Cheating Pan's shimmering nothingness absorbed the taunt and the Australian idiom with as little reaction as it had done in lapping up the sun for a million years.

Kepler's remark seemed to pass Rencha by, too. Had he been in the car with the two of them, Bossiere would have been disappointed at Rencha's follow-through after her brilliantly-executed 'getting-to-know' feminine ploy. It was, in fact, nil. She sat silent and withdrawn – and still a little pale – in the passenger's seat, staring sightlessly at the Pan's heat-struck surface. They had left the crash site about a kilometre behind in the car's dust; there were about another three to go to Corbel Camp.

'There's no black stump – anywhere. There's nothing.' The double-take seemed prised out of her, reluctantly.

'The black stump is not for real – not even in Australia. It's a way of speaking,' he answered. 'It stands for a kind of symbol of immense distance – horizonless. Beyond are the gibber plains, treeless and waterless. I guess the guy who coined the phrase must have seen Cheating Pan beforehand.' He tried, unsuccessfully, to jolly her out of her dark mood.

'It's a good thing, in a way. You can lose yourself. Men have.'

'And women?'

She did not miss the innuendo, nor the sympathy. And she needed that, after the empty years. She pulled her glance away from the reflecting earth. Kepler's beard seemed the blacker by contrast. She wondered why his moustache grew only in the centre of his upper lip, leaving the corners untouched.

She jerked out. 'You wonder why I flaked out. My husband was killed in a car crash. The demonstration reminded me of it.'

'Long ago?'

Kepler realized immediately that he had said the wrong thing. Her face turned away again. She clammed up.

'Three years – a little more.'

'I asked because I was at Cheating Pan long before there was anything here. All I recall is one ruined stone hut where Corbel Camp now stands. It was once Sir Malcolm Campbell's racing headquarters, wasn't it?'

'So they say.'

As if she herself were aware of the offhandedness of her answer, she added, 'The first time I ever saw Corbel Camp, it was very much as you describe. You see, my husband was an architect and was very interested in the corbelled style you get in these parts. It is unique.'

'In what way?'

'It's a throwback thousands of years to megalithic builders on the shores of the Mediterranean. There are no trees or timber here. So instead the earliest settlers used the big stone

23

slabs you'll see everywhere. What makes it interesting is that the pioneers had no tradition of corbelling. They were untaught. It just cropped up as the natural way to build.'

'The beehive-shaped roofs remind me of inverted egg-cups.'

She still seemed unwilling to be trapped into conversation. She added, deprecatingly, 'I don't know anything about it, really. I'm only quoting what I heard.'

'It wasn't quotes which built Corbel Camp. You did.'

'Corbel Camp was on its way out – until you made your discovery. The shoestring kept breaking. My idea was a tourist camp en route to the spring flowers of Namaqualand – with the tarnished glamour of *Bluebird*'s old record attempt as a makeweight for those who were daring enough to venture . . .' she paused and added '. . . this side of the black stump.'

He smiled, and his teeth seemed very white against the blackness of his beard. She noted that they were regular, with spaces in between. Maybe he should have been a doctor, not a geochemist. What was there about herself that required and responded to a doctor's sympathy? Charles Laroche had had it in good measure – she had been just nineteen when she had gone to live with him in Paris . . . She winced and turned away from Kepler as the black mood swept over her again like a tangible blow to the head. What can of maggots from her past had the sight of the crash opened again? Dr Charles Laroche was dead; she had picked him off the floor after the Bakunin messenger of death had put a bullet between his eyes as he opened the door. It had been the pay-off for Laroche's having helped a wounded man – he was unaware that he was a terrorist on the run – who had knocked him up late one night. The doctor had patched him up; the Bakunin had got their claws into him and had blackmailed him into using his surgery as a safe house. Blackmail, too, had forced her into becoming the movement's courier. When Laroche had decided he had had enough, he had paid the Bakunin price, death . . .

Rencha shivered. Kepler glanced acutely at her. As if he had picked up something of her vibes, he said, 'My discovery would never have happened if I'd gone ahead with my original career, which was medicine.'

So he, too, had been in medicine!

She tried to sidestep the darkness which had come at her like an incoming tide. 'What made you start as a doctor?'

'Father's footsteps, I suppose. He was one of Sydney's leading physician-specialists.'

The track made a sudden left-hander off Cheating Pan's smooth surface and the car bumped over terrain of a different sort – patches of low scrub called *ganna* locally, ruined anti-erosion works and walls.

'Why did you give it up?'

Rencha immediately became aware of a change in the man next to her. At her question, a sense of smouldering inner force seemed to invest his words, a potential locked away like – she found herself surprised at her own comparison – nuclear atoms awaiting a detonating trigger.

'Part of my final studies involved the treatment of cancer and leukæmia,' he replied. 'It was unfortunate for the professors that they chose a group of Aborigines with radiation burns as human guinea-pigs. They came from Maralinga . . .

'Maralinga is out in the Centre – sorry, I'm speaking Australian again. It's a remote Aboriginal settlement on the edge of the Great Victoria Desert about one thousand kilometres west of Adelaide.' Kepler's voice hardened. 'It's one of the places where the British carried out their atom bomb tests in Australia years ago.'

Perhaps it was the way Kepler put it, the power of that inner fire rising to the surface, that communicated itself to Rencha and sidelined for the moment her own tragedy.

'Were . . . were they an awful sight?'

'It's wasn't the sight, though that was bad enough. It was the cause.'

'You said it was British atom bomb testing.'

Kepler wrenched the wheel unnecessarily hard to avoid a pothole in the road.

'What I saw at the hospital – and what the doctors were trying to do – was merely mitigation after the event,' he went on. 'It was too late. Nuclear radiation had to be stopped *at its source*, long before it got as far as being a bomb. From the manufacture of bombs, and other sources like nuclear power stations, medicine and the rest, are being produced thousands of tons of nuclear waste – radwaste – which are an ever-growing threat to all of us. And the world doesn't know how to get rid of it. It cynically proposes to dump it as best it can – which is not very well – and wherever it can.'

Rencha speculated to herself what the name Kepler meant. It sounded German. Medieval saint – alchemist, perhaps.

'The damage I saw to the men from Maralinga made me give up medicine. My father accused me of being yellow, not being able to stand the sight of cancer. I took up geochemistry. That, in my view, and not medicine is the route to the *cause* of radiation.'

'So that is what led to your discovery?'

He laughed. 'Not just like that, I assure you! To all the doctors, including my father, I was a crazy nut – not worth a zac.'

'Zac?'

He snapped his fingers a little impatiently against the wheel. 'A damn, a cent, a sixpence. I decided to go and look for myself, tell Australia and the whole world about Maralinga. I soon found out something: nuclear radiation and atom tests in the outback were a hot potato, too hot for public discussion. Even in a city like Adelaide, which is the nearest big town to the test site of Maralinga. I have a sister living there. She came close to disowning me. The storm blew up into a hurricane when I went to Maralinga itself and found the bodies of six dead Aborigines in a crater. The authorities and public practically chased me out of South Australia.' His eyes flashed like a stop signal. Rencha could begin to understand how the conventions of medicine would have laced him in a strait-jacket.

'Maybe that was a good thing, as it turned out. I went on

from there to Western Australia. The British carried out other atom bomb tests at the Monte Bello Islands, off the coast of Western Australia.' He gestured at the stark landscape around them. 'Believe it or not, a low-lying collection of half-awash rocks over nine thousand kilometres from here had a big part in the story of my discovery at Cheating Pan.'

'How did all this fit in with your studies?' she asked. 'Somehow you seem to have found time to have become a distinguished geochemist.'

He smiled at her. 'I'm giving you rather a compressed time-wrap. It didn't happen all at once. It was spread over a matter of years. I took my degree and my doctorate, and was given a lectureship at the Australian National University in Canberra. Travel to the atom bomb test sites came in between. I'm surprised the university ever gave me the job – there was a lot of criticism in the media over my stand regarding the British atom tests. A great deal of public feeling was also generated. In fact, one night when I was working alone in my lab I was attacked by an unknown intruder because of it. After that, a police friend of mine taught me unarmed combat and how to use a gun. He'd been specially trained himself in Chicago by a crack anti-terrorist police unit.'

He had a strong athletic body, and she could believe that he kept himself in trim.

'The link between your Monte Bello Islands and Cheating Pan sounds like a detective story.' For the first time she smiled, but it only partially reached her shadowed eyes.

'The powers-that-be wouldn't let me near the Monte Bello Islands,' he resumed. 'My firebrand reputation had cast its shadow ahead. Looking back on the refusal, it seemed rather like the finger of fate. Because I couldn't go there, I headed instead for the desert area of Western Australia. It's called Kimberley – same as the South African Kimberley, and for the same reason – I wanted to examine some kimberlite deposits, what we call blue ground. Diamonds are found in it. It formed part of my geochemistry studies. However, before I reached the area I came across a sample of kimberlite at the

West Australian Institute for Technology which intrigued me. It was that sample which changed my life.'

Chapter 4

Ahead, a neat notice nailed to a wooden pole said, 'Corbel Camp'.

The light striking back from the score of white beehive stone huts was as hard as a neon-lit morgue slab. Some of the huts were grouped round a central stone complex of conventional design with a thatched roof (Rencha was to tell him later that it had been a farmhouse long ago) while others stood further away on hillocks of the black basalt ridges which were everywhere and formed a kind of flattish, raw, exposed platform in front of the main building. A wall of unmortared stone slabs fenced off the complex to one side: it had once formed part of a cattle enclosure. Adjacent to it and the farmhouse proper were two corbelled huts, one with the typical egg-shaped roof, about three times the height of a man, and the other with a rectangular, cut-off top. Some of the huts scattered about were taller than these two. A feature of all the huts, however, were the rows of stones which had been left to project from the upper walls and roof. These formed a kind of ready-made scaffolding or ladder for repairs and renovations.

As the car passed the signpost, Kepler asked, 'Your work?'

'My husband taught me to draw.'

There were further signposts dotted about, carrying hut numbers and direction arrows for the benefit of the IAEA delegates.

Kepler looked inquiringly at her for the way. She indicated the twin huts adjoining the central complex. To reach them, the car had to make its way round the buildings. The black rock platform fronting them was a scene of activity. Groups of men and women were piling wood at various points; there were also what looked like metal spits at intervals.

'What gives?' he asked.

'There's an entertainment tonight for the delegates,' she replied. 'What South Africans call a *braai* – a barbecue.'

'On spits?'

'It's a sheep barbecue,' she explained further. 'We'll have a whole sheep barbecued on each spit. The process takes about four or five hours. Guests circulate and take their wine or drinks with them, have a chat while the cooking proceeds. That's the drill.'

When he remained puzzled and a little doubtful, she added, 'I've got the best *braai* experts helping me. You see those three women there? They're local farmers' wives. One of them is Mrs Bonsma, whose husband's family has been in the Cheating Pan area for generations.'

They parked in a demarcated area near Rencha's twin huts. One was a sitting-room, leading in through a low door to her bedroom beyond.

When she had asked to be taken away from the demonstration, Rencha had had only one thought – to get away, to be alone, away from the sight which had seared her mind with recollections of the past. She had had no intention even of asking Kepler in. Now, however, she said, 'The sample that changed your life – you can't leave me hanging in mid-air like that. Come in and have a cup of tea and finish your story.'

They entered through a halved, stable-type door. The hut had only one small window, directly opposite the door. A timbered loft, occupying only half the roof space and reached by a flight of wooden steps, rose above their heads. The place was simply but tastefully furnished with cane furniture and bright rugs on the stone floor.

She went to a niche in the left-hand wall which seemed to have been specially built.

'Keeping-hole,' she explained. 'You'll have to get used to the Cheating Pan way of life. Keeping-holes are part of the original way corbelled huts were built. I keep special tea in mine.'

'Local too?'

'As a matter of fact, it is. It's called *Jacob-jong*, the real McCoy. I'll get some hot water from the kitchen – it's close.'

'When I first saw Corbel Camp, there wasn't a roof, let alone a kitchen,' he observed.

Kepler sat down in one of the comfortable cane armchairs. It was a feminine room, with cheerful curtains and chair covers and a rather surrealistic painting on one wall which could have been Cheating Pan under mirage – or anything at all. However, something was missing. Kepler was puzzled, then he had it. There was not one photograph, not even on a small writing desk. It was as if Rencha had wanted no trace of her past in her present.

She returned, dispensed the brew.

'If it tastes awful to you, don't be polite,' she said. 'It is, literally, not everyone's cup of tea.'

Kepler sipped cautiously. 'The taste is better than the bouquet – the way some wines are.'

'I'm glad. It's supposed to bring good health. It's used in these parts for all sorts of ills. If you don't like it as tea, you can use it as an eye-wash.'

She had regained her colour, and taken off her loose-fitting flowered jacket. Her breasts were prominent under that cream-and-brown shirt blouse. She sat on a high-backed chair at the small desk.

'That sample which changed your life,' she prompted him.

'Kimberlite – blue ground,' he repeated. 'There was a note with the sample at the West Australian Institute which said that it had been found by Sir Malcolm Campbell while hunting for a treasure hoard buried by the notorious seventeenth-century pirate, Captain Kidd, on the Cocos Keeling and Monte Bello Islands.'

'Sir Malcolm Campbell – the same racing ace who was here at Cheating Pan?'

'The same.'

'I had no idea that he was a treasure-hunter. I thought his life was devoted to high-speed cars.'

'So did I – until I began researches after I'd got back to Canberra.'

'I notice Monte Bello crops up again.'

'You're going too fast,' he remarked.

'If I'd only known about Campbell for the benefit of my tourists . . .' She got up, went to the keeping-hole again, and came to him carrying a tiny teddy-bear.

'Mister Whoppit – Campbell's lucky mascot for *Bluebird*'s attempt,' she said. 'His son, Donald Campbell, also carried it when attempting the world's water speed record, and his granddaughter Gina reckoned it saved her life in 1984 when her speedboat – also named *Bluebird* – flipped only moments after she had broken the women's water speed record. Mister Whoppit was thrown clear of the boat with her.'

'Is this really Campbell's own original mascot?'

'Sorry, no, I'm giving the wrong impression. I made replicas to give away as part of the Campbell legend at Cheating Pan. My tourists loved them.'

'May I have this?'

She eyed him for a moment and then her voice, which had become animated and full of interest a moment before, went flat and distant. 'If you wish. It's my own.'

'That would make it – special.'

She sat down again, avoiding his eyes. 'You were telling me, Campbell was a treasure-hunter.'

'Here's the replay. It took me a lot of delving into the past to unearth Campbell's love of treasure-hunting. But I did, and I memorized his own words – "I am sure there is nothing as fascinating as hunting for buried treasure. There is a lot of it hidden all over the globe, waiting for some adventurous soul to find it."'

'Monte Bello,' she murmured.

'That's what flashed through my mind when I saw the sample first.'

31

'Still, I don't know where Cocos is.'

'It is also off Western Australia, but well offshore – quite far out in the Indian Ocean, in fact.'

'Did Campbell visit Cocos?'

'Yes, he did. I managed to check. He described the "haunted atmosphere" of the place.'

'Did he find anything of Captain Kidd's treasure?'

'No. But I found a bigger treasure in the form of his sample.'

'Go on.'

'You see, I had a hunch about that sample from the moment I first saw it. I can't explain it – something intuitive, unconscious, call it what you will. The West Australian Institute was simply not interested – it had lain about there for years. They had no objections whatever to my taking it back to Canberra. There I found under scientific examination that it wasn't only kimberlite. It contained two minerals with a metallic lustre I couldn't identify. They *looked* like ilmenite and rutile . . .'

'You're talking to a mere layman,' she reminded him. He was pleased to see that her interest and a faint smile had returned.

'Ilmenite and rutile are two minerals from which titanium, the space-age metal, is derived,' he explained. 'But my two were more than black like rutile and ilmenite, and distinctly lighter in colour. However, I didn't have the equipment at Canberra – or anywhere else in Australia, for that matter – to prove my hunch. The kind of electron microbeam analysis techniques for that sort of thing you'll find only in the United States. So I sent my samples off to Los Alamos in New Mexico, to the University of Massachusetts, and to the Geophysical Laboratory at the Carnegie Institution in Washington.'

'It sounds terribly high-powered,' she observed. 'You must have led a very full life.'

'It all took time, of course,' he went on. 'I'm giving you another condensed time-wrap. While the two minerals were being subjected to the most stringent investigations in the United States, I made a journey to the Cocos Islands to try and track down the source of Campbell's sample. There was not a trace of kimberlite on the islands. My journey was a saga in itself – I won't bore you with the details.

'But when I got back to Canberra, I received preliminary reports from the United States . . . the two nodules were minerals new to science!

'Next, I *had* to explore Monte Bello and check it out there. I was in a fever of excitement, but officialdom thought otherwise, in the light of my public comments about the British atom bomb tests in the islands years before. Every trick of red tape was tried to block me. Finally, however, I won my clearance. I had no idea of what I was going to. I found a scatter of half-awash islets stretching for fifty kilometres. The highest of them had cliffs only twelve metres high. There were some stunted, low bushes and no fresh water at all. I took one look at them and knew that kimberlite never originated from Monte Bello – they were all limestone and coral.

'I returned to Canberra and resumed my detective work. I was certain now that the note with the sample was wrong. Where, though, had Campbell found the kimberlite? The scientific world was buzzing with my discovery – it is not every day that anyone finds one mineral, let alone two, unknown to science.

'I gave the minerals names – I christened one lindsleyite and the other mathiasite. Professor Donald Lindsley was a famous American geochemist, and Professor Morna Mathias an equally noted South African who had done magnificent pioneer work on the type of rock my discoveries came from . . .'

'A woman!' exclaimed Rencha.

He grinned. 'Of course, the discovery provoked jealousies. One scientist even tried to debunk it by saying the two were in fact a related mineral called priderite which came from the Kimberley region of Western Australia itself. I'm glad I didn't know that at the time I saw Campbell's sample first in Western Australia – it might have confused the issue.'

'But *where* did Campbell's sample originate?' To Rencha it seemed that the scientist's eyes had become more inscrutable than before; she noticed for the first time the deep scoring of flesh between them.

His laugh broke his concentrated look. 'I guess I know more about Campbell's racing career than any man living. I tracked down every location he'd ever been in – an in-depth investigation. One place stood out – the track where he had made his attempt on the world land speed record in 1929.'

'Cheating Pan,' she said softly.

He inclined his head in agreement. 'I said, Corbel Camp wasn't like it is today, when eventually I got here. Some ruined stone structures, remnants of the place where Campbell and the world's press congregated. There was not a soul here either – just a vast, waterless, hostile stretch of sand reaching into eternity. The nearest habitation was about ten kilometres south of the Pan, a place called *Kareeboomleegte* . . .'

'Karee Tree Hollow, it's the Bonsmas' place still,' interjected Rencha. 'Remember – it's the Bonsmas who are helping me with the barbecue?'

'I struck out on to the Pan. I carried my own food, water and tent,' went on Kepler. '*Bluebird*'s track was there, just as it is today. There were piles of flints alongside it, millions of them. Campbell maintained that they would cut *Bluebird*'s thin tyres. So they were removed by hand. It cost him thousands to engage teams of locals for the task.'

'Those heaps are still there,' remarked Rencha.

'Except they weren't flints, as Campbell thought,' said Kepler. 'Some of the so-called flints were kimberlite. They finally proved to contain nodules of mathiasite and lindsleyite. I made an inspired guess that this could be so, and, working on that assumption, went on to locate the main kimberlite deposit on the south-eastern edge of the Pan. That's where we're doing our open-cast mining now – at New Rest.' He drained his cup. 'That's the story. The rest you know.'

'I certainly don't!' she exclaimed. 'How, for instance, did SYNROC-R come to be born and how did it get into orbit? How does South Africa come to be pioneering your discovery when you are an Australian? What about your own people? I'd like to know what the significance is of mathiasite and lindsleyite in regard to SYNROC-R . . .'

He smiled wryly. 'So would a lot of people! However, broadly speaking, my two new minerals have a special structural ability to act as host to positively-charged ions, which include radio-active material which is discarded during manufacturing processes, as well as rare earths and akalies . . .'

'You're talking right over my head!'

'Sorry. What it means is, that using the two together with nuclear waste products, an artificial rock can be manufactured whose rate of decay is known, and can be monitored over a given time period. It is absolutely safe compared to the guesswork involved in using containers made of glass, metal or ceramics. Science simply doesn't know how other radio-active substances will act upon these kind of containers once they themselves start to break down.'

'You perfected this artificial rock – SYNROC-R?'

'That's it.'

'Just like that!'

He grinned. 'When I returned to Australia from Cheating Pan, I found that my popularity ratings by both the Aussie public and Canberra University had nosedived. I decided I was no longer welcome at home, and offered my discovery to South Africa – to Nucor, the Nuclear Development Corporation. They jumped at it. I returned to Cheating Pan with Nucor's top geologists and geochemists about six months afterwards.'

He regarded her acutely. 'On my first visit to Cheating Pan, there was nobody here, as I told you. But the second occasion, some restoration work was in progress on a couple of huts. The Nucor men and I were allowed by the builders to sleep in them. We stayed about ten days. I am puzzled that I missed seeing you.'

Rencha's eyes became wary. 'When exactly was this? I'm trying to figure how it fits in with my own arrival at Corbel Camp.'

'About three years ago, perhaps a little more.'

The mention of a specific date seemed to cause Rencha to

withdraw into herself. 'That would be about right,' she answered carefully. 'I wonder how I went through with it. It was pure heartbreak.'

Kepler considered her again. Corbel Camp wasn't her only heartbreak. She also seemed to stall deliberately about times.

She went on. 'I worked against time – tried to drive builders who did not wish to be driven – for six to eight months, I can't remember how long, in order to get Corbel Camp in a fit state for the following season's spring-flower tourists. To start with, there were only a couple of huts and the farmhouse central block. The place was never intended as more than a shoestring affair . . .'

'Yet – where were you when I came with the Nucor men?' he persisted.

'I had a spell in hospital. Pneumonia. It was caused either by the overwork, the tension, or the dust. I finished up in Carnavon, the nearest town, about two hundred and twenty kilometres away. That must have been why our paths didn't cross.'

Rencha seemed to be getting tenser. Then she broke out. 'Please don't ask me more about that time . . . it's something I prefer to forget.'

And a lot of other things, Rencha.

'I haven't been back in the meantime,' added Kepler. 'Setting up the SYNROC-R plant in conjunction with the nuclear power station at Koeberg has taken up all my time.'

'What I can't understand is why South Africa has established a second nuclear waste repository near Cheating Pan when they already have one in operation elsewhere, in Namaqualand?' asked Rencha.

'It's a good question,' replied Kepler. 'The first radwaste dustbin has been in use at Vaalputs – about three hundred kilometres west of here – for some years. But it is intended for conventional containment methods dating from before SYNROC-R – metal, glass and ceramics. Our new one at Gougo will be solely for SYNROC-R waste. There's no sense in mixing the two containment systems – it would only be self-defeating.

Even Blind Freddy could see that. We're gambling here with a time-ticket of one hundred thousand years, at least. Radwaste from the Koeberg power station as well as other – mainly medical – waste will be trucked specially to Gougo. It is the only repository of its kind in the world. The first transporter-load of SYNROC-R will leave for Gougo the day after tomorrow . . .'

There was a knock at the door.

It was Henri Bossiere.

Chapter 5

It was not kisses, but handcuffs, he should be slapping on those slender wrists and hands, Bossiere told himself as he introduced himself. But it was a kiss nevertheless he planted on Rencha's, with a mixture of impertinence and charm which is the hallmark of a French bachelor who has reached forty without being snared into matrimony.

'If this had happened to my hostess in France,' he said gallantly, speaking in English, 'I would have brought flowers, but in this god-forsaken place there is not a blade of grass, let alone a flower.'

His mouth pulled up leftwards, giving him a slightly questioning, insouciant air, like a wine steward querying a diner's choice of vintage. What neither Kepler nor Rencha could see was the scar underneath – a terrorist legacy – which no plastic surgeon's skill could conceal.

'Nothing happened really,' answered Rencha. 'Nothing.'

Bossiere still held her hand. She was beautiful, he told himself, how did she come to be mixed up with a shower like the Bakunin? On his way from the Pan to Corbel Camp, he had stopped and checked the photograph in his wallet. It *was* the same face. He'd never kissed the hand of a terrorist before, nor let a terrorist go free. Bossiere's heart turned to steel as he recalled the companion picture to Rencha's – Ledoux and Carlos the Jackal together, on the freighter's deck escaping from West Beirut . . .

'The President, Professor Jaboulet, who leads our French IAEA delegation, has also asked me to convey his felicitations for mademoiselle's recovery.'

Rencha was embarrassed. 'I didn't know I had attracted anyone's attention except . . .'

'Her bad turn didn't last more than a second or two,' interrupted Kepler.

Long enough to have established a relationship with the scientist who could turn out to be Number One Bakunin target, Bossiere thought cynically.

He said to Kepler, 'You are a lucky man, being in the right place at the right moment. I wish I had had the privilege of escorting such a beautiful young lady home.'

'Madame,' Rencha corrected him. 'Not mademoiselle.'

'Surely not!' the Frenchman protested. 'Such charm surely cannot go husbandless! And buried in such a place as Cheating Pan! I cannot believe it!'

Rencha switched into French. 'I lost my husband, that is why I am here. Corbel Camp was his brain-child before he was killed. That is what upset me. The crash reminded me of the accident.'

'You spoke to me in French last night, and I heard you speaking German to the West Germans.'

'I have an ear for languages. I have even learned to speak some elementary Afrikaans, which is the language of everyone round here.'

'Italian?'

'Yes.'

Bossiere fiddled with an affectation he wore in his jacket buttonhole, a little enamelled shamrock medallion. In a restaurant, it might have been his waiter's number. Here, it wasn't. It was an ultra-sensitive recording microphone. It was as if the DST man wanted to direct it still more accurately at Rencha so that there could be no mistake whatever about her own words and true identity. He knew he was hard on the trail.

'And not one language from behind the Iron Curtain to add to that formidable accomplishment?'

He had switched back into English; Bossiere had grabbed centre stage; he had not missed the relaxed atmosphere and teacups on his arrival. Rencha had been working fast. It had been a pity, in a way, to interrupt them, but he had to make doubly sure of the identity of the Bakunin woman.

'A few words of Czech and Hungarian – no more than a tourist courier would pick up,' she answered.

Bossiere had finally got the clincher – Anna-Kai Cerny! Nationality, Czech-Hungarian, her dossier recorded. Courier – of course she had lied. Not tourist, but terrorist. But she let slip the half-truth of saying she had been a courier. Her use of the word was her own gallows-drop.

Bossiere pushed his luck too far. 'Rencha – surely that is an unusual name? Not French?'

He could have bitten off his tongue. The presumption brought a coldness to her voice, a halt to her previous acceptance of his small flattery. He must find out how long she had been – without a man – at Corbel Camp.

'It was my late husband's name for me. He was South African. He liked it. I like it.'

'It suits an unusual person,' Bossiere tried to retrieve his mistake. 'It is altogether unusual, this Corbel Camp. We congratulate you on it – madame.'

'That is what I was saying in the car coming here,' added Kepler. 'You should have seen it as I did first: just a heap of ruined stones, not even a jackal nosing about.'

'You knew one another before, then?' If they had, he would have to do a hard rethink on a lot of things . . .

'No.' Kepler was rueful. 'You wouldn't think it possible in a remote spot like this for two people to miss meeting, but we did.'

'I was ill, I was in hospital,' Rencha cut in abruptly.

When had the DST lost track of Rencha, of Anna-Kai

Cerny? Bossiere asked himself. He wished he had her dossier in front of him to correlate the pieces of her time-place jigsaw. Perhaps there was not even a specific date for her disappearance from France; maybe there had been a gradual realization of it over months, years even.

Bossiere surreptitiously threw her another searching look. This was the woman in his picture all right. The too-large slanting eyes and generous mouth – a little wide for classic beauty but perfect for the balance and proportion of the cheekbones. He wished that the photograph had been in colour; there would be no mistaking her green eyes and auburn hair.

He addressed Kepler. 'I would like some time to hear about your great discovery from yourself,' he said with more politeness than sincerity. As a top Intelligence man, he was not likely to have neglected his homework about the track record of the most distinguished of a number of nuclear experts gathered at Corbel Camp.

'It sounds like a fascinating detective story,' said Rencha.

So, she'd got the story out of him already! All the pointers were there, Bossiere told himself. He had only to fill in some tantalizing gaps.

'Imagine spotting those two unknown minerals in what everyone regarded as piles of useless flints alongside *Bluebird*'s track,' she added.

Bossiere was surprised at the warmth in her voice. Be careful, little girl! Some spies get themselves emotionally involved with their would-be victims, and the result is hell.

Kepler laughed in a slightly embarrassed way, but Bossiere came to his rescue. 'More than ever, I should like to hear the story from you, Dr West.'

'There was luck in it . . . there always is, in something big,' Kepler answered.

'We will drink a glass of wine to that tonight at the . . . sheep roast . . .?'

Rencha laughed. 'Barbecue. Here they have the name, *braai*. They pronounce it to rhyme with "why".'

'*Braai.*' A South African would have cringed at the end result. They all laughed.

'Au revoir,' said Bossiere.

Kepler and Rencha stood for a moment after the Frenchman had gone. Neither wanted to break it up, neither knew what to say to keep it going.

Then Rencha said diffidently, 'Perhaps it would help if I told you about the accident which killed my husband. What I did say must have sounded very bald and ungrateful.'

'If it would help you.'

'It would help, does help, just to talk to you about it.' The skin on her face became strained, as if the tension inside her were pulling it taut. 'John and I were motoring down a steep pass in the Cape mountains called Bain's Kloof. It is a tremendous pass, with fantastic drops from the road. In places, the old stone walling along the verge had crumbled. It was raining, a little misty. The road was very slippery.

'At one of these spots, there was a bang. The next thing I knew was that the car was cartwheeling and thumping down the mountain-side – it sounded just like the car in the crash today. It finally came to a stop against an outcrop of rock. John was dead. I was unhurt. The police said a tyre had burst. A one-in-a-million accident.'

Except it had not been an accident. The Bakunin had not meant to kill John Krummect. Their target had been Rencha.

Chapter 6

The group did not look like angels of death with a seven billion dollar sidestake on the table.

And the scene was as incongruous to their project as Campbell's choice of Cheating Pan had been to his world record attempt.

That evening, the German Radchem troika – Dr Waldegg, Ledoux and Louis Maurette – stood, drinks in hand, at a fire over which a whole sheep was barbecuing over a spit. Ledoux passed under the name Carl Lentz, and his fellow-Bakunin, Maurette, as Ernst Fichte. As Bossiere guessed, the two men's credentials as members of the Radchem team were impeccable. With them were two men who did not need Dr Waldegg's Fu Manchu beard to assert their claims to Oriental origin: Professor Chillun To, a tubby little man who was sipping whisky, and Dr Chang Nakanishi, bald and remarkably tall for a Chinese, whose drink was fresh grape juice. Both were members of the China Nuclear Energy Industry Corporation, and as such official Red China representatives to the IAEA gathering. Dr Nakanishi was known in scientific circles for some outstanding work on kimberlite deposits at Yimeng, in China.

The cold of late autumn struck up from the black basalt platform fronting Corbel Camp; the dark had rushed ahead with almost undue haste as if it could not wait to demonstrate that stars could seem twice their normal size out here on the edge of the great pan and so low that it appeared possible to reach up and touch them. Desert chill lurked like a gatecrasher on the fringe of the party: delegates were glad to stand close to the big fires. The logs threw strange shadows; as the flames flickered and flared they picked out the stark whiteness of the beehive roofs in the background.

Ledoux threw his cigarette impatiently into the fire. He had come here to do a job – a big job – and not to fraternize and put over scientific chit-chat (he and Maurette had undergone a crash course at Radchem in Germany) and exchange smiles with a lot of eggheads. Nakanishi, with his high bald head, could have symbolized the types now chatting round the fires – French, British, American, German, South African.

Except Nakanishi didn't. Behind his bland façade was a cold-blooded schemer who had come to Corbel Camp to see that Dr Waldegg, head of Radchem, carried through a masterplan (propounded originally by Waldegg himself) to topple South

Africa's scientific credibility regarding SYNROC-R into the dust of Cheating Pan.

If Waldegg and Ledoux failed, China would stand to lose seven billion dollars.

South Africa had not been alone in spotting the potential of remote radwaste desert disposal sites for the convenience of industrialized nations; world accumulation was calculated at some seventy-five-million gallons of liquefied military waste and two thousand five hundred metric tons of radwaste from nuclear reactors. China had offered a deal to take four thousand tons of radwaste from Western Europe over the next five years at a price tag of seven billion dollars and bury it in the Gobi Desert in Mongolia. Agent in the negotiations was the West German nuclear chemical firm Radchem, headed by Dr Waldegg. This radwaste would be stored in conventional containers made of metal, glass and ceramics.

However, transport, environmental and safety problems involved in the Red China deal, especially the long haul by train from the coast to the Gobi Desert site, had placed China at a disadvantage compared to South Africa's Cheating Pan 'nuclear dustbin'. More than these factors even was the fact that SYNROC-R offered the first safe and scientific solution to the long-term environmental hazard posed by radwaste storage.

To discredit Kepler's SYNROC-R discovery (as yet unproven by time and experience) Dr Waldegg had conceived the idea of planting a bomb in the radwaste disposal area of the Gougo repository situated near Cheating Pan and detonating it during the official inspection by IAEA delegates of the site. It would appear, therefore, as if a SYNROC-R container had exploded spontaneously. The explosion, Dr Waldegg had reasoned, would not only discredit SYNROC-R as a storage medium but would immobilize the repository area for years through the resulting radiation contamination. If some of the IAEA delegates were killed by the bomb, it would draw the world's attention in no uncertain way to the danger of using the untried invention.

Red China, which stood to lose the seven billion dollars if the nuclear industrialized nations should opt for SYNROC-R, enthusiastically endorsed Dr Waldegg's scheme.

To implement the audacious bomb plan, Dr Waldegg had commissioned, via underground contacts in West Germany's Red Army Faction, the Bakunin Movement. He had selected this terrorist body because its hostility to South Africa dated back to 1982 when it had threatened the French government over the supply of a second nuclear power station. The sale had been abandoned.

The discrediting of SYNROC-R involved a two-pronged operation: the bomb attack was the second phase. The first was to be an offer to buy off Kepler with a bid of half a million dollars and a lifetime job with Radchem in return for the secret of SYNROC-R. If this failed, the bomb project would go ahead.

Obtaining the large amount of high explosive for the job so far from the Bakunin's home base in France and conveying it secretly to Corbel Camp posed major problems for both Ledoux and Dr Waldegg. Their late arrival with Maurette, separately from the other IAEA delegates, by station wagon the previous evening, accounted for this. Their visit to the Kruger National Park shortly after their arrival by air in Johannesburg had been a bluff. Their purpose had been to collect a cache of about 40 kilograms of Soviet SZ demolition charges and detonators from a supply laid down on the wild, guerrilla-frequented Mozambique–South Africa border; the Kruger Park formed the joint international boundary for over three hundred kilometres. This they had conveyed to Corbel camp.

The principle of the bomb attack was simple enough; the logistics of getting high explosive past the tightest security and radiation checks seemed at first glance an almost insuperable hurdle.

It was this problem which gnawed at Ledoux's mind and nerves as he stood by the fire, chain-smoking Gauloises, longing for another drink, which he denied himself. The day, as far as he was concerned, was a dead loss: he was no nearer getting to grips with the logistical problem of how to smuggle a bomb into the repository. The delegates had not even gone near the place that day. It happened to be fifty kilometres away to the south.

The bomb had been tentatively scheduled to explode during the IAEA delegates' final day's inspection of the nuclear dustbin.

That was a week from now.

Ledoux cursed inwardly. Dr Waldegg had postulated the idea that Kepler might have his secret SYNROC-R formula with him at Corbel Camp. He had ordered Ledoux and Maurette to search Kepler's hut while Kepler was involved in the barbecue and remove his briefcase. The two men would then take the briefcase to the hut which Dr Waldegg and Ledoux shared. Here Dr Waldegg would check Kepler's documents for the formula, after which the briefcase would be restored.

As if he hadn't enough on his mind without being engaged on a petty break-in!

Ledoux glanced at his watch, threw his half-smoked cigarette into the fire.

'Let's go,' he snapped at Maurette.

Maurette was considerably younger than Ledoux. He had a sulky, rather truculent air and a fighter's nose.

'Watch your step,' cautioned Dr Waldegg. 'You don't want to be caught red-handed . . .'

'Oh, for Christ's sake!' retorted Ledoux.

They moved off.

Their place with the group was taken within a couple of minutes by the suave Sir Edward Nayland, head of British Nuclear Fuels, who was circulating round the fires with the head of South Africa's Nucor, burly Professor Frans Dreyer.

Ledoux's target, Kepler's hut, lay out of sight behind a long new-thatched building which had been built at right angles to adjoin the old farmhouse complex and thus form an open square on to the basalt platform. It served as lounge and relaxation area.

The central complex of Corbel Camp occupied the only really flat area; its surroundings were flanked on all sides by low, irregular hillocks of bare, black rock. Some of these were hollow, like little volcanic craters, others were simply mounds of rock slabs. Rencha had turned these cleverly to account, perching beehives (their white a striking contrast to the natural black) on some, and sitting others inside the 'craters'. Access was by gaps in the rock, giving considerable privacy. Signposts with hut numbers were everywhere.

The opposite flank of the main platform where the barbecue was in progress was formed by the unmortared stone wall of the old cattle *kraal*. This wall doubled its height when it reached the line of the farmhouse. The former *kraal* was now in use as an official car park. The beehive which Ledoux and Dr Waldegg shared was behind the farmhouse proper, out of sight of Kepler's. Bossiere, on the other hand, had quarters tucked away in a natural secluded nook formed by the kitchen on one side and the high section of the *kraal* wall on the other. He could see without being seen, come and go via half a dozen narrow passageways between buildings, car park, and rocky hillocks.

Bossiere eyed the scene. He wished he could be joining in, drinking the South African wine which he had heard was so good, instead of the insipid soft drink in his glass. But what he was about to do would require every gram of grey matter to be in top form, not even shadowed by alcohol. Otherwise the pay-off could be a bullet or a knife. He must go about the operation as carefully as porcupines making love. The comparison cheered the DST man. He needed cheering, among the dark thoughts about Ledoux which seared his mind. He hadn't got over the face-to-face meeting the previous evening with the killer he had trailed for so many years.

Bossiere poured the dishwater from his glass on to the ground and reached inside his loose windcheater to check, unnecessarily, the Walther 9mm P38K. Bossiere loved this gun – its short barrel and smooth, double-action trigger pull which operated on the first shot. It was a man-stopper – the butt he touched had proved just that. If he came face to face with Ledoux again tonight, he wondered whether he would be able to hold back. Perhaps not.

Bossiere had decided, as he lay on his bed that afternoon (delegates had had their only 'off' afternoon of the eight-day inspection tour) that he must search the Waldegg-Ledoux station wagon and their shared hut for clues. The mere thought of it had sent the adrenalin pumping through Bossiere's veins. Unlike his verbal approach to Rencha, that to Ledoux would be one of action. And action would provoke the counterpunch from Ledoux, a natural killer. That was why the frivolous porcupines simile had brought amusement to his grim face.

When to search? The next day would be ideal. All the delegates were due to make a detailed hydrological inspection of the Cheating Pan catchment area to the south from the air in five helicopters. However, Bossiere asked himself, how could he enter and case the Waldegg-Ledoux hut in broad daylight with Corbel Camp's staff about? He discarded the idea. The sooner the search, the better – the barbecue offered the opportunity. Riskier, by far, with the possibility always of Waldegg or Ledoux visiting the hut unexpectedly.

Bossiere moved swiftly along the *kraal* wall, through a narrow gap past Rencha's quarters, and on to the rear of the farmhouse-kitchen complex. He collected a flashlight from his own place, double-checked the number of the Waldegg-Ledoux hut against one of Rencha's neat signs. There was hardly any need: the station wagon was parked outside the hut.

It took Bossiere only seconds to check through the glass of the hatchback that the vehicle was empty.

The hut door was locked. He had expected that. He was no stranger to this sort of break-in. The lock was a simple, standard fitment. It sprang open under his master-key. He flicked the torch beam round the interior. It was spartan, tidy, bare. A wooden loft, reached by a flight of steps, occupied most of the ceiling area. Leading off the main two-bedded room was a smaller one, taken up by a shower-toilet. As originally built, this little enclosure had been a threshing-floor. Rencha had skilfully converted it to modern needs.

Two suitcases, unlocked, lay on the stone floor. Bossiere rifled expertly through the clothes. Nothing there. The only unusual item was a scale with a hanging hook for weighing air luggage – an unnecessary precaution for VIPs, Bossiere thought in passing. Bossiere crossed quickly into the shower-toilet. Even less incriminating or significant items there.

Bossiere returned to the main room. He shaded the torch with his hand: he was a little worried by one small, high curtainless window over the loft opposite the door. Because the loft planking did not cover the entire ceiling space, it would be possible for anyone outside to spot a light inside. However, since it was in a basalt 'crater', Bossiere rated the chances of his flashlight being seen as minimal.

Next, the beam picked out the characteristic keeping-hole in the left-hand wall. There was a tape recorder/cassette in this recess; on a venerable-looking small yellow-wood bedside table was a small transistor radio.

The place was as virgin as a nun.

Bossiere slipped up the short flight of steps to the loft. Had he had time, he might have admired the old yellow-wood planks resting on joists of the same timber. The only articles in the loft were a pair of matched suitcases, securely locked. From the airline tags, they were Waldegg's and Ledoux's. Why stash them away up here? Bossiere queried inwardly. Why not have them below with the others if they held personal possessions?

Bossiere weighed the two suitcases in his hands. They were heavy, a kind of dead weight. He shook them. No rattles, nothing loose inside. He carefully wiped his fingerprints off the handles. He paused, before going for the locks. They were well made; his door master-key was, of course, useless. He would have to force them. Bossiere went down on his hunkers, considering. Altogether the four suitcases would make Waldegg and Ledoux very much overweight on a flight. Yet they had gone to the trouble of bringing along an air luggage scale – why? He had to establish what was in the cases! He reached into his pocket for a finely-machined stainless steel probe to test the locks' mechanisms.

Bossiere froze, snapped out the torch.

From the doorway came the sound of voices.

One was Ledoux's.

Chapter 7

Bossiere was trapped.

And, like a cornered wild animal prepared to sell its life dearly, he shrank back well out of sight in an enclave of shadow where the heavy loft beam met the wall. He pulled out the stubby-barrelled P38K. That deadly double-action on the first shot would get two of them for a start, if they came at him. Revenge-lust rose like sour vomit in his throat. He hoped the first up the loft steps would be Ledoux. It would be a shabby little place for it all to end; often he had fantasized where the final shoot-out would take place.

From their voices (they spoke French) the other man was definitely not Dr Waldegg. Waldegg had a deep, resonant voice which broadsided from the depths of his pseudo-Chinese beard.

The electric light clicked on. Bossiere winced, cowered further into the shadows. The bulb fitting was sited below the planking so that its full illumination did not reach into the loft proper. Another bulb, shadeless and as yet unlit, hung on a flex from the apex of the beehive roof. If that went on, he would be in full view.

Ledoux said, 'Louis, I tell you I didn't come all this way to filch a diddly-shit briefcase out of a VIP's hut. I've had it. And I'll tell Waldegg so.'

'It was a piece of cake anyway. You've been a tight-ass all day,' came the reply.

Louis! Who was Louis? Was he the man Bossiere knew as Ernst Fichte? It could be. The voice was young-sounding.

'Why shouldn't I be?' retorted Ledoux. 'See here, you're in on this job as much as I am. A big-time job, not a small-time robbery. And what do we know after a whole day and night in this dump about our target? Damn-all. We haven't even clapped eyes on the repository. It's fifty bloody kilometres away to start with! No one in Paris told me that. What sort of security have we got to get past . . .?'

'Security!' exclaimed Louis' voice. 'We don't have to get as far as security before my guts start turning over! It does so every time one of those egg-heads starts talking to me! What in hell do I know about negative groundwater aspects of the floodplain or about seismic stability?'

'You did your homework on the crash course.'

'Yeah, yeah. So did you. But sooner or later one of these scientific guys will trip us up.'

'I want to get on with the job, not be told off to carry out a piddling little burglary!'

'That's the third time you've said that – I get the message,' retorted Louis. 'But Dr West's briefcase may turn out to be more than a petty burglary – depends what the boss finds in it.'

Bossiere laid the Walther silently on the planking and switched on the shamrock microphone in his lapel. With luck, it might be strong enough to record the terrorists' conversation. It was indeed pure gold. The repository! He hadn't been wrong in his deduction that the Bakunin were after a major target. Now also, the Bakunin had broken in and stolen Kepler West's briefcase for Waldegg to check. It had been a piece of cake because Rencha had made it a piece of cake. She had obviously given them the key to the Australian scientist's hut.

Bossiere wished he could see. Dare he risk a glance?

He picked up the gun again, edged forward, spreadeagling

himself and holding the Walther in a firing position. He got his eyes over the decking's edge.

A briefcase, which hadn't been there previously, lay on a bed. Louis – that was Ernst Fichte of the Radchem team. Also a Bakunin! Bossiere eased back into the shadows.

He was just in time. The door opened. The angle of sight from doorway to loft was much greater than from the spot where Ledoux and Maurette were grouped. Bossiere's head could have been spotted by the newcomer.

Bossiere didn't have to see to know who it was from the deep, tough voice.

'Did ye get it? Ledoux? Maurette?' barked Waldegg.

Maurette! So that was the name of the second Bakunin! Bossiere had never heard it, but then the DST's roll-call of the Bakunin muster amounted to only one, and that was the leader, Ledoux.

'No sweat,' answered Maurette. 'There – on the bed.'

'Do you expect us to screw up a miserable little job like that?' demanded Ledoux. His voice was truculent, rhetorical.

'Where'd you learn American slang?' countered Waldegg. 'Don't work it off on me. It makes you sound like a retread gangster.'

'Listen,' went on Ledoux. 'We came here to do a job, a big job . . .'

'And you're being handsomely paid to do it,' interrupted the Radchem chief.

'And for one whole day we've sat around being put in the pressure cooker and the best you can do is to tell us to go and break into this Australian bastard's hut and steal his briefcase. When are we going to the repository?'

Waldegg ignored the outburst. 'You haven't opened West's case?'

'What do you take us for?' demanded Ledoux in the same tone. 'If his papers are going to be buggered about with, it's going to be you who does it.'

'Neither I nor anyone else is going to bugger around with his papers,' replied Waldegg coldly. 'Every paper will be replaced in exactly the same way and in the same order as it is at the moment.'

'There can't be much of value, it's not even locked,' said Ledoux.

There was a sound of catches being snapped open.

'What if his secret formula is there?' said Ledoux. 'Does it mean that our job is off?'

Bossiere decided to risk another glance. Kepler's briefcase was open and the three men were concentrating on it. Ledoux was smoking his acrid Gauloises. As he peered, ash dropped off his cigarette into Kepler's papers.

Waldegg straightened up. 'Can't you be careful?' he snapped. 'Do you want to advertise that someone's been looking in the case?'

Ledoux brushed the ash away with his handkerchief. Waldegg carefully laid the first document face-down on the bed, after glancing at it and blowing off more ash.

Some other papers followed, then Waldegg stopped and considered one which obviously contained scientific formulae.

'Any luck?' asked Ledoux.

Waldegg laid the paper among the others. 'Nothing to do with SYNROC-R.'

Maurette said, 'He'd be crazy to leave it lying around in an open briefcase.'

'It's an outside chance . . . wait a moment, what's this?'

Bossiere was torn. He wanted to see what Waldegg had discovered, and at the same time he knew the colossal risk he was running. He decided to glance only long enough to see what interested Waldegg.

Waldegg was examining what looked like two small pebbles mounted between plastic covers.

'Lindsleyite and mathiasite.' Waldegg's deep voice gave a note of drama to the exhibit.

'I can also read the labels,' sneered Ledoux. '"Present as discrete crystals in a single vein of periodite . . ."'

'These tell us nothing,' retorted Waldegg. 'They are obviously for the benefit of the IAEA delegates when West takes

52

us all to the open-cast kimberlite workings at New Rest in a couple of days' time. They're meant for public showing. No secrets.'

'That guy must be pretty smart to have hatched up something which left all you other egg-heads flat-footed,' observed Maurette.

'If he wasn't, you wouldn't be here earning yourselves good money,' responded Waldegg caustically.

Bossiere decided to withdraw his eyes. No sense in taking risks, now that the trio had decided that there was little worthwhile in Kepler West's briefcase.

There was silence from below as Waldegg went through the few remaining papers in the briefcase.

'You didn't examine anything else in West's hut – his suitcase or anything?' The tension in Waldegg's voice underscored his lack of success with the briefcase.

'Briefcase,' answered Ledoux. 'That is all you told us to bring. There it is. Anyway, his suitcase was there, standing open. It's not likely to have held valuable secrets.'

'You've made your point,' responded Waldegg. 'Now we'll get this repacked, item by item, just as you found it. Return this exactly where it came from, and then get yourselves back to the barbecue before you're missed.'

'*We* won't be missed,' answered Ledoux. 'And, see here, I don't like being ordered around – do this, do that. After we've returned West's briefcase, Louis and I are coming back here for a smoke. Neither of us can take too much scientific bullshit.'

'Very well, if that's the way you want it.' There was a note of menace in the Radchem man's voice. 'But I am planning the strategy of this thing, and I am paying you. You'd do well to remember that, Ledoux.'

'For crying out, all I want is to go for *action*, and stop frigging around on the sidelines – like this. We know what we want – let's get moving, that's all I ask. That means also, forget about approaching West the way Nakanishi insists. When do you plan to do *that*, anyway?'

Bossiere felt the hairs rise on his spine. It was like listening

53

in to the secrets of a couple making love. He hoped his little microphone wasn't losing its head.

'At the first opportunity,' answered Waldegg.

'What does that mean?'

'I'm the judge of that.'

'Okay, okay. I only wanted to know because if West accepts, then Louis and I might as well go home to Paris.'

'You will have had a nice free ride to a fascinating country.' Waldegg could not keep the sarcasm out of his voice.

Ledoux missed the thrust. 'Fascinating! This bloody Cheating Pan gives me the shits . . .'

'You'll fly over the repository tomorrow by helicopter – you can start building your strategy from that,' Waldegg said incisively. 'You're entitled, remember, to ask the pilot to show you what you wish. To everyone but me, Nakanishi and Chillun To, you're a couple of top Radchem technicians. Tomorrow's inspection is the start of a critical appraisal of the groundwater system . . .'

Ledoux emitted a sound between a belch and a raspberry.

Waldegg kept his cool. 'It's your plan of action, Ledoux, you've got to work it out. It's not got to fail or go off at half-cock either, do you understand? If it does, Radchem stands to lose billions.'

'You're saying what I've been yelling all evening,' retorted Ledoux. 'I want *action* – action, action, not jaw-jaw.'

Waldegg cut him short. 'I'm on my way to the barbecue. Professor John Ankey is waiting for me. I told him I'd come to fetch a magazine criticizing the US Department of Energy and its dumping sites.'

'That the Yank?' interrupted Ledoux.

'His home base is the Los Alamos Scientific Laboratory in New Mexico.'

'No tie-up with Radchem?'

'Why do you ask?'

'I like to know where I stand. See you at the barbecue after we've had our smoke.'

Bossiere heard the sound of the door open and close.

Then Maurette said, 'Tomorrow – is it going to be enough for us to get a quick sight of the place from a chopper? It's the precise security checks we have to know about.'

Tension replaced truculence in Ledoux's voice. 'It seems it's one hell of a thing we've got to beat. Let's get rid of this damn case and talk it over. It's bugging me.'

'Leave the light on?'

'We won't be more than a couple of minutes.'

The door sounds were repeated. It made no creak, however, when Bossiere, gun at the ready, slipped noiselessly from his hiding-place and out into the night.

Chapter 8

'. . . the family guards the Haunted Graveyard out there on the Pan. They're very jealous of the place. Strangers are liable to get shot at,' Rencha was saying.

'I'm glad I didn't know that at the time I came ferreting about for kimberlite,' replied Kepler. 'I remember passing it as I worked my way eastwards from *Bluebird*'s track.'

'Hot on the trail of mathiasite and lindsleyite,' smiled Rencha.

They grinned at each other. The light from the barbecue fires, dying now that it was late, sketched her outline – black slacks, high heels, black top with a splash of violet over the left shoulder – only amorphously. Rencha felt good. The evening had done that for her. Whenever she could, she had taken time off from her duties as hostess circulating among the guests to be with Kepler. For the past hour, with the festivities winding down, she had been continually at his side.

'The graveyard – all this and haunted too?' quipped Kepler.

'It's a sort of local Romeo and Juliet tale,' explained Rencha.

She indicated. 'That's Chris Bonsma over there. Marie his wife has been a tower of strength to me over the delegates' visit; she's been my right-hand man.'

'Woman,' Kepler corrected her.

'Woman,' repeated Rencha. They both laughed, sharing a wavelength on a word of no consequence.

'The Bonsmas are probably the oldest family in the entire Cheating Pan area,' Rencha went on. 'They came from over the mountains with their flocks of sheep. They also must have been among the pioneers to develop the corbelled style. In fact, there's a splendid old example on their farm *Kareeboomleegte* . . .'

'Karee Tree Hollow,' added Kepler.

Her eyes locked with his in the firelight, and she interrupted. 'It's just this side of the black stump.'

'I asked for that!' Then he said, 'Where does Romeo Bonsma come into the picture?'

'He was called Nel, another old name hereabouts. The tragedy apparently happened shortly after World War One. Nel Bonsma had a girl on the other side of Cheating Pan. Her family didn't approve. To visit her, he had to walk across the Pan. On this particular occasion, Nel set off and never came back. The mirages got him. They found his body three days later, tragically quite close to the edge of the Pan and safety. He'd become hopelessly lost, although he knew the Pan like the back of his hand. The girl shot herself over his body. The two were buried in the same grave.'

'Is that why the graveyard is haunted?'

'Maybe. But apparently what makes it spooky is that the family has a light which they keep burning on the lovers' headstone, a kind of living flame, I'm told. The Bonsmas consider it their sacred duty to keep it alight perpetually.'

'What keeps it going?'

'I don't know – I haven't been there. I told you, the family doesn't allow strangers. In fact, it was Chris over there who came and warned me when my first tourists arrived to keep them away from the Haunted Graveyard. He told me the story himself. The tragedy is kept alive – in this kind of isolated region that sort of thing strikes very deep roots.'

The on-off effect of the firelight illuminated the Tartar-like features of the coloured servants helping Bonsma and two or three other farmers at the spits. They sliced off strips of mutton with long butchers' knives. Their Bushmen and Hottentot origins were plain in the flat noses, high cheekbones and small bone structure. It was their ancestors who had fired their poisoned arrows at the windows of the first settlers' corbelled huts; their darts had been deflected by openings – firing slits, in fact – traversing the upper walls obliquely.

Rencha indicated the coloureds. 'The local population won't go near the Haunted Graveyard because of its reputation. Some of them claim to have seen – from a distance – ghostly lights wandering about at night.'

'Maybe the "living flame" had another purpose as well?' suggested Kepler.

'I don't think so, it's simply a spin-off, a very effective deterrent. Nobody goes near the place.'

Men were dismantling some of the spits and hefting sheep carcasses towards the kitchen.

'Why don't you leave the clearing-up for the morning? The party's just about over,' observed Kepler.

Rencha laughed. 'If we left the carcasses, you wouldn't get any sleep tonight for yapping. Cheating Pan's jackals would hold their own barbecue.'

'It seems my visit that first time from Australia was a case of ignorance being bliss – I never saw a jackal then.'

'You were too hot on the trail to notice anything except stones.'

'Too right.'

Bossiere was among the party's bitter-enders. He could see what progress the Bakunin girl was making with Kepler West. Had the scientist only seen what he had just seen, heard what he had overheard from the loft!

He walked over to them. 'A very unique party, madame.

57

Congratulations! I shall remember this night and the big stars.' He spoke in French.

'The stars are for free,' Rencha smiled.

Not all the colour in your cheeks is from the fires, thought Bossiere.

He switched into English, for Kepler's benefit. 'I am pleased to see that madame has completely recovered.'

'That was this morning,' she answered.

Yes, that was this morning. Before you had started on your conquest. The DST man was trying to get the hang of the situation, to decide where this attractive woman fitted into the scheme of whatever Ledoux was up to. There had been no mention of her as he had skulked in the loft above the terrorists' heads.

'And you've got a heavy day tomorrow, a lot of flying,' said Kepler.

Bossiere got the message. 'That goes for all us delegates.'

'Not for me,' laughed Kepler. 'I'm staying put at Corbel Camp. The intricacies of Cheating Pan's groundwater system are for the open-air types – hydrologists and geologists. My home base is the laboratory.'

Bossiere said to Rencha, 'With these scientists, one never quite knows where the one discipline begins and the other ends.'

Bossiere admired her poise. She was either a consummate actress to chat so easily and naturally, or else her training had been better than he had imagined. Perhaps shock tactics would be the answer to break down her barriers. He had the shock, right there in his wallet. For a moment, he felt pity for her. He wondered how the imploded courier façade would look once he'd sprung the explosion. He shrugged to himself. If you played Bakunin games, you had to take the rap.

'Goodnight,' he said suavely.

'Goodnight, Monsieur Bossiere.'

Kepler could have gone then, but he stayed. The farmers and their wives also came and wished Rencha goodnight. The two of them were almost the last left.

Rencha said obliquely, 'They say my *Jacob-jong* tea promotes a good sleep.'

'Tea instead of beer at a barbecue!' exclaimed Kepler. 'It's a good thing there aren't any other Australians present!'

She turned aside quickly. Kepler realized what a tightrope her emotions walked, how easy it was for her to trip into whatever dark chasm lay continually at her feet.

He went on, deliberately light-heartedly, a trifle mocking. 'The practice is considered highly eccentric amongst a race of beer drinkers. But why shouldn't I be eccentric? There's not a countryman of mine within thousands of kilometres. And *Jacob-jong* is also the real McCoy as far as I am concerned.'

Her large eyes were steady on him. There was a pause. 'Thank you for that,' she said finally. 'We can't drink it here – over at my place – it'll take a few minutes to make.'

Together they walked over the uneven outcrop past the last embers to Rencha's twin huts.

The interior of her sitting-room was like an icebox. Rencha switched on an electric heater. 'This is something you have to thank the IAEA visit for,' she said. 'As well as for the electricity itself. It's the first winter we've had either. I used to go to bed with a couple of old-fashioned stone hot water bottles filled with boiling water, but by morning they'd be too cold to have in the bed.'

You needed a man in your bed, Rencha, a man to love you warm. Why wasn't there one?

Kepler said, 'The barbecue was a brainwave. The fires made everything and everybody warm and cheerful. Better than sitting around inside and making small talk.'

She went to her keeping-hole in the wall and went through a ritual of bringing out her tea and heading for the kitchen and boiling water. 'I won't be a moment.'

Kepler waited. He warmed himself close to the heater. Again, he was struck by the room. It contained no impress of her personality, only an elusive trace of perfume, a lingering Lanvin ghost.

When she returned, they stood together at the fire, cups in

hand. 'What happens next to Corbel Camp, once all the delegates have departed in a week's time?'

'I don't have to worry about optimum occupancy any more, as they say in the hotel business,' she answered. 'All the technical staff from the repository will move here in their place. No more tourists.'

'Why do you say it like that?'

'Just because then Corbel Camp won't be mine – the way I built it – any more.'

'And what was that?'

'A road from nowhere to nowhere.'

'Your own life story?'

She put down her cup so unsteadily that the liquid slopped.

'It's been a wonderful evening, Kepler. Don't spoil it. Just don't – *ask*!'

'You must have loved John Krummect very much.'

'No more than another man in my life. But John –' She walked away from Kepler, spun on her heel, and faced him – 'he was as Corbel Camp became: sanctuary. A safe place. Like this keeping-hole. Hidden away. Safe and secure. That's the way I loved him. I saw that he never regretted it.'

'Meaning?'

'I have a capacity for loving. I lost John. I am losing Corbel Camp. It's slipping away. I feel it going – and I can't do anything about it.'

'Taken to its logical conclusion, you're losing it because of me.'

'I don't get that.'

'If I'd never discovered mathiasite and lindsleyite on Cheating Pan, you'd have gone on having Corbel Camp for ever and ever.'

She didn't seem to hear him, rather talked half to herself.

'It wasn't the winters that were bad. It was the summers. When it was cold, little groups of people used to come and I tried to amuse them and keep them entertained. Then, when the heat and winds arrived, it went empty. The long, empty months. Empty of all life as the Pan itself. I'd be like one of those giant frogs in these parts which hibernate for years until they feel the first touch of water from a thunderstorm. Then they revive and shout. I wanted to shout, winter, come!' She sat down in a chair and buried her face in her hands and whispered, 'For God's sake, come! Don't leave me alone to rot!'

Kepler went to her and put his hand on her shoulder. He said very gently, 'That's all done now, Rencha. You've got permanent people. Corbel Camp is a going concern from now on.'

She took the long strand of hair which hung down over her left breast and twisted it so that it concealed her lower face from him. 'A going concern! Yes, that's what it is now, I suppose. But I don't want a going concern. I want a funkhole.'

'Why?'

There was a long pause. She remained with her head down, hidden by the strand of hair. Then slowly she shook it from side to side.

'No! That "no" is part of the reason why I flaked out this morning. No, Kepler. The present is all that counts.'

'You've got a future.'

'Not with Corbel Camp.' She returned her hair to its position over her shoulder. 'Nucor has made me a very handsome offer for it – much more than it will ever be worth.'

'It's worth that to them. It's the only accommodation in the whole region. There's not a hotel for . . . for . . .'

'One hundred and fifty kilometres,' she supplied. Her mouth twisted. 'I know. Part of the occupancy story. Nucor's being very generous. They know my attachment to the place. They're willing to buy it and let me continue to run it – indefinitely.'

'You can't go wrong. Your bets are hedged.'

She got up and stood in front of him, her hands on his shoulders now, looking into his dark eyes.

'Because it won't be a road to nowhere any more. But I'm being unfair to you. You can't expect to understand, not knowing what went before.'

He took her hands. 'Why don't you tell?'

Her eyes suddenly went opaque, as if a blind had been drawn. 'Because I'm scared of losing what little I've found of you tonight. It's something which I can't afford. You asked for the reason. That's it. I can't explain. That's all.'

She stood simply looking at him. He knew that if he kissed her, he would lose her. Yet, paradoxically, she wanted to be kissed.

Instead, he said, 'Some old stone huts – bursting with a woman's heart.'

'Maybe you could understand, but I can't risk it. You see, Kepler, Corbel Camp is just one step away from the megalithic man who dragged a few stones together over his head to keep off the sun and the wind. In direct line, you might say. For me it serves the same purpose.'

'A funkhole.'

She suddenly dropped her hands from his shoulders and said in a completely different tone, 'Here I've lured you to my funkhole in the middle of the night with a bribe of tea and instead I've abused my hospitality by crying on your shoulder. I'd like to make amends.'

Her eyes were bright, now. Kepler wondered what was coming. If she had been an ordinary girl, he would not have needed three guesses.

She said, 'The day after tomorrow I'm going to the railhead at Sak River in my truck to collect supplies. I know you're not joining the other delegates to inspect the groundwater set-up. Come with me?'

He smiled at her. He was glad and sorry she hadn't let him down.

'It's a date.'

She took his arm and opened the door. 'We have a date.' He noted her changed wording.

He walked towards his own hut across the deserted platform where the barbecue lay in ruins. It was situated at the back of the new lounge complex. Cold squirmed off the black rock like a desert viper. He couldn't get his mind off the thought of the beautiful woman behind him alone in her morgue-like bed with hard stone bottles as companions. Three winters!

Kepler unlocked his door.

He stopped, sniffed. There was something strange, alien, on the air, like the first time you smell the Underground in a London winter. It wasn't his tobacco. Someone had been here!

There was no place to hide in the hut itself. He crossed swiftly to the shower/toilet. It, too, was empty. So was the loft.

Was he deceiving himself? The night air which had come in with him had diluted the slightly acrid tang which had accosted him on arrival.

He searched around. Nothing seemed out of place. He tried the suitcase. If someone had been through his clothes, they had done it masterfully. He checked hurriedly for the one thing which any burglar would have gone for. He pulled out a black metal shaving case and snapped it open. Only it didn't contain an electric razor. The compact .45 Colt Commander's stainless steel butt smiled up at him as it greeted the light. The special long ten-round magazine was securely in place. This was the gun which he had been trained to use by his friend Mike, the unarmed combat specialist, following the mysterious attack on him in his Canberra lab. Mike, a believer in both guns and fists, had himself fine-honed the ramp and trigger-pull so that it was a gun in a thousand. Since the attack, Kepler had always carried the Colt. The bogus razor-case had also been Mike's idea.

So was the method by which he carried two extra twenty-round boxes of Winchester centre-fire shells. No boxes for them. The straps which secured the lid of his suitcase had been converted to bandoliers, into which the shells latched invisibly. No customs man had yet woken up to the trick.

More out of force of habit than suspicion, Kepler balanced the Colt Commander in his hand. Nothing seemed amiss. Yet – he was certain he had smelt that alien smell on entering.

Then – Kepler noticed. Before he had left for the barbecue he had seated Mr Whoppit – the Campbell mascot replica Rencha had presented to him – in a rakish pose on top of his briefcase. The briefcase was in exactly the same position – but Mr Whoppit was to one side on the table.

Kepler opened the case. The pungent tang of tobacco was plain. Something strong, certainly not his own John Player mild. The papers were in order. But, as he lifted out the kimberlite folder with the two mineral specimens of mathiasite and lindsleyite, the light showed an opaque smear on the transparent plastic. Kepler sniffed. Cigarette ash!

Nothing was missing. Kepler checked and rechecked the case's contents. What had the thief been after?

Puzzled, Kepler finally decided to go to bed.

He sat Mr Whoppit next to his pillow. The barrel of the pistol rested across his legs.

Kepler paused with his hand on the light switch.

'I may need your good luck yet,' he said.

Chapter 9

'Half a million. In American dollars. A Swiss banking account, if you want. I can fix that. A lifetime job with Radchem. Your own private lab. Complete freedom to pursue your own researches. Adapting the Gobi Desert repository to SYNROC-R containment would be a major challenge in itself. Eh?'

The broadside from the depths of Dr Waldegg's Fu Manchu beard, meant to sweep the decks clear, came out instead as staccato single-gun phrases. Dr Waldegg was rattled; the morning's events and pressures were crowding him; he had intended his buy-off approach to Kepler to be urbane, delicate, roundabout, but in the event the way it had taken shape could not have been jerkier, less diplomatic, more straight-from-the-shoulder.

It was next morning, the third day of the IAEA inspection,

focused on the Cheating Pan 'floodplain' system. Dr Waldegg and Kepler were alone in the hut the German shared with Ledoux. Bossiere's microphone would have given its ears to be once again eavesdropping from the loft above.

Dr Waldegg had intercepted Kepler coming away from the phone situated in the central complex building. Kepler was feeling pleased with himself. Koeberg had reported that everything was running smoothly with the SYNROC-R production and that the first transporter-load would leave the next day as scheduled for the Gougo repository. Kepler was looking forward to having Rencha to himself for most of the day.

Had Waldegg been able to go back in time, he would have seen the same flash like a stop signal go into action in the dark, almost inscrutable eyes of the scientist as on the occasion when he had been ordered by Canberra University to lay off the British atom bomb tests in Australia. The compelling, powerful face above the sloppy collar of his jogger's tracksuit seemed to tauten at the German's words.

'You must be joking.'

'If you're concerned about the size of the amount, I am authorized to tell you that it has been underwritten by the China Nuclear Energy Industry Corporation.'

'And therefore a party to this underhand offer.'

'There is nothing underhand about it.' Dr Waldegg was glad to fall back upon a defensive response – the hostility in the other man's eyes disturbed him. Nakanishi had warned him of the almost crusading zeal the Australian was known for in scientific circles, allied to a brilliant, single-minded purposefulness. Heaven alone knew through what remote leads he had tracked down the kimberlite deposit on Cheating Pan from faraway Australia, but he had done it. Waldegg felt uneasy about being at the receiving end of a crusader's sword.

'Let us be realistic, pragmatic,' Waldegg went on. 'You have made a discovery which will progressively become worth more and more as the world's stock of radwaste builds up, as it must. We in Radchem recognize that fact. South Africa is a small country. Fair enough, it was the first bidder for SYNROC-R. But we are *big* – and we are offering big accordingly.'

Kepler said, 'There's a remote station called Wallatina in the Australian outback. A black mist came in one day and enveloped the Aborigines' settlement there. Many died. Others had sore eyes, sore mouths, vomited, had green diarrhoea after the cloud passed through. Drinking water turned greasy. They said it was a *mamu*, an evil spirit. It wasn't. It was fall-out from a British atom bomb test.'

Kepler got to his feet. 'Your offer is like that cloud, Dr Waldegg, one thing posing as another. To me, it is poison, as if an evil spirit had passed over me.'

The pronounced V on either side of the scientist's nose seemed to have become deeper, fashioning the face stronger, more powerful.

Waldegg knew he had missed his trick.

'You're being fanciful,' Waldegg replied. 'This is a straightforward business offer. You have the commodity, we have the price. That is all there is to it. No evil spirits.'

'How do you intend to protect those unfortunate Mongolian nomads who wander into your Gobi Desert site and get themselves irradiated? Have you ever seen a man or a woman suffering from radiation burns – or the resulting cancer?'

'There'll be plenty of warning signs and keep-out notices round the repository site . . .'

'The same story as the Aborigines,' retorted Kepler. 'No one thought – or gave a damn – to the fact that they couldn't read what the signs said, or what it was all about. They simply wandered in where the tribe had been used to wander for generations.'

Waldegg shrugged. 'You can't have omelette without breaking the eggs. A few dead peasants – what does it matter in the broader context of world radwaste disposal?'

'You callous bastard!' breathed Kepler. 'You'd let them die! Innocents – your Mongolians, my Aborigines!'

'You're slipping into sentiment,' answered Waldegg curtly.

'I am talking business. Half a million. A lifetime meal ticket. Your own lab – your own research –'

'A dog on a chain – and don't bark at the radiation,' responded Kepler.

'You refuse then?'

'Haven't I made that clear?'

Waldegg held himself back. He was off-balance from the flak Ledoux had thrown at him before the meeting. Ledoux's nerves were stretched: he was demanding to know the lay-out of his target, how he could insinuate a load of SZ demolition charges into the repository, clamouring at the delays which the official IAEA schedule made inevitable. Nakanishi had been at him also. Maybe he should have left the offer to his devious Oriental mind to hatch. Anway, he'd blown it, Waldegg told himself.

Waldegg tried to sound cool, businesslike, unperturbed by Kepler's rejection. 'See here, Dr West, we're all here together for another week. I am not taking no for an answer today. Maybe when you have had time to think it over you will reconsider. I am available any time . . .'

Kepler shrugged, and walked out.

'Confidentiality . . .' Waldegg called after him.

'You needn't worry,' replied Kepler. 'I wouldn't like anyone to know even that I had been approached with such an offer.'

Waldegg watched him go. As if he'd not had enough of human problems, South Africa had pitched Radchem a real fast ball also that morning. Even Nakanishi had found it hard to field; Chillun To was definitely depressed.

The main shot in China's armoury – a legitimate scientific shot which, they hoped, would persuade the IAEA against authorizing the Gougo repository – was serious objection to the groundwater aspect of the so-called 'floodplain' at the extremity of which Cheating Pan was situated. That day (and the next, at China's prior insistence) was to be devoted to an in-depth inspection of the geology, hydrology and geography of this 'floodplain', which stretched back southwards for hundreds of kilometres to the mountains of the Western Cape, great ranges named Roggeveld ('Wild Rye') and Nuweveld ('New Steppes'). It was on this great plain that the hard men who had built the first corbelled houses had fed their flocks of sheep and goats after thrusting their way through the mountain barrier.

The almost level plain was a complex of pans, both big and small, of which Cheating Pan was the most extensive. A century ago, these pans were flooded regularly to a depth of a few inches by run-off from silt-rich soil eroded from the mountains. A farming system, called 'saaidam' (meaning 'sowing dam') developed, which closely resembled that of the Nile Delta in Egypt. Low-earth contour walls or embankments were thrown across the flat valleys and watersheds to delay the flow of the floodwaters and provide the soil with enough moisture for the germination of a wheat crop.

Despite periodic droughts, the scheme worked reasonably successfully before farmers in the catchment installed conservation works and blocked the flow of life-giving silt. Great hopes were held at the beginning of the twentieth century that the area might develop into a 'little Manitoba' and one big company poured millions in money and expertise into the 'saaidam' system. However, the scheme foundered on a changed climatic cycle, years of pitiless droughts, and the progressive use of modern conservation methods in the mountain catchments. It was this danger of periodic flooding in relation to radwaste buried at the Gougo repository – itself sited at what appeared at first glance to be the heart of the floodplain, with its resulting dissemination of radio-active chemicals – that China hoped to exploit and so possibly prevent the establishment of the international 'nuclear dustbin'.

However, at a pre-flight briefing that morning before Dr Waldegg's interview with Kepler West, South Africa had thrown down a card calculated to trump China's objections. An impressive array of documentation regarding the geography, hydrology and geology of the area was laid before the delegates, plus scientific proof and statistics to show that there was no continuous water table, and that only after occasional 'good' rainy seasons were there isolated pockets of underground water which in themselves were no threat to the spreading of radwaste lodged in SYNROC-R containers at Gougo.

The South Africans had also given a detailed historical account of the failure of the old 'sowing dam' system and its abandonment at the time of World War I as a going concern; although there were still irrigation projects along the main watercourses such as the Sak River ('Sinking River', whose waters disappear into the earth as it nears and passes Cheating Pan), the massive floodings of the past had sunk into history, and drought was the order of the day.

China had hoped to have Britain as one of its main allies in support of its objections. Britain was not uninterested in the fate of the Gougo repository; she had a £3000 million stake during the next decade in processing nuclear waste sent from all over the world to British Nuclear Fuels. Endorsement of the Gougo repository would hit this lucrative business.

Both China and other objectors could not contest other vital aspects of the Gougo repository siting: the sparsely inhabited countryside, its extremely limited carrying capacity for stock (one sheep to nine hectares), the lack of evidence of seismic activity for millions of years, and a twenty-metre protective blanket of clay over the entire radwaste disposal area (clay is the ideal type of soil for radwaste).

Dr Waldegg and Professors Nakanishi and Chillun To had, moreover, been thrown back on their heels by something else the South Africans had kept secret and produced like a rabbit out of a hat at that morning's briefing. A sophisticated space-age technology system had been installed at key points throughout the 'sowing dam' waterways and canals to provide instant data on water levels. Monitoring transmitters relayed data on water levels, temperatures and water quality via a satellite which retransmitted it to computers, which enabled repository engineers and irrigation scientists to assess at any given moment, should it rain, what threat, if any, existed to the repository. This sophisticated system replaced the old method of having stone pillars (not unlike the nilometers of Egypt which had been in use for thousands of years) from which visual readings were telephoned (should the cranky telephone system be working) by farmers to a central point.

There was no denying that South Africa had struck a body-blow at its opponents and had largely pre-empted the air-to-ground and on-the-ground inspections of the next two days.

Kepler's contempt was still cauterizing Dr Waldegg when Professor Nakanishi came in. The tall Chinese had to stoop for his bald, cupola-like head to pass. Dr Chillun To accompanied him.

'Well?' demanded Nakanishi.

'He refused – of course.'

'Why – of course?' went on the Chinese. 'The money was good. Wasn't it enough?'

These two hadn't encountered the fire which had sprung up in the Australian's smouldering eyes nor his contemptuous rejection – more the spirit of it than the words – which had followed. Had he been capable of feeling guilt, Waldegg would have been experiencing it after the interview with Kepler West. Whatever it was, it had left him rattled, angry.

'He doesn't care about money. Or about the sort of things with which you'd expect to buy off an ordinary man.'

'We were watching from a distance. The entire interview took only a couple of minutes. I have a strong feeling you rushed your fences. You should have been more diplomatic, talked round the subject . . .'

He was right, of course, Waldegg conceded inwardly. But he would never admit it. He remembered how his offer had come out – abrupt, calculated to be a verbal knock-down. The blows had only bounced off Kepler.

Waldegg resorted to hectoring. 'If you didn't trust me to make the offer, why did you ask me in the first place? You've met the man before at scientific conferences. If you know him better, why didn't *you* try?'

'For the simple reason that the China Nuclear Energy Industry Corporation is employing you as its agent and, moreoever, it does not . . . not . . .'

'Descend to doing the dirty work?' sneered Waldegg.

Nakanishi stared at him, a disconcerting, fixed stare.

At length he said, 'Is that all?'

'The door was left open . . .'

'How far open?' Dr Chillun To interjected.

'I gave him time – till the end of the IAEA gathering – to think it over. I will approach him again.'

'And if he says no again, we will have let the golden opportunity of the IAEA gathering slip between our fingers.'

'We don't and won't,' snapped Waldegg. 'We go now for the second option.' He jerked his head in the direction of the loft.

'The option in those two suitcases.'

'Jaw-jaw – nothing but jaw-jaw. For heaven's sake, let me and Maurette *get on with it*!'

Ledoux entered suddenly. A half-smoked Gauloise was stuck between his lips. His pale, almost transparent eyes reminded Waldegg of an overbred Rottweiler. Ledoux was just as uncertain – and dangerous.

'That's exactly what you'll be doing in less than an hour from now,' retorted Waldegg. 'And, talking of jaw, keep your mouths shut in the helicopter when we fly over the repository. The IAEA men who'll be with us know what they're talking about. Dr Dieckmann and I will carry on what conversation is necessary. And, don't either of you try and be clever. You'll be with some of the world's biggest experts in their fields. Pretend to be sick, if you like, but don't make an ass of yourselves.'

Ledoux took the cigarette from his lips with a curious, slow-motion action. It was the way a torturer might adduce his next hellishness. In this case, it was an idea.

'Bluff sick – that's it! That's what I'll do!' Ledoux responded. 'Listen. Once we've flown over the repository and Louis and I have had a good look-see at the security set-up, I'll bluff I'm air-sick, really taken bad. I'll get the pilot to bring me back here to Cheating Pan. Then Louis and I can drop off and later we can motor on our own and investigate the place from the outside. Get the feel of it, if you know what I mean.'

Waldegg considered. 'I think it might work.'

'The IAEA schedule calls for a ground inspection by all the delegates as well,' went on Ledoux as the idea caught on. 'What I would be doing is short-circuiting that. We want to get ideas, how we can get that load of peanut butter into place.'

'Peanut butter?' Nakanishi, Waldegg and Chillun To were puzzled.

Ledoux explained, as if to a child. 'There's about forty kilograms of peanut butter above our heads in two suitcases.'

'Shut up, you fool!' hissed Waldegg. 'The door's open. Anyone can overhear.'

'The sooner we get that stuff out of here, the better,' went on Ledoux. 'I don't like it here any more than you do. I need a safe place to stash it away until the right moment comes.'

Waldegg said incisively, 'That is the plan then for today. Ledoux, you feign sick. You and Maurette get back here afterwards. Take the station wagon and spy out the land as best you can.'

'What happened? Did West refuse?' asked Maurette. 'Is our job definitely on?'

'Dr West wasn't very – ah, amenable,' replied Waldegg uncomfortably. 'All the eggs are now in one basket.'

'The bomb basket,' added Nakanishi.

'Good. Then we know exactly where we are,' replied Ledoux. 'I'm to be sick . . .'

Ledoux was sick, genuinely sick to the stomach, at what he saw an hour later when a helicopter carrying himself and Maurette, Dr Waldegg and Dr Dieckmann, the other Radchem expert, together with Dr Hans Pienaar, a South African from Nucor, and Professor Louis Jaboulet, President of the IAEA, clattered over the Gougo nuclear dustbin. The presence of the President himself with the Radchem team showed the importance which was attached to China's objections.

They had flown for about twenty minutes from Cheating Pan in a southwesterly direction to reach a great tableland about sixty kilometres long and half that distance broad which was situated between two huge dry watercourses, one to the west, the other to the east. They converged like gigantic brown-grey pincers on Cheating Pan to the north. The repository site, on some of the highest ground in the northern sector of the tableland, was 100 square kilometres in extent. However, the repository complex proper took up only about a square kilometre of this, and the site where the nuclear waste was actually buried was (to Ledoux's surprise) barely the size of a rugby field. Only a helicopter-eye view could give an idea of the immensity and starkness of the countryside: square kilometre after square kilometre of aching emptiness, sand, rock outcrops, pitiful stunted bushes, an occasional tree rising out of the dun wilderness like a lighthouse to mark the location of a '*puts*' or waterhole and a more occasional farmhouse and windmill. The sun blurred the outer limits of the tableland with curtains of mirage.

The helicopter came low over Gougo. Ledoux shielded his eyes against the glare; even dark glasses were not enough. A massive double security fence – sharp-edged two-metre mesh topped by razor tape and barbed wire – led from an outer gate along a tarred entranceway (dog-legged to prevent a vehicle making a sudden reverse turn and dashing for safety) to an inner gate and on to three low, adjoining buildings. One of these, on the left, had four entrances.

Dr Pienaar pointed to the outermost entrance. 'Reception area,' he told Ledoux, who was craning to see. 'All incoming vehicles' documents are checked there. The special transporters carry manifests and clearance papers from Koeberg and if anything in a load doesn't tally, it is stopped immediately. The vehicles are then tested for freedom from radiation contamination. Only after that can they be off-loaded. The whole lay-out is similar to our conventional containment repository at Vaalputs in Namaqualand. You delegates are going there to see for yourselves later in the week.'

Ledoux indicated the double security gates and an approach road which turned to gravel and disappeared into the distance.

'Only one entrance, I see.'

'Sure,' replied the Nucor man. 'Everything heading for the repository is channelled down that one road. It links up with the main road to Koeberg about twenty kilometres south of here.'

'What is that other smaller road, then?'

Ledoux pointed to a dirt road coming in from outside the wire from one side and joining the main entranceway near a small hill.

'Airfield road – there it is in the distance.'

'Gougo has its own airfield?'

'Yes. Inside the general repository area but not the inner security section. It comes in handy as a link with Cheating Pan.'

'I'd like to have a close look at the security gate itself. After all, that's where the trouble can start.'

Dr Pienaar smiled. 'We'd check out even a radio-active mouse if he didn't wear protective clothing.'

Dr Pienaar instructed the pilot and the machine hung over the heads of a group of security men at the gate. Ledoux wasn't bluffing himself when he felt that the pit of his stomach was falling overboard. How could he get a load of about forty kilograms of high explosive past that lot!

Shortly after, the helicopter hovered over the biggest of the three adjoining buildings to which the gate led: for reception, transfer of loads, and decontamination, if necessary.

Dr Pienaar indicated the middle entrance to these buildings. 'In there, our site vehicles, which are quite separate from the big flatbed transporters which convey the radwaste from Koeberg, are loaded up for the excavation and disposal area.' Some distance away, Ledoux saw a huge trench the size of a rugby field where bulldozers and front-end loaders were throwing up clouds of dust.

'What happens if you suspect something – I mean, if a drum . . .' Ledoux tailed off.

'That's the decontamination and re-encapsulating centre next door to the transfer area,' explained Dr Pienaar. 'If we should find a drum which is contaminated radio-actively on arrival, it will be treated there and made safe.'

'You mean, if you are suspicious of a drum for any reason?'

'There is only one reason to be suspicious about here – radio-activity,' laughed Dr Pienaar. 'That's all we check for. Anyway, we don't expect that section to get much use because there is a prior check of all drums before they leave Koeberg and it's unlikely that they would be damaged en route.'

Ledoux eyed with dismay the raw new buildings (builders were still clearing rubble and tidying up) and the road leading from them to the clay-topped trenches. That would probably be the best place for his explosion . . .

Maurette was on the same wavelength: how far would the blast effect extend? The trench was too far away from the main buildings to do more than perhaps blow the roofs off . . .

'How deep do you bury the radwaste?' he asked Dr Pienaar.

'About sixty metres finally,' replied the Nucor man. 'The twenty-metre layer of clay is the perfect insurance in itself. The depth for burial really hinges on the structural, tectonic, host rock and groundwater characteristics of the region. In the United States, for example, they consider a hundred to two hundred metres a necessary burying depth. But we're fortunate here. We don't need to go as deep as that, particularly since we have SYNROC-R.'

It all came back to Kepler West! Dr Waldegg, who was listening, reminded himself.

Both Ledoux and Maurette, with their highly sòphisticated training in explosives, realized that unless the IAEA delegates could be caught at the moment of inspecting an open trench itself, few of them would be killed or injured. But that, after all, was not their main objective. It was to discredit SYNROC-R. And a blast, wherever it took place inside the repository area, could not fail to do just that.

If the demolition charges could be smuggled in.

Ledoux didn't want to see more. On the morning's showing, he couldn't win. It was high time for his air-sickness act.

Chapter 10

Only Bossiere would not have been surprised at the sudden reappearance at Corbel Camp of Ledoux and Maurette. But he was far away, enduring another helicopter flight and the aching wilderness under the machine's belly. Certainly, Rencha and Kepler were taken aback. They were together, as they had been all morning, in the old farmhouse lounge facing the basalt courtyard. Bossiere's microphone would have long since run out of tape recording what they had to say to one another.

'Airsick,' answered Ledoux cryptically to Rencha's question.

'Bad,' added Maurette. 'The pilot wanted to drop him off at the Gougo airfield, but we thought it wiser for him to come back here. I'll make sure he's okay.'

'It was the air pockets – must be a special sort hereabouts,' said Ledoux. 'They knocked my socks off.'

'About the only thing I didn't cater for for the delegates was airsickness tablets,' said Rencha. She was wearing a white sleeveless cotton dress. She looked like the spring that never was at Cheating Pan. 'What about some tea, Herr Lentz?'

Ledoux caught himself in time not to look round for Herr Lentz. He must not forget either that Maurette was Ernst Fichte.

'Thank you, no,' Ledoux replied as germanically as he thought would sound right. 'Water, and that I have had. My colleague and I must pursue our investigations into the floodplain, in spite of this temporary setback.'

Kepler eyed the two men. They were from Radchem, only he found it hard to accept that anyone as young as Maurette (he was no older than his middle twenties) had achieved

76

enough, even academically, to be rated company among the world's top radwaste scientists. They were described officially as 'laboratory technicians'. There was also an air of jauntiness about him which jarred. Ledoux? He could pass muster on the score of age. There were premature lines round the angle of his jaw which could have been caused by anything from illness to pain, the latter either suffered or inflicted.

Kepler had deliberately pushed into the background the ugly taste Dr Waldegg's buy-off bid had left in his mouth: Rencha had seen to that. Now it was back. Would these two from Radchem be in the know? Were they high enough in the hierarchy for it to be confided to them?

'How do you intend to do that?' asked Kepler, perhaps more pointedly than he intended. 'The chopper's gone again, presumably.'

Ledoux tried to smile, but his pale eyes made it a failure.

'That machine of torture is no longer for me. No, we go this time by road. We have come for the station wagon – and road directions. This countryside seems to swallow anything. We do not wish to be swallowed.'

'That's one way of putting it,' smiled Rencha.

'The IAEA schedule calls for ground reconnaissance as well as air,' went on Ledoux. 'All we are doing is – how do you say it in English? – jumping the gun a little. We will be one step ahead of the other delegates, who will do the same road journeys later, no?'

There was a crack in the bell-tone somewhere, Kepler decided inwardly. Ledoux's sounded like a rehearsed speech, deliberately a little stylized. If he knew about Waldegg's offer, he certainly wasn't showing it. His attitude towards him was neutral.

'You can't really go wrong,' explained Rencha. 'There's only one road in and out of Corbel Camp in the direction of the repository. If you follow that road for about fifty kilometres, you hit the main east-west Gougo road at a T-junction. Again, it's the only way . . .'

'We saw it from the air,' interrupted Maurette. 'Near the

repository itself, there's another branch which leads to the security gate. How far is it?'

'Gougo is about one hundred and ten kilometres by road from Corbel Camp, but it will take you a couple of hours. The road isn't good, especially at this end. Sandy and twisty. Do you want a sketch map? Where exactly do you plan to go?'

Ledoux improvised. 'We saw what appeared to be some interesting groundwater lodgement areas to the south of the main road, but my unfortunate disposition prevented our investigating them this morning,' he replied. 'I think that will be our objective for this afternoon.'

'Groundwater lodgement areas' – that was a new one! Kepler had never heard the phrase. Either Ledoux was pontificating, or else he was phoney.

'In that case, you probably don't need a map. You can easily work your way off the main road along some of the small side roads leading to the pans you spotted,' said Rencha.

'Roads – or tracks?' asked Maurette. He had a brittle know-all way of putting ordinary things which set Kepler's teeth on edge.

'Something in between,' laughed Rencha. Her mood was sunny. It owed nothing to Cheating Pan's sun.

'If we don't come back, you'll know where to send a search party,' responded Ledoux heavily.

The two men wondered whether they had indeed pre-empted their afternoon's target area by the time they had travelled only a few kilometres south of Corbel Camp. To Ledoux, accustomed to smooth urban tarmac, the rough, sandy narrow road was a tribulation. True, they had come this way on their arrival, but then the station wagon had been stable with the weight of three men, their luggage – and the twin suitcases. Forty kilograms of high explosive ballast makes a vehicle sit harder on the road than you would think. Now, the empty station wagon slewed, bumped, and yawed its way. Had the two terrorists been the least interested, they would have seen on their right, about ten kilometres after starting, the single tree from which the Bonsmas' farm took its name, Karee Tree

Hollow. Further on, outlandish names such as Jan Louw se Leegte (Jan Louw's Hollow) and Klaas Titus Vier (Klaas Titus the Fourth) materialized out of the countryside. To Parisian eyes, it was hell. Their objective was to kill time; despite that, they couldn't get themselves on to the smoother main repository road quick enough.

'I wonder whether we'll get West with the bomb? That broad will cry for him if we do,' remarked Maurette. His tone was conversational: he might have been discussing the weather, had there been any weather to discuss at Cheating Pan.

'She's making one hell of a go at him,' answered Ledoux. 'Not that I wouldn't mind a slice there myself.'

They reached the main road T-junction, turned left or east towards Gougo. Immediately their discomfort was doubled. A wind from the west, which on the Corbel Camp sector was merely an irritating crosswind, now blew the dust from their wheels up their exhaust and over everything inside. They could scarcely breathe. Ledoux was driving slowly to kill time; the corrugated surface of the road made this a progression of bangs and bumps. On corrugations you either travel fast or dead slow. The station wagon was caught between speeds.

After about twenty kilometres of this, the level road resolved itself into a series of sharp bends cutting through a steep, rugged defile. Had the terrorists accepted Rencha's offer of a map, they would have learned that this prominent landmark, which pushed up the altitude of the road by some forty metres over a short distance, was known as Hartogskloof. The pass was the entrance, in fact, to the great tableland on part of which the nuclear repository was sited.

The terrorists first crossed a concrete causeway into a small haven of stunted trees and green bushes which had established themselves precariously on the roadside as it began its upward twists. Hartogskloof was, in fact, the main by-pass channel round the great plateau to the west round which any flowing water drained in a series of pans and flats in the general direction of Cheating Pan. By virtue of this rare occasional water, it was, compared to its surrounding starkness, an oasis.

Ledoux pulled the station wagon off the road under a tree on to a wide sandy space immediately beyond the causeway. The first bend of the pass lay immediately ahead.

He got out, lit a cigarette.

'You'll be running out of Gauloises before long if you go on like that,' observed Maurette.

'Don't needle me, man – I've got enough on my mind already!' He took a gulp of the hot coffee which Rencha had insisted on providing before their departure.

'It'll make you feel worse, when you have to smoke English cigarettes which you hate – the only brand I've noticed around here,' went on Maurette.

Ledoux glanced about him. 'Give me a back alley in Paris any day, rather than this!' he exclaimed. 'Hell, it's like some invisible creature out there, watching, watching, watching, and you've got no place to hide! Bloody countryside, bloody open spaces!'

'We'll make a plan, we'll get it right, somehow,' said Maurette.

'Make a plan – with what?' demanded Ledoux. 'Didn't you see what I saw at the Gougo gate? You couldn't fart there without being checked for radio-activity!'

'I saw, and I don't know any more than you,' answered Maurette. 'Let's get back there and take another look-see from the road.'

'No,' replied Ledoux. 'The less you're seen, the less you are remembered. Close, yes, but not right up to the gate where we're bound to be spotted.'

'What's the idea then?'

'I haven't got an idea, or a plan, or anything – that's what's bugging me! We've got Lichine of course, but he's going to be of no use. How the hell is anything of any use with that kind of security?' Ledoux pitched the dregs of his coffee on to the ground. 'We're now on the third day – we've only five left! And we're no nearer a plan than when we arrived!'

'Let's talk it through, maybe something will strike us,' suggested Maurette.

'Jaw! That's all I hear, jaw, jaw!' Ledoux went on angrily. 'Look, every time I think of those SZ-6 and SZ-3 charges above my head in the loft, I want to piss myself! We've got to get them out of there!'

'They won't go off,' observed Maurette.

'Of course they bloody well won't of their own accord,' snapped back Ledoux. 'But what if some nosey-parker decides to take a look in those suitcases . . .'

'You never saw such a polite lot as those South African Security guys,' sneered Maurette. 'Far too gentlemanly ever to dream of searching an IAEA delegate's luggage!'

'It's not Security I'm worrying about. It's the kind of outside chance that can bugger a whole plan. The sort of thing you never thought could happen. Something piddling, a servant taking a chance.'

'The suitcases are locked. No one would know what an SZ charge was, even if they saw it.'

'Don't be too sure,' answered Ledoux. 'A petty thief would be forgiven if he went to the police and split the beans about suspicious-looking containers and detonators stashed away in a loft.'

'What do you propose to do?'

For a moment, Ledoux looked as if he would explode again. Then he pulled himself together and said levelly, 'Our plan resolves itself into two parts. First, we have got to find a place, a hiding-place which no one will suspect, where we can hide away those demolition charges. Second, we have got to think up a plan how to get them past the security gate at Gougo.'

'Car bomb?' suggested Maurette. 'This station wagon?'

'Even if you wanted to make a kamikaze run through the gate, I wouldn't let you,' replied Ledoux. 'It's not merely an explosion we're aiming at. It's an explosion that has to look like a SYNROC-R drum going up. A car-load of SZ would be – a car bomb. Finish. It wouldn't affect the value of SYNROC-R in the least in the eyes of the delegates. We have got to smuggle our high explosive right in there among the SYNROC-R drums – somehow.'

'Somehow!' echoed Maurette.

Maurette was to echo that another thirty-five kilometres further on after they had turned off the main road on to the subsidiary leading to the repository proper. They carried on only a limited distance along it, stopping well short of the outer security fence they had observed from the air.

They drew a complete blank.

After an aimless halt, they finally drove in tense silence, burning heat and a rising north-westerly wind away from their target, Gougo, and headed into a constellation of pans flanking the main road to the south in order to give backing to their statements that they had inspected the groundwater catchments in the vicinity of the repository. Psychologists would have found Ledoux's dread of open spaces, called agoraphobia, interesting. He longed to find even a tree or a rock behind which to shelter. His temper deteriorated with the afternoon. The whole area was to him a derated version of his desert exile island off Yemen, in the Red Sea. There, at least, he had had the mastermind of terrorism, Carlos the Jackal, to dream dreams with. Here, there was – nothing.

Several times, as the day wore on endlessly, they sighted helicopters in the distance carrying the IAEA delegates, and on one occasion a machine came and hovered over their vehicle. They got out and waved. At least their cover story – geographically speaking – would ring true. So would the dust-covered station wagon.

They finally sought sanctuary again, in the late afternoon, on Hartogskloof's sandy causeway and green trees.

Maurette rinsed the dust from his mouth with a last swill of Rencha's coffee and spat it out on the sand.

'This dump too – good for nothing but an ambush,' he said savagely.

'Ambush – here? What? Who?' retorted Ledoux. The Bakunin was on his last Gauloise and it was a long way home.

Later that night, he was to remember Maurette's throwaway words.

Chapter 11

'Code – KO-RAD-003. KO for Koeberg. RAD for rad-waste, contaminated medical and laboratory discards. 003, number three drum loaded singly on left rear saddle of transporter . . .'

The light voice at the other end of the phone to Ledoux was bored. The fluctuations in volume provided by the cranky telephone, now loud, now light years away, served as a welcome counterpoint to the monotonous recital.

Recital it was: Ledoux was being fed details of the first transporter-load of SYNROC-R destined for the Gougo repository. He had been called from a council of war to take the call – it was more in the nature of a critical post-mortem on the inspection day's non-events – in Dr Waldegg's hut.

It was early evening, before dinner.

Both Professors Nakanishi and Chillun To were carping, accusing. Both men were tired, rattled by their own lack of success in putting over China's scientific objections to the groundwater set-up of the Cheating Pan floodplain. The images persisted before their eyes of those awful parched plains below the helicopter.

The voice at the other end of Ledoux's phone was French. Roger Lichine was a Bakunin 'sleeper' at Koeberg. He had been planted at the nuclear power station years before to await, like the Sleeping Beauty, the resuscitating kiss of life. Roger Lichine did not want to be activated. He had dug himself so well into the good life at Koeberg that he had become part of the scene. Now, the Bakunin foray into the IAEA gathering at Cheating Pan had brought him out of mothballs, into the front line.

Lichine was a bachelor. He was a small man with a ready,

almost elfin, grin, and a puckish sense of humour which gained clout from his French accent and foreign twist with words. Men loved to go fishing with him up the rich west Cape coast beyond Saldanha; women wanted to stroke his soft brown hair which aroused their maternal instincts as it fell across his forehead in a cutesy-poo wisp like a child.

Roger Lichine was the man who killed Rencha's husband.

If the DST had lost touch with Rencha – Anna-Kai Cerny – after she had fled from France, the Bakunin had not. They traced her to Cape Town. It had taken time. By then, she had married John Krummect and was living happily in Cape Town. Together they had visited the ruin of Corbel Camp as Campbell and *Bluebird* had forsaken it. They made plans for its restoration.

Lichine, on orders from the then head of the Bakunin, Detroyat (Ledoux had not then returned to France from exile with Carlos the Jackal in the Middle East), had approached Rencha secretly. She had been petrified by the reappearance of the Bakunin in her life. Become a sleeper at Koeberg, they said – which at that stage had been a target of the Bakunin (the French government had, in fact, knuckled under to its threat not to supply more nuclear power stations to South Africa) – or else.

Rencha, terrified, had refused. Retribution had been sure and swift. Lichine had staged a fake accident; Rencha and John Krummect's car had rolled down a mountainside in Bain's Kloof, one of the Cape's major passes, as they had been returning from inspecting an old Cape homestead in need of restoration.

Lichine believed in keeping his yardarm clear. He had watched the car somersault down the mountainside in the rain; he did not go near in order to leave no footprints or other clues; there could have been no survivors from such a wreck. He took a flight back to Paris that same evening.

Nonetheless, he returned. It was he who became the Bakunin sleeper at Koeberg in Rencha's place. He slotted into the job naturally because of his early scientific training. His security clearance was watertight: the Bakunin did its homework well. Of Rencha there was no trace. Cheating Pan had buried her as securely as a grave.

'. . . weight, fifty kilograms. There are three of this type of drum, loaded in saddles at the rear. The other twelve drums on the transporter all contain SYNROC-R, loaded at the cab end . . .'

Lichine's voice faded away into almost nothing.

Ledoux waited, phone in one hand, pencil in the other, to jot down Lichine's information. What possible use it could be, he had no idea. It didn't matter to a bomb whether a SYNROC-R drum weighed fifty or a hundred kilograms. The phone, in an enclosed cubicle for privacy, was situated in the old farmhouse complex, down a passageway leading to the kitchen. The two men had little fear of being overheard; even if they were, they were speaking French, which would not be understood by the operator.

'For crying out!' Lichine's voice was audible again now. 'Can you hear me? Tell the bloody exchange to give us another line . . .'

'The exchange is a hundred kilometres away, at a settlement called Brandvlei, they tell me. It's useless. The wind blows, the phone blows. It's a way of life here.'

'How am I supposed to supply you with information when every time there is a gust . . .?'

'You're wasting good time – get on with it!' snapped Ledoux. He was the boss, but he felt like a kid on the carpet after his grilling by Waldegg and the two Chinese.

'Every flatbed transporter carries fifteen drums – three of discarded medical and lab equipment, clothing and so on, the other twelve are SYNROC-R . . .'

'You've already told me all that,' interrupted Ledoux. 'What else?'

'You've got the whole story now,' said Lichine. The phone had stopped playing up. 'There's nothing else, except that the first transporter is standing by all loaded up. It's the first vehicle of the shuttle. It leaves here at 7 a.m. tomorrow.'

'Where are you speaking from – is it safe?' Ledoux felt he had to pull his rank to show he was in charge.

'My flat. Of course it's safe. You wouldn't expect me to go through the Koeberg exchange, would you?'

'Not if you wanted to save your skin.'

'How is the IAEA gathering progressing?' asked Lichine in less businesslike tones.

'It progresses. The delegates have been flying all day. The schedule is being kept.'

'You don't sound very enthusiastic.'

'You wouldn't be either, if you saw this place. Corbel Camp! Jeez, what a dump and what a country! Not a woman in sight either – sorry, there's one, and she owns it. Name of Rencha Krummect.'

Ledoux thought the phone had gone dead again. There was no voice from the other end. But the line was open: he could hear Lichine's intake of breath. Stunned intake.

'Repeat that – *what did you say?*'

Either Lichine was half shouting or the line had miraculously doubled its decibels.

'Rencha Krummect.'

The half-hiccup the phone gave was due to Lichine, not to the instrument.

'Describe her!'

'Sort of auburn hair, green eyes, a pair on her that any girl would go crazy for, carries a load of sex, I'd say – what are you getting excited about?'

Lichine replied as levelly as he could. 'You have just described Anna-Kai Cerny.'

It was Ledoux's turn to take a verbal left cross to the jaw. The name was spoken of with awe by terrorists in Europe – dedicated killers like the Action Directe, the German Red Army Faction, the Belgian Fighting Communist Cells. She was the only Bakunin who had double-crossed the movement and got away with it. The Bakunin had a fearsome code. It was rooted deep in a line of comradeship descent via the Japanese. Red Army terrorists from a medieval society of

assassins. Any Bakunin who failed in a mission or was identified, either committed suicide or was executed.

'*Anna-Kai Cerny!*'

Lichine's words boiled over. 'It was before your time with
the Bakunins – in Detroyat's. We traced her to the Cape. I
was assigned . . . we gave her the choice . . . she could have
been the Koeberg sleeper . . . she refused . . .'

'Why didn't you kill her?' Ledoux's voice was impersonal.

'I did. That was my mission. I saw her car hurtle down the
mountainside . . .' Lichine explained rapidly how he had laid
the trap for Rencha and her husband in Bain's Kloof. There
had been no need to double-check. No one could have come
out of that smash alive. He had returned post-haste to France,
reporting success. Subsequently, a Bakunin stringer had reported no sign of Rencha. The reasonable assumption was that
she was dead.

'But you didn't wait to make one hundred per cent certain?'
Ledoux was judicial.

'If you mean, did I open her coffin and look inside,
the answer is no.' Lichine was waspish. He knew what
Ledoux was driving at. 'If you want any further proof,
I have been here for years, and when I got the job at Koeberg I left no stone unturned in Cape Town to trace Rencha
Krummect just to make doubly certain. She was gone –
gone!'

'That's what happened previously in Paris also,' Ledoux
said coldly. 'She just vanished utterly.'

But he wasn't really thinking of sitting in judgement on
Lichine after all this time. As head of the Bakunin, he was its
executioner. He'd have to kill Rencha, of course. A quick
bullet would be too surgical, too merciful, too impersonal, to
fit the crime of her defection from the Bakunin. The thought
pulsed through his brain, how some of those bodies had been
brought naked to him in the Argentine death squad . . . This
woman had a better body than most of them . . . His knuckles
went white. The pencil with which he had been taking notes

snapped between his fingers. The phone booth was suffocating from the heat which swept over him.

He deliberately pushed the subject of Rencha from the forefront of his mind. She might well prove to be of use to him in regard to SYNROC-R before he finished her off. How, he couldn't think at this stage. In any event, that would have to stand in the queue of events. The bomb blast was priority number one.

Suppressed emotion made his voice harsh. 'Get on with it!' he rapped out at Lichine.

'You mean . . .?'

'The drums, damn you! What do you think we were talking about?'

Lichine babbled repetitively, thankful to be let off the Rencha hook, for the moment. 'The flatbed is standing by now, like I said, all ready loaded up. It leaves tomorrow at 7 a.m. . . .'

Perhaps it was the charge of adrenalin which had surged through his veins at the thought of executing Rencha which dredged up out of Ledoux's unconscious Maurette's throw-away remark that afternoon.

Ambush! Hartogskloof!

He'd ambush the flatbed!

Hartogskloof was the place!

Lichine had just said, one of the drums at the rear weighed fifty kilograms. Allowing for the weight of the drum itself, he could assume that it could probably hold a quantity of about thirty kilograms of high explosive – enough to blow the Gougo repository sky-high to hell . . .!

He broke in excitedly. 'Repeat that! Three drums, each containing something like thirty kilograms of contaminated lab equipment and clothing – right?'

'Thirty-five kilograms, to be exact. What's eating you?'

'You said saddles. What do you mean, saddles? Are the drums secured to them? How – how, man, how?'

'The saddles are wooden supports fixed to the floor of the flatbed. The drums fit into them. They're fitted for size.

The saddles at the rear are smaller because the drums of contaminated equipment are smaller than the SYNROC-R drums. They are up forward.'

Ledoux rushed on. 'How are they secured? Are they locked?'

'No. Straps. Ordinary leather straps, with buckles. No locks. What is all this about?'

Bossiere and the DST would have borne long and grudging testimony to Ledoux's bomb plans. They were always simple, with an imaginative, innovative flair which had kept him out of their clutches for more times than they cared to remember.

Ledoux dropped his voice a little, as if there were a danger (which there was not) of being overheard. He spoke rapidly and incisively; the print-out of his masterplan flashed and formed even as he outlined it.

'Maurette – and I – are going to ambush that flatbed. There's a pass, a tailor-made site, about an hour's driving distance from the repository. I am going to grab one of those drums at the back and substitute a drum of high explosive. The transporter will carry on to the repository and deliver the loaded drum. Remote control detonation on the final day of the delegates' inspection! They'll all be concentrated at Gougo – perfect target!'

'You must be out of your mind!' burst out Lichine. 'Ambush the flatbed! You'll never get away with it!'

'Why not?'

'Every drum in a load is clearly marked with its own code. I've just given them to you. Then there are the loading manifests. The flatbed crew carries the originals, and every drum is checked through the reception area at Gougo on arrival against a duplicate copy already telexed to it. That's not all. The drums and documents are checked again at the transfer area before the site vehicle is reloaded on its way to the trenches for off-loading and burial . . .'

Ledoux was hardly listening. 'What colour are those drums at the rear you were talking about – the ones with the discarded equipment?'

'Drums are colour-coded according to their contents . . .'

'Don't throw shit at me!' snapped Ledoux. 'Answer my bloody question! What colour are those rear drums?'

'Green. SYNROC-R drums are grey.'

'That code again – the one you first gave me!'

'KO-RAD-003. But I tell you, it won't work. It's straight suicide! You won't – can't – get a drum of explosive past the checks!'

'Why not?' demanded Ledoux. 'They don't check for explosive. My drum won't – can't have – a millirad of radiation leakage. Their sole concern is radiation. They told me that myself today as we flew over the place!'

'The manifests . . .' bleated Lichine.

'My drum will have the same manifests, the same code, the same colour, and the same weight!' went on Ledoux. He rapped out, 'How is the code put on? Paint? What colour?'

'There are special stencils, but they haven't arrived,' Lichine explained unhappily. 'It's part of the hassles we've been having with SYNROC-R. So we've chalked them on . . .'

'With what, man?'

'Ordinary packing pencil.'

'Ah!'

'This crazy plan is going to blow open the whole Bakunin involvement here,' whimpered Lichine. 'It's the road to suicide for all of us!'

'Don't worry about your skin – yet,' retorted Ledoux. 'This plan is going to work. I'll make it work!'

The sleeper's voice suddenly became confident, stronger. He had had time to collect his thoughts after the avalanche of Ledoux's plan had swept over him.

'You've overlooked the most important snag of all,' he said. 'When any sort of accident happens to a transporter, there are strict procedures laid down which have to be followed by the driver and co-driver. They've been in operation for the other repository in Namaqualand for a long time. I can't see a hold-up not being regarded as an emergency. All transporters carry their own radio and are in touch with Koeberg during their trips. Progress is monitored at regular intervals. In an emergency, the driver radios Koeberg. Emergency procedures go into operation. A standby crew, specially trained in handling nuclear material, is rushed to the spot. The area is sealed off. The drums are recovered. Affected drums – which would include your drum of high explosive – are opened and tested at a special decontamination facility. There is no way you can get away with this crazy idea.'

Ledoux laughed. 'I can't spend all night explaining my plan, even if it was wise to go on using this phone for so long,' he said. 'I've got the answers. It *will* work, I tell you.'

Lichine added, 'You haven't even got a green drum to substitute for one on the flatbed . . .'

'Haven't I?'

The prospect of action, daring action, always had the effect of clearing Ledoux's brain laser-sharp. Only torture did it better. At Lichine's words, his mind had leaped out to Cheating Pan. That's where the answer was!

'Haven't I?' he repeated derisively. But there was one important aspect to which he had not yet found a solution: he'd by-pass that, like an army in full pursuit by-passes a troublesome pocket of resistance.

He had to get on with it – tonight!

'Keep in touch,' he told Lichine briefly. 'There may be some minor details that need clearing up.'

'Minor details!' bleated Lichine. 'Listen . . .'

Ledoux rang off.

Lichine might have been a Bakunin sleeper. But he wouldn't sleep tonight.

Chapter 12

'Tomorrow?'

'Just about this time.' Ledoux checked his watch. It was shortly before seven, following the call from Lichine.

'We first shoot the driver and his mate, and then . . .?' Maurette was agog, elated. Ledoux had rejoined his fellow-Bakunin at the hut; he had waited to pass on an angry message from Dr Waldegg that he and the two Chinese delegates had gone on to the main lounge – what had kept Ledoux so long on the phone? He was ordered to join them immediately and explain his absence.

Ledoux had simply laughed off Waldegg's instructions derisively. He was so hyped up over the ambush plan that he had left the phone at the double and in doing so had almost collided with the little Frenchman he knew to be one of the official French team. He offered no apology; his mind was too full of logistics. What he did not know was that Bossiere had been hanging around the cubicle, out of sight, for more than twenty minutes, trying to eavesdrop (unsuccessfully) on only a few words of the conversation. What was keeping Ledoux glued to the phone? Who was at the other end? At one stage he had heard Ledoux's voice raised, excited, and from then on, it seemed, it had become brisk, full of a purpose it had lacked before. The impatient brush-off bore out, in Bossiere's mind, that Ledoux was up to something – what?

'We don't shoot anyone – this is an ambush with a difference,' answered Ledoux.

'A hijack, but no shooting? How's that possible?' Maurette was cast down. His killer mind worked from A to Z; there were no grey areas in between. But he was one of the best; he never allowed his brains to cloud his trigger-finger.

Ledoux played with his words to Maurette the way a cat does with a mouse. It was his nature.

'The driver and his mate may live to thank us, if it works out the way I think.'

'Tell me what you think, Jean.'

It wasn't often Maurette dared call him Jean. The prospect of action, however, forged a closer tie than was otherwise possible with the stand-off personality of the Bakunin leader.

'We're going to change drums on the transporter – put our own, stuffed with high explosive, in place of one which is

92

carrying discards, like contaminated lab equipment and clothing.'

'Ah!'

Ledoux lit a Gauloise from a new packet, but threw it away. He didn't need any stimulus now that he had his plan.

'You said yourself, nothing, but nothing, will get past the security checks at the repository. So we must have them think they are conveying their own stuff in. But in fact it will be ours. Thirty kilos or thereabouts of SZ charges . . .' he raced on.

'The SZ-6 canisters are big – we'll have to see how they fit into a drum.' Maurette's mind, trained in sophisticated bombing techniques, had simply accepted the main fact of beating the Gougo security and leapt on to the mechanics.

'We'll get to all that in a moment,' replied Ledoux. 'What we need right now is a drum – a drum of our own – which is an exact match to one of those on the flatbed.'

'You've got something in mind,' observed Maurette.

Ledoux laughed. 'Yeah. That's where we're headed for right now. Remember the crash demonstration?'

'Hell's teeth!' exclaimed Maurette. 'The end of the runway and *Bluebird*'s track was lined with drums!'

'Marker drums,' added Ledoux triumphantly. 'We're on our way to pick up one of them. But we must have a *green* drum – do you remember any such?'

Maurette thought for a moment. 'Naw. There were lots of drums, could have been any colour. I seem to remember that some were different from others. That's all.'

'We're getting ourselves out there right away – hope they haven't cleared the place.'

'They hadn't this morning when we returned in the chopper.'

'Let's go.'

'What about Waldegg?'

'Stuff him. This is our show.'

The two Bakunins moved quickly outside to where the station wagon was parked. They debated for a moment whether or not to lock the door for Dr Waldegg, then decided (both their minds were now acutely focused on the suitcases in the loft) that it would be safest to do so.

Ledoux started the engine and they shot off. He switched on the headlights only when they were well clear of the lighted area of Corbel Camp in case their departure should have been seen.

It was. Their hurried take-off was witnessed by Henri Bossiere.

It would be foolish, the DST man decided, to rush after the terrorists in his own car. Headlights would be a giveaway. For the moment, he could only watch and wait. He walked slowly towards the main lounge where the delegates were congregated for a pre-dinner drink, a deeply troubled man.

The distance from Corbel Camp to the site where the crash had been staged was about four kilometres; from the Pan's edge proper it was about a kilometre and a half.

'Those short, steep bends on the pass couldn't be better for our job,' exclaimed Maurette. 'Do we go for them once the flatbed's over the causeway?'

Ledoux liked Maurette's unqualified enthusiasm for his plan, by contrast to Lichine's objections and backtracking.

'That's the place,' he replied. He hadn't worked out the plan in detail, but what Maurette was saying made sense.

'We play it absolutely natural – that is what Carlos said, and that's why he always got away with it the way he did,' continued Ledoux. 'He told me he was once doing a job with five kilos of Samtex in a shopping bag he was carrying and an old dear came up to him and started chatting. And there the bomb was, ticking away with only five minutes to go! He didn't get flustered. He spoke to her for a couple of minutes, and then went off and planted it with almost no time to spare. Afterwards the police questioned her, and she told how the kind gentleman had been chatting to her almost right up to the time of the blast. So, said the police, it couldn't have been the kind, unhurrying gentleman if he had been intending to plant a bomb.'

'Where do we hide ourselves and the station wagon in the pass?' asked Maurette.

'We don't,' replied Ledoux. 'I said, we play it natural. We'll park on the strip of sand near the causeway and just be standing there having a smoke and a cup of coffee when the transporter comes in sight . . .'

'They'll identify us in their headlights,' broke in Maurette uneasily.

'Sure they will. We're also going to speak to them as the transporter goes up the pass. They'll know our faces anyway.'

'What's up your sleeve?' asked Maurette.

'The flatbed goes past us at the causeway – right? Those bends are steep, steep. She'll change right down into lowest gear. Snail's pace. Only for us, it's a running pace. We run after the transporter, jump aboard, loosen the straps of our target – one green drum at the rear – heave it aboard . . .'

'Jeez!' exclaimed Maurette. 'You said this was a hijack with a difference! And our bomb drum? Carrying all those kilos is bloody heavy to go sprinting after a vehicle, even if it's moving at a snail's pace.'

Ledoux jerked his thumb in the direction of the station wagon's capacious loading area behind his seat.

'We have *our* bomb green drum all coded up and ready, right here. We *drive* after the flatbed, stop it, and say, please mister, a drum fell off the back of your transporter and here we're bringing it back to you.'

'I don't believe it!' exclaimed Maurette. 'I don't believe it!'

'Objections?' Ledoux's voice turned hard.

For a reply, Maurette laughed. 'Jean, you're a genius, that's what! Play it natural – what could be more natural?'

Ledoux relaxed. He said a little tentatively, 'Think it will work?'

'Like a bomb.' Maurette grinned at his own simile. 'So the transporter will carry on with our drum containing the bomb! What about checks at the repository?'

'If the codes are right and the colour of the drum is right, and the weight is right, all they check for is radiation leakage. High explosive doesn't leak radiation.'

'I won't even need a gun,' said Maurette.

Ledoux leaned forward, peered through the windscreen. A strong, hot north-westerly wind, known locally as a 'berg wind', which generally preceded the onset of a cold front from the south, was bringing dust from the Pan and obscuring the stars. Visibility seemed to be getting worse, the nearer they drew to the Pan itself.

'That's what I said. This is hijack without a gun.'

'When do we blow her?'

'Five days from now. The last day of the delegates' inspection. You've seen the official schedule. They'll all be at the repository being shown how the SYNROC-R drums are buried and covered over in the trenches. Our bomb will be amongst 'em. It'll take the SYNROC-R and the delegates with it sky-high.'

'Thirty kilos or so should make one hell of a mess,' observed Maurette appreciatively. 'But we've got a problem. How do we set her off – remote, command or timer detonation?'

'What do you think is best for this job?'

'Five days is a hell of a time to wait. Timer mightn't be all that exact. Can't we set it off before the last day on another suitable occasion?'

'Not if we want to catch some of the delegates too. They'll be spread out at other times. For instance, they are visiting the other repository in Namaqualand, and on another day Dr West is scheduled to demonstrate the kimberlite workings. No, none of those occasions is suitable. It must be the last day at Gougo.'

Maurette said, 'There's a new-type photocell detonator amongst the stuff we collected in the suitcases. I rather fancy it. I've never used the sun's rays to activate a bomb before.'

'It's out,' answered Ledoux. 'What if the photocell is covered over by the backfilling in the trench? The sun's rays will be cut off from it. Or maybe, if it's not covered by earth, other drums could be stacked on top of it and prevent the light reaching the detonator.'

'I hadn't thought of that,' conceded Maurette. His wizardry with microcircuitry placed him among the most skilful bomb-masters in Europe. 'Command detonation?'

Ledoux shrugged. 'You need a wire – how could we manage that here? It's okay for a built-up area like a city, but here a wire running from the burial trench would be a complete giveaway, even if it were possible for us to rig it. No, my money's on remote control – by coded radio signal – the best in the book, as far as I am concerned. We've got the trigger back there at the hut, that harmless-looking so-called transistor radio of mine.'

Maurette grinned appreciatively. Both men were keyed up at the prospect of action – killer action. They'd been through it before.

'I watched you go through the customs when we arrived,' he said, shaking his head at the recollection. '"Anything to declare, sir?"' He mimicked the South African accent. 'And you shoved the radio at him. "Personal use, sir?" And bloody how, you should have said. He never suspected a thing.'

'No transistor radio ever looked like mine inside!' replied Ledoux.

'What's its range – three kilometres?'

'Not as much as that. Two is the optimum, I'd say, with the bomb being located below ground level in the trench. Three at the outside.'

'We've got a problem, then. Where do we fire it from?'

'There was a small hill near the entrance gate, remember? I want to have a closer look at that. It will give us the elevation we need.'

'And the secrecy. We will have to keep out of the way. We don't want to get hurt.'

'We won't, not at two kilometres' range. But neither do we want to draw attention to ourselves. We can't just sit in a parking lot in the repository and trigger a radio device. The scheduled ground inspection is tomorrow. That could give us the opportunity for a close look-see at the best spot.'

'No more messing about like today! I've had a gutsful of this countryside.'

'Today gave us Hartogskloof.'

'Is that what it's called?'

'Yeah. I checked on the road map there in the cubby on my way back from the phone,' said Ledoux.

'Bloody name.'

'All names are bloody hereabouts.'

'The skin of the drum could mask our detonation signal. We must fix something outside. Any idea how thick a steel casing like that would be?'

'We'll judge when we find one tonight.'

'We'll have to rig some kind of antenna on the outside to catch our signal, with a lead wire to the charges inside.'

'Our drum mustn't appear the slightest bit different from any others of the load,' said Ledoux. 'It has to look, seem, weigh and be coded the same as all the others.'

'Then the sooner we find a drum, the better.'

A signpost showed in the headlights. It was one of Rencha's neat hand-written signs. An arrow indicated 'airfield' one way and 'Corbel Camp' the other.

Ledoux stopped. 'Just what the codeman ordered!'

'What are you talking about?'

'Lichine said the codes of the first radwaste loads were written in packaging pencil.' He indicated the sign. 'Red, on a green drum. We'll borrow a pencil from the lady who wrote these.'

Mention of Rencha brought to mind the secret of her Bakunin connection which Lichine had unmasked. He was about to recount it to Maurette when a gust of wind plucked at the station wagon. It brought with it a load of dust as fine as talcum powder, as impenetrable as fog. Ledoux lost sight of the track. He was not to know that Sir Malcolm Campbell had had to postpone his attempts on the speed record several times because of Cheating Pan's dust storms, nor the stories of men who had tried to walk across it, only to wander in circles until they died.

Ledoux braked almost to a standstill.

'For crying out loud!' exclaimed Maurette. 'Do you think you can find the way?'

'The whole pan can get up and walk but we will carry on – whatever,' retorted Ledoux. 'Tonight's our night. Either we find the drum we want tonight, load it and prime it, or else we call off the hijack. Now is our opportunity. I'm not letting it go. Understood?'

'Left a bit,' said Maurette for an answer, peering out his window. 'I can make out tyre marks.'

Ledoux regained the track; they were on course again, and travelling now over the surface of the Pan itself. The bumpy basalt had given way to a smooth, billiard-table flatness.

They headed into the thickening murk.

Chapter 13

'We load and prime the drum tonight – but where?'

Maurette fired the question which Ledoux had deliberately thrust to the back of his mind. It was one of those troublesome 'pockets of resistance' which, he had decided after he had put down the phone to Lichine, he would work out later. Mopping up, the army called it. Now he had to face it.

He resorted to generalities. 'We have to have a place which is secluded and where we can be sure we won't be disturbed.'

Maurette gestured beyond the windscreen. 'Plenty of that here.'

The station wagon was picking its way. It seemed to Ledoux that the tyre marks were remarkably faint, considering that scores of vehicles must have travelled back and forth to the airfield during the past couple of days. What he did not know was that by carrying straight on they had missed the main track to the airfield proper, which branched sharp right the moment the Corbel Camp road met the Pan. They had, in fact, taken a side-route: this headed towards the south-western terminal-point of *Bluebird*'s track. A hill called Kranskop – a flying hazard – blocked this extremity.

Ledoux did not reply. Maurette continued. 'Okay, we find our drum tonight, take it back to camp . . .'

'Noways,' broke in Ledoux. 'Too risky.'

'No one is likely to come nosing round in the middle of the night to see what we are doing.'

'That part of it isn't too bad. But what to do with a drumful of high explosive for the next five days? Where do you propose to hide it?'

'The loft . . .'

'Out!' retorted Ledoux. 'Any servant or the housekeeper could spot it, and certainly questions would be asked. Guests don't keep drums – big drums – in their lofts.'

'I hadn't thought of that,' admitted Maurette.

'Skip it for the moment. We'll go into it when we've located our drum.' Ledoux's voice was tense. Meticulous attention to detail was the keynote of success. One small giveaway would make the hijacked drum suspect. The plan would then abort.

As they travelled further, visibility became poorer and poorer. Ledoux cursed the station wagon's lack of foglights. Even on maximum dip, the headlights threw back more light into his eyes than they cast forward against the brown, swirling barrier.

'Hold it!'

A faint reflection lanced back from Maurette's side, light off metal.

Ledoux clicked the lights on full. The ghost of the Hercules transport, great and grey, showed.

'Got it!' exclaimed Ledoux. 'It's the airfield, all right!'

'But not where we wanted to hit it. This is the aircraft parking bay, right at the end of *Bluebird*'s track.'

'So what? All we need is the runway as a guide to the crash site, and we've found it.'

He turned towards the big machine. Four smaller ghosts showed up, helicopters which had played workhorse all day to the delegates on their groundwater inspection flights. The airfield was deserted. Ground crews and flying personnel were accommodated in temporary quarters at Gougo, since Corbel Camp was full to the seams. They commuted by means of a single spare helicopter from the repository's own airfield.

'We'll follow the runway and pick up the position of the crash. That's where the drums start,' said Ledoux.

The hard surface of the airfield was easy to follow. In minutes, the unmistakable black-and-white concrete markers of the demonstration showed up in the headlights.

'Look – drums! There they are!'

Ledoux speeded up towards them. Drums lined both sides of the crash site. Ledoux stopped. Both men jumped out. There was no need for the flashlights they had brought along. The headlights revealed the drums' colour. Grey!

'The wrong thing completely.' Ledoux's voice was bitterly disappointed.

'They look bigger than some of the others we saw on the TV monitors,' added Maurette.

'These must be SYNROC-R containers. Lichine said they were different from what we are after.'

'Apart from being green, how different, did he say?'

'He didn't. I was a fool not to have questioned him more closely. I thought we couldn't go wrong.'

'I seem to remember that some of the drums had ridges – kind of flanges – round them,' went on Maurette.

'It's no good standing here and crying about it,' snapped Ledoux. 'We'll press on. Maybe our kind of drums are further up the runway.'

They weren't. The double row of drums, grey as Soviet sentries, came to an abrupt end after a few minutes' motoring.

'What now?'

'If I knew, I wouldn't have stopped.' Ledoux was becoming more uptight by the minute.

'Couldn't we improvise with a grey drum?'

'No! It's a case of all or nothing. We'll press on.'

Maurette said eagerly, 'I seem to remember now! There was a gap in the lines of drums before the final run-in to the transporter. Hell, yes, I'm right! I thought, the car's slowing down, but it was only an illusion because there was a gap in the line of the drums. They gave the impression of speed.'

'Let's go.'

Ledoux accelerated. The blowing murk came at the station wagon from every side. If he had been less disappointed, he would have taken more trouble to watch the amorphous surface under his wheels. There was nothing to guide him any more. Tyre marks – whether planes' or vehicles' – seemed to have vanished.

Neither Ledoux nor Maurette were sensitive men. But now they were scared. Ledoux was scared in a different way from his fear earlier in the day of the wide-open spaces. Maurette in his turn longed for a friendly street corner. Both were overcome by an awful, isolated feeling of being adrift, rudderless and without compass, in a hot blanket of sand which reached for their throats, their palates, their tongues. They were undergoing their preliminary baptism of fire in Cheating Pan's foyer of death and darkness. There was a frightening feeling of vacuum, of non-being. It was ultra-real; it began to assume the proportions of nightmare.

'Any water?' Ledoux's words were thick.

'I didn't bring anything at all to drink. I never guessed it would be like this.'

Ledoux increased speed, then turned. The manœuvre – only worsening their plight – was the measure of his inner panic.

'See anything?'

'Shut up! Of course I don't. Can you?'

The station wagon pushed on, shouldering aside the curtain of darkness. It closed remorselessly behind.

Maurette asked, 'Which way *was* the wind blowing? Maybe we could get ourselves oriented – by all that's holy, look!'

For a desperate moment Ledoux thought they must have wandered all the way back to Corbel Camp.

A corbelled white roof loomed ahead.

He flicked the lights to full to get a better view. A stone wall rose up in front of the hut also, like a stage effect.

'I know where we are!' Ledoux's fears were behind him. 'I know this place! I saw it from the chopper this morning! It's away to the left of the runway as you come in to land, two or three kilometres, I'd guess. There's a hill behind it. I've got my bearings now! If we head back dead on the course we've come, we'll land right back at the airstrip!'

The vehicle's lights picked up a big double wrought-iron gate.

'Gravestones!' exclaimed Maurette. 'A bloody graveyard!'

A notice on the gate, picked up by the lights, read: '*Keep out. Private property. Trespassers will be severely dealt with.*'

Ledoux stopped, cut the lights. It took a few seconds for their eyes to adapt to the darkness.

A light showed among the gravestones.

Neither man had survived Bakunin assignments because of poor reflexes. Before Ledoux had even time to hiss, 'Down, out!', Maurette and he had thrown themselves prone on the ground by the side of the station wagon and had their guns aimed.

They waited. The soft dust played games with their breathing. Both men stifled giveaway coughs.

Finally Ledoux whispered, 'Is it coming this way?'

Maurette was better sighted, on the passenger's side, than Ledoux on the driver's.

'Dead still. Can't make it out,' he hissed back.

They waited.

Their night-vision increased every minute. Yet the night was fuzzy with fog. Maurette couldn't judge whether the light was weak in itself, or half-hidden by dust.

'Looks as if someone's holding a light at an inscription, right at the top of a headstone,' whispered Maurette.

'See him?'

'No. It's funny though, the light's shining this way, not at the stone.'

'You take one side of the gate and I'll take the other,' Ledoux ordered. 'Maybe we'll make out who it is, from close. If he comes at you, give it to him!'

'Sure I will.'

The steady light was an easy snapshot target for gunmen as experienced as the two Bakunin. They wriggled to the gate and peered through.

'I'm damned!' exclaimed Maurette. 'The light's *fixed* on the headstone.'

'See anyone your side?'

'This place is empty,' replied Maurette with assurance. 'There's nobody *shining* that light. It's there of its own accord.'

Ledoux took a long look.

'You could be right,' he replied. 'What is a light doing burning here?'

Neither of them had, of course, heard the legend of the two lovers buried in the same grave, nor the Bonsmas' jealous guardianship of the old cemetery. Had Chris Bonsma been around, the least the Bakunins would have got would have been a charge of buckshot in the backside. Nor did they know the legend of the living flame which burned perpetually to the memory of the dead lovers.

'Keep me covered,' ordered Ledoux. 'We'll take a close look-see.'

He opened the catch of the big gate with one hand, keeping his gunhand free and aimed. Maurette provided the back-up.

Nothing moved. The light flickered yellowly. It was more a glow than a light. It hadn't the sharpness of electricity.

The two Bakunins advanced, guns cocked and ready. They reached the source of the light.

The headstone in the top of which it was set was taller than any of the surrounding stones. The light burned inside a tiny glass chamber set inside the granite. The two men could see the tiny flame, bickering now and then as air entered from some unknown source. But the flame itself was protected against being extinguished by the wind.

'Sort of thing you see in war memorials,' said Maurette. Instinctively, he had dropped his voice.

'Wonder what this is in aid of,' said Ledoux. He was able to read a name at the top of the Afrikaans inscription, carved in bigger letters than the rest, 'Bonsma'.

To Maurette's astonishment, Ledoux gave a loud laugh and thumped the top of the gravestone.

'Thank you, Mister Bloody Bonsma or whoever you are!' he exclaimed. He pocketed his gun. 'Thank you!'

'What the hell's got into you?' demanded Maurette.

'We've got it! We've found just what we were looking for – the perfect place to hide our drum, the perfect place to prime it!' Ledoux went on excitedly. 'A graveyard – what could you have more private?'

'I don't care for this dump,' replied Maurette uneasily. 'It gives me the creeps. We haven't got our drum, to start with.'

'We will, we will,' went on Ledoux confidently. 'I reckon I know where the airstrip is now in relation to the graveyard. We'll head straight back there for our drum.'

'We tried that before.'

'Get a flashlight from the station wagon. We're going to have a look also inside the hut.'

Ledoux waited at the headstone until Maurette whistled from the gate. Ledoux took the torch and tried the hut door. It was not locked. The purpose of the place was clear. There were several spades, and a jar or two of battered plastic flowers. It was cold inside, despite the warm wind. The stone walls and a stone ceiling (an unusual feature for a corbelled hut) provided a measure of natural refrigeration for bodies awaiting burial.

'Better and better!' exclaimed Ledoux triumphantly. 'Just the place where we can work in perfect safety! Then tomorrow we can come again, pick up our explosive drum, and take it to the pass for the hijack.'

'Okay, okay,' replied Maurette. 'You've got everything except the drum.'

'It's simply a matter of heading back now in the direction of the airfield and collecting one the right colour.'

'*If* we find one, *if* we can find our way back here again.'

'We'll be okay, you'll see.'

Maurette vented his uncertainty on the headstone light. 'That bloody light gives me the heebie-jeebies – it's like an eye watching every movement we make!'

Don't you wish you were that eye, Bossiere?

Ledoux bulldozed Maurette's fears out of the way. 'I've been worried all along about those two suitcases in the loft at Corbel Camp. There'll also be some explosive charges over after we load the bomb in the drum. Now we can leave them here in safety. Same thing goes for the detonators. Let's get moving!'

At the gate, Ledoux shone the torch beam on to the ground.

'Here it is – a track! The way to the airfield!'

'We lost our way before,' repeated Maurette.

'Aw, put a sock in it!' retorted Ledoux.

The living flame watched their departure.

Chapter 14

The station wagon headed directly into the wind. It seemed to be scraping up handfuls of dust and throwing them against the windscreen. Ledoux craned out of the driver's window to try and pick up the line of the track; on the passenger's side, Maurette used a flashlight to supplement the headlights, calling out directions to Ledoux and conning the vehicle like a ship through a tricky waterway.

They achieved more confident progress than on their previous aimless wanderings. Once or twice they thought they had indeed lost the track; however, by casting around, they picked it up again.

Both men were so absorbed in their task that they almost overran a line of small scrubby bushes.

'Got it!' Ledoux exclaimed triumphantly, braking to a halt. 'I knew we'd hit it if we kept on!'

Maurette spat dust. 'Got what?'

'*Bluebird*'s track. See the bushes? They told me on the day of the crash demonstration that there's a line of them for about twelve kilometres dead straight across the Pan. When *Bluebird* made its speed runs, the tyres cut up the surface and left a furrow. When it rained, water gathered in it and the bushes established themselves. They're so tough, they'll even grow out of a crack in solid rock.'

This gem of environmental lore was lost on Maurette.

'So what? How does it help us?'

'We can't miss our way now. All we do is turn, follow the bushes and carry on till we strike the marker drums.'

'We lost them last time.'

'We approached from the opposite side then. Now we're dead on course. We're following the route of the drone car down *Bluebird*'s track. We can't go wrong.'

'Anything can go wrong on Cheating Pan.'

But it didn't. Ledoux hung on to the line of bushes and motored down *Bluebird*'s track.

'Look!'

A double row of marker drums showed up suddenly in the lights.

Green drums!

Ledoux halted. 'We could have a dozen now, if we wanted.'

The drums were slightly larger than the standard forty-four gallon (two hundred litre) fuel drum in general use. The green ones had been specially manufactured for the conveyance of radwaste. Unlike the smooth exterior of a fuel drum, these had four flanges on their sides. In these were set eyelets. A wire cable, which served to seal the drum at one end by means of a simple click-on locking device, traversed these apertures.

'Now take a look at that!' exclaimed Maurette, whose professional enthusiasm at the sight of the drums now swamped his earlier gloom. 'An antenna – ready-made for remote-control detonation! Just what the doctor ordered!'

'Needs a bit of adapting,' added Ledoux. 'I didn't expect a bonus like that.'

'We'll easily fix a wire leading to the charges inside . . . we'll have to make sure we keep it out of sight . . .' Maurette enthused.

'We can go into all that later,' answered Ledoux.

'The drums look a bit of an awkward fit for the SZ charges,' went on Maurette. 'They'll need some sort of padding.'

'What the hell did Corbel Camp give us blankets and pillows for?' said Ledoux.

Both men burst out laughing. They were excited, exhilarated.

'How does the locking device work?' asked Maurette, fiddling with the wire strop.

'Try snapping it back,' said Ledoux, focusing his torch.

The tension snap-on, snap-off device moved easily to the 'open' position; Maurette was able to loosen the securing cable accordingly.

'There must be an additional inner seal when the drum's packed full of radio-active material. That catch in itself wouldn't be enough,' said Ledoux.

'There's a place here for a padlock also,' pointed out Maurette.

'We're not really concerned with anything escaping from the interior of the drum or not,' said Ledoux. 'The anti-radio-activity seal must fit snugly out of sight on the inside. We can count on no check being made, unless the drum shows signs of contamination.'

'Let's get back and prime her,' said Maurette.

Ledoux spat on a finger and traced a line of wetness across the top. 'Do your thing well, little one.'

'Not so bloody little,' said Maurette, getting a grip on the drum prior to hefting it, with Ledoux's help, to the station wagon.

They loaded the drum into the back of the vehicle, then Maurette said, 'What about taking along another one on the roof rack and using it as a marker at the *Bluebird* track turnoff to the graveyard?'

'Good man!' said Ledoux. 'It'll back up the speedometer readings I've been taking so we won't get lost again.'

They found another drum and secured it to the rack with a length of thin, strong nylon cord which had been in the vehicle for the journey down-country.

They set off. Now Ledoux had the line of scrubby bushes (called *ganna* locally) on his other side. They could easily have overshot the graveyard turnoff without the back-up mileages. Here they positioned the second drum from the roof-rack. Their progress slowed over the three-kilometre stretch to their objective, but the fresh tyre marks of their earlier journey kept them firmly on course. It was only a matter of time until the ghost-white roof of the lying-in hut and the tracery of the wrought-iron gate showed up out of the blowing murk.

The unblinking cyclops-eye of the lovers' headstone watched as they off-loaded the drum and rolled it through the gate.

'There's never been a corpse like this one here before,' remarked Maurette as they steered the drum into the lying-in hut.

'Some corpse!' rejoined Ledoux. 'The difference about this corpse is that it's going to come alive again in less than a week from now. And how it is!'

They left the drum, closed the door, and made the return run in high spirits. The route was easy now that they had the signpost drum as well as the mileage readings. It was easy also, once they had left behind the double row of marker drums flanking *Bluebird*'s track, to steer right ahead and find the big parked Hercules and helicopters. This time, they found the main track from the airfield back to Corbel Camp instead of fiddling about on the side-road which had originally misled them.

Lights were still on all over Corbel Camp. It was about an hour after dinner. There was no sign of Dr Waldegg at their own hut.

'I expect he's over at the main building with the rest of 'em,' said Maurette. 'Hadn't we better keep the boss informed?'

'Forget it. From now on, I'm the boss,' retorted Ledoux. 'We've put our show on the road, and we're going to keep it that way – our way, not his way, or Dr Bloody Nakanishi or anybody else's.'

'Sure, sure,' replied Maurette, startled at the Bakunin leader's vehemence.

'Suitcases – SZ charges!' went on Ledoux.

They did not know it, but the sight of the two suitcases being carried from the hut to the station wagon had an electrifying effect on a watcher nearby. He was Bossiere. Earlier in the evening the DST man had ensconced himself in one of the basalt mini-craters, a vantage-point which enjoyed a view of the Waldegg–Ledoux establishment. Bossiere had had a long vigil. He had taken up station as soon after dinner as he could manage to slip away. His hide-out was a miniature version of the craters in which Rencha had sited entire huts. It was out of sight at the back of the kitchen quarters and also close enough to his own hut for him to observe if anyone should approach it.

Now, Bossiere drew in his breath sharply. The two terrorists moved fast and purposefully. They dumped the suitcases in the back of their vehicle, returned indoors. Ledoux then emerged carrying in one hand his transistor radio and in the other the air luggage weighing scale he had spotted earlier in his search of the hut. Bossiere noted the care with which he laid the radio on the front seat. Maurette followed with an armful of blankets and several pillows. Ledoux made yet another trip, returning with several flashlights.

By the vehicle's interior light the two men seemed to be checking over the items they had brought. What the devil were they up to? No one, argued the DST man, goes off into the night – especially in a place like Cheating Pan in a dust storm – for an assignation between males, if that is what the blankets and pillows were intended for. Nor did they need an extra radio for sweet gay music when the station wagon already had its own. Neither of them seemed gay (you could never tell, of course) but Bossiere's instinct told him that women would be the sex to appeal to Ledoux, at least. Perverted women, or perverted stimulus via women, he noted. That radio – Bossiere cursed himself inwardly for not checking it when he had the opportunity. He knew, from his long experience of terrorists, what devices an apparently harmless radio could conceal. He couldn't prove it, but his fears were that the two suitcases contained explosive and that the radio was a front for an activating device of some kind. As puzzling as anything else was the air luggage weighing scale. What was their destination?

Bossiere had hardly to wait for an answer. The station wagon started up and took the road which led to one place only – Cheating Pan. The other remaining road out of Corbel Camp was to the south, to Gougo ultimately.

Bossiere considered briefly whether he should risk following the Bakunins, but discarded the idea. Headlights, as he had reasoned before, would be a complete giveaway. He had to let them go! Were they on their way to the airfield to plant a bomb in one of the unguarded helicopters, or in the Hercules itself? This idea gained weight from the fact that the two had got out of flying that day on the grounds of Ledoux's illness. Whether genuine or not, he had no way of telling. A bomb set to explode during the delegates' continued inspection flights next day?

All this was speculation. He must have *facts*. Had they left any incriminating facts behind them now? There was only one way to find out – to go and see.

Bossiere threw a swift glance round to make sure that nobody was about, and headed for his second break-in of the terrorists' hut.

Chapter 15

Death's fingerprints were microcircuitry and microchips.

Like miniature steel coffins, too, were the SZ-6 and SZ-3 demolition charges which lay scattered about Ledoux and Maurette in the graveyard lying-in hut. The air luggage weighing scale hung from a projection on the ceiling: its hook could have been a miniature hangman's noose awaiting its victim.

The terrorists were busy priming and arming their green drum to blow up the Gougo repository.

One pall-bearer was enough to pick up and carry one of the small steel coffins of high explosive. This was by means of a collapsible handle set amidships. One end of each coffin was sealed; the other had an open circular mouth agape to take a wire connection which would turn it into a mindless killer at the touch of Ledoux's coded radio signal.

These were Soviet explosives – rough, tough, reliable – the sort which terrorists had insinuated into towns and cities from Belfast to Beirut, from Dusseldorf to Durban. They were durable and could be kicked around in the same way as the Soviet AK-47 rifle, the most popular terrorist weapon in the world.

Ledoux and Maurette knew their expertise: Ledoux was arming the internal impulse detonator which would relay his signal on its lethal journey along seven wires to seven charges – three SZ-6s (weighing six kilograms each) and four SZ-3s (each weighing three kilograms) – which the two men had set aside for the bomb. Maurette, working with a limited-life, high-performance miniature soldering iron and pliers (they looked more like forceps than a tool), would couple the detonator and charges for their tumultuous mating.

The first thing the two Bakunins had done on arrival was to weigh the green drum by suspending it from the weighing scale.

Both men had peered at the tiny indicator.

'Fifteen kilos,' Ledoux noted.

'Let's double-check that, just to be sure,' insisted Maurette. 'This is critical. It's where we could blow the whole plan, if the weight doesn't tally exactly with the Koeberg manifest when they come to check the drum at Gougo.'

They lifted off the drum from the hook, returned it, and

checked a second time. The result coincided.

'Makes our job with the SZ stuff easier. We can work with whole canisters. No need to cut 'em to an exact weight,' observed Ledoux.

'It was something which was worrying me,' added Maurette. 'It's easy when you've got all the time in the world and the facilities. Here you could go wrong.'

'Let's get on.'

Now they were in the middle of their task, both men working swiftly and expertly. Maurette had spread out the connecting wires to the charges in a pattern on the floor like thin outspread cancers. Where each terminated, a demolition charge had been placed ready for connecting up, seven in all.

'Seven's too many for comfort. I'd rather have fewer charges in one bomb, just to make sure,' grumbled Maurette.

'Trouble is, the SZ-6 charges by themselves are too damn big for the drum,' answered Ledoux. 'Five of them would have weighed the thirty kilos we required, but we have to make up the weight with the small three-kilo sizes in order to fit 'em into the drum. We've no choice.'

'We don't know how rough this drum will be treated at the Gougo check-points,' went on Maurette. 'The connections could be bumped loose. I can't go over them twice with the soldering iron as I would like because the battery will be kaput before then. Let's hope it lasts out for the job on hand.'

'Even if one or two connections are poor it won't spoil the show,' replied Ledoux. 'Sympathetic detonation. That will set 'em off anyway. The end result will be the same.'

Maurette shook his head. The prospect of a slipshod explosion offended his professional skill. He was a bomb-armer whom any terrorist group, from the Action Directe to the IRA, would have been glad to have on their roll. His fingers worked, even as he spoke – sure, deft, seemingly with a life of their own, like a fine surgeon's or a concert pianist's.

'You'll cope,' said Ledoux reassuringly. 'You always do. Don't rush it.'

Apart from the seven charges laid ready for connections,

two further spare demolition charges lay to one side. One was a larger SZ-6 and the other a smaller SZ-3. With them were several conventional timer detonators and the photo-cell impulse device which had been included in the cache they had collected on the border of the Kruger National Park. Maurette rather fancied this gadget, but both men had discarded it as impractical because of the nature of their target.

The two Bakunins had made it back to the Haunted Grave-yard in less than half the time it had taken them originally. They now welcomed the fogginess which had bedevilled their first journey, since the deadly part of their mission had begun. They even doused the station wagon's headlights on approaching their destination as a precaution and kept them off. They would have been a considerable help focused into the lying-in hut where they worked. Instead, they used three flashlights.

'Bringing blankets and pillows to stuff into the drum was a brainwave,' said Ledoux. 'I myself didn't think the damn thing's shape would have been so awkward to accommodate the charges.'

'We can't use too much padding,' replied Maurette. 'Our total overall weight must be fifty kilos, no more, no less.'

Ledoux patted the internal impulse detonator he was busy on. 'This little beauty doesn't weigh much.'

'All the bits and pieces add up,' answered Maurette. His fingers continued to work deftly, swiftly, a maestro playing a concerto for killing.

'Maybe we should cut off the handles of the canister charges,' went on Maurette. 'It would do away with any possibility of rattles.'

'The padding will muffle them – I'm not worried,' replied Ledoux. The Bakunin leader sat back on his hunkers. 'Ready! Can I hold the torch for you?'

Maurette nodded, without looking up. 'In there.' He indicated one of the big charges. Ledoux's light probed the SZ-6 as if for an iron ovariectomy; Maurette went in with the glowing tip of the soldering iron and forceps. In seconds, the connection was made.

He switched off the tool. 'I'll give the battery a breather for a minute or two.'

Ledoux gestured at the redundant gear. 'We've got a problem with this stuff. It's too risky, like I said, to keep it at Corbel Camp.'

'Why not simply leave it here at the hut?'

'Also too risky.'

'We're leaving the drum.'

'Only for one day – tomorrow. We'll collect it tomorrow late afternoon for the hijack. But the other stuff – no, there'll be five full days after that until the Gougo blast.'

'What if someone *does* come here tomorrow and see our drum?' asked Maurette.

'It's a million-to-one risk we've got to take,' replied Ledoux. 'But I reckon that even if someone should come, all they'll see is what could be one of the drums from the runway. It might seem strange how it came to be here, but outwardly there'll be no giveaway what's inside. It won't be obvious like a detonator or a demolition charge.'

Maurette snapped on his soldering iron and went to work again. One by one the SZ charges were linked: then came the task of wiring them to the internal impulse detonator. Before the final connection was made, Ledoux, whose specialized field this was, tested and retested the device. Once connected, there was no going back. The next signal would be for real.

Then, the two men carefully tamped in the seven lethal charges of explosive with an expertise which would have made bomb disposal experts blink. Padding of blankets and pillows damped out any sound, movement or rattles from within. A single length of wire remained loose; it came from the internal impulse detonator.

Before sealing the drum's lid, the two Bakunins once again hefted it on to the weighing scale. Maurette concentrated on the calibrations.

'It's a fraction over – something will have to come out. Half a kilo, to be safe.'

'Keep the pillows,' said Ledoux. 'A blanket?'

'Too much. A bit of one.'

Ledoux pulled out a knife and sliced off a piece of blanket.

'Okay. Okay now,' replied Maurette.

Ledoux checked. He, too, was satisfied.

'Now for the last operation.'

It was Ledoux's turn to demonstrate his skill. Before firming the lid into position, it was vital to feed the all-important connecting wire from the internal impulse detonator to the exterior of the drum. The Bakunins had no drill with which to make a hole. But a hole they had to have. They found that the metal eyelets through which the wire cable enveloping the drum passed were secured on the inside of the container by means of screwthreads fastened by nuts. There were two of these eyelets on each end of the drum, and four on each side, set in the flanges. They loosened one of these eyelet nuts in the lid using a spanner from the station wagon, broke off the screwthread, and passed the thin wire through the resulting empty aperture. The broken thread end completely masked the wire's exit; only the most minute examination would have revealed the wire on the inside. In turn, this was connected by means of a drop of solder to the inside face of the enveloping cable. This latter was to play the all-important role of an antenna in receiving the coded radio signal which would detonate the charges.

Ledoux finally straightened up, patted the drum like a whore's bottom. 'You'll ride the beam all right, you beautiful bitch.'

'What's that supposed to mean?'

'American – plays the innocent, but inside is as guilty as hell.'

Ledoux stepped back both to examine and admire his handiwork. As he did so, he stepped on the blade of one of the spades lying about. The shaft thumped his leg.

'That gives me an idea! Sure, I've got it!'

'About what?'

'Those spare charges and detonators. We'll bury 'em! Here, in the graveyard! Who'd ever think of looking in a grave?'

'You intend to open up one of the graves?'

'Bodies don't bite, if that is what is worrying you!' went on Ledoux excitedly. 'In fact, we'll use the grave with the light burning over it – we can't miss it when we come to collect the stuff later.'

'I don't like it,' said Maurette. 'I don't stand back from any man when he's alive and kicking. But when he's dead . . .'

'Forget it – kid's fears,' went on Ledoux roughly. 'Grab yourself a spade and help me – quick!'

The two men took spades, the spare charges and detonators (which they restored to their original plastic yellow wrappings) and headed for the lovers' grave. The living flame burned yellow and baleful in the blowing dust.

Ledoux stepped over the low metal railing surrounding the grave; Maurette hung back, directing the flashlight beam.

'Scared?' jeered the Bakunin leader.

Maurette shook his head. 'No, but this sort of thing brings bad luck. That's all I'm saying.'

'Luck runs the way you make it,' retorted Ledoux. 'Now!'

'How deep are you going to dig?' persisted Maurette.

'Usually they bury bodies six feet,' replied Ledoux sarcastically. 'We haven't got time to go that deep, even if we wanted to. Just a hole deep enough to hide our stuff in.'

He attacked the surface with the spade. It was loose, friable stuff. The main problem was the way it kept sifting back into the hole.

'Now you!' Ledoux said. It wasn't a request, but an order. He handed his own spade to Maurette, who reluctantly climbed over the railing and started shovelling away at the loose ground. Soon they had a shallow grave within the grave. In this they buried the two remaining charges, one an SZ-6 and the other an SZ-3, along with the detonators. The plastic wrapping might have doubled for a body sheet.

When they had done, they flattened and smoothed over the

disturbed surface as carefully as they could, and left the rest to the wind to sweep away traces of their activities.

'Now – Corbel Camp!' said Ledoux. 'We've got a hell of a lot to tell Waldegg since we saw him last.'

The living flame kept a malign eye on the two terrorists as they leaned against the wind to walk back to the lying-in hut, collected their equipment, and made off in the station wagon.

But Maurette had been right. To dig up a grave brings bad luck.

Chapter 16

Ledoux equals Bakunin: Bakunin equals bomb.

The simple equation kept going through Bossiere's mind. It was late – after 11 p.m. The DST man was cold in his spy-perch. The chill struck up from the black basalt against which he sat propped, whorled and contorted as if it had been scooped out by some outsize spoon to fashion the mini-crater which he was using yet again that night to keep the Waldegg–Ledoux hut under surveillance. Its lights were on; they had been for over an hour now since Dr Waldegg had returned alone from Corbel Camp's main complex where he had spent the evening in company with the other IAEA delegates.

Where were Ledoux and Maurette? Bossiere asked himself the same question which, unknown to him, Dr Waldegg had been asking himself all evening and now, as it grew later, with growing anger and concern.

Bossiere had had plenty of time to ponder the question: after a safe interval after watching the two terrorists depart with their two suitcases, blankets, pillows, radio and weighing scale in the direction of Cheating Pan, Bossiere had slipped from his vantage-point, edged through the hut's unlocked door, and cased the place. He did not expect to find anything: these men were far too experienced to leave incriminating clues behind them. Nor did he. All that was left was negative evidence – the two suitcases gone from the loft, the missing radio, and beds apple-pied for their blankets and pillows. If only he had had time previously to open those twin suitcases!

Bakunin equals bomb.

The alliteration drummed through Bossiere's brain. It *was* the answer, *had* to be the answer! Yet, somewhere, somehow, along the line, to his inner intuitiveness regarding terrorists, the simple answer became simplistic. He checked over the facts, the concrete evidence of his own eyes. He had seen two terrorists, one as notorious as any loose in the world, go off with two heavy suitcases which he was sure contained explosives, along a road which led in one direction only, namely, to Cheating Pan's airfield. Target? You could take your pick of five – either the big transport Hercules, or any (or several) of four helicopters. (The fifth was at Gougo, acting as ground crew ferry.) The IAEA delegates were due to fly all day again tomorrow over the groundwater approaches to Cheating Pan. Backing his deductions was the fact that the two men – who had been in such a hurry that they had not turned up to dinner that night – had opted out of their helicopter flight earlier that day on the grounds of airsickness.

What did the Bakunin hope to achieve by destroying an aircraft full of IAEA delegates? Deep down, this is where Bossiere felt his reasoning was going astray. Yet, superficially, he could not fault it. Who was the target? Professor Jaboulet, the IAEA President? What would it achieve if they did kill him? Jaboulet was an international figure – but the Bakunins had already won their battle over further French nuclear power stations in South Africa. The best Bossiere could think of was that the Bakunins wanted to draw attention to, and demand the release of, some terrorists in custody, either in France or elsewhere. Who? Bossiere could not think of one big name offhand: he hated this kind of wholly, academic speculation.

Bossiere allowed another consideration to emerge from the shadows of his mind where he had deliberately avoided examining it. Say Ledoux and Maurette *did* blow up a helicopter(s) and succeed in killing a dozen IAEA delegates, what chance had they of escape? Corbel Camp wasn't Europe or Paris: South African Security would certainly put everyone through the hoop after such a blast. Yet – another dark possibility – what if the escape had already been planned by someone with local knowledge? Rencha Krummect!

Bakunin equals bomb.

It was too simplistic.

These were terrible waters, Bossiere told himself. He reached for a cigarette, stopped himself. He'd have to sit this one out.

At intervals during the evening he had made his way back from his spy-hole to the main building and had mingled with the other delegates. Rencha Krummect! If she was aware of what was going on outside (and Bossiere felt certain that she did) her poise and finesse were magnificent. No wonder she had escaped the DST's net in France! He himself might almost have been taken in, had he not known her background. On one occasion he had deliberately intruded on a conversation between Rencha and Kepler. He had observed them come back to earth, to everyday things, from their own wavelength, at his arrival. Had he not known she was Anna-Kai Cerny, the courier, he would have said that what was going on between her and Kepler was for real.

Bossiere shook his head and smiled in the darkness at the recollection. His natural romanticism read the Indian signs of powerful attraction: his DST assessment, cold as the rock against which he leaned, was of an actress playing her part with superb skill. The game was going on still: the light was on in Rencha's quarters (one of the few left on in camp) and Bossiere had observed her at one stage go through to the kitchen, which was a stone's-throw away from his hide-out.

Suddenly Bossiere stiffened. A pair of headlights cut through the darkness on the Cheating Pan side of the camp, approached, made their way towards Dr Waldegg's hut. Finally, the station wagon drew up. No illumination was needed to reveal its occupants. The hut door was thrown open, and the interior light cut into the darkness. Ledoux and Maurette jumped out, each with an empty suitcase. Bossiere recognized them immediately. With equal perception he recognized something else – those suitcases were now empty! The two men swung them with an air of jauntiness which was patently clear. Jauntiness – or maybe triumph?

The sound of raised voices – Waldegg's from its deep note – reached the DST man in his spy-hole. He strained to hear what was being said (there was anger in the tone) and longed for a high-powered directional microphone. Ledoux gave the suitcase a twirl like a drum-majorette's mace; had he been a schoolboy, the gesture would have been rated as silent insolence. Bossiere could not make out the Bakunin leader's reply either: he was clearly unabashed by what Waldegg had to say.

The three men went indoors. For the next hour, Bossiere fought his own lonely fight with himself seated alone there in the blackness while the chill struck up from the black rock. He knew he was witnessing a council of war – and he could do nothing about it, let alone hear what was transpiring!

He had to do something!

The desire to break out, sprint across to the lighted hut and gun down the murderer he had tailed for so long was almost irresistible. The image of the man arrogantly brandishing an empty shell of what must have contained explosive to send more innocent people to their deaths provoked in Bossiere's mind the nightmare vision of his three colleagues with their smashed-in faces, bloodied eyeless corpses, which Ledoux had caused with those same hands. The madness became so potent that Bossiere got out his wicked little Walther, slid out the magazine, and cocked and decocked the weapon over and over again in a kind of out-of-control compulsive reflex action, like a flagellant flogging himself with his whip. The decocking movement, which also brought down the hammer at the same time, made a sinister sound, like a man grinding steel false teeth together.

Ledoux was his!

But Bossiere remained sane enough to know that if he went

out there and killed him, along with Maurette (and probably Waldegg) it would serve no purpose. He'd never get away with it. He'd be rounded up for murder, rightly so. What he *had* to know was where the two terrorists had planted the bomb. There was only one way to find out, to go to South African Security . . .

A figure moved from the direction of Rencha's quarters through the gap between the old farmhouse and the new complex heading for his own hut: Kepler. Bossiere recognized the beard; in a moment or two his identification was confirmed when Kepler's hut light went on. There was another puzzle there. He knew that Rencha as the Bakunin courier was involved in Ledoux's plot somehow, but why the head-over-heels attraction to Kepler? It could only complicate her role in the post-bomb process. Bossiere remained persuaded in his own mind that she was playing a deep, deep game.

Bossiere forced himself to face an unpalatable decision. There was only one way to go about the bomb problem – to go to South African Security.

The way Bossiere could hardly bring himself to uncock the Walther and restore the magazine revealed how against the grain the decision went. He had always gone it alone. He himself could not go out to the airfield and conduct a search of the Hercules and helicopters at this time of night. The bomb, of course, would be cunningly hidden, if a Bakunin had anything to do with it. There was also the possibility (a strong one) that Ledoux, Maurette and Waldegg would hear any vehicle leaving Corbel Camp and arouse their suspicions: the exit road passed on the far side of their hut.

How would he approach Security? Bossiere had no intention of revealing his DST connection, or what he had seen that night. Then the solution came to him ready-made. He would prevail on Professor Jaboulet to request Security, taking a precedent from European practice, to search the aircraft before take-off tomorrow. The reason? The aircraft were left alone and unguarded at night, and anything could happen. The French delegation could stand on their high horse. They would be unpopular with Security. They could insist on adequate safeguards for their delegation. It was splitting hairs, of course – Bossiere himself knew as well as anyone else that there was no one about at night on the lonely wastes of Cheating Pan. It would be a way of getting round the situation, Bossiere reasoned, although it might alert Ledoux and Maurette to the fact that someone was keeping tabs on them. On the other hand, the request could be framed as a generalized safety requirement, with no specific allegations attached.

The Walther magazine gave a frustrated, irritated click as it snapped back into position; Bossiere put the weapon on safety. It would not be needed tonight, after all. He got up stiffly and eased himself out of the hide-out.

It was a tame way for a Happening to end.

Chapter 17

'. . . left dead on schedule? So the transporter will clock in at Gougo twelve hours from now – at eight this evening? Good!'

Kepler put down the phone, glanced automatically at his watch. It showed a minute or two after eight, shortly before breakfast next day. He thrust open the door of Corbel Camp's phone booth abstractedly and almost thumped the passer-by in the passage, which led from the lounge to the farmhouse kitchen.

It was Rencha.

She dodged out of range of the door and grinned. 'That must have been either very good or very bad news for you to do that with the door.'

'Sorry,' he answered. 'Good news. Couldn't be better. Koeberg tells me that the first flatbed transporter loaded with SYNROC-R left there at seven this morning. It's due at the repository at eight tonight.'

'I'm glad for you.'

Behind their everyday words was a close-packed package of exchanges ready to take off. It had been a small ploy of Kepler's to use the booth early in the hope of seeing Rencha without making his intention too obvious. It had worked, and he had his reward. She was dressed in her favourite green slacks, with a sweater against the early chill, over a pale tangerine shirt.

It was the fourth day of the IAEA delegates' tour, during which they were due to finalize their inspection, both by road and air, of the approaches to Cheating Pan.

Kepler added, 'Koeberg had also just received its first radio report-back call from the transporter. All systems go. No problems. They'll be monitoring the flatbed all the way, of course. Seeing it's the first load, it's very special.'

'You'll be relieved to have the first SYNROC-R safely under wraps tonight, Kepler.'

'I will indeed.'

Neither of them noticed the figure which had approached from the direction of the lounge and had stopped short when he overheard Kepler's news. It was, in fact, what he himself had come to establish from Koeberg, although from a very different source from Kepler's. The man was Ledoux. Perhaps Rencha and Kepler were too engrossed in their recollection of how the previous night had ended for them. Had Bossiere remained at his post, he would have witnessed something to add to his log of the night's events.

About half an hour after Bossiere had packed up, Kepler's door had opened. The scientist retraced his route across the basalt forecourt to Rencha's quarters. Her light still burned in the bedroom; the one in her sitting-room was out. Access to her bedroom was via this hut. Kepler hesitated, then knocked gently but firmly. There was no response. He tried a second time.

Then Rencha was there, in her dressing-gown. The light was behind her, so that he could not see what was going on in her eyes.

He said nothing, she said nothing. Then she was in his arms, her lovely auburn hair mingling with his black beard. There were kisses, strange affairs aborted by grief and regrets. The broken-hearted sobbing had in it her tears for the courier-years with the Bakunin killers, the panic-stricken escape from France, the interim happiness with John Krummect, the nightmare return of the terror with Krummect's death, the empty funkhole life of Corbel Camp.

When she had done, she held his face in her hands and looked at him as if she had never seen him before. He felt her breast hard against him and she said so softly that he wondered afterwards whether she had really said it, 'I haven't had a man's love for three years.'

Then she was gone; her door was closed.

Now Kepler said, 'Even the telephone is on my side this morning. It wasn't playing its usual tricks. So it looks as if SYNROC-R is literally and figuratively on the road . . .'

'Congratulations!' It was Ledoux. Neither of them had heard him approach. 'I could not avoid hearing you communicating your news. So – your first transporter is now on its way, Dr West? It reaches the repository tonight?'

Ledoux's pale eyes picked up no light from the passage: it was like viewing a face masked by pigmented contact-lenses. There were words, but no spirit.

'Yes.'

'I was looking for you, madame,' continued Ledoux. 'I want some advice. You see, yesterday my stomach refused to put up with the flying, and there is no reason to think it won't be the same today. So a plan has been made. I am to rendezvous with one of the South African Nucor experts, Dr Hans Pienaar, on the ground after he has done some preliminary flying. The name of the place is . . .' he consulted a slip of paper '. . . Brospan. His helicopter meets my station wagon there.'

'Brospan.' Rencha gave better value to the pronunciation. 'Yes, I know Brospan.'

'What should a name like that mean?' went on Ledoux. He was trying to be amiable; he could not forget that here was the Bakunin traitor he had unmasked to Dr Waldegg the previous night, someone whom he might yet have to execute with his own hands. Never took into their eyes, was the terrorist motto. It was the only way to do it.

'Crisp Pan – it refers to the water. Everything in these parts has to do with water.'

'Even the IAEA inspection.'

She laughed, a little reservedly. Ledoux was an uneasy person to be with. 'Brospan is about fifty kilometres from here, Herr Lentz. Just follow our road until you reach a T-junction with the main road running to the repository. Instead of turning left to Gougo, you bear right. Brospan is very close to the junction, about five kilometres. You can't miss it – the edge of the pan comes right up to the main road. There's also a trading store a little further on.'

Something he couldn't place worried Kepler about the man he knew as Lentz. He was being pleasant enough, but somehow he didn't seem to have the bearing of a professional scientist. He lounged against the door of the phone kiosk, taller than either of them: in his sloppy windcheater he looked more like a street-corner drop-out than a nuclear technician. The impression was heightened by his overlong Arab-like nose and thick hair which spilled down the slope of his head to his forehead like a schoolboy's.

'Thank you. That sounds easy enough. There is something else . . .'

Suddenly the thought crashed home on Kepler. Cigarette odour! The man smelt the same as his briefcase had when he had opened it and decided it had been searched! The unmistakable smell of stale Gauloises. Kepler pulled himself up. You can't point a finger of suspicion at a man because he smells of cigarette smoke. It would need the nose of a sniffer dog to distinguish among twenty-five delegates who most resembled his briefcase's odour. It was certainly not his pre-rogative, being a smoker himself.

'All over the camp I see your fine signposts,' Ledoux was saying. 'I need one of those marker pencils, a red one. Have you such a one to spare?'

Rencha looked a little surprised. 'Yes, I am sure I have. Just wait here and I'll fetch it. Red, you say?'

'Red.'

Ledoux smiled to himself. So much for Lichine's fears and the mountain he had made out of a molehill.

The two men were left standing in the passage. Kepler tried to will Ledoux to offer him a cigarette in order to confirm his tobacco suspicions. Instead, the Bakunin said, making conversation, 'You are flying today . . .?'

'All flying is delayed.'

Both men turned. It was Bossiere. He came down the passage to them, his mind racing, his pulses beating with a surge of adrenalin. He couldn't help it. Last night he had fought himself at the sight of that arrogant, triumphant swinging of the empty explosives suitcases; here now was his prey at close quarters. He had spotted the two from the lounge: what in hell were they doing together, he asked himself.

He had just come from pulling his rank – and that of Professor Jaboulet – with Captain Fourie, who headed the small security force of three men stationed at Corbel Camp. Bossiere had approached Fourie, who had scoffed at the idea of a bomb in any of the aircraft. Bossiere had then become tough: unless the aircraft were searched and declared safe, Professor Jaboulet would refuse to allow the delegates to fly; Captain Fourie would have to face the music with his superiors. Aircraft which had stood out all night unattended and un-guarded were a potential threat, and the IAEA president had a serious responsibility to all delegates in these times of terror, he had pontificated.

Captain Fourie had at first been incredulous at the demand; when he had finally bowed to Bossiere's pressure, he had given Bossiere the task of informing the delegates. He himself, he said, would not take the responsibility for such flimsy reasons for postponing the inspection tour. Bossiere had accepted with alacrity; Fourie and his two assistants had motored off post-haste to Cheating Pan.

Bossiere had already formulated the way he would announce

the delay. He would not mention a bomb scare. He would revert to the time-worn euphemism, 'because of technical problems'. But when he saw Ledoux, Bossiere changed his mind. The short, sharp shock might jerk the terrorist into some kind of giveaway.

'There is a bomb scare. All the aircraft are being searched. Take-off is delayed for at least an hour.'

Bossiere watched Ledoux like a hawk. He was taller and rangier than he appeared in that revealing shot on the deck of the Beirut freighter with Carlos the Jackal. The nose resembled that of an Arab, and he deserved to have escaped the eagle eye of the Mossad cameraman. But those eyes!

Ledoux's face registered – nothing. All he said was, 'It shows there is something to be gained from being prone to airsickness.'

Inwardly, he felt his stomach muscles crimp. Bomb! Surely nothing could have gone wrong last night! He dismissed the thought the moment it surged up into his mind. The little Frenchman had said aircraft bomb scare. His hijack drum was three kilometres away, safely hidden in the lying-in hut. Nobody could have got on to that!

'Here – Cheating Pan?' Kepler echoed the Security man's incredulity. 'Who would want to plant a bomb here?'

'A bomb?' It was Rencha, who had returned. Bossiere watched her hand Ledoux the marker pencil. 'Red – I only had three reds left.'

Double-talk? Bossiere regarded the pencil: he had seen booby-traps masquerading as a host of things, even as a toilet roll.

As if to refute him, Ledoux snapped off the cap and revealed the red marker wick. He tested it, and the colour came off on his finger.

'Just what I wanted – thank you.'

'What's this about a bomb?' she repeated.

Bossiere was watching Rencha as closely as he had done Ledoux. There was not an overt exchange of glances, not the slightest giveaway sign.

Bossiere explained. 'The South African Security officers are about to search all the aircraft being used today in case bombs have been planted.'

'You can't be serious, Monsieur Bossiere! Here, at Cheating Pan!'

'I am deadly serious, madame.' Bossiere was deliberately stiffly professional. It was the sort of yarn he himself would not have believed, if anyone had come to him with it. 'At least, Security is concerned about the threat. Four helicopters and the Hercules have stood out all night on the airfield – anything could happen. The fifth helicopter is due in soon from Gougo with ground and flying crews.'

'This isn't Europe – those sort of things don't happen here!' exclaimed Rencha.

'Who knows where and how terrorists will strike in today's world, and for what way-out reason?' said the DST man. He was saying it for Ledoux's benefit. The pale eyes absorbed the thrust without a blink.

'Perhaps, Herr Lentz, you would be kind enough to pass on the news to your delegation? The take-off times will be announced as soon as the search has been completed.'

'Of course,' replied Ledoux. He was glad Bossiere had made the request: he would frame it to Dr Waldegg in such a way as exonerated himself and Maurette from any shadow of carelessness. Not that he credited that they had made any slip-up the previous night. But, coming hard on the heels of their activities on the Pan, it was worrying. It would, moreover, be highly unwise to venture anywhere near the gravcyard until the countdown time came tonight to collect the drum.

Hartogskloof! He must be familiar with every stone of the pass in readiness for tonight's ambush. The pass had been his first objective all along for the coming morning's drive. The Brospan rendezvous had been an irritating if necessary side-issue.

'The delay will make no difference to my plans, seeing I am going by road,' he said. 'I will simply arrange a later rendezvous time with Dr Pienaar and his helicopter.'

'Provided there is no bomb,' said Kepler.

Ledoux eyed him. 'I am sure there is no bomb,' he said. 'Do not forget security men have to earn their living by keeping other people on their toes. A bomb scare is an easy way of doing it. If nothing is found, it doesn't reflect upon them. Everyone says, they're doing their job.'

Bossiere considered the terrorist. In some ways, it was better being close to your prey; at a distance, like last night, the nightmare things ate into your reason, even into your gun-hand.

Ledoux went. Bossiere followed, to carry out his mission of informing the other delegations that the start of the day's inspection would be delayed. Neither Rencha nor Kepler had any intention of letting the bomb scare or the delay interfere with their plans to spend the day alone together motoring to the nearest railhead at Sak River, one hundred and fifty kilometres to the west, to collect supplies. Both realized (and welcomed) instinctively that their journey might turn out to be an ambush of the emotions.

East of their route, an ambush of another sort was in train. Hartogskloof.

Chapter 18

As a matter of form, Ledoux and Maurette did wait long enough for the all clear to come through from the airfield before setting off in the station wagon down the rough, dusty road towards the main repository route – and Hartogskloof.

This was necessary to synchronize their rendezvous time at Brospan – twenty-five kilometres away in the opposite direction from the ambush site – with the helicopter carrying the South African Nucor official, Dr Pienaar, who had been delegated to accompany them on a ground tour of the endless, dreary complex of pans, big and small, immediately south of the tableland on which the repository was situated. In hydrological terms the area was called a floodplain; of water, there was no sign, either above or below the ground.

It was a foregone conclusion to the two Bakunins what the result of the aircraft search would be, but they dared not pre-empt it by setting off until Dr Pienaar was satisfied that take-off would indeed take place, and when.

Bossiere observed the two terrorists leave, and Dr Waldegg vacate his hut and join the other delegations mustered in the main lounge complex in preparation for being transported by mini-bus to the airfield.

Now!

The idea hit Bossiere with the suddenness of a piece of space junk falling out of the sky – go for it! Case the joint! Search the terrorists' hut! Prove or disprove your suspicions about those two suitcases! If caught, you have a watertight excuse, you are summoning Dr Waldegg for the flight, looking for Ledoux . . .

Bossiere moved quickly towards the Waldegg–Ledoux bee-hive, keeping the old farmhouse complex between himself and the assembled delegates so that he could not be spotted.

The door was open. He went in.

No radio. Both the keeping-hole and bedside table were vacant. That in itself was significant. Blast! One glimpse behind what he was certain was a false front to the instrument could verify or disprove a major sticking-point in his mind. The place was tidy – the German in Dr Waldegg, no doubt, said the DST man cynically to himself.

He went up the steps to the loft two at a time.

There they were – twin suitcases, twin Gemini split personalities, so outwardly harmless, so inwardly – what?

Bossiere didn't have to wait long for an answer. This time they weren't locked. They were as empty as Cheating Pan. Bossiere knelt down, smelt. Samtex, a favourite Czech explosive with terrorists (which was packed in small briquettes) left an acrid, bitter smell. There was nothing like that here. That in itself was inconclusive. There were half a dozen other types of explosive for terrorists to choose from. What did strike the DST man, however, were a number of fresh scrapes and scratches. The interior of both cases had been scuffed by what could have been sharp objects or metal. The marks were the more noticeable because the cases were brand-new. They showed no signs inside of previous use.

Then – Bossiere froze.

From below, came the sound of two voices.

Dr Waldegg's deep tone was unmistakable. He was speaking fast, urgently.

'See here, Dr Nakanishi,' he was saying. 'It was simply an excuse of mine to the others that I'd forgotten my notes. I had to speak to you alone, before the day's flying.'

'Nucor is very keen to get started. We'll have to be quick. You have some news for me?'

'Yes, Ledoux is turning out trumps. He's a clever and daring opportunist. I want you to know the final option is in train. Well in train.'

'How so?'

'It's too involved a story to go into now, we haven't the time. But you can take it from me that it will happen, just as we hoped. Ledoux is seizing his opportunity – right under everyone's nose.'

Bossiere sat like a yoga in a seventh heaven trance. Not a muscle moved, only his fingers crimped with satisfaction at what he heard. He was right about the Bakunin!

Nakanishi said, 'This thing will create one hell of a stink afterwards, you realize, don't you?'

'We haven't got any other cards left,' replied Waldegg. 'Look at the case the South Africans have built up in regard to the hydrological and groundwater aspects of the repository – it was to have been our strong point of objection. It can't be overthrown, you know that yourself.'

The admission was wrung from the Chinese. 'I know that. Their surprise about their system of satellite monitors really killed any valid scientific objections we had. True, we're going out again to inspect, but you can't dispute their facts and figures. The IAEA's approval is almost a foregone conclusion.'

'The final option . . .' repeated Waldegg.

'As an Oriental, I would still prefer a more circumspect, less drastic method,' went on Dr Nakanishi.

'What do you propose? You don't intend to call off Ledoux now that he has set it all up, do you?'

Bossiere opened his mouth and breathed through it, afraid that his indrawn breath through his nose might alert the men below.

'No. Although I cannot judge completely until I know the details. Nevertheless, I want you to approach Dr West again. It could come off, now that he has had time to reconsider.'

'Our offer failed the first time, and there's no reason to think it will succeed on the second occasion. You weren't there to get his brush-off. You can't realize the dedication and determination of the man, until you touch on SYNROC-R. It's not merely an invention with him, it's a way of life.'

'We'll offer him a new way of life,' replied Nakanishi thinly. 'I authorize you to double our previous offer.'

Waldegg gave a low whistle. 'That puts him on the gravy train all right, as our American friends would say.'

'China *must have* SYNROC-R.'

'Or else SYNROC-R must be totally discredited,' added Waldegg. 'That's the route I opt for. It's what Ledoux is out there busy with today.' He added with an ugly laugh, 'There is still another way – via the girl. You can be sure we won't neglect that aspect. She's making pretty good progress with him, by the looks of it.'

Bossiere bit his lips. He hadn't been wrong there, either. Once a Bakunin, always a Bakunin. She was simply playing the terrorist's game with Kepler West. He was fishing in very deep waters.

Waldegg glanced at his watch. 'We'd better get going before they send someone to look for us.'

'Who started the bomb scare anyway?' asked Nakanishi.

Waldegg laughed his deep belly-laugh. 'There's no bomb *there*, I assure you.'

When they had gone, Bossiere remained sitting in his frozen posture for a few moments. Now that the shock of not being discovered had passed, he felt his socks wet with sweat inside his shoes. The innuendo in Waldegg's final remark was plain and gave substance to what he had only suspected before that morning: there *was* a bomb, and Ledoux and the girl were in the plan up to the eyes. Now that he had established it, his next imperative task was to find out where, and when.

Bossiere closed the lids of the suitcases carefully, again using his handkerchief to mask his fingerprints.

He tiptoed down the wooden stairs, threw a cautious glance round before stepping out of the door, and then walked quickly to where the other delegates were assembled.

As he hurried into the passageway between the old and new complexes, a light pick-up truck came from the direction of Rencha's quarters. Rencha herself was driving, Kepler West was with her. They were laughing, and waved to the DST man as they passed. Bossiere returned the salute – with no smile. Anna-Kai Cerny! In his mind was the ruthless two-pronged Bakunin code: identification or failure on a mission was punishable by death. By nailing her, he had imposed the first penalty and thus passed sentence on her. He intended that she should fail – together with Ledoux – on the second score also. He crushed down his sense of pity: she had looked so young, so scared, in that old photograph . . .

'There's the Bonsma homestead over there, the Haunted Graveyard family,' said Rencha. She gestured to her right. They were about ten kilometres south of Corbel Camp. Rencha was making better time than Ledoux and Maurette had done a short while before. Also, she knew the road; the light truck gave better clearance over the rough, bumpy surface than did the terrorists' station wagon.

'Did you warn the delegates that the Bonsmas were so sensitive about the graveyard?' asked Kepler.

'No, I didn't think it necessary. They're not going sightseeing like my tourists used to do. At that time I stuck up notices in the huts warning visitors. In fact, there may still be some of them left in the older huts.'

They were now on a straighter section of road, which continued more or less directly southwards, except for one big loop past a spot known as Jan Louw se Leegte – Jan Louw's Hollow.

'You drive well,' remarked Kepler.

'I like driving – in this sort of countryside,' she replied. 'The horizons are as wide as the sea.'

'The only difference being the water,' said Kepler.

They both laughed. Their mood was in total sync.

'They say driving has a lot in common with riding – I rode horses once.'

'When was that?'

The moment Kepler said it, he realized that his unthinking question had cut into that no-man's-land of hers, that tight-shut, no-beginning, no-ending territory.

Rencha did not answer, but speeded up instead, and gave all her attention to holding the fast-moving vehicle on the road. He realized that the day would die if he allowed the silence to continue and become corrosive. The fear crystallized in his mind a decision about which, up to then, he had not been certain whether or not he would tell her.

'If we go on at this rate, we could intercept the flatbed with the load of SYNROC-R – then you'd be in for a surprise.'

Her sideways glance held her question: he also noted that her eyes were shuttered against what she had interpreted as his previous prying question which, she judged, he had no right to ask.

'Can you keep a secret? Nobody at Corbel Camp knows.'

For a reply, she let go the wheel with her left hand and clenched his hand in hers. He was surprised at the vehemence – and the intimacy.

He went on. 'The transporter is carrying something rather special which I intend springing on the delegates tomorrow when I address them at the kimberlite workings.'

'Your big day, Kepler.'

'Others might call it my day under the whip.' They were communicating again now; this woman was lovely and sensitive, with a hurt inside her as big as a crater blasted by an atom bomb test.

'SYNROC-R is somewhat of an unreal myth to most people,' he went on. 'Nobody has ever seen it, except workers at the plant, and then the view is from behind all sorts of anti-radiation screens and remote-control arms and hands. Nobody either knows what it looks like, or its colour . . .'

'But you have seen it.'

'Yes, I have. But once it is amalgamated with radio-active waste, it is mechanically sealed into big drums and that is the end of it. It will be discreetly buried for the next hundred thousand – maybe million – years.'

'Why are you telling me all this?'

'I want to punch it home to the IAEA delegates that here is a rock – an artificial rock – which they could see and touch, if only it were not radio-active. I want them to *see* SYNROC-R as a physical reality, believe in it. So I had a shop-window model made for their benefit. The transporter is carrying it, plus the first load of SYNROC-R drums for the repository.'

She shook her head so that her long hair masked the side of her face closest to him.

'You're making the secret only more tantalizing without revealing it.'

'The driver has in his charge a special radiation-proof glass bottle about the size of a jam jar. It is filled with SYNROC-R. Genuine SYNROC-R, alive and dangerous. The container was subjected to the most searching checks against radiation leakage and is, of course, totally sealed. It will be rechecked again tonight at the repository when it arrives. Then tomorrow I will pull it like a rabbit out of a hat in front of the delegates during my talk on how I came to discover mathiasite and lindsleyite on Cheating Pan.'

'You don't really mean us to carry on beyond Sak River and intercept the flatbed, do you, Kepler?'

'No, I was only joking. The driver wouldn't hand over my display jar anyway. He has the strictest orders that after the journey it has to go for test immediately on arrival at Gougo.'

'How can you then have it in time for your address to-morrow?'

'Captain Fourie, who, as you know, is the head of Security at Corbel Camp, will be waiting at Gougo for the flatbed's arrival at about eight,' explained Kepler. 'Once my jar has been checked and cleared, he personally will bring it by car to Corbel Camp and hand it over to me.'

She said, in a completely neutral tone, 'We'll have to wait up for it, then.'

'Yes. Nobody else knows about it.'

'Why did you tell me this, Kepler?'

She knew his reason; yet she was surprised at the fire which surrounded his rationalization of it to her.

'I have got to stop this madness in the world about nuclear waste,' he answered. 'We are rushing headlong at high speed in harm's way. I will use every means in my power to stop the uncontrolled burial of radwaste in out-of-the-way places in containers made of metal, ceramics or glass, which in time will break down and contaminate entire regions – the Gobi Desert, for example. It's fine to shrug off the responsibility and say, we won't be around in a hundred years, or a thousand years, so what does it matter? I'm not talking about a mere hundred years, or a thousand – I'm talking of a hundred thousand at least. Anything up to one million years! Radwaste as it is being carried out today is as primitive as pit sanitation. The epidemic which is going to follow is a million times more ghastly.'

She broke the high-pitched intensity of the moment by gesturing at the road ahead.

'Look!'

A long plume of dust, like a high-speed landing chute, tailed a vehicle they were overhauling.

'Isn't that the Radchem station wagon?'

Kepler screwed up his eyes. 'Looks like it.'

'We're too close to the main road to catch them before the T-junction, unless we want a mouthful of dust,' said Rencha. 'I'll hang back until after the turn.'

Rencha eased her speed, keeping well clear of the dust.

'There's the main road. We turn right, and so do they to reach Brospan. But it's only a few kilometres to the Pan. The main road's not as dusty as this one, anyway.'

The two vehicles approached the main road T-junction. They could see a dozen miles in any direction. The station wagon reached the junction.

Then Rencha exclaimed, 'They've turned *left* – they've gone wrong.'

'I heard you tell them explicitly, turn right,' said Kepler.

They themselves were now approaching the main road. They could make out the station wagon travelling in the opposite direction to Brospan, towards Gougo – and Hartogskloof. The terrorists were picking up speed.

'Hadn't we better chase after them and put them right?' asked Rencha.

There was a note of doubt in her voice. Kepler heard it; he had found himself almost resentful at their first sight of the station wagon. This was their own day, exclusively. He sensed that Rencha, like himself, wanted to be alone, each with the other.

Kepler checked his watch. 'They're more than an hour too early for their rendezvous with the helicopter. Maybe they've gone off in the other direction simply to kill time.'

'Better than hanging around at Brospan,' Rencha agreed. 'There's absolutely nothing there to do or see.'

Their pick-up now reached the T-junction. She said, 'It's your decision, Kepler.'

'It's yours also, Rencha.'

She did not reply, but put the pick-up into gear, turned

right, and accelerated away in the direction of Sak River, the opposite way from the station wagon.

They soon passed Brospan, continued westward. If it hadn't been for its down-at-heel trading store opposite a small pan, Brospan wouldn't have been any different from the rest of the godforsaken countryside. A paint-stripped petrol pump stood like a lighthouse planted by science to mark the conquest of progress.

Their road was taking them towards the long chain of dry pans and 'floors', hundreds of kilometres long, which ran due north–south to mark the 'course' of the Sak River. River was a misnomer. It was simply a route water had of finding its way when it did not sink into the parched ground – 'sak' means to sink into the ground. The 'river' could vary in width (when it flowed) from a couple of metres to ten kilometres. The inter-linked 'floors' alternated in size from a hundred to five hundred square kilometres. At the southern end of this complex of nothingness was a railhead; midway was a village called Brandvlei; far to the north lay the impassable barrier of the Orange River, which swallowed the puny discharge of the Sak and its nameless tributaries without even a hiccup.

Rencha said, breaking the silence, 'If we look hard enough along those rock ridges, we might spot a specimen or two of the bush which produces your favourite *Jacob-jong* tea.'

'I can understand where its underlying harsh taste comes from,' observed Kepler.

'You get used to it. I've got used to coming this way alone so often.'

'Yet it attracts you, that is why you stay.'

A moment before she had been relaxed and smiling; now her mood changed like a plummeting barometer.

'You're wrong, Kepler,' she replied quickly. 'It frightens and repels me. Only when you've known fear yourself, can you come to terms with it. But love it – never!'

If ever they were to be close, Kepler knew that somewhere, sometime, she would have to relax her 'no-beginning, no-ending' barrier which she had thrown up round herself. Now could be the time. They were alone, in complete harmony.

'Rencha . . .' he began.

She didn't seem to observe the changed note in his voice.

'They say that a true desert in the physical sense takes on a mystique for one's psyche – it becomes a mirror reflecting no more and no less than what is going on inside you,' she hurried on, not picking her words, as if she were bringing into the open something over which she had mulled many times, in darkness and agony, perhaps. 'This –' she made a sweeping gesture at the countryside '– it's like a dull hot mirror reflecting – what? Something harsh and uncompromising, something as inescapable as the heat, as terrible as the thirst which is always lurking . . . That's what it is all about to me, Kepler. I'm not attracted, I'm scared. Scared all the time.'

'Of what, Rencha?'

'You call me Rencha, but that was John's name for me. I wasn't born Rencha but Anna-Kai . . .'

She stopped short, bit her lips, bit back further admissions.

A moment or two passed, and then Kepler said gently, 'In Australia, we have an Aborigine name which sounds very like Kai – Kylie.'

'And what does that mean?' Kepler was surprised at her tone. If she had meant it to reflect the harshness of the countryside, she had succeeded.

'It means a curl, or a curled stick, even a boomerang. I guess the curl part stands for a girl's hair.'

'Kylie.' She turned the word over on her tongue so softly that Kepler could scarcely hear it above the rumble of the pick-up's wheels.

Then she said briefly, 'Tell me more about you. I know all about myself.'

He realized the razor's-edge he was walking. A wrong inflexion, a misguided question about her past, would lose her.

He made up his mind in a flash. 'There is something I wanted to tell you, Rencha.'

'I know, you're married.' The words were jerked from her.

He laughed with genuine amusement. 'Noways! No, this

has to do with what is going on right here and now at Corbel Camp.'

'Going on?'

'I'm telling you something which is for your ears alone, Rencha. Nobody else must know.'

'You give me so much, I give you nothing,' she said.

'Here it is, then. Would it surprise you to know that yesterday I was offered half a million dollars to sell out the secret of SYNROC-R?'

'Half a million dollars as a bribe! But these men are the most respected in the scientific world, they're their countries' top representatives! They should be beyond reproach!'

'That's what I thought, too. I'll tell you who it was. Dr Waldegg, of Radchem, representing Red China. Half a million dollars in my lap, a meal-ticket for a lifetime, my own laboratory, freedom of research . . .'

'It just shows how little they must think of their own radwaste disposal methods. In a way, it's a kind of inverted compliment to you, Kepler.'

'I could have accepted. The world patent rights haven't gone through yet.'

'You didn't *give* them away to Nucor, did you, Kepler?'

'The South Africans have been very generous. Nucor itself pointed out what the patent rights could mean financially if I chose to hold them myself. I didn't. Listen, Rencha, this isn't what interests me. I want to try and make a world safe from nuclear radiation, and SYNROC-R is the way to do it. So that in fifty or a hundred years there won't be kids running around with awful deformities, hideous cancers, and the like. Can you understand? That's what I'm after, not a handful of dollars!'

'It's the way I would have expected you to reply, Kepler. It makes Corbel Camp and its shoestring problems all seem very insignificant.'

He leaned forward, took her left knee in his hand and held it firmly. 'Corbel Camp is the focus of SYNROC-R, never forget, Rencha. And you made Corbel Camp. If there hadn't been a Corbel Camp there might never have been . . .'

'There would have, Kepler, and you know it. It's sweet of you to say it, but I've told you before that Corbel Camp – Rencha's Corbel Camp – is on its way out, if it's not already disappeared.'

'I don't accept that.' He steered the conversation away from the turn it was taking. 'There's something else I had in mind to tell you. It's also about SYNROC-R – at least, I think so.'

'I don't know whether I'll be glad or sorry when that first transporter-load arrives tonight.'

He asked, obliquely, 'Were you surprised today before we set out when I asked you to lock my briefcase in your safe?'

'Yes, I was a little. The Corbel Camp servants would never touch anything.'

'The night of the sheep barbecue – maybe while you and I were chatting – someone searched my briefcase.'

'In Corbel Camp? I can't believe it! Was anything taken?'

'Nothing was taken. But today I included something of value with the briefcase which happened to be lying around previously in my suitcase. My pistol.'

'You carry a gun?'

'Yes, ever since I was attacked in my lab at Canberra. I supplemented it with a course in unarmed combat.'

'If nothing was taken, how can you be sure your briefcase was tampered with?'

'I can't, that is the trouble. It was something I couldn't quite put my finger on – the way the papers had been put back, it wasn't quite the same. Most of all, the case smelt of cigarettes, not my brand, that I am sure of.'

Rencha said incisively, 'I think you should go straight away to Professor Jaboulet and make a formal complaint. Captain Fourie can take it up.'

'On such flimsy grounds? No security man would listen.'

'It's also an insult to try and buy you off!' she went on hotly. 'It's another matter which should be brought into the open with Professor Jaboulet!'

'Dr Waldegg would naturally deny it. Besides, it's not a crime.'

'It's underhand and it's despicable!'

He shrugged and laughed. 'It's all that. But I wanted you to know.'

She slowed down and held his glance. 'You didn't have to tell me any of this, Kepler. Why did you?'

'Because you are you.'

Her eyes filled with tears: suddenly she looked defenceless – wildly, madly desirable. She said brokenly, 'I have nothing to give you in return.'

Far to the south, the flatbed with its seventeen drums of lethal radwaste plugged northwards. By afternoon, it would be traversing Rencha's and Kepler's road on course for the repository.

Chapter 19

'Let's go!'

Ledoux ground out the half-smoked Gauloise on the hut floor, started towards the keeping-hole where the radio detonator stood.

It was five o'clock that afternoon. Ledoux, Maurette and Waldegg were together in the Waldegg hut. The two Bakunins were about to launch themselves on the night's hijack. First, they would have to collect the drum of high explosive from the Haunted Graveyard.

'Thank heavens! – no more poisonous cigarette smoke! You're becoming a smokaholic, Ledoux.'

'Cut out the fancy names,' retorted Ledoux. 'Rencha brought plenty of fresh supplies back with her this afternoon, didn't she?'

'That's not the point . . .'

'Listen,' snapped Ledoux. 'In the next half hour or so we're going to load up thirty kilos of HE – if it goes up by any mischance while it's in the back of the station wagon, all you'll find of us afterwards is a pair of balls hanging in a tree a hundred metres away.'

'There aren't any trees in these parts,' responded Waldegg.

'Aw, shit!' snapped back Ledoux. He looked round as if seeking yet another Gauloise to ease his tension, then said, 'Louis, check everything, see? We don't want any loose ends. Got your gun?'

'Sure.' The only outward sign of his own uptightness was the way he fumbled slightly as he checked the magazine. Ledoux did the same, then slipped the weapon back into his leather windbreaker pocket, and pulled out a grenade.

'I thought this was a peaceful ambush,' began Waldegg.

'Keep out of this!' retorted Ledoux. 'Louis and I know our business. We always carry a gun – just in case. It *is* a peaceful job. The driver is no more going to know he has been bushed than a tart knows she's been stuffed.'

'Keep it that way,' responded Waldegg tautly. 'Now remember, if anything goes astray . . .'

'Yeah, yeah, you're not implicated, I know, I know! It can't and won't go wrong. Play it natural, that's what Carlos always said. That's the way we're doing this job tonight. If you start pissing yourself inwardly, it sets up vibes, and somehow things go sour. It's all going to be so natural that the driver will want to thank us.'

The tension between Ledoux, Maurette and Waldegg dated back to the morning. The two Bakunins had been late, almost irresponsibly late, for their helicopter rendezvous at Brospan with the Nucor man, Dr Pienaar. After Kepler and Rencha had seen them turn off in the wrong direction, the two men had raced towards the Hartogskloof. Ledoux had reconnoitred the mouth of the pass: the initial causeway with its sandy platform, the first steep, rugged, tight bend which was ideal for their purpose. A series of similar bends projected the road upwards for some forty metres in a short distance. They stamped every detail on their minds to draw upon when it was dark that night.

The Bakunins' unpunctuality and Dr Waldegg's anxiety and irritation forced the Radchem chief into changing his plans and accompanying the Nucor man and Ledoux and Maurette on their road inspection. Both their minds were preoccupied with details of the ambush – fertile ground for a slip-up with Dr Pienaar. It was a wise decision: it turned out to be a high-tech day as they threaded their way through and inspected endless pans and dry floors on the southern approaches to Gougo, a day which left the two terrorists bored and impatient. Dr Waldegg did most of the talking. They also visited the sites of two of the space age 'nilometers' whose function was to transmit water level data to a hovering satellite.

Before the day was over, Dr Waldegg also had reached the conclusion that China and Radchem had lost their scientitfic battle. Later, back in camp, Professor John Ankey, the United States Department of Energy representative, had summed up the two days of groundwater inspection: 'Gougo is probably the finest and safest nuclear repository site in the world, twice as good as anything in the United States.'

The only option left to Dr Waldegg was Ledoux's bomb.

Now Ledoux checked his watch and started for the door.

'Good thing it gets dark so early in these parts. We'll have its cover once we leave the graveyard.'

'Can't you wait until it's a hundred per cent dark? It's only dusk now,' said Dr Waldegg.

'It's seventy kilometres from the graveyard to the ambush site,' answered Ledoux. 'That will take us forty-five minutes. We have to leave the graveyard by five thirty – and we still have to get there.'

'There's still a danger now of being spotted by the air and ground crews,' said Dr Waldegg.

Maurette interrupted. 'Noways. All the choppers were back at the airfield at four. The ground staff has long since dispersed. Danger from that quarter is out.'

The two Bakunins left, jumped into the station wagon,

which kicked up a spurt of dust from its wheels as Maurette, who was driving, gunned the engine. Ledoux held the radio detonator carefully. He had already taken the precaution of disconnecting its small batteries to guard against a premature detonation signal, should the delicate internal trigger be activated by a bump.

There was no dust curtain on the Pan this time, only a thin murkiness kicked up by a light breeze. The station wagon put the four kilometres to the airfield behind it in excellent time. The place was deserted, as Maurette had stated it would be. The light was waning; nevertheless, they could still make out the distant loom of Deelkop, the hill backing the graveyard. They raced towards it, pulled up by the wrought iron gates.

'Not even a ghost watching us,' quipped Maurette.

'Keep your gun handy, just in case,' warned Ledoux. 'We haven't checked the hut yet.'

They sidled in the gate, and approached the hut door, one strategically on each side.

Ledoux pushed it open cautiously.

The drum stood where they had left it. 'Like you said, not even a ghost here,' remarked Ledoux.

'We'll have to roll it to the station wagon,' said Maurette.

'First things first,' replied Ledoux.

He took Rencha's red packaging pencil and a slip of paper from his pocket on which he had noted Lichine's code.

'KO-RAD-003' he repeated. As he wrote, he addressed the drum. 'That's your passport into Gougo, sweetheart – nothing's going to stop you now.'

Maurette, standing by the door, exclaimed, 'Hey, look at this!'

He indicated a thin clear plastic pipe running down the outer wall and then up along the line of stones projecting from the roof which formed the customary 'ladder' for painting and repairs. Although the pipe was buried where it met the ground, it was clear that it ran in the direction of the 'living flame' headstone; its dim light was becoming visible in the gathering dusk.

'Maybe there's another room above there – I'm going up,'

said Maurette excitedly. 'If there is, it's the perfect place to stash away the radwaste drum off the flatbed.'

'Make it quick!' said Ledoux.

Maurette raced up the stone 'rungs' to the top.

'Just come and look at this!' he called down.

Ledoux followed, at the double. The traditional egg-shape of this beehive hut had been so built as to foreshorten its tip, forming a hatchway open to the sky. Inside was an upper chamber above the lying-in hut, having a stone floor/ceiling.

'There's the secret of the living flame – hell, could anything be more corny!' Maurette indicated. The plastic pipe reached over the lip of the hatchway: it led to a standard 44-gallon power paraffin drum which had been set up on a special wooden cradle or 'bed'.

'Simple gravity feed,' went on Maurette.

'If that fuel drum could fit through the hatchway, so can our radwaste drum!' exclaimed Ledoux excitedly. 'The perfect hiding-place!'

'That's what I reckoned,' answered Maurette.

'This solves our problem,' went on Ledoux. 'Our hijacked drum will be as safe here for the next five days as . . . as . . .'

'Inside the repository trench at Gougo,' grinned Maurette. 'We'll bring it back here and heave it up step by step!'

'No problem,' responded Ledoux. His gratified grin was as rare as a rainy day at Cheating Pan.

The two men quickly descended the stone steps, tilted the drum containing the SZ charges on its side, and carefully rolled it to the rear of the station wagon. Both were strong, and the wire cable strop provided a ready-made grip. One heave, and they had it safely stowed. Ledoux threw a blanket over it.

'What's that for?' asked Maurette.

'Carlos said, play it natural always,' he replied. 'We have to drive back past Corbel Camp – there's only the one road, as you know. If someone spots us, what does he see in the back? – something, under a blanket. No giveaway. See?'

Ledoux took the wheel; in high spirits, they headed for Hartogskloof.

Their spirits would have been dampened had they noticed, on their return passage past Corbel Camp, a man crouched by a car apparently changing a punctured tyre who checked his watch as the station wagon whipped by and covered him with dust. Bossiere cursed the Bakunin vehicle for its lack of consideration. Even as he spat out the dust, his mind was racing to complete a time-distance calculation. He had also observed their departure earlier. It was from his favourite vantage-point, the 'little volcano' crater, at the rear of the old farmhouse. He had seen the 'transistor radio' being handled with such care; because he guessed what it really was, it filled him with disquiet. To have followed the terrorists to the Pan would have been a straight giveaway; he knew they must use the only road back. By staging a flat tyre outside the camp on the sole other exit, namely, that to the south and Gougo, he could not miss their return.

Bossiere had set his watch then; the station wagon had returned quicker than he had expected; like a ranging radar beam the conjunction of time and distance provided him with a fixed radius inside which their target must lie.

Eight kilometres!

Somewhere within an arc of eight kilometres from Corbel Camp lay the terrorists' target!

Target?

Bossiere kicked impatiently at the jack he had positioned under the wheel. Target? Maybe. Perhaps only a staging-post – he had observed, as the Bakunin vehicle had passed, something which he knew had not been there when it set out. A bulky object in the back, covered with a blanket. He had spotted it for a split second as the vehicle tore by. He had jumped to his feet to observe it further, but the cloud of dust had blinded him. Bastards, he cursed softly to himself. But he knew now – somewhere, within eight kilometres of Corbel Camp. There was nothing but the airfield within that radius. Nothing at all.

But there was.

Shortly after, he got back to his hut and washed the dust off his face. He reached for a towel. Then he stared in incredulous disbelief at the notice – an old, typed notice hanging from a hook on the shower-room door. It thrust itself at him. It read:

> *Visitors are warned that under no circumstances should they venture alone on Cheating Pan or stray from Bluebird's track, due to the danger of becoming lost. Visitors should also take note that an old graveyard in the vicinity is private property and entry is strictly prohibited by the family owning it for personal reasons.*

A graveyard! A prohibited place! Near the airfield! What better funkhole could a Bakunin want? He must find out exactly where it was!

Bossiere only half-dried his face in his hurry, dragged on his shirt, and went in search of Rencha.

Chapter 20

Smokaholic, bombaholic, drumaholic . . .

Dr Waldegg's taunt attached itself to the trappings of the ambush and made a nonsense drum-beat in Ledoux's mind.

He had not felt so keyed up since he had blown up the Paris–Toulouse express. The rhythmic clickety-clack of the express' wheels pulsed through his mind as if they were yesterday. They had thumped out a similar beat, deep-beat music, in his brain on that occasion. Then, however, there had been the train's lights, the passing brightness of the French countryside, the lighted stations, the car headlights waiting at level crossings. Here, in this god-awful countryside at Hartogskloof, there was nothing, nothing, nothing but blackness and silence like a wild beast waiting to pounce . . .

Smokaholic, bombaholic, drumaholic . . .

This wasn't going to be the clean in-and-out job he was used to with a bomb or a gun. Those were straightforward, uncomplicated missions: the frantic nervous build-up, the rush in, the orgasmic discharge of tension as the eardrums bucked and the flames leapt. Tonight's assignment would need more finesse. It was more devious. It would be – Ledoux searched for a word – more diplomatic.

Smokaholic, bombaholic, drumaholic . . .

Ledoux longed for a cup of coffee from the vacuum flask which had been set out for show with two mugs on the bonnet of the station wagon – he'd throw up at another lungful of the acrid Gauloises he'd been using since he and Maurette took up station on the patch of sand on the far side of the causeway in Hartogskloof, at the critical point where the road launched itself into the first of the series of steep, narrow bends which took it on to the plateau beyond.

It was 6.50 p.m.

Ten minutes more at the earliest before they could expect the flatbed with its cargo of radwaste, if the massive vehicle was running on schedule . . .

'Listen!' Maurette was next to him, keeping his voice down to a hiss, as if it mattered. 'Listen, for Chrissake!'

The blatant roar of a distant heavy diesel engine cut through the watchful silence. The forty-metre backdrop of the pass constituted a natural echo curtain. It sounded closer than it actually was.

'That's the flatbed!' snapped Ledoux. 'See it?'

'No.'

The approach road to Hartogskloof was hidden from their view by the hollow, with its trees, formed by the causeway.

'Get going!' ordered Ledoux. 'You know what to do.'

Maurette started to move quickly past the station wagon into the shadows. He stopped. 'Hey, it's not the transporter! It's an aircraft! Look at the lights!'

The down-road horizon lighted momentarily, flickered with a yellow-orange flash, one, two, three.

'Can't be!' exclaimed Ledoux. 'It must be the flatbed!'

Maurette hung back; Ledoux paused uncertainly in the act

of pouring himself a cup of coffee from the flask on the bonnet.

The triple orange-yellow flash sparkled above the trees at the start of the pass. There was a glimpse of white light under it.

'Cab lights – she's got flashers high above the cab, that's why we're seeing 'em first!' rapped out Ledoux. 'Get going, man, get going – she'll be here any minute!'

Maurette vanished; Ledoux splashed a dollop of hot coffee into a mug, lit a cigarette he did not want. He moved quickly to the station wagon's dashboard and switched on the sidelights.

All at once, it seemed, the pass seemed filled with the roar of a powerful diesel, blinding white light from the flatbed's highly-positioned headlights, and yellow-orange flashing lights above.

The transporter reached the causeway.

Maurette reappeared out of the shadows, zipping up his pants. What more natural – in Carlos' dictum – than relieving yourself by the roadside?

The flatbed's headlights went on to high. Like searchlights, they picked out the scene: the flat sandy stretch beyond the causeway, the station wagon with its sidelights on facing it, two men grouped at the bonnet drinking coffee and smoking. The lights penetrated beyond also, and showed the road ahead swinging right, climbing up steeply between the small trees and shrubby bushes clinging to the sides of the pass.

The driver saw the steep ascent, too. He changed down into lowest gear, gunned the engine. The racket of low-gear acceleration as he headed for the first bend filled the pass.

It was useless for Ledoux to shout above the racket what he wanted to say to Maurette – the louder the better, for our purposes!

Then the flatbed was abreast them. Ledoux raised a hand in salute; he could not distinguish against the headlights' glare the driver or co-driver's features. All he saw was the driver's hand go up in return salute and the co-driver, on their side, as a passing, grinning face and waving hand.

The driver was rushing the pass; the long length of the

transporter slid by; the dazzling St Elmo's Fire of the flashers spurted across the cab-top, stage-lighting the scene momentarily.

There they were! Fifteen drums of radwaste, encased in their SYNROC-R coffins for the next hundred thousand years, stacked (as Lichine had said) in saddles at the cab-end of the multi-wheeled vehicle.

Ledoux registered with surprise that the flatbed was lower than he remembered the same type used for the crash demonstration on Cheating Pan.

The rear, the rear! That's what they were interested in!

And there they were too! The trio of drums – green drums – smaller and differently shaped from the rest of the load, every one with its enveloping wire strop. They sat in their saddles like triplets in a carry-cot. Two were on one side of a central dividing gangway; one sat apart on the left, or kerb-side. Lichine had been dead accurate with his information.

Ledoux and Maurette's mugs were back on their vehicle's bonnet even before the stop-lights on the big tailgates of the flatbed blazed by, in contrast to the flashers' orange-yellow, which suddenly cut.

The cab or mechanical horse section of the transporter put its nose to the first steep bend, started to swing sideways.

Ledoux had to yell at Maurette; he had not bargained for such a racket. The driver was now giving the engine everything to haul the massive load up the pass. Already, speed was down to a snail's pace.

The two Bakunins sprinted after the flatbed.

They caught it up.

They vaulted over the low rear, among the drums.

Twin roll-on, roll-off ramps, gridded with cross steel battens for grip, were folded up to form a tailboard across the rear. This was a double safety precaution, in case a drum should work loose in its saddle. The ramps' main function – in conjunction with a forklift – was to facilitate on-and-off loading.

Ledoux and Maurette crouched low. The oscillating lighthouse beam of the flashers illuminated the drums in yellow. There was also some local lighting from the big rear reflectors, but it was directed mainly backwards.

Ledoux smacked the drum sitting singly in its saddle with his fist and mimicked by means of hand signals to Maurette.

They had to get the tailgate lowered!

How was it raised and lifted? Was it manual, or hydraulic, perhaps even controlled from the driver's cab? If the latter, the hijack was doomed. They might heft the drum over the back by brute strength, but the extent of the drop to the road would more than likely rupture it . . .

Both men were at the back, searching for the tailgate cable. Maurette found it, and passed on the news by grabbing Ledoux's shoulder. Speech was impossible.

Maurette now crawled forward, trying to trace the source of the cable.

A different note came from the cab. It penetrated even the engine-gears noise. It was a voice – harsh, metallic, a radio voice.

The crew was reporting by radio to their base! Lichine had said the flatbed's progress was monitored regularly, and a landmark like Hartogskloof was an obvious place from which to give a position.

Another plus factor in Ledoux and Maurette's favour! There was little likelihood that the co-driver, busy operating the radio, would glance around and spot them.

On hands and knees, the two Bakunins worked their way rapidly to the immediate rear of the cab. Low in shadow behind it, they were out of sight to the crew.

The cable! Maurette grabbed Ledoux's wrist, guided it firmly on to a barrel-shaped piece of metal to show his discovery, and ran it further to meet a handle. A winch, a manual winch!

There was a ratchet, too, securing it. In a second, Ledoux had snicked it loose. He indicated by hand signals to Maurette that he should lower the tailgate until he himself came back and stopped him, when it was in position.

Ledoux squirmed the length of the gangway on his belly; the ramp had already started to tilt over the back edge of the transporter. It made a light metallic clatter as Maurette lowered it still further; then there was the accursed oscillation of the flashers. Ledoux went down spreadeagled until it passed.

By feel alone, Ledoux let the ramp go further, further down towards the road's surface. He knew he dared not let it go full stretch. The thing would scrape along the road, kick up a racket or vibration loud enough to alert the driver. Nor dare he maintain it too high, out of danger of the extent of the drop.

The rear red lights helped. When the ramp had gone low, but not low enough to touch the road, Ledoux hurried back to Maurette. He secured the ratchet in its locking position.

Now!

The two men flung themselves at the straps securing their target drum to its saddle. They were ordinary simple buckles. In a moment they were loose.

How far up the pass had they progressed? Ledoux had lost count of time. Now his morning's reconnaissance paid off. They were – he was almost sure – at the third bend of the pass. It was vital to pinpoint where they jettisoned the drum. They could go on searching all night for it afterwards, especially if it rolled well clear of the road.

Maurette had already started to position himself for the final step when Ledoux remembered something. They had decided beforehand that, in order to give authenticity to their story of the drums working loose, they would also slack off the straps of another green drum. Ledoux held Maurette back, mimed his intention. For a moment Maurette did not comprehend, then, when he did, he and Ledoux worked at a second strap round one of the other drums (which were grouped together) and loosened it.

Then, they were back at their target drum. They threw their combined strength at the fifty-kilogram burden. It moved more easily than they had bargained for – the downward inclination of the flatbed added its own push.

Next, Ledoux put his shoulder against the drum as it hovered above the ramp leading to the road. He signalled to Maurette: he would climb down on to one of the metal cross-pieces before letting it go. This would cushion its final fall.

Ledoux got a foothold, braced himself. The drum was heavy and mobile: any moment it could carry him with it and crush him on the roadway. Maurette had the drum – eager to be away – by its wire strop. Together they manœuvred it on to the securing crosspiece. Sweat poured off their faces.

Ledoux gave the pre-arranged signal, a bump with the shoulder.

Away she goes!

The drum made a soft landing. In the limited range of the red rear lights they saw the drum roll and vanish over the verge of the bend.

Again the flashers vomited their jaundiced light; from inside the cab came another crackle of radio.

Ledoux and Maurette dropped over the rear of the flatbed, sprinted back down the road towards the causeway.

They left the drum where it had landed; they did not pause even to mark the spot.

Chapter 21

A Le Mans sprint-start had nothing on the two Bakunins. They flung themselves into the station wagon. Ledoux grabbed the wheel, gunned the engine, slipped the clutch. The tyres dug into the soft sand. The spinning wheels retarded rather than accelerated progress.

Then they were on the hard surface of the pass. Ledoux gave the engine everything it had, skidding and swinging wide on the lip of the first bend. The drum of explosive in the back aggravated the sideways slew; it was heavier than Ledoux had bargained for.

Maurette snatched off the blanket masking it. He was careful not to brush away more dust than necessary – before the flatbed's arrival, he and Ledoux had daubed the drum with dirt (apart from that which it had accumulated when they had rolled it from the graveyard). They had also scuffed the paintwork, to add realism to their story to the driver.

'We've got to catch the flatbed before it reaches the top of the pass!' snapped Ledoux. 'See anything yet?'

'It's too soon – we're just about where we dropped the radwaste drum.'

Ledoux threw the vehicle savagely into a lower gear, thrust the throttle hard against the floor.

'Take it easy!' exclaimed Maurette, hanging on. 'We don't want to finish up over the edge.'

'See it?' repeated Ledoux.

'No – wait – yes, there! Flashers!'

Ledoux did a racing change. The pass steepened. They must be close to the final ascent.

'There it is!' Maurette craned forward. 'Look at that ramp hanging!'

The flatbed rocketed within headlight range: Ledoux put them on to full. They illuminated the back of the massive vehicle ahead. On the inner side they could see the tailgate ramp swinging and clattering loose. It was surprising that the crew had not noticed it, even above the diesel's racket.

Ledoux did not slow or hesitate. He aimed the station wagon into a narrow gap between the transporter and the road edge where the road took a sharp turn.

Maurette gave a gasp. From the passenger's seat he was confronted by an array of drums, spinning multi-wheels, and a blast of hot diesel exhaust smoke.

The driver held course.

Ledoux went as far out as the narrow road would permit. He flashed his lights, gave a long blast on the hooter.

He powered level with the cab.

The driver glanced down. Even in the restricted light, his fury was plain. He waved them savagely aside – 'Give away, give room, you stupid sons-of-bitches!'

'Tell him!' shouted Ledoux to Maurette. 'Tell him!'

Maurette screwed down his window. He yelled, but his words were lost in the noise of the two vehicles jockeying within inches of one another. One yaw, and the spinning wheels of both would lock.

Maurette yelled again, gesticulated, pointed rearwards at the flatbed's body, trying to pass on the message that something was amiss. The driver waved him off, clamped both hands on the steering wheel, swung hard left and away into the final leg of the pass.

Ledoux did not give ground.

'He's coming into us!' screamed Maurette. 'Give way, for God's sake!'

Ledoux was made of sterner stuff. Instead of slowing, he accelerated. The station wagon's rear wheels came abreast of the huge vehicle's fore end. Ledoux turned slightly inwards, forcing it to slow.

The two vehicles, decelerating, went in tandem up the last bend. Ledoux, in the best cops-and-robbers style, slewed progressively inwards, gradually slowing the flatbed.

Finally, it came to a halt.

'What the hell do you think you're playing at?' shouted the driver. 'Trying to kill us all? What's your game . . .!'

Ledoux jumped out, went to the cab. He kept his voice cool and level, despite the driver's anger.

'You dropped a drum off the back – that's what we're trying to tell you!'

The driver throttled back the engine so that now, at least, words could be heard.

'What did you say!' He turned to the co-driver and shouted, 'Lost a drum – bullshit!'

Maurette joined Ledoux at the cab.

'You saw us next to the causeway – remember?' Ledoux

went on. 'As you passed we noticed that the ramp at the back was hanging loose . . .'

'Rubbish!' snapped the driver. 'I don't believe a word of this!'

Maurette intervened. 'See for yourself.' He gestured towards the back of the flatbed. 'It's still that way.'

The driver remained in his seat. 'Check it,' he told the co-driver. 'Check this nonsense.'

Ledoux and Maurette looked into the cab. The driver was a heavily-built man, shirtsleeves rolled up to show muscular forearms. He was sweating from the effort of piloting the heavy vehicle up the pass. The co-driver was tall, lean and wiry. He indicated to the driver what looked to the Bakunins like a jam jar fixed to the front seat.

'See that nothing happens to this.'

'Too damn right,' growled the driver.

The co-driver edged himself clear of the radio paraphernalia above his head and joined Ledoux and Maurette on the roadway.

'For crying out loud!' He stared in disbelief at the transporter's rear. 'Now the fat's in the fire!'

He rushed to the cab. 'Bill, quick, we've lost one of the drums – *quick*!'

The driver jumped down and rushed to the scene. The diesel still idled noisily.

'Now I've seen everything!' he burst out. 'It's not possible . . .!'

Ledoux broke in. 'As you passed us, the ramp was hanging down. When you went into that first bend, one of the drums rolled off . . .'

'I can't take it – *a drum rolled off*!'

'See here – there's another strap loose! – another one is working loose!' exclaimed the co-driver.

'Hell's teeth!' the driver got out. 'After all the delays and hassles in getting this first shipment on the road, this has to happen! How's it possible! The whole SYNROC-R operation has been dogged by bad luck. Nothing has gone right!'

Ledoux said equably, 'I think we should introduce ourselves. We are both members of the Radchem team to the IAEA gathering – Herr Ernst Fichte, Carl Lentz.'

The driver seemed scarcely to hear. 'This snookers everything!'

'In more ways than one,' added the co-driver sombrely. 'Gougo is waiting for that demonstration jar of SYNROC-R there in the cab. There's also a security man waiting to rush it back to Dr West once it has been cleared by the decontamination checks.'

Bossiere had always maintained that Ledoux's biggest asset – like a good general – was a talent to exploit an unexpected breakthrough.

'For Dr West?' he asked, trying to keep the excitement out of his voice. A plan was born that moment in his mind.

'Dr West is giving a demonstration tomorrow, as you know, at the kimberlite deposit,' explained the co-driver. The driver himself still seemed too shocked to join in. 'The glass jar in the cab is a special radiation-proof container with his own invention, SYNROC-R. It was touch-and-go whether Koeberg would have it ready in time. I heard that Dr West was keeping it secret because he wasn't sure whether Koeberg would manage. We were entrusted to get it here tonight.'

'I see,' said Ledoux. 'No, we IAEA delegates certainly did not know about it. You say it is being taken to Corbel Camp tonight?'

'Forget it!' interrupted the driver. 'You can forget about everything after this.' He waved at the empty saddle.

Ledoux picked his words and said carefully, 'We didn't only see the ramp hanging down, you know. I said, at the first bend, a drum rolled overboard. It finished up on the edge of the road. We collected it. That's why we chased after you the way we did. It's in the back of our station wagon.'

'You collected it – it's in the back of your station wagon.'

The man repeated the words like a concussed boxer automatically mouthing a doctor's word-test after a brain-damage knockdown.

'That is correct.'

The driver supported himself on the tailgate. 'You – collected – a – drum – of – radio-active – waste – which – fell – off – and – damaged – itself.'

The co-driver added, in an awed whisper, 'You've been handling a radio-active drum! You're dead men!'

The histrionic way Ledoux took Maurette by the shoulder would have been play-acting in any other circumstances, had the Koeberg men not been blinded by their deadly earnest.

'We never thought of that. All we wanted was to help you.'

'This gets worse and worse!' exclaimed the driver.

'The drum only fell a short distance,' said Ledoux reassuringly. 'We didn't see any damage, did we, Ernst?'

For a moment, Maurette missed his Radchem name, then stumbled out, 'No, no damage. It rolled right down the ramp. The sand on the roadside was pretty soft.'

'It's in the back of your vehicle, you say?' went on the driver. 'Let's go and look.'

Ledoux said, as if the thought had just occurred to him, 'I see you're wearing your radio-activity detection badges. Mine's still in my pocket from our Koeberg visit. We can easily check whether there's a radio-active leak or not.'

'What do you say about that, Pete?' the driver asked his mate. He seemed too stunned to make further judgements himself. 'Should be okay, I guess.'

Ledoux pulled out his badge and showed the flatbed crew. 'Neutral – we've been handling it, as you know.' Maurette also exhibited his neutral badge.

'Thank heavens for that!' breathed the driver. 'If anything's amiss, our own badges should start to register close to the station wagon.'

They didn't, of course. Like sniffer-dogs approaching a mine, the four men closed on the drum propped in the back of the vehicle with radiation badges held at full arm's stretch.

'No sign of damage here,' observed the co-driver, Pete, at length. 'Let's lift it out.'

The drum was easy for four men. They stood it in the roadway.

'Pete, switch off that bloody engine – I want to think. The row is knocking the thoughts out of my head.'

The engine went mercifully quiet. Ledoux said, 'Well, there's no harm done. Let's load it up and you can be on your way.'

'We stay right here,' responded the driver.

'What for?' asked Ledoux. He was sweating, despite the early night chill. It was make or break now for his masterplan.

'Regulations,' answered the driver. 'There is a strict procedure laid down in case of an accident. We radio Koeberg, stay exactly where we are. A standby relief crew and decontamination crew will be sent to the spot. All traffic must be diverted . . .'

Ledoux had his reply ready; he had been expecting this.

'It's going to take a relief crew a whole day to get here from Koeberg,' he said. 'You're almost within sight of the repository here, aren't you? You can be there in less than an hour. I guess no one is going to thank you for snarling up the rest of the IAEA delegates' visit just because you stick to the letter of your regulations – why not simply load up the drum and carry on? We'll back you up. There won't be a mention of the incident from our side, if you want it that way. We're in the same game, we understand the implications. And you can see for yourselves that there is no damage.'

The driver stood lost in thought, wavering. Ledoux tried to will him to his own viewpoint. Through the open door of the cab, he could see the exhibition glass jar of SYNROC-R, a pale colour, like caramel toffee. He *had* to get his hands on that jar! A plan started to avalanche in his mind, but he pulled himself back into the present to listen to what the driver was saying.

'. . . if Koeberg knows there's been an accident and I've gone on, I'll be fired,' he said. Ledoux latched on to the defensive, weakening note in the man's voice. 'I'd be fired, for sure.'

'Was it an accident – in the strict sense of the word?' Ledoux asked blandly. 'A drum rolled off the flatbed through no fault of yours, was undamaged, and some understanding friends picked it up and returned it to you. Can you call that an accident?'

Pete, the co-driver, said, 'He's right, you know, Bill.'

'Remember, we're out to help you,' added Ledoux sententiously.

Maurette also joined in. 'What will the IAEA delegates' reaction be when they hear – as they must – that everything has been fouled up because of a non-accident situation?'

'The regulations . . .' muttered the driver.

'You haven't contravened the regulations,' repeated Ledoux. 'There hasn't been an accident.'

The co-driver said, 'Bill, you gotta make up your mind, damn fast. I radioed our position when we started up the pass. I gave our ETA at Gougo as eight o'clock, approximately. If we don't make it thereabouts, questions *will* be asked.'

The driver squared his big shoulders. 'Listen, Herr . . .'

'Lentz,' supplied Ledoux.

'Herr Lentz,' repeated the driver. 'If I take that drum aboard again as if nothing had happened and fix the other straps into place, you swear you won't say anything about the incident?'

'Why should I?' answered Ledoux. 'It's what we all want. No harm's been done – to anyone. We'll help you load it up.'

The driver shook both Ledoux and Maurette by the hand.

'I can't tell you what this means to me,' he said. 'There would have been a board of enquiry, if I had reported this. I was given the job as the best of a short list of drivers – reliability, judgement, all that crap, you know. They would have derated me, for sure.'

'Forget it – we're all in this together,' said Ledoux, smiling. 'Eh, Ernst?'

Maurette again did a double-take on his unfamiliar name. 'Sure, sure. Let's get moving.'

It was easy for the four men to heft the drum of explosive by its wire strops on to the saddle via the ramp.

'We'll have this winch and ratchet checked when we get in,' said the driver. 'Can't understand how it came loose.'

'Vibration – bad roads,' said Ledoux cryptically.

'Could be, but one wouldn't expect it.'

Ledoux and Maurette stood by as the flatbed crew returned to the cab. The jar of SYNROC-R mesmerized Ledoux: a plan churned through his mind.

The driver fired the big diesel; further conversation was drowned out. He leaned out, shook hands once again. The two Bakunins went round to the co-driver's window and repeated the goodbyes.

The way the driver crashed the gears in starting off was evidence of his state of mind. Finally, he raised a hand in salute: the huge vehicle roared up towards the top of the pass.

Maurette turned to Ledoux with a grin. 'Talk about a piece of cake! – What's eating you?'

The Bakunin leader was silent, his face withdrawn and abstracted.

'Something wrong?' went on Maurette. 'I thought everything went as you wanted it to.'

'Nothing went wrong. That part of it is fine. There's nothing now to stop those demolition charges getting inside Gougo.'

'Then what the hell . . .?'

Ledoux broke in impatiently. 'You saw that exhibition jar of SYNROC-R in the cab?'

'Yeah – for West's address tomorrow.'

'What if it didn't?'

'Didn't? I don't know what you mean.'

'You heard him say, no one except West and the Security man knew about it, didn't you? That means, no one can expect what they don't know about, can they?'

'For Pete's sake, don't talk in riddles!'

'So if the jar came to us, the only person to miss it would be West . . .'

'To *us*? Whadderyamean, *us*?'

'A small sample of SYNROC-R, that is what Radchem has needed all along, isn't it? Dr Waldegg could analyse it – against

163

strict control checks against radiation, of course – and find out its composition, apart from the lindsleyite and mathiasite we all know about. Radchem would then have the formula, no problem. That's what Waldegg has been after. He's even prepared to buy it for half a million dollars.'

'What about our bomb?'

'Hedging our bets,' replied Ledoux confidently. 'One or the other, maybe both.'

'But West . . .'

'Listen carefully,' snapped Ledoux. 'Listen to what I have to tell you while we go and locate the drum we pitched off the flatbed. It is what *you* have to do once we have taken it to the graveyard and safely stashed it away . . .'

Ledoux talked as he manœuvred the station wagon to head down the pass again in search of the drum. His words came faster as the logistics of the plan took shape in his mind. It was neat, clever, opportunist; Maurette was the kingpin.

In his excitement, he almost overshot the bend where, both men felt sure, the drum had disappeared into the undergrowth by the roadside. Marks in the sand confirmed where the drum had gone sideways; it had rolled over the edge, they could see from the deeper tracks. The sand had also cushioned its fall. Best of all, the wire strop had snagged on the branches of a small tree close to the lip of the bend, and the drum was as safely hooked as a carrier plane doing a deck-landing.

Ledoux examined it with his flashlight. 'Damage?'

'No. I'll try a spot check with the radiation badges. If anything's wrong there, we're in trouble.'

'Don't cross your bridges. Try it first.'

The men's radiation badges moved across the surface of the captive drum, showed no reaction.

'Now let's load it up,' ordered Ledoux.

It was a muscle-cracking task for the two men to haul it bodily up the bank on to the road, but they managed it. They gave themselves a breather, then got it safely aboard the station wagon.

They drank the remains of the coffee in the vacuum flask,

and set off with Maurette at the wheel for the long drive back to the Haunted Graveyard.

Chapter 22

It was after 9 p.m. when the two Bakunin passed the lights of Corbel Camp on their way to the graveyard and Cheating Pan.

Bossiere had had another long vigil. The patience for such a wait was fretted ragged by the turmoil going on in his mind. He *knew* instinctively that he was right about the graveyard. But, as he had rushed off to find Rencha after reading the old tourist notice about the place in order to establish where it was in relation to the airfield, he had suddenly stopped in mid-stride.

For a moment he had forgotten – Rencha was the enemy!

If he unexpectedly started probing about the graveyard, she would suspect and pass on the fact to her bosses, the two Bakunins. They would then be alerted to the fact that he was – somehow – on their trail. Once that took place, anything could happen.

Bossiere had paused, gone back to his hut. He had to set about ruthlessly being his own Devil's advocate, testing every one of his suspicions. He wanted *fact*, not supposition. The two biggest facts of all lay snug in his wallet, those two photographs, one of Ledoux and one of Anna-Kai Cerny, the Bakunin courier, now passing herself off as Rencha Krummect. The rest was a cloud of deduction and suspicion springing from that . . . the bomb, its target. Where, when?

He threw his mental spotlight ruthlessly on what he knew of the two suitcases, the conversations he had eavesdropped on. How would it all stand up to scrutiny in a court of law? It wouldn't. But as a train of significant pointers, it was good. And the law, Bossiere told himself, was only the last stage in a security agent's chain, when everything else had been sewn up.

Latest pointer had been his sight of a large, blanket-covered object in the back of the terrorists' vehicle as it had swept past ... Bossiere got up, paced the small hut. If he got out his car now and went to the airfield, where would he head from there to find the graveyard? It could be in any direction. It must be close, he knew, from his time-distance calculations, but then distance didn't mean on Cheating Pan what it meant elsewhere. Besides, fiddling around and searching in the dark by means of headlights would be inviting disaster if Ledoux and Maurette returned from whatever mission they were now busy with and surprised him ...

There was no alternative but to wait until morning. The IAEA assignment for the day was to visit the site – on Cheating Pan, he understood – where Kepler West had made his historic kimberlite discovery. He knew it was not far from Corbel Camp, and that delegates were to be conveyed there by mini-bus and returned for lunch. He cursed inwardly that he hadn't bothered to check the geography of the place.

Bossiere felt as if he were being pinioned into a strait-jacket. The only movement he could make until he had fact to back suspicion was to watch for the return of Ledoux and Maurette.

Dinner was an agony for Bossiere. He tried to keep one ear on the road outside the camp for the sound of the Bakunins' engine; with the other, he had to listen to politeness and conversation from other delegates. He even imagined he saw Rencha eyeing him curiously at one stage when he had obviously made a wrong reply.

Back at his spy-hole, the tension finally broke when he spotted the station wagon's lights coming from the south. Bossiere kept his night-glasses on it: he was surprised when it by-passed Corbel Camp and headed for Cheating Pan. Yet, it was long enough in his vision for him to see three things: a bulky, blanket-covered object in the rear, the dust-streaked vehicle and Ledoux in the passenger's seat hugging his transistor radio.

Bossiere fought the temptation to jump into his own car and follow. He gritted his teeth, noted the time. All he could do was to check their return.

Maurette, too, glanced at the time as they passed Corbel Camp.

'The flatbed will be safely inside the repository by now.'

'So will the jar of SYNROC-R,' replied Ledoux.

'How long did the driver say it would take to check out?'

'He didn't.'

'Then it could be any time that the Security man brings it to West.'

'West's expecting it, so the driver said. If it's late, it will spoil his fun for the evening with the woman.'

'He's got work to do.'

'So have we.'

They had, once they reached the Haunted Graveyard.

It may have been over-eagerness to get the back-breaking task done of levering the drum up the stone ladder to the top of the beehive roof and upper chamber, or it may have been the darkness (they had switched off the headlights as a precaution and had only a partial moon to see by) which caused the drum to cannon into the low metal railing round the lovers' grave. The wire cable snagged, a short section of railing broke off, another section was bent.

'Careful, dammit!' exclaimed Ledoux. 'We don't want to damage the drum.'

'If it could stand falling off the flatbed, it won't be worried by a little bump like that,' retorted Maurette. 'I couldn't care less about the railing.'

Both men were uptight, and sweating from their effort.

'We'll catch our breath for a moment,' said Ledoux.

When they had got their breath back, they rolled and shoved the drum to the wall of the hut. They had brought with them the thin, strong cord from the station wagon's roof rack, the cord they had used to lash on the marker drum previously. Maurette now looped it over a thick, flat stone slab at the upper corner of the door lintel. These stone slabs were a feature of corbelled construction; from this course, the beehive dome sprang; they also formed the lowermost step of the stone ladder up its sloping side. From ground level to the summit of the dome was something over three times the height of a man.

'Heave!'

Both men threw their weight on the rope and the drum swung clear of the ground. Sweating like sailors on a topsail haul off Cape Horn, they got it shoulder-high. Ledoux held it in position – the projecting slab provided purchase – while Maurette scrambled up, grabbed the strop, and added his strength to the upward heave.

The drum came level with the underside of the first stone step, which now blocked further upward progress.

'What now?' panted Maurette. 'I can't hold this thing much longer.'

'I'll pass up the slack – tie it round the slab – I'll come up and help.'

'Can't see,' panted Maurette. Their hands were too occupied to manipulate flashlights.

'Here!'

Ledoux threw him an improvised lassoo which Maurette looped securely round the stone slab. Ledoux joined him. The drum hung like a bale in a sling.

'There are four more steps to the top,' said Maurette. 'We'll never make it this way.'

'We've got to move it on to the top of the step so that it can carry the weight,' said Ledoux. 'I'm shit-scared this rope could break. If it does and the drum falls, it's tickets.'

Both took hold of the cable strop and by sheer muscle-power manœuvred the drum the few inches necessary to position it on top of the slab.

'Now we'll run the rope up to the top and use it as a safety anchor,' said Ledoux. 'You and I will drag the drum up step by step and at each one we'll make the rope secure again . . .'

This they did. The rope was tied inside the upper chamber to the wooden 'bed' on which rested the barrel of fuel for the living flame. It was heavy enough in itself to provide a counterweight should the radwaste drum slip. Finally, for the last hurdle – the lip of the hatchway – Maurette sprawled full-length on the roof with his shoulder propped against the drum and Ledoux completed the lift from inside with the rope.

Then Maurette climbed thankfully into the chamber, now illuminated by Ledoux's flashlight; the fuel barrel stood on its altar like a full-bellied, headless Buddha. It was only possible to stand fully upright in the centre section; towards the walls, they had less headroom and had to stoop.

Maurette said, 'Let's fetch the spare demolition charges and detonators from the grave, and then the job's done.'

'I've changed my mind about them,' replied Ledoux. 'They stay buried.'

'I thought you regarded this as the safest place!' replied Maurette in surprise.

'The grave is better,' answered Ledoux. 'Look, we know that whoever has charge of this living flame gadget will return as far as we know when he reckons the fuel needs replenishing. What does he see in here? A strange drum. That's mighty odd, in itself. But if he also happens on a couple of demolition charges and a collection of detonators, the association will be clear – somehow the strange drum and an explosion are linked.'

'You're assuming that he'll recognize demolition charges and detonators.'

'This country is sensitive to explosives,' said Ledoux. 'They've had a lot of bombing in the towns. The public is aware of the danger. You can bet your life that even if the guy himself who locates these in here doesn't know exactly what they are, he'll have the security police round post-haste. No, the charges stay safely where they are – in the grave.'

'Okay. I see your point. We've still got to brush out all our tracks.'

The two Bakunins returned to the ground via the stone ladder. They used the blanket from the station wagon to brush out the drum's trail. They also worked over the surface of the grave in the belief that the next wind – it always rose with the dawn – would finish the job naturally beyond any suspicion They even took the final precaution of walking backwards to the station wagon, sweeping out their footprints as they retreated.

The living flame watched their departure with a lidless, malignant eye. It also held focus on the broken, buckled railing with its smear of green paint from the Koeberg drum. No blanket would ever mask that track.

Chapter 23

The glass jar of SYNROC-R lay in ambush in the cleavage between Rencha's breasts; its nuclear radiation seemed to be concentrating on searing and burning the right alone. It was inflamed livid red, and the nipple appeared to have come loose on its foundations and was hanging down at a grotesque angle. Kepler tried to yell, keep out of harm's way, for God's sake, keep out of harm's way! Throw the jar away! But he couldn't manage anything: the violent energy which the sight generated burst out through another channel, and he fought his way upwards through the nightmare and the strange, elusive fields of premonition to jerk to full consciousness in his own hut.

Maurette was already on his way across the floor to the keeping-hole in the wall opposite Kepler's bed.

The hectic, overcharged dream vanished as dramatically as the reality of the sight crashed in on Kepler.

The radiation-safe jar which had been of such concern to the flatbed's crew stood in the hut's keeping-hole. It had completed its journey that night to Kepler from Captain Fourie's hands after being cleared as top priority at the repository on the transporter's arrival.

There was no need for Kepler to bark the histrionic, redundant question, 'What are you doing here?' at the crouched, balaclava-capped figure moving towards the SYNROC-R jar. His dream had forewarned him of evil: here it was: he went for it.

Kepler, wearing only pyjama shorts, flung himself from his bed at the man. The pale light of the fading moon made the scene as unreal as the dream from which he had just emerged.

Kepler's intention was to grab the intruder, hold him, force him into submission with a deadly hold like a Boston Crab or a full nelson. After that, the game would have to play itself out.

Maurette chose otherwise. He had learned his trade in the garish world of punks, whores, knifemen, drunks, bars and bouncers where the catchword was opportunism – the first to send a kick to the groin or a stab to the back came out winner. If there were winners, in that society minus the Queensbury rules. And he had only his hands and feet as weapons. Ledoux had insisted that he should not take a knife or a gun.

He swung at Kepler, straightening and sidestepping. But Kepler had learned, in his unarmed combat course after the Canberra lab attack, to be cagey. He saw the signal in the other's dropped right shoulder, ducked inside the swing. Maurette's fist singed the side of his throat. He staggered sideways, off-balance, wide open. Kepler's right went hard in to the body. The response was a quick adenoidal gasp and a left to the side of Kepler's head which spun him round like a top.

Kepler covered his face, but Maurette's fists powered in under his elbows and jack-knifed him over – the perfect target for the kill. But, instead of backtracking or trying to hold on, Kepler moved forward and had all the weight of his straightening-out behind an uppercut which whip-lashed Maurette's head at the loft's half-ceiling.

Kepler set himself to finish him off with an orthodox straight left lead and a straight righthand cross fired from the shoulder – the fastest punch in the book.

But Maurette was faster. He jerked clear with a little dance step, jumped backwards, and tore from the wall near the keeping-hole a relic of the days when the hut was a tourist stop-over – a small buck's horn, fixed on the wall as a hat-rack.

Now he had a weapon!

He came at Kepler with a weaving, stalking approach and, if Kepler could have seen behind the balaclava, a smouldering viciousness in his eyes. He had broken in expecting a swift, clean job of larceny in an unoccupied room; instead, he had been confronted by a powerful, knowledgeable fighter. Maurette realized one thing now: he had to kill his opponent, if he wanted to get clear.

Kepler moved forwards, whipping a short hook for Maurette's head. It missed. Out of the corner of his eye he saw the sharp, serrated edge of the horn descending. Then it raked and burned across the top of his head, and the crash of the butt completed the delivery. The eggcup roof above him whirled like an inverted outer-space body; it steadied into position as he hit the floor.

He was up in a second to counter Maurette's killer rush, gripping the sharp horn with his left hand, aimed for Kepler's ribs or stomach. As he jabbed, he brought his hooked right over. The chop sent Kepler back to the floor. He got to his knees, rode out a kick which he didn't quite manage to turn to his own account by tipping over his opponent, as he should. But it was enough to send him staggering.

Kepler went after him, went after that primitive weapon in his hand. Maurette showed how deadly it was: its point seared across Kepler's forehead, bringing a rainbow of blood into his eyes. Kepler went in, bulled inside Maurette's guard, dropped his left for a feint to his body, cross-switched, and smashed a right squarely to the side of Maurette's jaw. It sent him reeling across the hut towards the keeping-hole. The improvised dagger shot from his hand.

Through a holo of pinkish blood from his wound, Kepler saw Maurette get up, pivot, reach for the jar of SYNROC-R.

For the first time during the fight, he uttered something. 'Leave it, you crazy fool!'

For an answer, Maurette raised the jar in both hands above

his head as if he meant either to throw it or brain Kepler.

Until now, Kepler had been fighting coolly, professionally, assessing, countering Maurette's blows and moves with his own. Now, at the sight of the SYNROC-R jar, a sweet, burning rage spread through him, a blazing truculence that fuelled power to his arms and limbs.

He measured Maurette fractionally, went in hard. Maurette had already begun his move, a rush made clumsy by his hands held high. They stayed high, came down with all the force they had.

The container missed Kepler's head but jarred and burned the muscles at the back of his neck. Maurette's arms were round and over him, still hanging on to the jar. Kepler was jammed up against his chest. The man stank. There was a legacy of stale sweat from the work of the ambush; another from hefting the drum up the graveyard hut; and now the bitter stench of fear joined with it.

He flung Kepler from him by sheer force and precipitated himself backwards, free of his hold. He could still get away clear – with the jar. But – he would first have to stop Kepler from coming after him.

But there was no stopping him. Maurette saw the menace in the crouch of the bearded, hairy body in front of him as he moved forward at him. There was only one way.

He raised the jar to smash it on the floor.

A new fury swept over Kepler. Through his fuzzy vision he saw the balaclava moving in and out round the intruder's mouth with his panting like a turkey's wattles. He didn't hesitate.

His body was hard against the Bakunin's, his hand at the wrist holding the lethal jar.

Maurette's reflexes were not sluggish. He shifted his left over for a two-handed grip, chopped the jar down to brain Kepler. Kepler moved in hard on his right arm, threw a Mexican armlock round the shoulder. He heard Maurette's muscles start to stretch, crack. No man can take that hold, banned from the ring, for long. Kepler bent the sweating torso double and spilled the jar out of his hands on to the floor from a height of only a few inches.

Fear surged through Maurette. He had lost everything – except his identity. It was only a matter of seconds now before Kepler ripped the mask from his face.

He squirmed, kneed Kepler in the groin.

It had been the move Kepler had been half expecting – almost hoping for – earlier in the fight. It was the foulest sort of blow, but he had learned how to turn it against its perpetrator.

Kepler unleashed the armlock as he sensed it coming, threw his right arm under Maurette's upraised knee, swung him bodily off his feet to his own full height. Still grasping his victim horizontal, he himself went down on one knee, his left. Across his other outstretched knee he would break the other man's back as he descended with his full weight behind it.

Maurette came down. Perhaps Maurette had some knowledge of the deadly grip, or perhaps he was so frantic to escape that he managed to shift slightly as he crashed down. Whatever it was, the back's fulcrum-point where the spine would snap like a crunchie bar evaded the waiting knee; he landed on the more solid lower back instead.

In a trice, the odds turned against Kepler. His hands still gripped Maurette as part of the back-breaker; they were no good for offensive work where they were. You can do almost anything to a kneeling man.

Maurette did. A mule-kick from his recumbent position exploded against Kepler's head and spun him across the floor to the far wall, sweeping the glass jar along with him. The impact knocked the breath from him. He could only lie and gasp desperately as the hooded figure went into a crouch like a hunted animal, saw he was safe, then dashed for the door, empty-handed.

Kepler was aware enough to register the door key being turned from the outside.

Chapter 24

It was mid-morning next day. '. . . so you see, my two new minerals are so similar to ilmenite and rutile that they are, at first glance, practically indistinguishable from them. As you know, ilmenite and rutile are reasonably common and the source of the space-age metal titanium. The biggest difference is in the colour. You can see for yourselves how the pale tan colour of lindsleyite and the darker tan of mathiasite persists in the SYNROC-R mixture.'

Kepler gestured at the glass jar of SYNROC-R which stood on the trestle table in front of him. It was the same jar which had been the target of Maurette's abortive heist.

Kepler West stood under an improvised awning on the edge of the open-cast site where kimberlite – the host substance for mathiasite and lindsleyite – was being mined by mechanical grabs and shovels. The place was known as New Rest, and lay on the south-eastern fringe of Cheating Pan, about fifteen kilometres east of Corbel Camp. This was also the spot where Kepler had made his momentous discovery after tracing to Cheating Pan Sir Malcolm Campbell's specimens which the racing ace had left behind at the West Australian Institute for Technology.

The awning sheltering Kepler against the already fierce sun was strung between two mechanical grabs with buckets extended like giant orange-yellow muzzled dinosaurs. Grouped in front of it were other earth-moving machines, also draped with shade tarpaulins. Under them stood or sat the twenty-five delegates and agencies of the International Atomic Energy Agency. All of them had travelled from Corbel Camp by mini-bus, taking a road which ran as straight as a laser beam along the Pan's edge through a series of retaining walls and anti-erosion works, designed to catch rain-borne silt before it spread itself across the uncompromising surface of Cheating Pan itself.

The exhibition jar of SYNROC-R had upstaged the proceedings. It had created a buzz of excitement when, after holding his audience with his account of his detective work in establishing that Campbell's specimens had originated from the piles of so-called flints which had been painstakingly collected from *Bluebird*'s track so as not to cut the ultra-thin racing tyres, Kepler had uncovered a workaday plastic shopping bag to reveal the SYNROC-R jar. The IAEA delegates' mass reaction, however, had been less than that earlier of one individual who was present. He was Captain Fourie, the South African Security officer who had been entrusted with the mission of conveying the SYNROC-R jar from the repository to Kepler the previous night.

Kepler had gone to Captain Fourie's quarters before breakfast and demanded that Fourie and an assistant should be present at his New Rest address – with guns in their pockets. Kepler had been taut, authoritative, and had offered no explanation for the precautions. Nor had he told the Security man that he had sat up most of the rest of the night with his own pistol (which had been locked in his suitcase at the time of the attack) guarding the jar in case the intruder should venture a second attempt.

Immediately after Maurette's escape, it had taken Kepler a couple of minutes to recover from the mule-kick. He had hauled himself to the window in a too-late attempt to see if he could spot where the intruder had gone – he did not, of course, risk the light. There was no sign of the man. He had then inspected the locked door and inner keyhole with a torch. In his haste, the escaper had left the key outside in the lock. It was a tough effort for Kepler to get himself through the small window aperture adjoining the door after he had again carefully checked the surroundings. He finally managed it, unlocked the door, and returned inside, shivering with the cold.

At his interview with Captain Fourie, Kepler had noted the other man's eyes stray to the plaster on his forehead – he had offered no explanation of that either, nor to Rencha at breakfast.

At first, Fourie had objected to the New Rest guard, but Kepler had insisted on having an armed escort for the SYNROC-R jar. He had gone further: once his address was over, Captain Fourie and his colleague, both armed, were to convey the jar back to the repository for safe-keeping. Fourie had dismissed his request as exaggerated fussiness. Finally Kepler had pulled his rank and now the two Security men sat next to him under the awning.

'So the Australians could be forgiven for overlooking Campbell's specimens because of their similar optical properties to ilmenite and rutile?' The question was from Sir Edward Nayland. His supercilious English drawl got under the Australian scientist's skin.

'Yes. If all you do is to look at a specimen without investigating further.'

The delegates laughed. Kepler added, 'It could also have been another related mineral, priderite. Priderite is found in the Kimberley region of Western Australia — right on the Institute's doorstep.'

Kepler regarded the gathering. His neck and shoulders were still stiff from the battering they had taken from the masked intruder — which was he here among his audience? He must be young, to have put on a show like that. And from a background which didn't tally with what might be expected of a scientist's sheltered academic environment. You don't learn the kick to the groin or the slash to the face in a laboratory curriculum. Top men like Professor Jaboulet, Professor John Ankey (who happened to be a friend anyway) and Sir Edward Nayland were naturally disqualified. Round these stars were clustered constellations of lesser men, some of whom were young and fit enough to have grappled with him. On his way to Captain Fourie that morning he had encountered joggers — would any of them have qualified? Among them, the stocky Frenchman Bossiere had greeted him. However, decided Kepler, Bossiere's body wasn't the one he had tangled with, although he was far from flabby and tough enough to take a punch.

The Red China-Radchem team were automatic suspects in Kepler's mind. They had shown their hand in making the outrageous half-million dollar offer for his SYNROC-R secret. However, would they have resorted to such thuggery to get their hands on the material itself?

Kepler eliminated Nakanishi and Chillun To from his suspect list. They simply didn't fit the bill. With them was the deep-voiced, Fu Manchu-bearded Dr Waldegg and faceless Dr Dieckmann, a paunchy discount. Kepler was willing to believe anything of Dr Waldegg after his offer, but could not equate him with physical attack.

The other two Radchem men, the technicians Lentz and Fichte? Kepler focused on them as if awaiting a question from their direction, but it was really to try and see whether either of their faces were marked from his blows. That was no criterion either – the balaclava would have cushioned their impact and left little bruising. He hadn't been able to observe whether either of them walked stiffly or had any problems boarding the mini-bus – surely that last abortive back-breaker must have left some damage?

Kepler was brought back to the present by a question from the brittle voice of Dr Nakanishi. 'Isn't it a fact, Dr West, that a mineral from the kimberlite deposit at the Yimeng mountain in Shandong in my country bears a close compositional similarity to your mathiasite? In fact, you may simply be calling it by another name.'

Remembering Nakanishi's involvement in the buy-off bid, Kepler was tempted to take a crack at him and ask if what he was asking were correct, why China simply had not made its own version of SYNROC-R. But he decided that it would serve no purpose; he replied levelly.

'I am familiar with your Yimeng mineral, Dr Nakanishi, and have tested it. It lacks – like priderite – an essential constituent of mathiasite and lindsleyite.'

'I see. However, I am still not convinced that your new

minerals may not be relatively common – they may just have been overlooked because of what you have told us is their resemblance to ilmenite and rutile.'

Kepler did not respond. It was clear that Nakanishi was trying his best to talk down his discovery, without any real ammunition to back him.

Then, to his surprise, Kepler was confronted with a question from the man he knew as Lentz, of the Radchem team. It had been Dr Waldegg's decision that a question from Ledoux would draw off possible suspicion which Kepler might have regarding the attack having come from the Radchem team by presenting Ledoux and Maurette as they were supposed to be, nuclear technicians. Waldegg had been furious and upset by Maurette's failure to get his hands on the jar of SYNROC-R. He had questioned Maurette over and over: had Kepler gained any clue to his identity? Finally, he was reasonably satisfied that Kepler remained in the dark. Waldegg was now convinced that the bomb was the only option – except one, perhaps . . .

In spite of Ledoux's initial objections, Dr Waldegg had coached him about what he had to ask.

Ledoux put Waldegg's question, carefully, well rehearsed.

'Dr West, my colleague Herr Fichte and I are nuclear technicians and as such we are concerned with the refractory properties of mathiasite and lindsleyite. In other words, can they withstand safely the high temperatures they are likely to encounter after a long period of burial, without fusion or decomposition?'

Kepler was surprised enough to find himself replying like a book. 'Yes, they are highly refractory. That, coupled with their structural flexibility in hosting large and small radii cations . . .'

Dr Waldegg rushed to the rescue before Ledoux made a fool of himself. 'That is where Radchem and my colleagues from British Nuclear Fuels part company with SYNROC-R, Dr West. We maintain that glass is the ideal first barrier containment medium for radwaste. I am talking of specialized types of glass, naturally – metallic glasses, alkali or zinc-based boro-silicate glasses, high-silica content glasses and the like.'

Kepler knew a professional when he heard one. 'The major disadvantage of glass as a containment medium is its inherent thermodynamic instability over a long period of time – I am referring now to historical as well as geological time. The instability springs from the deterioration of glass by devitrification in which the glass is transformed into a crystalline state. In the natural processes of decay, the radwaste will generate temperatures of between a hundred and five hundred degrees for periods of at least a century, and glass would simply not stand up to that without undergoing a change in structure.'

Dr John Ankey, the American, broke in. 'All that is being said now is a rehash of the arguments which were put forward at the time of Dr West's discovery. We haven't come here for a geochemical discussion on the merits of mathiasite and lindsleyite. I myself originally put them through the hoop at Los Alamos. You can rest assured that the International Mineralogical Association would not have accepted mathiasite and lindsleyite without the most meticulous examination of their credentials – you don't get so many new minerals coming along any more, as you know.'

Kepler threw Ankey a glance of appreciation; he had never made any secret of his admiration of SYNROC-R.

Now he added the massive weight of official American scientific opinion to it.

'I'd add that I consider the Gougo repository site probably the best in the world, better than any of the five we have earmarked for use in the USA. Most of all, here we have a completely new site devoted to a new containment technique and uncluttered by conventional forms where the stabilities of the various constituents of SYNROC-R and their element-retention capacities can be assessed in a geological setting over geological time. Anything up to a hundred thousand years, in my opinion.' He gave a grin. 'In short, I buy Gougo and SYNROC-R.'

Kepler was not the only one present who had been surprised

by Ledoux's entry into the discussion. Bossiere had hardly followed the scientific exchanges – they were above his head, anyway – and he had his own problems. First and foremost, *where* was the location of the graveyard described in the old tourist notice stuck behind his door? At first he considered it an easy thing to find out; when he did, he would motor there and check it out. Reference to a road atlas showed a small-scale map of Cheating Pan, so small as to be useless for his purpose. Who could he ask? The obvious person, Rencha, was out.

Bossiere had reckoned that the road to New Rest must pass the graveyard and answer his question. It didn't. It did not traverse the Pan itself but ran along its southern fringe, branching immediately outside the camp from the airfield road. There was no sign of a graveyard on the New Rest route, and the little he could see of the Pan was hazed by heat mirages. Yet, it must lie within that eight-kilometre radius he had calculated!

The sound of Ledoux's questioning voice was like the jab of a red-hot hypodermic needle into Bossiere. It jerked him out of his contemplative state of mind, and his mouth clamped hard. This was a killer talking, a killer with blood on his hands, the companion-in-terror of the arch-terrorist Carlos the Jackal – and he had the nerve to embark on a scientific discussion! Bossiere stifled the upsurge of hatred which rose within him. It was situations like this which were the most dangerous – a harmless, everyday setting which could suddenly be ripped apart by explosive into a hideous pantomime of torn bodies and dismembered limbs . . .

Today was the fifth day of the IAEA delegates' gathering. They had only three more left. Two of those, the next and that following, would be spent away from Corbel Camp at South Africa's original nuclear repository some three hundred air-kilometres to the west. Had the killers earmarked that opportunity to detonate their bomb? Unlikely, if they planned to include IAEA delegates in their target.

Bossiere could have spat when Ledoux finished his high-falutin' question.

Three days! He'd have to act fast!
Tonight he would take that graveyard apart!

Chapter 25

You can stun a man with bootleg rye, or with a blackjack, or
with a woman's body. Corbel Camp, being beyond the black
stump, lacked the first two commodities. For the third, it had
Rencha.

And Rencha looked stunning.

IAEA delegates, gathered that night in the big communal
lounge for what Rencha termed a finger supper – it was one of
her novel meal improvisations, a kind of kebab dish on skewers
which the delegates themselves roasted on the two big open
fires – stared when Rencha made her entry late enough and
woman-like to ensure that they were all present. Relaxed they
were, too, over bottles of wine and a day spent at the New
Rest kimberlite site.

Had Bossiere been present – he was unaccountably absent
– he would have double-checked against the photograph in his
wallet of Anna-Kai Cerny the Bakunin courier to make sure
he was looking at the same person. He would have found it
hard to reconcile the face under a pulled-down beret of a scared
girl scarcely out of her teens with the exquisite creature which
walked into the room. She wore a light-green loose jacket
patterned in bold flower motifs of muted pale pink, black and
darker greens, a champagne-coloured waistcoat and open-
necked blouse, olive-green pants, and high heels. The real
eye-catcher was a wide nappa belt in pale grey with a large
silver butterfly clasp; it divided into two over the body section
to form the clasp with wings almost as wide as the belt itself.

Rencha had changed her hairstyle, too. The long waft of
auburn which customarily hung down almost to her left breast
had been formed into a soft upward-sweeping chignon at the

back of her head; where the weight of hair usually levelled her hairline in front, it was now relieved of it and formed a soft, loose coif, full of unexpected lights from the fire. Flecks of fire came, too, from her crystal earrings – only a Frenchwoman could have worn them.

There was no secret for whom all this was intended: when she came into the room, she went straight to Kepler, who was sharing a glass of wine with John Ankey. It was an act of accepted intimacy which brought him an inner thrill. It also rounded off a successful day. At New Rest, Kepler had been uptight all the time the jar of SYNROC-R had been on public show. When he had finished his address, the two Security men had loaded it up and started for Gougo, with strict instructions to telephone immediately their safe arrival at the repository. Ledoux and Maurette also had watched them drive off; that was one hijack they would not attempt.

Now, finally, the evening's party was over, and Kepler and Rencha were alone in her quarters. Drinking *Jacob-jong* tea had become a shared late-night ritual between them.

She handed him the cup. 'There'll only be three more times of doing this after tonight. Do you realize that?'

'Yes, I know. But there will be other occasions – later on.'

'Meaning?'

He smiled at her. 'I suppose previously there was no real technical justification for my coming back and checking what was going on at the repository. It was the other chap's job – mine was getting SYNROC-R into production. Now I can find reasons for visiting Gougo. The shipments are flowing – I heard again by phone this morning that there's a whole convoy of flatbeds ready, one for each day.'

'You're assuming that I'm staying, Kepler.'

'Aren't you?'

'I seem to move into other people's lives, and then move out again.' She made a little illustrative gesture at the bland, unresponsive room as if it knew to keep its eyes closed against her past and its mouth shut about what had gone before. 'Once everything was as fresh and new and now it's . . .' She fumbled for a word to go on.

'Routine?'

Kepler wondered what was coming. She had already gone further than she ever had about what lay behind her.

She backtracked, evaded the route her words were taking her.

'You'd like the routine – me at Corbel Camp, you at Koeberg, routine weekend visitis . . .?'

You're lying to yourself, Rencha. No Bakunin defector's head ever lies easily again. Nor will yours, after tomorrow.

He laughed, a little uneasily. 'What will happen to us? Just grow old and run out of ourselves?'

'You're talking of a different kind of life from Corbel Camp, Kepler. A city life, where that sort of thing happens – just happens, insidiously, quietly, unnoticed, and before you know, you're part of it and the gloss has somehow vanished and all you're left with is a pile of empties. The wine and the intoxication has gone. Cheating Pan isn't like that. It dies, it comes alive, fresh and new each spring . . .'

'Here, the spring?'

'It isn't flowers, it isn't the rain. The butterflies. They take its place. Millions and millions of butterflies. Suddenly, one day as unexpectedly as love, they burst upon you. Out of the northeast. The world – the Pan – is white with a kind of pulsing life. Fresh, new, vibrating.'

She stood up, talking rapidly, animatedly.

'Go on.'

'One of my earliest tourist guests at Corbel Camp was a butterfly-hunter. He wasn't old, not like the conventional picture of a butterfly fuddy-duddy nut. He was a young scientist who had come to study the butterfly migrations. They are like the great migrations the buck used to make once in these parts of the world, millions and millions of animals who would go past at a steady trot heading in a fixed direction, across whatever barrier lay in front of them – rivers, mountains, anything. The Bonsma grandfather remembered them, they told me. Like the lemmings of Canada, if you like. The butterfly man waited, weeks. He believed in them. He knew the great cloud of new life would come. And it did. I need the new life myself, too.'

'Is that all he came for? Just to witness the sight?'

She moved closer to him, and stood above his chair.

'He came to study the visual, touch and sound stimuli which provoked mating between the butterflies.'

Kepler put down his cup. His eyes locked with hers.

'Your belt is shaped like a butterfly.'

'I got the idea from them.'

Kepler moved forward and took the wings of her belt, one in either hand.

She said very softly, 'Pre-love demonstrations are a feature of the sex-life of the butterflies. It is followed by copulation, which can last from half an hour to all night . . .'

The two halves of her buckle were loose in his hands. His head and lips were buried in her groin.

She picked up his head sharply, almost roughly, to hers. He could not tell whether the wetness was tears or passion. Her lips were all over his face, his eyes, his mouth. Her tongue sought out his, caressing it with hers. Her right arm went round his waist and one thigh jammed itself between his legs. Her words were jumbled by her sobs, or pants. 'Half an hour . . . all night . . .'

She took him and led him through to her bedroom.

He knew then what she meant when she said she hadn't had a man for three years.

Chapter 26

When larks sing for lovers, there is always someone around to shoot them dead out of the sky at their feet.

Next morning, that person was Bossiere.

And the larks were singing for Rencha and Kepler when the DST man confronted them after the IAEA delegates had flown off to the Namaqualand repository at Vaalputs – the site of South Africa's first radwaste repository. A quantity of radwaste, much of it from the nuclear power station at Koeberg, had been buried there, using conventional container storage methods. The layout at Vaalputs had served as a prototype for the new Gougo repository, which was exclusively for SYNROC-R. The South African authorities had decided not to deposit any SYNROC-R at Vaalputs since it might confuse the long-term evaluation of the merits of Kepler's discovery.

It was Saturday. Bossiere had scarcely waited until the delegates were clear of Corbel Camp before finding Rencha and Kepler together in Rencha's sitting-room. Bossiere alone of the twenty-five delegates remained at Corbel Camp. He had told Professor Jaboulet briefly that he was staying (the official explanation could be an attack of enteritis) and the IAEA President, himself a Frenchman, asked no explanations from the DST man. One glance at that taut face was enough. He knew Bossiere – and his formidable reputation.

Bossiere's absence from the previous night's meal had nothing to do with enteritis. What had happened, however, had put him into a rough, ruthless mood and had made Rencha his target. Time was running out, fast. He had taken his car and gone off in the dark in search of the graveyard – and Ledoux's hypothetical bomb. Cheating Pan had palmed the ace with a wind and a shroud of dust and left him a frightened man at the end of several hours of hopeless, fruitless wandering.

Like Ledoux and Maurette on their first sally, Bossiere had headed for the airfield. He had finally found it, as they had done, by locating the parked Hercules and helicopters. What next? The Bakunins at least had known that the graveyard lay somewhere to the east of the airfield; Bossiere did not know where to begin. He hoped to find a road, perhaps a signpost. But he was to learn later, after somehow drifting away from *Bluebird*'s track, that the only signposts on Cheating Pan, were thirst, fear, and an awful sense of plunging into an unknown amorphous curtain which could lift to show that the final destination was death. Bossiere was not a man easily scared; he pressed on. The fragment of moon which hung above the dust cloud as a diffused glow went down; his car's petrol gauge went down; he knew the first upsurge of panic at nothing – nothing except the blowing, shifting surface of the Pan under his headlights.

Where was he?

He cut the engine and the lights, tried to orientate himself. Panic plucked at him like the wind. At least, while the engine ran it gave the illusion of life. He feared that if he tried to sit it out until morning, he might be half out of his mind.

He fired the engine, wheeled the car in a blind circle, accelerated off in a direction which he hoped was against the wind; it could have been blowing from the north-west, he wasn't sure. He was equally unsure what lay in the north-west. The ten-minute high-speed plunge into nothingness was worse than his patient searching previously. Bossiere started to sweat. Then – a brief sight of something ahead, a scrape under the chassis, something harder under the wheels – he had crossed the small barrier of bushes which demarcated *Bluebird*'s track as straight as an arrow for more than a dozen kilometres across Cheating Pan.

Bossiere stopped, pulled himself together, then followed the line of bushes, keeping them on his left. Now he went slowly: those bushes were his lifeline; he knew they must lead him eventually to the parked aircraft.

They did. No sailor in a storm was gladder to see a lighthouse than Bossiere was to sight them. He was in no frame of mind to search further, even if his fuel gauge had permitted. It registered only a few litres left. He motored slowly and economically back to Corbel Camp.

He came to the conclusion: the way to short-circuit the bomb problem was to go for Rencha first thing next day.

Bossiere walked quickly from his own hut, past the high stone wall blocking off the car park, to Rencha's sitting-room which adjoined it. Her door was open, Kepler was there. Kepler had no reason to go to Vaalputs – he had seen it all before.

Rencha greeted Bossiere with a surprised smile. She had no time to assess that tension had pulled the DST man's once-fractured jaw slightly more askew, and that the extra missed bristles on his jaw after shaving were the result of it. Bossiere had broken down many suspects. If Rencha's inner glow affected his Gallic heart in any way, it was swept aside by the recollection that now was about to begin the revenge for the bullets Ledoux had used all those years ago to smash in his three colleagues' faces.

'M. Bossiere! I heard you were ill . . .'

'I am not ill, madame. I stayed behind with a purpose. I wanted to speak to you – and Dr West.'

There was a grate in his voice, like Cheating Pan grit between the teeth.

'To me, and Dr West? Come in.'

But Bossiere was already in the room. He pivoted to face Rencha. He wanted the best results from the shamrock microphone in his buttonhole.

'First, let me introduce myself.'

Rencha laughed. The thought flashed through Bossiere's mind, you won't laugh again like that. Perhaps never. A pity.

'We both know who you are, M. Bossiere.'

'You don't,' he replied roughly. 'You will not disclose to anywhat what I say – is that clear? First, I am not monsieur. I am a colonel. A colonel in the DST – French Intelligence.'

Bossiere was watching Rencha closely. Yes, that laugh, that smile, were now instant history. She'd been so clearly in love – Bakunin-type love, maybe.

Rencha glanced at Kepler, and then back at Bossiere. Kepler went to her, as if the mere mention of an organization as alien to themselves as the DST were drawing them physically closer.

Bossiere produced his DST accreditation card and formally passed it to Kepler.

He glanced at it and asked, 'What has French Intelligence to do with us? Any security hereabouts is the concern of the South Africans.'

'The point is debatable at what point the security interests of one nation impinge on those of another.'

Bossiere would have sounded pompous, had he not been in such deadly earnest.

'In other words the DST, by putting you in here with the front of being a scientist, is trying to upstage local arrangements? It's a pretty reprehensible way of doing things. I wonder what Captain Fourie will say when he hears? In any event, what in hell should you want that you think the South Africans can't handle?' Kepler threw the words at the Frenchman.

If they could have seen it, the scar under Bossiere's moustache pulled up cynically. 'All security is reprehensible to a greater or a lesser degree, Dr West.'

'That's your second generalization in as many minutes.'

Bossiere shrugged. 'It wasn't you I primarily came to see. It was the lady.'

He moved half a step closer to her and fired the question.

'What do you know of the Bakunin?'

The question imploded the structure of her face, leaving the skin slightly stretched and pale where a few minutes before it had been relaxed and glowing. The green eyes snapped into blank portholes outwardly, shutting off an inner hell within.

'I've never heard the name.'

'Yet you were a courier . . .' he gave the word a value which puzzled Kepler and exacerbated Rencha's emotions '. . . moving backwards and forwards in and out of France. But you never heard of the Bakunin? Your courier duties may, for example, have taken you on the Toulouse express. You would not have known that the bomb which went off aboard it and tossed bodies about the surrounding countryside was planted by the Bakunin.'

'I did not know.' Police court denial.

'For the second time, Colonel Bossiere, what has this to do with Rencha, Corbel Camp, or the IAEA?'

'The Bakunin is France's most mysterious and dreaded terrorist movement, Dr West.'

'So what?'

Rencha stood frozen. Kepler could almost detect the withdrawal of the person with whom he had shared so much in such a short time sink away like the vanishing waters of the Sak River into the unfriendly ground. He felt the onset of some unnamed fear for the future.

Bossiere threw his verbal punch in the same way as Kepler had done his lightning straight right from the shoulder at Maurette.

'Where is the bomb?'

He had expected the knock-down, the tearful breakdown into confession, but it didn't come. Instead, she stood there like a boxer who had taken the anaesthetizing punch but by some freak remained on his feet.

'Bomb?' The word was spoken from a nightmare past where bombs, bullets, Bakunin and terrorist hunts were everyday life; she had buried it all when she had fled to South Africa . . .

'Yes, bomb,' retorted Bossiere. 'I have reason to know that the Bakunin has a bomb planted . . .'

'At Corbel Camp? Don't be absurd!' interrupted Kepler.

Bossiere ignored the interjection. 'You can save yourself a good deal of agony – and the lives of other people – by revealing the bomb's whereabouts and detonation time. I guarantee that if you do, it will never be traced back to you.'

Rencha looked about her like a half-awake patient emerging from an operation.

'I don't know anything about a bomb.'

Bossiere shrugged in a 'you-asked-for-it' way. 'You weren't a travel courier, madame. You were – and are – a courier for the Bakunin Movement. Your name isn't Rencha Krummect. It is Anna-Kai Cerny.'

'I am none of these things. I am the owner of Corbel Camp. I have been ever since my husband – my late husband – and I bought it.' She put up her hand across her eyes, as if trying to hide her secrets from Kepler.

Kepler put his arm round her shoulders. The muscles were as taut as a violin string.

'You are fantasizing, Colonel Bossiere,' he said. 'I myself have been through this sort of interrogation, after I had been attacked in my laboratory at Canberra. Security men see shadows, detect men lurking round corners where there aren't even corners. It's their job – a nauseating one. I found it more worthwhile to learn to look after myself than trust in security rubbish. The same goes for this terrorist nonsense you've hatched up. Now – get out!'

Bossiere rocked backwards and forwards on the balls of his feet. He might have been waiting for a snap pass from a scrum.

'I don't get out, Dr West. Do you know what a sleeper is?'

'No more than a Bakunin or Anna-Kai Cerny.'

Rencha may have winced when he said the name, he wasn't sure, or it might have been a convulsive nerve ripple lancing through her taut shoulders.

'A sleeper, Dr West, is someone whom a terrorist or spy organization plants – often years before – at a particular target. That sleeper becomes part of the landscape, so to speak. He or she identifies completely with the surroundings. They are accepted. No one suspects, just because they have been around for so long.

'I say, this woman is a Bakunin sleeper.'

Bossiere saw Kepler bite back his anger. He made a big attempt to give a controlled reply.

'You've made some mighty big accusations, Colonel Bossiere. I intend to make you eat them. Them, plus anything else you care to add to this wild fantasy of yours.'

'I have more to add.'

Bossiere's tone had the measured inexorability of a bulldozer approaching a wall to demolish it.

He addressed himself to Kepler, as if Rencha were in another room.

'I say Anna-Kai Cerny was planted here as a Bakunin sleeper for the express purpose of the IAEA gathering at Cheating Pan.'

Kepler shrugged. He did not trust himself to reply.

Bossiere went on, 'How does it strike you, Dr West, that the lady has made the running, eh? From that first time at the crash demonstration? In other ways far beyond her duties as hostess of Corbel Camp?'

Bossiere saw the anger flare in the scientist's face. 'Be careful of what you are saying, Colonel Bossiere!'

The DST man went on quickly, 'I have reason to think that you yourself might be the Bakunins' prime target, Dr West.'

Rencha said in a strangled voice, 'No, no! Not him, too!'

'*Too*, madame?' Bossiere never missed a trick.

Kepler made a contemptuous dismissal of his words. 'You are seeing more and more shadows, Colonel Bossiere. How could I be a terrorist target when an offer has already been made to me of half a million dollars to sell out the secret of SYNROC-R.'

It was Bossiere's turn to be shaken. 'By whom, Dr West?'

'The head of Radchem, Dr Waldegg. It is common knowledge that if the Gougo project goes ahead, China stands to lose a seven-billion dollar deal to bury radwaste in the Gobi Desert. Radchem is China's agent in Europe. What is half a million compared to seven billion? I suggest you concentrate on sleazy commercial sabotage before letting your imagination run riot over terrorists and bombs.'

Bossiere swallowed hard. Kepler's revelation put a different complexion on his suspicions. Kepler could not be the main Bakunin bomb target. Ledoux, as one of the Radchem team, must have been wise to the offer. The time had come to break open Ledoux's identity and get from the girl what it was all about.

'Was the man called Lentz concerned in the buy-off offer?' he demanded.

Kepler laughed, without humour. 'Lentz is a technician, so he says. A small fish.'

'So he says,' repeated Bossiere. There was something in the way he echoed it which made Kepler pause.

Bossiere said levelly, addressing Rencha as well, 'I want you to listen to this. Lentz's name is not Lentz. It is Ledoux. Jean Ledoux.'

The DST man marvelled at her acting. She showed no reaction at all.

He threw the next part of it at her. 'Ledoux is the head of the Bakunin Movement.'

She said in a whisper. 'Ledoux – head of the Bakunin – here!'

Kepler broke in. 'You are fixated about Bakunins, Colonel Bossiere. You haven't produced a single fact to back up what you are saying.'

For an answer, Bossiere fiddled in his inner coat pocket, found what he wanted, and passed it to Kepler. It was the Mossad photograph of Ledoux in Arab clothes on the deck of a ship escaping from West Beirut.

Kepler started to say, 'This means nothing . . .'

'Look at the back, Dr West.'

Rencha seemed to be in a state of shock. She made no attempt to read with Kepler.

'I can't read the French,' he said. 'But I see the official French Intelligence stamp.'

Bossiere read aloud, 'Photograph by courtesy of Mossad, Israeli Intelligence. Jean Ledoux, now head of Bakunin Movement, on board freighter *Alkyon* in company with . . .'

Bossiere stopped. His throat was tightening up with hatred. He said thickly to Rencha, 'The man there with Ledoux is the world's most notorious terrorist, Carlos the Jackal. Ledoux is a friend of his. The same Ledoux who is now your guest at Corbel Camp.'

Rencha shook her head wordlessly, not looking up.

'I have information that two suitcases of high explosive were smuggled into Corbel Camp, weighing I reckon between thirty and forty kilograms. That is enough to bring down half a skyscraper, Dr West. Nor do you move that amount of explosive around just anyhow. It requires an infrastructure, someone on the spot, someone to organize. That is where the couriers, the women couriers, come into it. It is they who open lines of communication, bring in explosive, the detonators, the guns, the grenades. The experts carry out the final job. The couriers also carry orders, verbally, and as such are the kingpins of terrorism. A great responsibility rests upon them. In France, Anna-Kai Cerny was one of the best. The DST never trapped her, although we tried many times. And then, just as our net was closing, she vanished. Utterly, completely disappeared. We made the mistake of writing her off. She had only gone off for her next job.'

He jerked out savagely at Rencha, '*Where is the bomb?*'

Rencha replied in a voice which Kepler hardly recognized. 'I told you who I am. Rencha Krummect. I know nothing of Anna-Kai Cerny or the Bakunin.'

Kepler intervened harshly, 'Leave her alone, Colonel Bossiere. You've had your say, now leave it, do you hear? You've had her answer . . .'

Bossiere went on quietly, 'You make me do this, Anna-Kai Cerny. Maybe I might have spared you, if you'd come clean.'

He pulled out the wallet again and took out a photograph. This time he did not let it out of his grasp. He held it out for Rencha and Kepler to see.

Kepler could not have taken it away, his hand was shaking so. He stared in stunned disbelief at Rencha and then at Bossiere.

'I see you recognize her,' said Bossiere. 'A little younger, a little scared, but unmistakable. Do you believe me now when I say Rencha Krummect is Anna-Kai Cerny, the Bakunin terrorist courier? This was taken by one of my agents outside a Metro station in Paris . . .'

The floodgates which years of lonely isolation at Corbel Camp had held tight shut suddenly collapsed inside Rencha.

She spoke rapidly, almost uncontrollably, the words tumbling over one another into occasional near-hysteria. 'Yes, yes, it is me, that photo? I am Anna-Kai Cerny! My name is changed – you can see the deed of poll in Cape Town! I was a Bakunin courier! I was forced to be a courier . . . I loved Charles, he was a doctor, one night he attended a man with a gunshot wound who came to the door begging help – he was a Bakunin on the run – they got at us, blackmailed us, those Bakunin devils did. Then, when they saw that Charles was no longer willing to play along with them, they killed him! I fled, broken-hearted, blindly from France to South Africa – that is why you couldn't find me, Colonel Bossiere! I was here, trying to make a new life. I did make a new life. I married a man I loved dearly, John Krummect . . . together we discovered this place, Corbel Camp . . . it was our dream, but they got him too . . .' Rencha turned away from Kepler, evading his comfort. Her sobs were as uncontrollable as an out-of-orbit space shot. 'When I saw that car crash out there on the Pan that first day, it brought it all back . . . that's the way they killed him, John, with a grenade thrown against a tyre on the mountain pass like a burst tyre . . . it somersaulted . . . I was with him . . . I still hear those awful thumps . . . the police wouldn't believe that it was anything but an ordinary burst . . . what could they know of the Bakunin and their methods? Even in this faraway country?

'I swear I know nothing of Ledoux, have never heard of him! Detroyat was the head, in my time. Everything to do with the Bakunin is in the past, it is behind me! I know nothing of this bomb, this plot, I will do anything, anything you say, Colonel Bossiere, to get rid of this albatross which hangs round my life and my loves . . .'

Her inner agony, her face averted, her shoulders heaving, threw up an invisible curtain which kept both men at a distance.

Kepler broke the silence. 'If you are so sure of your facts, Colonel Bossiere, why don't you go to South African Security and tell them everything?'

Kepler realized that Rencha was not the only one under high emotional stress. Bossiere replied tightly.

'Dr West, Ledoux has evaded the world's top anti-terrorist units – including my own, the DST – who have hunted him for years. That goes for the Israeli Mossad also, and our new French Anti-Terrorist Co-ordination Unit, Uclat, which was created with the special function of beating the combined link-up of terrorist movements in Europe – the Bakunin, the Action Directe, the Red Army Faction in Germany, Belgium's Fighting Communist Cells, the IRA, the Corsican National Guerrillas. If I go now, today, to South African Security, they will check and find that Ledoux-Lentz's credentials as a member of Radchem are impeccable. You cannot go around levelling that sort of accusation against men of international standing in the IAEA, I will be told.'

Bossiere's voice became harder as he plummeted into his own private vendetta. Kepler thought his hand was going again to his inner pocket for his wallet, but it was an unconscious reflex reach for his Walther, which he had left behind in his hut.

'Ledoux is my man. I will get him. For ten long years I have hunted him. I have sworn that. I will, even if I have to shoot him dead in front of the assembled IAEA delegates. It has been a long, long chase. I am within an ace of him now. Any moment Ledoux will strike. It could come any time.' He gestured at Rencha and rapped out, 'Show me that bomb, so that I can get Ledoux!'

Chapter 27

Kepler went silent. The napalm-burst of emotions which had exploded from Rencha and Bossiere had left them standing in an almost stylized attitude, emptied of words. With Kepler, the blast went inward. Had he got the picture of Rencha all wrong, been totally carried away by her passionate responses, as Bossiere had inferred? He was too close to the previous night, too close to her physical beauty, to judge coolly. Only that morning, she had sat on the bed with her breasts swinging . . .

Could it all have been for an ulterior purpose? A Bakunin

purpose? Kepler deliberately kept his mouth shut to Bossiere about the fact that his briefcase had been searched, and about the attempt to heist the jar of SYNROC-R. Who knew what construction this clever Frenchman would put upon that? He winced away from the thought that Rencha had been the only person in Corbel Camp to know its presence. If Ledoux or Maurette had been informed, it must have come via her. He couldn't accept that treachery any more than he could face what Rencha herself had admitted – that she had been a Bakunin courier.

Bossiere broke the tight silence. He addressed Rencha.

'You say you are willing to do anything I ask to free yourself of the Bakunin?'

Bossiere didn't trust her, didn't believe her protestations, but ostensibly to enlist her on his side might yield further useful clues.

'Yes.'

'You say you don't know where the bomb is?'

Rencha's voice trembled. 'If I did, I would tell you.'

'Let me clarify the picture. Ledoux and Maurette had two suitcases of explosive. I myself saw them load them up.'

'If I knew what direction they took, perhaps I could help with a possible target.' Rencha was rapidly getting a grip on herself. Maybe too quickly, thought Bossiere. A woman in tears tells more than she should. 'I mean, I know the area. There are only two roads out of Corbel Camp, one to Cheating Pan, and the other to the main Gougo road, down south. Either way, there is no possible target for a bomb.'

'No?' asked Bossiere. 'They took the road to the Pan.'

'There is nothing there,' she insisted.

'No?' repeated Bossiere. 'Think again, think hard. There was a batch of unguarded helicopters and the big Hercules transport on the airfield. Do you wonder there was a search on Thursday of all aircraft before they took off?'

'So you were behind that,' Kepler interjected.

'Correct.'

Bossiere was waiting his opportunity to slip in his sixty-four-dollar question – without emphasis, hopefully – so that Rencha would not see its significance.

He dropped his interrogator's tone in favour of a questioner's seeking information.

'What did they do at the Pan?' he asked. 'Their suitcases were full when they left; they were empty when they returned.'

'How do you know all this, Colonel Bossiere?' demanded Kepler.

'I see lots of things in my business that I shouldn't. That is why I am still alive today.'

'There is nothing out there!' repeated Rencha in puzzlement. 'There is only *Bluebird*'s old track and a line of bushes . . .'

Bossiere saw his opportunity. 'There is a typed notice on the back of my bathroom door which warns tourists against a graveyard somewhere on the Pan.'

'I don't include *that*,' answered Rencha. 'Who would want to blow up a graveyard? It's secluded, away from everything. It lies about three kilometres from *Bluebird*'s track, to the east, near a hill. The track leading to it is hard to find, unless you know where to branch off. The correct spot is just about opposite where the planes touch down.'

Turn-off at touchdown point! Three kilometres from there!

Bossiere gave no sign of his inner exultation. He shrugged. 'As you say, a graveyard is unimportant.'

'I've never been there – the Bonsma family is very sensitive about it,' continued Rencha.

'So the notice says,' added Bossiere.

'Ledoux and Maurette . . .' she went on, stumbling over the names, '. . . couldn't possibly have known about it. They don't know the lie of the land. Why, the day before yesterday when Kepler and I were on our way to Sak River – I'd given them directions how to find the helicopter rendezvous at Brospan by turning right at the main road – we spotted them turning left instead. They obviously have no sense of direction.'

Left! Rencha's word smacked Bossiere's brain like a rocket from a launcher. Left! All his mental computer connections dropped into place. The terrorists had taken the road *left* following the activities which he himself had observed. The graveyard could be ruled out as their main target – perhaps it had only served as some kind of staging-post. *Left!* The road left would take them to Gougo repository!

The repository was a natural prime target for a bomb!

The IAEA inspection of Gougo was the last item on the official schedule. That was Monday – today was Saturday!

One microchip in Bossiere's mental computer was hiccupping, however. It had no data on Hartogskloof.

However, the pattern was becoming clearer in his mind. Somehow, Ledoux and Maurette must have smuggled thirty kilograms or more of explosive into Gougo! Sophisticated modern timers could detonate their bombs after months, let alone days. The bomb was probably already fused up and in position.

He had to get to Gougo – fast!

Bossiere was aware of both Rencha and Kepler eyeing him. He had been totally immersed in his own thoughts. Aware, too, that neither of them really wanted him to stop because he was serving as a buffer to cushion their own emotional shock and unwillingness to face one another. Kepler seemed more off-balance than Rencha. Bossiere at that moment needed someone on whom to cut his teeth, so to speak, to test the deductions racing around in his mind. Kepler would have been the right man. Yet – Kepler was still too much under Rencha's spell, in his opinion, to be of much use. Some unassailable concrete fact would have to be the shock tactic which would finally tip the scientist over the edge. Bossiere remained convinced that Rencha was playing a fast, duplicitous game.

'I revealed a lot of secrets this morning,' he said abruptly. 'If our conversation should become known, you realize what it will mean?'

'The whole plot should be exposed to South African Security,' reiterated Kepler.

'Forget it,' retorted Bossiere. 'If a hint of suspicion should be dropped, I believe the explosion will be triggered prematurely. If a bomb should go off while the IAEA gathering is in progress and South African Security should be tipped off that the lady who owns Corbel Camp is a former terrorist, there can be no doubt at whom the finger will point. Do I make myself clear?'

'Very clear, Monsieur Bossiere.'

The DST man went on harshly, 'I know the Bakunin. We are dealing with minds more ruthless and barbarous than anything to be found in the animal world. Nothing is too abominable for them. *You* know too, madame.'

Rencha went paler. 'I know.'

Bossiere glanced at his watch. It was after 10 a.m.! He had to get one hundred and ten kilometres to Gougo, and then back again . . .

'I have business.' He started to go, turned back at the door. 'I warn you again. Your silence protects a score of lives.'

Kepler and Rencha had been right instinctively to cling as long as possible to an outsider. What they had to say to one another could not be said, only left to fester and grow within each other.

'Rencha . . .'

She shook her head, turned her face from him. She was as cold and uncommunicating as a dead satellite in space. For the third time in her life, she felt as if a plastic body-shroud had been dragged over her head: through it, everyday things like this room where only last night Kepler had taken her to him seemed hazed, distant, unreal. Each time it had been the Bakunin, each time it had been a man. Charles, John, Kepler. The blood pumping out from between Charles' eyes – doctor, heal yourself! It was madness which had made her want to scream that when she saw where the Bakunin bullet had gone in . . . John's body, all mangled up with the upholstery of the car . . . now, the bearded scientist whom she loved probably more than either of the other two, standing there with his heart ripped out by a few words . . . Dear heaven, she should have told him everything herself, whatever the risk, before this French agent had had the chance to present his own construction!

'Go,' she said to him in a voice she didn't recognize. The

solace which previously had been Corbel Camp had now become part of her agony. The Bakunin were right here, right in the sanctuary. 'Please *go*.'

He hesitated for a moment, then turned and strode away.

Chapter 28

Tickety-tick.

The ticking of the car clock rippled through the silence. It was louder than the beating of Bossiere's heart after the spin. It was the only sound after the sudden cut-off noise of engine, gears, overworked dampers and springs. A shower of dust, like caster-sugar from a shaker, was a minute-old legacy from the car's skidding, churning wheels in the sand. It came filtering down through and past Bossiere's open window. The little clickety-click of the clock sputtered like a cauterizer attacking a wart. It reminded Bossiere, moreover, of two things: time wasn't on his side; somewhere, Ledoux's pre-set detonator was also ticking away.

Bossiere reached impetuously for the starter to refire the engine, and then checked himself. He knew he was accident-prone.

He also knew why. It was crazy to have high-tailed out of Corbel Camp like a Grand Prix start the way he had; he had spun off the road at the rough sandy place where Ledoux and Maurette had had problems with the road and now sat with a stalled engine and the car's nose against a bank. He was no more than a few kilometres south of Corbel Camp, on the road to Gougo.

Tickety-tick.

Blast the clock! Bossiere reached again for the starter, deliberately controlling himself. He reversed carefully, equally deliberately, back on to the road, and held back on his accelerator. To finish up in a road smash would be completely in line with the frustrations he had suffered ever since he had walked out of Rencha's hut. He had lost almost an hour of precious time.

The car itself had needed refilling with petrol after his previous night's peregrinations on Cheating Pan. The attendant at Corbel Camp had – rightly – gone off duty because of the delegates' absence at Vaalputs. It had taken Bossiere nearly half an hour to unearth him. A half-flat front left wheel, a lasting bequest from Cheating Pan where he had crashed across the tough little bushes marking *Bluebird*'s track, had required changing. The sulky petrol attendant worked to rule and took his time over the flat also. To offset his frustration, Bossiere had gone – without attempt at concealment – to the Waldegg Ledoux hut.

Tickety-tick.

Ledoux's portable radio was still missing.

Bossiere had guessed it would be. That was no comfort. The Bakunin was hugging the thing closer to him than his shirt. Neither was there any sign of a bomb. The two guilty suitcases stood in the loft, empty.

Karee Tree Hollow, the Bonsma homestead, showed up on his right. Muscles and nerves in Bossiere's right calf ached out of frustration. He longed to jam the accelerator hard against the floorboads, get moving. Get moving! Instead, he drove circumspectly, switching gears for the soft patches in the road rather than plunging through them at speed, as all his impulses cried out for him to do.

Beyond the Bonsma farm, the road hardened and Bossiere started to pick up speed. The physical feel of it brought relief, brought some discharge for the nervous build-up inside him. A ten-year build-up; now, for the first time, Bossiere knew he had his man in his sights. The long dreary road seemed to act like a truth-drug on Bossiere and evoke half-forgotten events and frustrations in his pursuit of Ledoux. Then he was upon Hartogskloof, down the gears, up the steep curves, and on and across the high tableland on which the repository was sited.

The blisters in the shape of pans on the face of the countryside were like the scars on the DST man's psyche from his past fruitless hunts after Ledoux. Now, if he played his cards right, the end was in sight.

Bossiere hadn't bargained for the extent of the security at the Gougo gate, having avoided all the red tape when passing through as one of the IAEA group. He had a story ready; all he really wanted to establish was whether Ledoux had passed through the Gougo gate in the past couple of days.

A middle-aged man in khaki flagged him down. The day was not old or hot enough to have ironed the creases from his pants. He was capless. His head was as bald as a puff-adder's. It swung and weaved, without corresponding motion by his body. He only lacked a forked tongue.

'Business? Identification?'

Bossiere passed over his IAEA accreditation.

Snake-head eyed him. 'All the other delegates are at Vaal-puts. Why not you?' The corners of his mouth were chewed with suspicion. For a moment, Bossiere wondered how a video of himself in action would appear.

'Stomach,' he replied briefly. 'Professor Jaboulet will vouch for me. Henri Bossiere, of the French delegation.'

'Why do you come to Gougo for medicine?'

That's the way a back-tracking security mind worked.

'I didn't come for medicine. I've been fixed up at Corbel Camp.'

'The official visit to Gougo is not scheduled until Monday. The delegates will fly directly from Vaalputs to the repository airfield nearby here. I am not authorized to admit anyone . . .'

The ravaged mouth took another chewing. Schutte was one of the best. He'd graduated from Vaalputs to Gougo. He was on his way to the top. If his mouth could stand the pace.

'I don't want to be admitted. As he left this morning, a friend of mine . . .' Bossiere had to pull himself up mentally in order to say it '. . . Herr Lentz, of the Radchem team, asked me to find out whether he had left a parcel here a couple of days ago.'

'Parcel?' Parcel is a dirty security word. A parcel can encompass a thousand sins.

'What sort of parcel?' Snake-head stepped into his own element. 'What was in it? He left it – *here*?' The way he said it implied that Gougo was sanitized regularly as a matter of routine.

Bossiere hadn't expected all this. All he wanted to know was when – if – Ledoux had checked through the Gougo gate.

He said placatingly, 'Herr Lentz was on the point of leaving Corbel Camp – he called to me from the bus taking him to the airfield. I might have misheard. I thought he said it was a parcel. It might have been something else.'

'You came all this way just to collect something you don't really know was left here?'

Bossiere found himself off-balance. Snake-head was on the job. He should have thought up a better story – he, a top security man himself.

'Have you tried phoning?'

It was a shot by Bossiere in the dark, and it worked. 'Jeez, how they expect a man to run a security outfit with these phones always breaking down, heaven only knows! Always out of order . . .'

Bossiere made sympathetic noises. 'The drive also gives me something to do. Corbel Camp's deserted now that everyone's at Vaalputs.'

He seemed to have made progress with snake-head. 'You could check and see when Herr Lentz was here.'

The man's lips chewed. You don't try and teach a puff-adder how to bite, unless you want to be bitten yourself.

'I'll decide what is to be done.'

He turned to go, paused, held up Bossiere's card. 'I'll keep this. Friend's name Lentz, you say?'

'That's it.'

'Stay in the car.'

Bossiere did. The man was away for about twenty minutes. The vehicle's interior started to heat like an oven.

'No record of Lentz,' snake-head said. Bossiere rode the

body-blow to his suspicions without blinking. The man's eyes were on him.

'Odd, isn't it?'

'It is.' Bossiere thought quickly. 'Anyway, on Monday we're all coming here . . .'

'Monday's a long way away.'

The man's snide platitude hit Bossiere like a brick. He'd drawn a complete blank at Gougo, when he'd been so sure. Where had Ledoux gone with his bomb? Now he had to get back to the graveyard! A mild sense of panic came over him. Ledoux must not outclass him in this last game of the series. And the last game Bossiere intended it to be. *He must get going!*

Snake-head said, 'You're not coming in?'

'No.'

He seemed disappointed, somehow. A spider has to let some flies go.

'Rules lay down, all non-entrants to be photographed.'

It was Bossiere's turn to bite his lips. Another time-waster!

He said, lying better than he thought he could with the ferment going on inside him. 'Anything to oblige. I've got all day.'

'Got all day.'

Repetition is an interrogation trick. You say the same thing over, in the hope that the victim will amplify his original reply and give himself away.

Bossiere replied, 'May I get out of the car? Otherwise there won't be anybody left to photograph.'

Snake-head nodded, went off. It must have taken another fifteen minutes to arrange a camera. He photographed Bossiere with the sort of care reserved for Vogue models. Bossiere dared not look at his watch – the graveyard!

When it was all over, Bossiere extended a hand full of fraternal bad will. He was scared the man would hatch up something fresh before he could get moving.

Snake-head ignored the gesture. 'Have a nice day,' he countered. The insincerity cost him a millimetre of skin off the corner of his mouth.

It was already after two o'clock. Bossiere did a quick calculation. He couldn't reach the graveyard before four, even allowing that he found the turn-off from *Bluebird*'s track without wasting time hunting for it. The hill which Rencha had mentioned as backing the graveyard would be a landmark, and fully visible in the afternoon light.

Bossiere knew that the graveyard was his last firm option. He was so lost in his thoughts that, beyond Hartogskloof and the Corbel Camp turn-off, he was upon a flatbed transporter before he realized it. It hammered towards Gougo in a cloud of dust. The SYNROC-R shipments were flowing. There'd be plenty on view on Monday.

Bossiere found himself at the graveyard so easily that he marvelled how he could have missed it, even in the dark. He used his odometer like a Muslim does the Koran as a signpost to heaven. He carefully noted the reading as he drew level with the airfield. He was surprised to see a number of ground crew about, and the air traffic control caravan appeared to be manned. The helicopters were all parked on the apron, clear of the central landing strip – *Bluebird*'s track. The north-west wind had started to churn up a fine dust cloud, not enough at this stage to obscure Deelkop hill behind the graveyard (he did not know its name.) Ironically, Bossiere used Ledoux's own marker drum as his waymark. It was clear that the track turned off at it.

Bossiere parked by the wrought iron gate, went in. He found his heart racing: would he find a bomb inside the corbelled hut at the entrance! It was the ideal hiding-place.

He threw open the door.

Spades, grave-junk.

Bossiere retreated outside. He thought at first the light from the headstone was a reflection of the late sun. Then he saw: it was a light in its own right!

Bossiere was intrigued, strode over to the grave. What interested him far more than the light now (any thought of seeking its origin was blanketed by what he spotted) was that a section of iron railing encircling the grave had broken off.

Newly broken off. There was also a smudge of green paint on the metal.

Bossiere went down on his hunkers to examine it. The humps and scrapes on the grave's surface rippled like an unquiet ghost.

The grave had been disturbed! Newly disturbed, just as that railing had been newly broken!

Bossiere's heart pounded as it had not done since the moment he had first recognized Ledoux at Corbel Camp. He scrabbled at the surface with his hands, kicking up some dust like a desert rat, but making no real progress. A spade! Tools for the job were to hand.

Bossiere sprinted back to the lying-in hut, grabbed a spade. The blade went in. The sand was so loose that most of it slipped back.

He wielded the spade again. He was rewarded by a metallic clatter.

Then, another clatter joined the first – this time out of the sky.

It was the clatter of heavy turbine airscrews.

Bossiere scanned the sky in the direction of the airfield – the north-west wind was jockeying the sound ahead of the plane. Bossiere realized immediately that the graveyard and his parked car would be visible to the approaching pilot; the landing strip was a mere three kilometres away. Moreover, if the pilot made a circuit to adapt his landing (as he must do) to the rising north-wester, he would do so low over the graveyard itself. In that case, he couldn't help spotting him, spade in hand, working on a grave . . .

Despite the risk, Bossiere couldn't tear himself away. He made a final attempt, scrabbled again with his hands. His fingers touched metal. He hastily scraped aside more loose sand.

Then he saw.

Bossiere recognized the object for what it was. An SZ-3 demolition charge.

The sound of the airscrews grew louder overhead.

Bossiere threw an anxious glance skyward. He had to probe further!

His fingers touched something resembling wire and something else like smooth plastic.

Now – he had to tear himself away!

He swept sand over the SZ-3 with untidy movements like a child scooping sea sand for a beach castle. It would have to do – until he could get back later that night.

Bossiere grabbed the spade, vaulted the railing, pitched the tool into the shed and made for his car. The car, distinctive in blue-and-white Nucor colours, could be a giveaway. Bossiere gunned the engine, moved off, then changed direction on a sudden thought. He decided to avoid the airfield altogether and hightail straight across the Pan to intercept the Corbel Camp access road to the airfield as near the edge of the Pan as he could. That would take him out of view of both the plane and ground crew.

Now Bossiere sighted the plane itself. It was the big Hercules which had ferried delegates to Vaalputs that morning. Why should it be returning? Bossiere asked himself. As he understood the IAEA schedule, the plane was due to remain at Vaalputs until Monday and then fly the delegates direct to Gougo for their final inspection.

Bossiere's car raced for the edge of the Pan and reached the airfield road close to where it dog-legged off it towards Corbel Camp. He was now safe, out of view. The big Hercules was just coming in to land.

Bossiere eased the car into Corbel Camp. The last sun was making magic with the beehive roofs. It all seemed so calm and tranquil.

It wasn't.

Chapter 29

The emotional punch-up had left Kepler as flatfooted mentally
as he had been physically after Maurette's mule-kick. He had
made his way like a sleepwalker to his own hut after Rencha
had asked him to leave. Not only had the day blown up in
their faces after Bossiere's accusations and revelations – they
had planned to spend it together, since Corbel Camp would
have been deserted, delegates and servants gone – but so had
their entire relationship.

Kepler, in a state of shock, refused to accept that Rencha
was involved in a bomb plot with one of the world's most
wanted terrorists, admirer and friend of Carlos the Jackal. It
simply seemed too much to swallow. Yet, he agonized as he
chain-smoked and paced up and down his hut, he had also
refused to accept that she had been a Bakunin courier, until
Bossiere had broken her down. There could be no doubt about
the authenticity of the DST photograph, nor who its subject
was. He felt a wave of emotion as he recalled the shy, scared
young face – last night, he had seen the love transform that
same face, and make it radiant, new . . .

Kepler cursed the DST man, cast about in his mind for an
Australian epithet strong enough.

Kepler pulled himself up. This was getting him nowhere.
He tried to assess Bossiere's allegations as coolly as he would
have given his mind to a complicated problem in geochemistry.
His statements about the Bakunin had seemed wild enough –
until he had been challenged. The bomb he kept referring
to, it was clear he couldn't prove that. Kepler himself had
reinforced Bossiere's suspicions of the Bakunins' plot by revealing the Radchem/China offer to him. How did they intend
otherwise to obtain it by the use of a bomb?

Through Rencha?

Kepler hardly dared face his own question. Had she – as Bossiere had inferred – made the running in order to extract from him (somehow) the SYNROC-R formula and pass it on to Ledoux and Radchem? The old pillow-talk ploy, the oldest spy deal in the book?

Kepler squirmed under his own scalpel. Postulate that construction underlying her approach and motives, then the series of events, starting with her so-called faint at the crash demonstration that first day, took on an altogether different complexion.

Spy – or compulsive mutual love?

The bells had rung for them both, even that first day. They had rushed together with the speed of atoms in a nuclear accelerator. Heart – and body.

Kepler winced at the recollection of her love-making. If it had been with an ulterior motive in mind . . .

He – and he alone – nonetheless knew that she had asked him nothing, nothing which could possibly be construed as relating to SYNROC-R. Perhaps, Kepler's Devil's Advocate needled, that was intended to come with more sex as the bait . . .

The brutal question provoked another more brutal. Kepler faced it for the first time. How had his unknown assailant *known* that the exhibition jar of SYNROC-R, which had been conveyed in total secrecy from Koeberg to Gougo, checked out, and then transported by a trusted security officer into his own hands, had been in his hut at Corbel Camp the night before his kimberlite address? The only person outside the security-Gougo circle who was aware of it was Rencha. He himself had told her in a moment of revelation on the way to Sak River. Had she passed that information on to Ledoux, who in turn had delegated Maurette to heist it, in expectation that Rencha would have pinned him in her bed and his hut be empty?

Kepler put her words, her actions, as ruthlessly under the microscope as mathiasite and lindsleyite had been scrutinized by the world's most sophisticated microbeam techniques. Like them, Rencha came out tops. Kepler remembered how she had even got him to leave that night, not without an inferred promise of the next night's passion.

Kepler threw away yet another half-smoked cigarette; he had made up his mind. Rencha emerged from his cross-examination in the clear. She was his. He had never felt for any woman – and there had been others – as he did for her. She had style, heaps of personality. He also found himself loving her for that half-scared face under the pulled-down beret; he loved her for the way she had made him part of her, even if (he recalled the omission with a pang) she had left her past a blank. To love, that had been a mystery and a challenge. Blast Bossiere! She would have come clean, in her own time . . .

Kepler knew what had to be done. The whole situation had to be talked through, the two of them, even if it meant temporarily hurting one another in the process.

Kepler reached his conclusion about the same time as Bossiere reached the repository gate. He had not realized that he had devoted most of the morning to sorting out his problem.

Kepler walked quickly from his hut round the corner of the new lounge complex where it was divided from the old farmhouse by a narrow lane. He headed for Rencha's quarters at the far side. As he passed the open main door, he heard her voice from the direction of the passageway where the phone was situated. He went in. It wasn't English she was speaking. He headed for the phone cubicle. Rencha must either have sensed someone coming, or perhaps seen his shadow across the open door.

She turned round, covered the mouthpiece with one hand. Her green eyes, which he had seen previously fill with unsaid and unsayable magic, were blank. She simply stared at him. A piece of rocket junk, whirling around in sub-zero space, could not have been colder or less responsive.

Kepler halted, stared back. Invisible cords seemed to be pulling his eyelids closed. He could still sense the upsurge of warmth he had felt on reaching his conclusions about her *bona fides*; it died inside him.

She waited, hand over the instrument. The day's earlier exchanges had tried to rephotograph her face into a semblance of what the DST operative had caught that Paris day outside the Metro – the face of a frightened woman. The shadows in the booth added to the illusion. Plus, now, the fact that the bottom had dropped out of her world. For the third and final time.

Kepler got the message.

He turned and went blindly back to his hut.

Solitary confinement makes a man's mind snap, sooner or later. With Kepler, it was later that afternoon. He had not moved from his hut all day. Rencha had slammed an unseen prison door closed on him; physically, he was free to go, if there had been anywhere to go. Psychologically, she had shut the door so tight that Houdini could not have slipped the lock. It was a day of misery; time had little meaning. It could have been six or sixty hours since he had seen her at the phone.

In the late afternoon, Kepler heard the sound of vehicles entering Corbel Camp. It was unexpected: no one, as far as he knew, was due until next day.

Kepler left his hut, walked slowly to the farmhouse complex. His motives were confused; somehow, the presence of other people might give him the opportunity of speaking – even if indirectly – to Rencha.

Bossiere, in his hut at the rear of the kitchen sector, also heard the sound of engines and voices. He made his way round via Rencha's own quarters to the farmhouse lounge.

Both Kepler and Bossiere converged together at the front door on the group inside.

Ledoux, Maurette and Rencha stood together. Ledoux hugged his radio.

Kepler arrived slightly ahead of Bossiere. The sight stopped his heart as a surgeon stops a would-be transplant heart with an electric shock. Rencha appeared confused, completely off-balance.

Ledoux, Maurette!

Six hours before, he had intruded on her speaking a language he did not understand – French? There was only one conclusion – the outcome of that conversation stood in front of him in the form of the two Bakunin terrorists. The corrosion of hours of introspective hurt shrank the time factor. She had been summoning Ledoux and Maurette back to Corbel Camp! She had informed them that the DST was on their trail! Now they were here!

Kepler couldn't face it. He half-crashed into Bossiere as he spun on his heel. He pushed his way out again past the DST man.

Bossiere had no emotional gallows-drop to serve as an eviction. Less than an hour previously, his hands had been on a Soviet SZ-3 demolition charge; it awaited the skilled hands of the men in front of him to activate it into a hideous instrument of death and destruction. For the first time that day, Bossiere was without his Walther. He knew, from the turbo-boost of adrenalin which surged through his veins at the sight of the two Bakunin that it was probably better that way.

There was no outward sign of any of this in him as he went forward.

'I thought I heard a plane. What brings you back? I understood all the delegates were staying at Vaalputs until Monday.'

If Rencha had not answered – over-rapidly and with words tripping to betray an inner confusion – Bossiere might well have had a fragment of pity for her. As it was, he was sure of her role, now.

'Herr Lentz and Herr Fichte also surprised me.' She tried a smile. She may have thought it worked. 'I haven't made any preparations . . . they tell me, they have come back to collect some plans and documents relating to the Gobi Desert disposal site . . . they were left behind by mistake . . .'

Ledoux said carefully, in English, 'Herr Fichte and I are acting as Professor Nakanishi's couriers. The plans and explanatory text are essential to China's case during the delegates' visit to Vaalputs.'

Bastard, thought Bossiere. Smooth, lying bastard! You've come back about the bomb.

'You'll take them back tomorrow, then?'

'No. We know what documents and plans are required and should be selected. The pilot can deliver them, once we have decided which they are.'

Bossiere could not keep the irony out of his reply. 'Very accommodating of the pilot and the Hercules to bring you all this way.'

Ledoux said ponderously, 'You will understand, this is a very vital matter for China, Monsieur Bossiere. All sides of the case have to be understood by the delegates.'

Bossiere's glance went to Ledoux's hands. They were square, with short, competent fingers, like a surgeon's. Their level of electronic technological know-how in the field of explosives could probably be matched by only a handful of boffins in Europe.

All sides of the case! Bossiere echoed Ledoux's words inwardly with irony. All sides, except the one which was the kicker – the bomb. He had to act fast, if he were to keep ahead of events. The unexpected return of the terrorists was the joker in the pack. He had to shock Kepler into accepting the fact and urgency of the bomb threat, and enlist him on his side. He might need a helper, before long. Kepler was his man.

Bossiere broke up the gathering; they all stood awkwardly as if posed by some unseen producer before some unseen camera.

'If possible, I would like a sight of the documents before they go off to Vaalputs. I am also involved, as a French delegate.' It sounded so banal that he could have laughed.

'If possible.' Ledoux's answer was level, without inflection. Maurette remained silent.

The DST man went.

Ledoux addressed Rencha. 'I have a matter to discuss with you – can we meet later?'

'With me? I am not one of the IAEA delegates, Herr Lentz.'

Maurette frowned. He couldn't stand all this flannel, this dancing round and round the subject like the love-making ritual of birds. Kill a man, or let him live. To him, there was little in between.

'It has to do with the IAEA, nevertheless.' The poor light found nothing to reflect in Ledoux's pale eyes. It was like looking into the lens of an unloaded camera.

Rencha felt the fear cramp her stomach. A Bakunin never forgets. And here was the master-terrorist himself! She wanted to cry out, come back, Monsieur Bossiere! Come, don't let him start on me, after all the years!

Instead, she replied, 'Of course. It will have to be after supper. I have to make preparations. Your return has caught me on the wrong foot.'

'At eight?'

'Here?'

'I would prefer somewhere more private.'

'In my sitting-room, then. At eight.'

Ledoux nodded. He was impersonal, a little stand-offish.

Those who had worked with Ledoux on the Argentine death squads said it always took him time to warm up. Like a woman.

Bossiere needed no warming-up. He was already hot. He gave himself time, after getting back to his hut and switching on the light – the dark came quickly at Cheating Pan – to collect and crystallize his thoughts in words before approaching Kepler. Then he walked quickly round the back of the farm-house complex to Kepler's hut on the far side, noting on the way that Ledoux's light was also on.

He knocked. 'Bossiere.'

Kepler opened. Perhaps Bossiere had been inadvertently wise by first announcing himself, when he looked inside. The .45 Colt lay in pieces on the bed. Two extra-length magazines, spare shells and cleaning material were scattered about.

'Going to kill someone?' Bossiere didn't care for the fazed look in the scientist's eyes.

'Yes. Kill time. There's nothing else to do.'

Bossiere went in. 'I didn't know you had a gun.'

'Some years back I was attacked in my lab in Australia. I learned to use a gun after that.'

'Would you like an opportunity of taking it for an airing tonight?'

'What are you driving at?'

'You saw. They're back,' answered Bossiere cryptically.

'I don't go around shooting unarmed men. Not on the strength of a lot of supposition and straws in the wind.'

Bossiere sat down on the bed, ran a trickle of shells through his fingers. 'Wake up, my friend. That is all I want you to do.'

Kepler shrugged. 'We've been through all this before.'

'We haven't,' retorted Bossiere. 'I intend to rub your nose in proof – tonight. At the place they call the Haunted Graveyard.'

'You become more and more romantic and absurd, Bossiere. It must be your French blood.'

'Listen to me!' retorted the DST man. He stood up. 'I found the Bakunin explosive – some of it. In a grave. A Soviet-origin demolition charge.'

Kepler said unbelievingly, 'Well I'll go to hell! Is this dinkum, Bossiere?'

'Don't go to hell, go with me. I'll show you specific evidence of what I have been stating. There's a cache in a grave out there on the Pan.'

'I'll come.'

'Bring the gun.'

Bossiere made the mistake of going further. 'Ledoux and Maurette flew back tonight against the run of the game – why? They were tipped off. By whom?'

Kepler froze. He still could not equate the loving devoted woman he had held in his arms with the picture Bossiere kept throwing at him. Half his mind accepted that she could once have been a Bakunin courier; the other half spat it out with scorn. That is what he did now.

'She never has had a chance to give her side of the story,' he said tightly. Still, he himself had come upon her that

216

morning speaking to someone in a foreign language on the phone . . .

He went on, 'I intend to give her that chance – before I come with you tonight.'

'Before, or depending on?'

'Before. I'll come, whatever.'

'I'll pick you up after we've eaten. We don't want to make it too obvious.'

If Kepler had any appetite for eating, Rencha killed it. He waited until Bossiere had gone, put the Colt together, tested the trigger pull, and snugged home a long ten-shot magazine. He locked it away in his suitcase, until later.

He intercepted Rencha on her way to the dining-room. In space, even a shuttle draws an out-of-orbit vehicle to it by some inherent mutual gravity. Here, mutual gravity was missing.

He said, 'I've been trying to get to talk to you all day.'

Her green eyes were expressionless. She simply stood. He was not to recognize the kind of defence mechanism a Bakunin tie-up built up in a woman. It was a screen as impenetrable as a battle-fleet's anti-missile electronics. It kept the enemy – and friend – just as far away.

'Can I see you – after supper?'

'I have an appointment with Herr Lentz at eight.'

Her voice had a knock-out flatness. She wanted to say, later, Kepler, for our sakes, come to me later, hold me, comfort me, tell me again that you love me . . .

All she could manage was, 'Later.'

It wasn't surprising that he misconstrued her tone. His hurt threw the jibe at her. 'You mean, Monsieur Ledoux.'

Fear leapt into her eyes. 'Don't say that, don't say that name!'

She turned and ran towards the dining-room, dropping a knife or spoon on the way.

Chapter 30

Kepler didn't eat. It seemed light years until Bossiere came and collected him.

But those light years of agonizing served a purpose. The basic discrepancy had come upon him like a laser-lance out of the darkness. Bossiere was wrong about Rencha – he could prove it. The fallacy had homed in upon his consciousness out of nowhere. He intended to wait his moment with the DST man. His inner certainty made him less communicative as they drove off in Bossiere's car from Corbel Camp.

'Know your way in the dark?'

The wind was up, but until they reached the Pan proper they wouldn't know how much the resulting sand curtain would obscure visibility. There would be some light, hopefully, from the fragment of last-quarter moon, the same ebbing light which had shown Kepler the hooded intruder crawling across his floor towards the SYNROC-R jar. He felt inside his windcheater now. The Colt would be better than bare hands in any further encounter.

Bossiere replied by indicating the odometer. 'I'll fly as it were on my autopilot, if it gets thick. I'll know where I am: I've checked all the distances.'

It was thicker – not nearly as dense as during Bossiere's first foray – when they reached the Pan's edge and headed towards the airfield.

'We call this sort of wind a cock-eye-boob in West Australia,' observed Kepler.

Bossiere didn't breach the subject of Rencha. Kepler's reaction had been too powerful and emotive previously. The fact that he was here, on his side, spoke for itself.

They found the turn-off (signposted by Ledoux's own drum) and finally halted outside the graveyard gate.

When the car's lights cut, Kepler exclaimed, 'A light – there's someone inside there!'

Bossiere was wryly amused. 'You won't need your gun. There's a sort of commemorative light rigged in a headstone. That's the grave we're after.'

A minute or two later, with Kepler directing the flashlight, Bossiere dug with a spade from the lying-in hut. He cleared a wider radius of the loose surface than he had done previously. His shovel went in. There was a clink of metal on metal. Kepler craned to see. Bossiere resorted to his hands.

The iron lips of an SZ-3 showed.

'There's a handle somewhere – this type all have carrying handles,' Bossiere said. He felt about in the sand. He hauled out the canister, shaped like a miniature coffin. Sand slid off it like ectoplasm from a ghost.

Kepler stared, mesmerized. 'Soviet SZ-3 demolition charge,' explained Bossiere. 'Favourite of terrorists.

'There's more in here.' He used the spade. The plastic bag he had merely touched but not examined before, emerged.

Bossiere laid the lengths of wire, fuse, pliers, mini soldering iron, detonators and timers along the brick edge of the grave. He held one gadget closer for Kepler to examine.

'You don't see many of these around,' he said with professional detachment. 'Photo-electric cell detonator. Uses the sun's rays. We'll check to see if there's more of anything in the grave.'

There was.

Kepler stood as withdrawn as a chief mourner while Bossiere shovelled aside more earth – it became more compacted deeper down – and located another object. The moonlight weakened all the time. Deelkop became a mere loom against the sky, standing out like a gigantic headstone above the graveyard itself.

Bossiere located another handle in the sand, withdrew the second object. It was bigger and heavier than the first.

'SZ-6,' he explained to Kepler. 'They make 'em in two sizes, this one weighing six kilograms, and the smaller weighing three. You can produce almost any suitable weight combination for the size of your target with the two sizes.'

The DST man examined the hole he had dug with Kepler's flashlight, and then felt about. 'I don't think there's anything more. The ground seems undisturbed deeper down.'

Kepler said in tight tones, 'You've proved your case against Ledoux. I accept that. You've drawn their teeth by discovering this cache. What do you intend to do now with these charges?'

Bossiere indicated the gadgetry set out on the brickwork.

'You're wrong. I haven't drawn their teeth. This isn't what I was after.'

'Then what in hell's name are you after?'

'These are chuck-outs, the things they don't want for their job.'

'How do you make that out?'

Bossiere replied slowly, 'My friend, I held in my hands their two suitcases – two deadweight suitcases. They totalled, at a guess, between thirty and forty kilograms. Here we have two charges, one weighing three and the other six kilograms. I ask myself, and I ask you, where is the remainder?'

'You're working on an assumption . . .'

'That's how I found this cache in the first place, by working on an assumption. If you don't accept what I say about more explosive, take a look at these gadgets. See these timers? They're hellishly ingenious – microcircuitry marvels inside. I'd guess that any one of these is sophisticated enough to detonate an explosion a month from now – or any given period in between – depending on what time Ledoux wants.

'There are three types of detonators the Bakunin use – timer, command, or remote control. There's no command here: it requires a long length of wire to the explosive charge itself and for your operator to be close, but not too close to kill himself in the operation, to touch it off. If they planned to use a timer, why didn't they use one of these? My guess is that they are going for the trickiest and deadliest of the three types – remote control.'

'I don't understand what you mean by remote control.'

'Ledoux brought with him what looks like a harmless small transistor radio. I could kick myself for not checking it when I had the chance. There's no use crying over spilt milk. I have kept watch on Ledoux. He has never been without his so-called radio – remember, he was carrying it when I found him and Maurette talking to Rencha?'

'I don't.'

Anything except Rencha had been blinkered from his sight.

'He was. I believe that instrument is a radio trigger to set off a quantity of explosive, over thirty kilograms, big enough to . . . to . . .'

'To do what, Bossiere? What, in Corbel Camp? What, in Cheating Pan?'

'We're going too fast. Let us first examine the logistics, if we are to work out what the target is.'

He picked out the photo-electric detonator from the others. 'This is activated by the sun's rays. That implies that the target is an outdoor one. One where the sun could get to it. Otherwise it wouldn't have been included.'

'Then why didn't they use it?'

'I suspect that Ledoux needs more time before the explosion takes place than this gadget would give him. Once it is exposed to the sun, it has to run its course. As against this, his radio-trigger would give to-the-second control of the explosion.'

'What sort of range does a radio-trigger have?'

'Depending on what obstructions – things like big buildings, hills, and so on – lie in between, an optimum range of about two kilometres. Three, at the maximum, but three would be dicey. At that distance it might not work.'

'So Ledoux would have to be within two kilometres of his target in order to detonate your hypothetical thirty-odd kilograms of TNT?'

'Not TNT, my friend. That's as out of date as an aeroplane

with a propeller. There are many much more potent explosives used by terrorists. The type inside here . . .' he touched the SZ-6 with his toe '. . . is pretty good. Not the tops – it's a bit too bulky – but nevertheless not to be sniffed at. Czech Samtex is also a front-runner.'

'You've built up your entire hypothesis that Ledoux has a big target in mind. It could be a small one. A person, for example.'

'Then this beauty here . . .' he indicated the SZ-3 '. . . would be the thing for it.' He regarded Kepler. 'There's only one individual in these parts it would be worth their while to bomb.'

'Who?'

'You. You're the man with the seven-billion dollar secret.'

A new note came into Kepler's voice. Bossiere realized that he had touched on the thing closest to the Australian scientist's heart.

'What good would it do killing me? Nucor has my SYNROC-R formula. They are patenting it world-wide on my behalf. See here, I didn't develop SYNROC-R to be a football to be kicked around by rival governments. Its purpose is to save mankind from itself.'

'That may have been your true motivation, but others don't see the discovery like that. You're the man in the middle, whether you like it or not. But I repeat, a man with Ledoux's know-how and cunning doesn't use all that amount of explosive to blow up one man. It's something much bigger he's after.'

'*We have got to find out what their target is,*' Kepler said vehemently.

Bossiere's heart lifted. He noted Kepler's use of the word 'we'. The scientist was powerfully enlisted on his side! That had been his objective when he had asked him to accompany him to the graveyard. Kepler had distanced himself from Rencha – it was better that way.

'*You* could find out.'

'I?'

'We will go back to Corbel Camp. You can join . . .' he

222

stumbled on the name '. . . Anna-Kai Cerny. If you play your cards right, she will tell you – tonight.'

'For crying out! A Judas trick! What do you take me for?' Kepler was angry, contemptuous.

'The Judas kiss was hers, my friend, in the first place. Do not deceive yourself. We are men of the world. Anything goes, in the Bakunin set-up.'

'Never!'

Bossiere realized that he had under-estimated the extent of Kepler's inner agony. 'Very well, but see her tonight anyway. Promise her the DST will indemnify her. Play it your own way, without telling her too much. Only, for Pete's sake, find out quickly! The bomb's ticking away!'

Kepler reached for a cigarette, but Bossiere stopped him. 'A cigarette is the biggest giveaway there is. We can't risk Ledoux even suspecting that anyone has been here.'

Kepler said, 'There is something else – of major importance. It struck me tonight while I was waiting for you. It means that Rencha cannot be part of your so-called bomb plot. If I weren't so sure, you wouldn't have got me to come.'

'Are you glad then you came?'

'Glad, and sorry. It doesn't alter what I have to say. Listen. When I first saw Cheating Pan, there was no Corbel Camp, only an old ruin from *Bluebird*'s day. I discovered the kimberlite deposit. Later, I came back . . .'

'How much later?' demanded Bossiere.

'I can't say exactly, but it was many months. I'd found mathiasite and lindsleyite to be present in the kimberlite in that interim, but at that stage they hadn't been authoritatively identified. That was a time-consuming process, although I was certain in my own mind about the two new minerals. Just because I was so sure, I approached Nucor. Their top geologists and I came to Cheating Pan together. When we did, work had been started on Corbel Camp. That was about three years ago.'

Bossiere was acute. He had already picked up the thrust of Kepler's argument.

'You saw – Anna-Kai Cerny here?'

'Stick to the name Rencha, Bossiere. That's the way I think of her.'

'Rencha Krummect, then. You saw her, spoke to her? She was at Corbel Camp three years ago?'

'She wasn't. She was in hospital at Carnarvon with pneumonia. But she had started building Corbel Camp.'

'Did she tell you about her illness?'

'Yes, and I believe her. What I am saying is, that if Rencha Krummect had started Corbel Camp three years ago, she could not have been put here as a sleeper by the Bakunin. SYNROC-R hadn't been invented. I should know. I'd only just discovered the two new minerals that are the basis of it.'

'Go on.'

'I will, because it puts Rencha in the clear. If no one but me and a couple of top Nucor men knew about it, it stands to reason that the Bakunin could not have. There was no question either at that stage of the Gougo repository. And – pay attention – accordingly no question of an IAEA inspection. You don't inspect institutions that aren't even in existence, aren't even thought of. So why should the Bakunin plant a sleeper – even assuming that she had not, as you accuse her, given up her terrorist connection and fled to South Africa? It doesn't wash, Bossiere!'

'I admit there is a time factor which I cannot at this stage explain,' he answered thoughtfully. 'But I will sort it out. Let me tell you something you don't know. Once a Bakunin, always a Bakunin. It is a terrorist movement which does not permit failure. It has a code, a rigid, inflexible code which it inherited from its fellow-terrorist organization in Japan, the Japanese Red Army. The Japanese movement in turn inherited it from a medieval martial sect called the Ninja. The Ninja were professional assassins. If a Ninja failed to carry out a mission or was identified doing so, there was only one way out – suicide. This is the reason we know so little about the Bakunins – the DST has never taken one alive.' His voice dropped. It might have been hatred, or his natural sense of drama. 'We nearly got one. A courier. Her name was Anna-Kai Cerny.'

Kepler realized immediately that there was no point in trying to talk down the ruthless purpose in the other man's voice.

'It has been a long hunt, but I have never deviated. I have Ledoux in my sights now. I swear to you, I will get him.'

The wind rose and became colder, as if underwriting the DST man's oath. The last scrap of moon vanished so that Deelkop had only the stars to backdrop it against eternity. Apart from flashlights, the only artificial light was the living flame, yellower now that the dust clouded it.

Kepler said, 'What are we going to do with these charges?'

'Rebury them, of course,' replied Bossiere. 'This isn't the big fish we are after. If Ledoux and Maurette find the charges and detonators missing, they'll realize that someone has got wise to them. That will make our main task doubly difficult. And time is running out! I want to think, think, think! We know there is a bomb, there must be a target – put your mind to work, man! We have got to find out where it is!'

Kepler said nothing. His brain seemed to be reeling with too many facts already, too many emotions . . .

Silently, he helped Bossiere with the recommittal of the charges and detonators. Then they smoothed over the grave, leaving the finishing task to the windspun shovel starting to blow powerfully from the north-west.

They returned to Corbel Camp, not speaking, each one lost in his own thoughts. Bossiere parked his car, and Kepler walked to his hut. On his way, he saw Rencha's light. He knew before he reached his own door that he was in for a sleepless night.

Once a Bakunin, always a Bakunin . . .

Chapter 31

Once a Bakunin, always a Bakunin.

The Bakunin code, as Bossiere had said, was rigid, uncompromising. It permitted no defectors.

That is what Ledoux told himself as he stood at Rencha's door after a scratch supper. As head of the Movement, it was his task to see that code was carried out – to the letter. If the letter spelled the execution of a defector, he would execute. That was why he had his gun with him tonight. That is, if the woman did not do what he ordered.

Professor Nakanishi had insisted that there must be another attempt to obtain the secret of SYNROC-R – Rencha was to be the means – before Red China made its final commitment to the bomb. This, Ledoux promised himself, would be the last chance he would offer.

Ledoux knocked.

Rencha opened. 'Come in. What can I do for you?'

Her tone was guarded, cautious. Her heart was racing – unnecessarily, she assured herself, because although she was aware of Ledoux's true identity from Bossiere, she was nevertheless certain in turn that he could have no idea of her Bakunin association. She had fled from France before Ledoux's return from his South Yemeni exile and his subsequent assumption of control of the terrorist movement.

Rencha waved to a chair.

'I prefer to stand.'

The way Ledoux refused made it clear this was no social visit. Time wasn't on his side. He had to work quickly. On Monday the bomb was due to go off.

Maurette stood a little aside, the apprentice watching the

master at work. It was a situation in which Ledoux was a craftsman: how to twist the arm of someone helpless who could not retaliate.

'I represent Radchem.'

Rencha breathed an inward sigh of relief and relaxed. He had not come to confront her with her Bakunin tie-up! Nevertheless, she wondered what was coming.

He threw what he calculated would be a knockdown punch without preliminaries.

'I want Dr West's SYNROC-R formula.'

'What has that to do with me? I am not a geochemist.'

'No, but you are a woman.'

'I don't care for the inference, Herr Lentz.'

'You don't have to,' he retorted roughly. 'It is plain to everyone that you and Dr West are emotionally involved, or should I say, entangled?'

Rencha flushed angrily. It exaggerated the shadows the day had left round her eyes.

'Leave him out of this!'

'On the contrary, he is part of it, whether you like it or not. Part of the emotion, part of the SYNROC-R . . .'

Ledoux was not a plain thug. There was a certain intellectual streak in him, a trait that had originally caused him, a natural anti, to rationalize his deep inner guilt feelings, and so led him to embrace the philosophy of the obscure nineteenth-century Russian Mikhil Akun.

He went on cynically, 'If you are thinking of making it permanent, you can become the wife of a very rich man.'

Righteous indignation is a very easy gear to slip into – when you are in the right.

'Is it necessary to have this man listen in on this odious conversation?' she flared and indicated Maurette.

'Our business requires a witness,' replied Ledoux pontifically.

'Business? I am not prepared to listen . . .'

'You will. I haven't started yet.'

Ledoux liked the shaft of fear he saw in her eyes. He was

starting to enjoy himself. The interview would have to become a lot rougher before it brought him satisfaction. But they always said he was a slow starter.

Rencha answered contemptuously, 'I have heard all I want to hear from you, Herr Lentz.'

He ignored her and went on. 'My principals are very generous. They have offered Dr West half a million dollars and a lifetime job – research of his own choosing and no strings – in return for the secret of SYNROC-R.'

She held her tongue that she already knew: she also knew her man. Her man that had been, she reproached herself.

'Then why bring me into it? Your business is with Dr West.'

'We encountered – certain difficulties, with Dr West,' he replied blandly. 'We feel we could resolve them by making an indirect approach.'

'What do you expect me to do then?' She allowed her anger to burn; it masked another surge of apprehension at Ledoux's calm, unreacting self-assurance. Intuition cast shadows before her.

He pitched the answer back. 'Pillow-talk. Get the secret out of him. In bed, or out of bed, it doesn't matter to me. You could earn yourself the half million dollars that way.'

The magic that had passed between her and Kepler suddenly appeared shabby, seen through the filter of Ledoux's outlook. She allowed her bitter resentment at the fact to inflate her reply.

'My reply to you – and your so-called principals – is, go to the devil! I will have nothing to do with you or your dirty schemes! Now – go!'

Ledoux switched into French. It was psychological warfare, perfect timing. Until that moment he had spoken in English. The use of her mother tongue fired the afterburner of new fears and she plunged into further conversation with an inescapable, sickening feeling in her stomach.

'You forget, you are obliged to. We are offering you the easy way, business combined with pleasure,' he sneered. 'If you refuse, you will learn the hard way.'

228

The sour fear rose like gall in her throat. She tried to keep a poker face, except she had never played poker.

'That sounds like a threat.' She tried to shore up her answer as best she could and crush the past out of sight again where it had lurked for so long. How could Ledoux possibly know anything of her Bakunin association? Let him rather think she was a sex-hungry female exploiting her one-woman advantage at Corbel Camp.

'It is. You refuse?'

All she could see in Ledoux's pigmentless eyes was a reflection of a trickle of smoke from his Gauloise. The smoke-machine bobbed in his lips as he continued talking without removing it.

Rencha spoke repetitively, trying to stave off anything further Ledoux might have to say. 'Bluntly, what you are asking from me is to go to bed with one of the world's leading nuclear geochemists, get his secret formula from him like a Mata Hari, and turn it over to you for half a million dollars. What do you take me for?'

Maurette stood by. Perhaps his empty face reflected his mind underneath; perhaps it was merely the perfect cover-up.

Ledoux coughed so that the ash spurted away from the cigarette tip. The rest stayed in position.

'The extraction of secrets and the exercise of sex are inextricably mingled with the history of spying,' he replied. A hard-shell Bible-puncher could not have sounded more phoney, more unctuous.

'As I read the situation, there would be no lack of willingness from either party involved . . .'

'Get out!' snapped Rencha. 'Get out of here! Both of you!'

Ledoux stood his ground. His voice hardened. 'If you won't do it for money, I order you to do it – out of duty.'

'Order? Duty – to whom?'

'Stop playing games. Can't you guess?' The way he said it frightened her. As much as when Bossiere had produced his DST photograph of herself.

Ledoux added, 'You know what I am talking about. I have

interrogated many guilty people. Your guilt is written all over your face.'

He pulled the remains of his cigarette from his mouth and threw the wet unpleasant thing on the stone floor. He did not bother to stub it dead. Its place was taken by a slit in his lips which showed a faint line of tobacco-stained front teeth.

Her panic became a physical thing, like an uncontrollable spasm of vomit hurling itself out of her gullet.

'What are you talking about?' Her whisper wandered across the room like the wind and ghosts of Cheating Pan.

'Once a Bakunin, always a Bakunin, Anna-Kai Cerny. My name is Jean Ledoux. I am head of the Bakunin.'

The faceless room suddenly became peopled with faces, for her. Faces twisted with terror. Dead faces. The face of Charles, with the bullet-hole between his eyes. The face of John Krummect, mashed beyond recognition over the wheel of their car . . .

The impact of the name Bakunin had the same effect on her face as it had had when Bossiere had thrown it at her. The skin, the muscles, seemed to be struck with an instant catatonia; they froze; all that remained of the beautiful face was an empty deadpan shell. The affliction took in her eyes also. Ledoux could find no answer in them.

'I have never heard of the Bakunin.' It was a standard clap-trap reply terrorists use to the police when they know the next stage will be the probe or the electricity. Ledoux had fine-honed his interrogation technique to a degree French Intelligence would have envied.

'What about Anna-Kai Cerny?'

'Likewise.'

'What about – Roger Lichine?' It was a sneak punch, perfectly executed, and it sent Rencha against the ropes. Her mind had been ready for anything to do with France; this cunning devil had feinted, like a boxer, and brought in the man who had hounded her in Cape Town . . .

'I . . .'

Ledoux smiled with satisfaction. 'I see you do. Roger

Lichine sends his regards, by the way. He feels he has rather got out of touch. You could have been in his job as sleeper at Koeberg all these years, if you had wanted a cushy position.'

Lichine was the man who had killed John Krummect. Her words slipped out uncontrollably.

'You bastard!'

'I will return your greetings to Roger – I see you remember him. The others you will undoubtedly recall, as we go along.'

Perhaps the effort was becoming too much for Ledoux himself. His voice lost its pseudo-coaxing, jollying note and became hard. 'Forget the cover-up and the bull,' he rapped out. 'You are Anna-Kai Cerny, once our best courier in Europe. We lost you. You are the only Bakunin ever to slip out of the movement. We found you again. You are back in business.'

Rencha's tongue felt four sizes too big for her mouth. She articulated with difficulty. 'I can't! I won't! You can't ask me to!'

For a reply, there was a gun in Ledoux's hand. It was a Czech CZ-75, probably the most deadly and accurate 9 mm parabellum in the world. It had a walnut butt with silver inlay. An Argentine who had crafted it had bought himself an extra month of life while Ledoux waited for him to finish before his hands were cut off so that his body would show no fingerprints.

He held it on Rencha. 'Sit down!'

She remained standing, immobile.

Ledoux nodded to Maurette. He grabbed her shoulders from behind, rammed her down hard in a chair, and stood ready for further duty.

Ledoux said, 'Stand clear of the shot, Maurette.'

Maurette knew the order was part of the breaking-down routine. He grinned and winked from behind Rencha, obeyed.

Ledoux sat and propped himself against Rencha's table and worked the slide of the CZ-75. The bullets pumped out like a litter of white mice from the womb, one to eight. They lay on the table. Ledoux kept his eyes on Rencha, except for a brief moment when he glanced down and selected one of the shells. He held it to the light like a vintner examining a fine wine.

Like a vintner also, he probably saw something that no one else did. Whatever it was, it seemed not to satisfy him. He returned it to the pile on the table, took another, and went through the same nerve-scraping process. Then he licked the percussion cap with the tip of his tongue and inserted the shell into the breech.

He lifted the pistol and aimed it at Rencha's face. Carefully, without taking his eyes off her, he drew back the hammer. He felt the tension of the spring, tested it by a slight pull rearward, moved it slightly forward again. The idea was to find just sufficient tension for the firing-pin to dent the percussion-cap. Too much strength would fire it; too little would be useless. It required great finesse and an intimate knowledge of the gun in hand.

He let go. Perhaps Rencha had spotted the movement of release, or perhaps her nerve had already cracked. She was half on her feet when the gun gave a tiny click. That was all. One tiny click.

Maurette knew the routine. He grabbed Rencha before she could rise fully and shoved her down again in her seat.

'It is some time since I practised this,' Ledoux said, grinning at the strained face in front of him. 'It's a good thing for you I haven't forgotten how.'

He waved Maurette aside for the second time. For the second time also, he started the sadistic routine – the studied inspection of the percussion-cap, the working of the slide, the measured insertion of the shell, the prolonged checking of hammer-pressure against his fingers.

Now, he held the hammer again in its critical position.

'As head of the Bakunin, I am both judge and executioner,' he said. 'Speak to my fingers, if you want to live. You know the Bakunin code. Defection means – death. I order you again, find out from Dr West the secret of SYNROC-R.'

Ledoux was enjoying himself. He had picked up the hammer trick from the Basque terrorists when he had fled to Spain after France had become too hot for him. He had only killed two prisoners while learning it, but that had been in the early days before acquiring years of skill in the Argentine death squads.

The pistol hammer stood poised.

A last-ditch, odds-against thought tore through Rencha's mind: dead, she was no good to anyone; alive, she might somehow be able to enlist Kepler or Bossiere . . .

'Don't let it go – don't let it go! I have no choice!' Rencha's voice emerged only as a distorted whisper.

Ledoux held the gun on her still. His voice was as menacing as the shell in the breech awaiting the hammer.

'Dr West and the Frenchman Bossiere went out tonight together. Where? For what?'

'I don't know.' Her voice was a flat monotone, like a deaf-mute's.

'Why did Bossiere remain behind when all the other delegates went to Vaalputs, eh?'

'He was ill.'

'Stow it!' Ledoux snapped. 'You're lying. Who is Bossiere? What is he up to? What is his association with Dr West?'

She shook her head silently.

'No matter. We will ask Monsieur Bossiere ourselves, eh Louis?'

Maurette caught the implication and grinned. 'We will.'

Ledoux went on. 'But West is the important one.' Rencha wondered how much longer Ledoux's finger could sustain the hammer to such a fine pitch. The pale eyes terrified her. A snake's held more animation.

Ledoux raised the gun a fraction. 'West?' It was an all-embracing question in one small word.

'I have no choice.'

'Ah!' exclaimed Ledoux. 'Ah! I see you agree.' He lowered the pistol, eased the hammer into a neutral position. 'You are a Bakunin, never forget. You are under orders. Fail, and you know what will come to you.'

'Meaning?' Ledoux could scarcely hear her question.

'On Monday, the delegates return from Vaalputs. You have until tomorrow night to get the SYNROC-R formula from Dr West.'

Rencha did not look up. The weight on her mind seemed heavy enough to keep her head down.

'Don't try anything funny,' he added. His voice was ravaged by lifelong mistrust. 'We'll be watching you all the time.'

They went.

Rencha sat, stunned, unable to think. All she was aware of at some stage was the sound of a car arriving, and then again, later, when she had dragged herself into her bed and sat propped up staring sightlessly, another leaving, followed by a second. Then, at another undefined time in the small hours, there was the noise of a vehicle arriving plus banging of doors. Later, much later, there was a rumble of freewheeling tyres from the car park next door to her hut, followed by the sound of a stealthy kick-start in the distance . . .

Chapter 32

You use an abacus to work out a mathematical solution – sideways, upwards, downwards, backwards. Repetition and practice are the key to its success. That is what Bossiere was doing to his brain. Instead of the brass beads of the traditional Chinese calculator, Bossiere was flicking his brain cells about – sideways, upwards, downwards, backwards – in an attempt to break the problem.

What was the Bakunins' target?

Where was the bomb?

It was just after eleven o'clock that night after he had returned from the graveyard with Kepler. His hut seemed as minute and restricted as a solitary-confinement cell. He needed endless cups of coffee to back up his chain-smoking; he had plenty of the latter, but none of the former. Ridiculously, he blamed his lack of a solution on it. He knew it was childish to do so, but it gave him something upon which to vent his frustration.

He had tried to outflank his problem by not approaching it directly in order to lick it – paradoxical intention, he had heard the method called. But his mind wouldn't deviate to trifling side-issues. It stuck pointing at the main target like a tank's gun whose aiming mechanism has jammed.

He tried going over in his mind every event, however small and apparently unimportant, since the start of the IAEA gathering at Corbel Camp. He pawed impatiently at the typed official itinerary which now lay cast aside on a table, in the hope of tracking down some ray of light: he knew the wretched thing by heart. Paradoxical intention – think round corners! Bossiere also cursed the psychologist who had hatched up that phrase. When your mind is racing like a Grand Prix engine, you can't deviate . . .

The one concrete fact he had to go upon was his discovery of the SZ-3 and SZ-6 demolition charges and detonators in the grave. He tried to work it backwards from there. He remained convinced that they were discards. If discards, that implied that the others of the same type were either sufficient for Ledoux's purpose, or that the two charges left could not be accommodated alongside the others.

Alongside? – *in*?

Bossiere cursed the lack of coffee. He was hot, as the golfers say, only his putts wouldn't drop.

Bossiere considered. He himself had tested the weight of those two suitcases in the loft, thirty to forty kilograms he reckoned. That meant a substantial target, not a single human, as he had stressed to Kepler West. That ruled out Kepler himself. However, that amount of explosive would easily obliterate the whole IAEA delegation, provided they were concentrated. Yet, Bossiere countered his own argument, he gave Ledoux with his sophisticated expertise in bombing more credit than to simply explode demolition charges in the open in the hope of killing a number of international experts. The demolition charges were lethal in themselves, but they were intended to be placed in such a way that they would do maximum damage – in other words, inside something in order to bring the maximum force to bear.

Inside!

Now he was on to it! If the majority of the demolition charges from the suitcases had been fitted into a container of predetermined shape, there could have been a couple over to spare – the ones he had located in the grave. Bossiere's mind avalanched.

There had been an object – was it the container he was postulating? – in the back of the terrorists' station wagon when he had seen them drive past Corbel Camp; it had been covered by a blanket. If only that blanket could talk!

Bossiere pulled himself up. This was no time to indulge in wishful thinking. What he needed was fact, more solid fact. Was there anything he and Kepler had missed at the graveyard?

There had been nothing in the hut at the gate, he was sure. True, they had not searched the other graves for signs of disturbance: would Ledoux and Maurette have buried their main bomb container separately from the SZ discards?

That broken railing round the grave!

Bossiere's mind was on to it like a homing Exocet on target. The railing had been buckled and broken off in one place – and that break had been new! The metal was still bright! It could have been caused by a heavy – *container!*

He must get back and check it out – now!

It was a few minutes before midnight.

Bossiere paused only long enough to consider whether he should invite Kepler to go with him. It was late enough for him to be asleep. Perhaps the scientist was making his peace with Rencha, in which case he would be less than welcome. On the other hand, the rift between them seemed to him, an outsider, pretty severe.

Bossiere could not see Kepler's hut light from his own. Even if it were still on, it didn't necessarily mean that Kepler was there.

Bossiere scrapped the idea. Instead, he scribbled a brief note to Kepler, pinned it on his own door, switched out the light and jumped into his car.

He shot off towards Cheating Pan – and the graveyard.

Midnight.

That was the H-hour Ledoux and Maurette had set to confront Bossiere.

Bossiere and Kepler had returned together while the two Bakunins were still with Rencha. When they had emerged from her quarters, both Bossiere and Kepler's lights were on, and Bossiere's car was at his door. They had no means of establishing whether Bossiere and Kepler were together: their business was with Bossiere alone. Maurette especially had no wish to encounter Kepler again – the only way, he told Ledoux, would be gun in hand.

The Bakunins' hut was sighted from both Kepler's and Bossiere's. The terrorists kept watch on them; after a time they decided they would wait until midnight at the latest before making for Bossiere's quarters.

Now, Ledoux checked his watch and his CZ-75. Maurette did the same with his own pistol; he had done so half a dozen times already, out of nervousness.

'Time!' said Ledoux. 'Let's go!'

'One moment.' Maurette fiddled unnecessarily with the magazine, removed it, checked it over, and reclipped it into position. Had he not wasted the time, they might have intercepted Bossiere.

'On our way!' repeated Ledoux.

They were just too late.

As if by some perverse psychic prescience, Bossiere raced away as the terrorists opened their door. The two Bakunins stood dumbfounded as they watched Bossiere's headlights follow the exit track through the camp to the main road beyond.

'He's . . . he's . . . got wise to us!' exclaimed Maurette incredulously.

'Don't be a fool! How could he?' snapped back Ledoux. 'After him – this is exactly what we want!'

'What we want?'

'We'll follow him – no lights – hold back until he stops – rough him up if he won't talk – it'll look like a roadside robbery – get going! We don't want to lose him!'

Ledoux sprinted for their station wagon, which they had made a routine of parking near their hut and not with the other vehicles in the official car park.

Maurette pocketed his pistol, threw himself into the vehicle as Ledoux fired the engine.

Action always appealed to Ledoux. 'Softee, softee, catchee monkey!' he grinned.

Then he exclaimed, 'He's taken the road to the Pan!' There was hardly any need for him to say it: Bossiere was driving with his lights full on; his rear reflectors shone muted red through his car's own dust.

'He's in a hurry,' remarked Ledoux. He himself, being without headlights, had to travel slowly through the dust which the light wind had not yet dissipated.

By the time they had cleared Corbel Camp's environs, Bossiere had drawn well ahead. There was no doubt what his destination was: Cheating Pan. Ledoux now picked up speed.

'While he's moving as fast as that, there's no chance of his hearing our engine,' he observed.

'What do you think he's up to at the airfield?' asked Maurette.

Ledoux replied enigmatically, 'You're assuming he's heading for the airfield.'

'Where else?'

'There's a graveyard out there, too.'

'He doesn't know about it.'

'If he does, it's his bad luck.'

It was also Bossiere's bad luck that he needed light at the graveyard because the moon had gone and he left his headlights shining through the wrought iron gate with its warning notice, and directed at the living flame headstone. It was also Bossiere's

238

bad luck that Ledoux and Maurette were so hard on his heels; given time, he was certain to have discovered the upper chamber above the lying-in hut. Once he had spotted the genuine Koeberg drum hidden there, a fuse of deductions would have led to the fake drum lodged in Gougo's repository.

Ledoux was clever in his stalking. He closed the gap between the two vehicles before reaching the airfield on the assumption that Bossiere could not see his pursuers. Once Bossiere stopped, however, it was a different matter. Sound would carry across the deserted landscape for kilometres.

The Bakunins observed Bossiere by-pass the airfield, then turn at their own marker drum.

'Graveyard.' It was the only word Ledoux spoke.

They took the turn also. It was three kilometres from there to the graveyard.

'The moment he stops, we stop,' said Ledoux.

'And then?'

'We go after him on foot.'

That was the way it worked out. Bossiere had already investigated the other graves and was busy exhuming the two demolition charges with a spade when Ledoux and Maurette, on foot, slid out of the darkness behind the DST man's car. Its lights illuminated Bossiere, back to them, at the living flame grave. The perfect unsuspecting target.

'Keep clear of the lights!' whispered Ledoux. 'Over the wall! We'll come from the side! I'll take him!'

Maurette gave a grunt of disappointment. But Ledoux knew his subordinate. Maurette would go in boots and all and kill the Frenchman. He didn't want him dead – yet.

The two terrorists slipped over the stone wall, converging on their prey like a pair of killer U-boats in tandem.

Then they were close to Bossiere, panting with exertion. He had opened his leather jacket to give himself air.

Ledoux reversed the CZ-75, holding it by the barrel. The wooden butt would ensure the Frenchman didn't die, as he might if it were a metal grip.

Bossiere never knew what hit him. The blow took him on that thin side of the skull just behind and above the ear where the brain below is so vulnerable. The strike was so swift that the blood from the broken scalp did not even have time to stain the silver engraving.

Bossiere pitched forward, crumpling untidily with his head at an angle against the headstone's lower plinth.

Maurette went down on his knees to finish him off.

'Hold it!'

'But . . .'

Maurette indicated one of the demolition charges, the smaller SZ-3, which Bossiere had already extracted. 'This means he knows the whole story.'

Ledoux turned the prostrate form over with his foot. Bossiere's eyes were rolled back, sightless. 'You can have your fun with that spade.'

'What do you mean, spade? I've got my gun . . .'

Ledoux gestured towards the graveyard gate. 'Remember what the notice says – "Trespassers will be severely dealt with." Deal with him severely.'

'I don't get it.' Maurette was like a sulky dog held back from a fight.

'This is a private graveyard, not so? That's on the notice also. So what happens when the owner comes along and finds someone –' he tapped Bossiere in the ribs with his shoe '– digging up his most precious grave? He tackles him. He grabs the trespasser's spade. He hammers him . . .'

Maurette went for the spade.

For the second time, Ledoux restrained him. 'Let's first check his pockets so that we won't get messed up with blood later.'

Ledoux felt inside Bossiere's jacket and pulled out something. He stayed on his knees in stupefaction as he read.

'Jeez!' he burst out at length. 'Look at this!'

He passed Bossiere's DST accreditation card to Maurette.

'The DST!' whispered Maurette. 'The DST – here!'

He raised the spade savagely.

'In a moment.' Ledoux's voice was hard. 'Louis, I want to kill him just as much, if not more, than you do – Henri Bossiere, French Intelligence! You bastard!' He kicked the unconscious man in the face. He was not too deeply unconscious to emit a groan.

Ledoux raised his foot again and then brought himself under control.

'He doesn't know – he *can't* know!' he burst out.

'He suspects – and that's enough for me.' Maurette's hands were round the shaft of the spade. 'Cut the cackle! Unless I kill him, I'll . . . I'll . . .'

Ledoux humped his shoulders and drew his breath in and out, like a fullback preparing for a difficult kick.

'If we kill him, someone will find him, sooner or later. If it's before Monday, the fat will be in the fire. Murder is one thing, a badly beaten trespasser is another. There'll be too many questions asked, too many nosey parkers, if we finish him off. Somehow, they might even get on to the bomb. You never know where things lead once they start.'

'For crying out loud!' exclaimed Maurette. 'What are you trying to do – talk yourself out of it, with that DST card in your hands?'

Ledoux took out his handkerchief, wiped the card.

'What's that in aid of?' demanded Maurette.

'Fingerprints,' he answered tersely. 'The same goes for the spade, once you're finished with him.' He thrust the card back inside Bossiere's jacket, held up his head to Maurette.

'Here.' He indicated Bossiere's hairline. 'Not too hard. Just hard enough for two days.'

The spade crashed on to the DST man's skull. Ledoux got clear of the blood which poured over his face.

He turned Bossiere over with his foot. 'Next, between the shoulder-blades – he was caught by surprise, remember.'

Again the spade crashed home.

'Maybe he'll die once the cold gets him,' remarked Maurette. 'Tough shit.'

Together they made of Bossiere a Bakunin picture of what

241

a beaten-up man should look like. Their concept of such images was very precise.

When they had done, they removed the two SZ charges from the grave and secreted them in the upper chamber above the lying-in hut, along with the detonators, lengths of cut wire and tools. They wiped the spade clean of fingerprints and left Bossiere, breathing stertorously, in the sand below the living flame.

The two Bakunins retreated to the gate, brushing out their footsteps as they went.

They switched off the car's headlights, carefully obliterating fingerprints, removed the ignition keys, locked the doors, and walked back to where they had left their own vehicle out on the Pan.

Chapter 33

It was intellectually-generated adrenalin which had robbed Bossiere of his sleep; with Kepler it was emotional adrenalin – and emotions cut deeper. He himself could not turn the spotlight on himself acutely enough to realize that he was in shock: he had been, ever since that moment in the morning when Bossiere had produced the photograph of Rencha as a Bakunin courier.

Her refusal to discuss it with him, her unapproachable iciness, the attack on him to heist the SYNROC-R jar, Rencha's mysterious telephone call in a foreign language and the equally mysterious reappearance of the two terrorists had all success-ively served to stun his feelings. He had spent most of the day desperately trying to exonerate her. Again and again, however, would come Bossiere's man-of-the-world reminder, 'the lady has made the running.'

His defences had crumbled like strongpoints falling to a creeping artillery barrage until only one bastion remained – the time factor of her occupation of Corbel Camp, when he had first visited Corbel Camp. Bossiere himself could not explain the 'sleeper' time discrepancy, but had tried to get away with the generality, 'once a Bakunin, always a Bakunin'. Kepler had hung on to that hope against hope – until that moment in the graveyard when Bossiere had produced the SZ demolition charges in support of his arguments. There was no contradicting them!

The thought that Rencha was playing games with him left him with the same kind of incredulous shock that a man might experience when he sees his leg has been severed in a car accident. The shock would overwhelm the immediate pain; that was hitting him now, wave after wave.

Kepler didn't even crave (as Bossiere did) cigarettes and strong coffee. What he did crave was the chance to talk the whole thing through with Bossiere. Not Rencha. He had noted her light when he came in; she would never, he promised himself, get another chance from him.

Kepler hardly heard the insomniac's comfort dispensed by the all-night radio service; it was only at the back of his mind that he half-recorded the sound of car engines, coming and going.

Kepler's thought snapped back to the explosives in the grave. Bossiere was so sure the two SZ charges were discards that he wasn't prepared to do anything about them. His attitude, as far as Kepler could define it, was to give the terrorists enough rope to hang themselves. The DST man had stuck to the assertion that there was a major bomb – somewhere.

The early hours of the morning do strange things to a man's thinking processes. Even rational thoughts can become irrational, and things are seen from an inverted viewpoint.

It was the early hours now.

The thought exploded in Kepler's mind – what if the cache in the grave *was* the bomb itself? And the array of detonators simply a choice, depending on immediate opportunist circumstances?

Kepler followed up the proposition excitedly. Bossiere himself had said that the SZ charges were ideally suited for a car bomb. Nine kilograms of high explosive would be available, more than enough to destroy a car. And a man in it.

Who would figure as the target?

The finger pointed unerringly. Himself.

Bossiere had also named him as a possible target, but had thrown the idea overboard, on the assumption that the terrorists would be using a bomb of thirty kilograms or more. What if they were not? What if that nine kilograms of explosive were intended to be insinuated into his own car – in the boot, under the chassis – and the moment he touched the starter . . .

Why should not the bomb be aimed at him? He was the inventor of Koeberg-originated SYNROC-R and his death would be a world-wide proclamation that the Bakunin had not forgotten their vow concerning the French-designed Koeberg power station.

Bossiere must be made to listen to his construction of the facts! Perhaps Bossiere's own relentless vendetta against Ledoux had clouded his judgement.

Kepler made up his mind. He would seek out Bossiere – now!

He checked his watch – 3.15 a.m. Where had the night gone?

Now that he had decided to act, he felt good. He pulled on his leather windcheater over his jersey and slipped the Colt into an inner pocket. He turned off the radio and light, unlocked the door cautiously, giving his eyes time to acquire night vision. Was he being watched? If he were No. 1 Bakunin target, it was possible. Or was he being fanciful, building up his own case for himself?

To reach Bossiere's hut, Kepler had to pass the rear of the farmhouse complex and also Ledoux's hut. There seemed no sign of light from that direction. But then, they would scarcely keep watch on him with their light on to advertise the fact.

Kepler decided on a roundabout route, but almost at once rejected it. It would have to be via the basalt platform and Rencha's door. Over the roofs now he could see a glow – Rencha's light, still on. Deliberately, he headed away in a direction which would take him to the top end of the car park through a cluster of hillocks or koppies. He worked his way down the length of the place and at its bottom end climbed the stone boundary wall to reach Bossiere's door.

He was about to knock when he spotted Bossiere's note.

By matchlight, he made out

> *11.55 a.m.*
> *Kepler – gone to graveyard.*
> *Henri*

Immediately Kepler noted the use of Bossiere's Christian name for the first time. That in itself presupposed a degree of intimacy. Also the mere fact that Bossiere had left a note implied that he had expected Kepler to call on him. Was the inference also that he should join him at the graveyard?

There was no hesitation in Kepler's mind. He crushed the note into his pocket, started for the car park. Then he pulled himself up. In the stillness, the sound of the car's starter would be heard all over Corbel Camp. His car was at the upper end of the park. The downward incline of its rock surface would enable him to make a relatively silent kick start in the direction he had just come, and thus head away from Rencha's quarters, away from the Bakunin hut.

Kepler again climbed the wall of the park, found his car. He eased off the handbrake, put it into gear. It rolled forwards, gathering momentum. The fact that he could not use the lights was nerve-racking: he feared that at any moment he might crash into the stone wall.

Then the engine fired. It sounded to his overwrought senses like *Bluebird* at full bore. He kept going. By good luck he found the track between the basalt hillocks, and picked his way blindly.

Then the roadway straightened; he could discern its faint demarcation towards the camp's exit.

Safe now! Kepler got his bearings by flicking on his lights briefly, then headed away towards Cheating Pan. Once he was well clear of the camp he put on his lights and made for the graveyard.

Kepler thought Bossiere was dead.

His first premonition of tragedy came when his own headlights picked up, from a distance, the metallic reflection of Bossiere's car by the gate. There seemed something unnatural in the sight of the car standing deserted on the measureless surface of the great pan under the stars. The lights were off, the windows shut.

Kepler pulled up alongside, cut his own lights. That left the night to the living flame which hung poised above the headstone. It revealed the crumpled body of Bossiere at its foot in the shadows between life and death.

Kepler grabbed the flashlight he kept in the car and sprinted for the grave.

He got the head and face out of the blood and sand. His hands were shaking from shock and savage anger against Ledoux and Maurette. He got his ear to Bossiere's nose and mouth. The answer came in the form of a half-gasp, half-choke. He was alive!

Kepler hastily spooned the sand and muck out of the DST man's mouth with his fingers. There was no response from his eyes to the light beam directed into them.

Kepler wasn't sure whether he was doing the right thing medically by propping him up. So he eased him flat again. As he did so, his foot grated against something.

There was no doubt about the attempted murder weapon. Kepler's flashlight showed the blade of the spade stained with blood.

Kepler now felt Bossiere's pulse: how long had he been lying there with that hideous wound? It looked awful. It was seeping still, and the bruise riding alongside it appeared wicked enough to have damaged half his brain cells. The pulse was there, but irregular.

Kepler was too shaken to make a cool assessment. All he knew was that he had to get Bossiere to hospital – to a doctor, to any skilled help – quickly!

He rolled the deadweight over in order to pick him up and spotted further evidence of the assault. The shadow of the dusty spade was outlined between Bossiere's shoulder-blades.

Then, for the first time, Kepler's mind swung to the SZ charges hidden in the grave. He paused for a moment. The surface seemed – surprisingly – undisturbed. Had there been no struggle at all? Had they (and there was no doubt in his mind that Ledoux and Maurette had been responsible) crept up and struck the unsuspecting Bossiere down from behind without his even having put up a fight? It looked like it. That is the way a terrorist would operate – the unsuspecting blow in the dark, from behind.

Kepler hefted the unconscious man on to his shoulders and made for his car at a shambling run. Why hadn't the Bakunins killed Bossiere? Why not a bullet in the back of the head instead of this messy, incomplete job? Kepler believed in the bomb now. Bossiere had been right. He had proved it, first by his discovery of the demolition charges, and second, the irrefutable evidence of the murderous assault. Yet – why had he gone back to the graveyard?

As he positioned the wounded man's head in as comfortable position as he could, Kepler sought an answer. Looking at that battered face, he might never find out.

To confront Ledoux and Maurette on his immediate return might be premature and a serious mistake. Kepler's mouth hardened. Like Bossiere and Ledoux, he plumped for the soft option. Rencha. He would force her to take the injured man to hospital or a doctor. She would know the nearest. Then he could sort matters out with the two terrorists.

It was a little over half an hour later that he knocked on Rencha's door – her bedroom light still burned.

He had made his way into Corbel Camp even more cautiously than he had departed.

He had Bossiere's body over his shoulders.

It was the first thing Rencha saw.

She had a small-calibre stainless steel pistol in her hand.

'Traitor!' he said.

Chapter 34

Because her back was to the light, Kepler did not see the surge of life come into her face at the sight of him, nor the instantaneous reversal of emotion at that of the body over his shoulders. She was wearing the jade-green dressing-gown which she had worn after their love-making.

He pushed past her. Bossiere's bloodied head came into full view. There was a smear of the blood and sand across his own left ear and shoulders.

Kepler eased Bossiere down on to the couch, found a cushion for his head.

He wheeled on her. She stood with the open door behind her, the little pistol hanging slack from her fingers at full arm's length.

Kepler was sure she wouldn't use the gun – on him. She might use it to signal the two Bakunin.

He walked past her, his eyes never leaving hers. He locked the door, pocketed the key.

'Why do you do that?' He could hardly hear her words.

He took the gun out of her unresisting fingers and put it in the drawer of a small table.

'Once a Bakunin, always a Bakunin,' he answered.

For the first time, a flicker of life came into her lovely eyes, charcoaled with the night's vigil and pain.

'You're hurt.'

'Not me. It was Bossiere who caught the broadside from your Bakunin bosses.'

'Bosses?' She might have been sleepwalking.

He took her roughly by the shoulders. Close like that, he could see the lift of her breasts under her nightdress.

Emotion backfired into savage anger. 'Don't play-act with me! I found him in the graveyard. I've had enough of it! You're going to take Bossiere – and me – to the nearest doctor. Now – get your clothes on!'

His anger exploded as she stood unmoving. He pointed at Bossiere.

'You organized this! Now try and talk your way out of it! I know why your light stayed on all night! You were waiting for Ledoux and Maurette to report back that they'd done the job you summoned them here from Vaalputs to do! Once you had found out that the DST was on your trail!'

'This is madness, Kepler!'

'Don't come up with the corny cliché that you don't know what I am talking about! I heard you phoning – remember? You put your hand over the mouthpiece, you waited for me to get out! You phoned Ledoux at Vaalputs! You told him the heat was on! Why did the two of them come rushing back to Corbel Camp when they were supposed to spend two whole days at Vaalputs – eh? You – you, Anna-Kai Cerny – called them back! That story of Professor Nakanishi's documents and the Gobi – my oath, what kind of sucker do you take me for?'

'Kepler, every word you say is killing our love.'

Again, emotion mutated into anger. He shrugged. 'You did it first.'

Her head went down for a moment, then she said in a different everyday voice.

'How bad is he?'

'Bad enough. I need a doctor for him.'

'*We* need a doctor.'

'You'll come with me, all right! I'm not giving those bastards the chance of following up!'

She interrupted quietly. 'All you say is wrong, Kepler. I'm not going to argue with you – not while a man lies dying. Just to prove it to you, I'll take him myself. There is no doctor in the entire Cheating Pan area. It will have to be the hospital at Carnarvon – that's two hundred and twenty kilometres away.'

'There must be one closer.'

'There is not. I know, from the time I had pneumonia here at Corbel Camp. We'll have to go by road, of course. We'll use my car. I'll drive. I know the route and the road.'

Kepler said, off-balance, 'Phone through first, tell them we're coming.'

She regarded him. 'I said, I will take him.'

'We're wasting time. Both of us.'

'Anyway, the telephone exchange doesn't open until seven,' she went on. 'We can almost get to Carnarvon in that time.'

She stood for a moment, as if wanting to say more. Then she added, 'I'll dress.' She eyed his bloody, dirty hands. 'First, you can clean up in my bathroom.'

His eyes locked with hers. She wasn't prepared for the bitterness in his reply. 'No! I couldn't. I used that bathroom when . . . when . . .' He dropped his eyes. 'Forget it. I go as I am.'

She started, as if towards her bedroom, then said, 'I love you, Kepler, and that is all there is to it. Whether you believe me or not, whether you think I am a Bakunin or not. There are no strings. There is no Bakunin involvement from my side. I've never known love like this – whether from my lover Charles the doctor in Paris, or from my dear John Krummect in Cape Town. Deep inside, you are all I ever want.'

'You are very beautiful and very persuasive, Rencha, alias Anna-Kai Cerny. But it's no sale.' He went closer to her and rapped out. 'What is the target?'

He might have been broadcasting on a different wavelength, unheard by her.

'The target is rapidly becoming myself.'

'What do you mean?'

She inclined her head towards the drawer where he had put

her little pistol. 'I had that with me tonight. It would have been so easy – several times tonight. A love as big as ours may require a death – the kind of sacrifice they made in ancient times when things got out of hand and they had to placate the gods when they went mad. Our gods have gone mad, Kepler.'

'I . . .'

She broke in imperatively, 'A man is dying while we waste time talking.'

She turned and went, closing the bedroom door on him.

While Rencha dressed, Kepler went through Bossiere's pockets; better that he should than the hospital authorities, in case of awkward questions. There undoubtedly would have been over the loaded Walther with two spare magazines; more so, over Bossiere's official DST accreditation card. Why had the terrorists left them untouched? Kepler had no time to consider how much or how little he would tell the hospital. Rencha came through as he finished carrying blankets and pillows for the injured man for the journey. She was wearing corduroy trousers and a thick sweater.

She started at the sight of Bossiere's gun. Kepler said nothing, put it into his pocket alongside his Colt. He then took the accreditation card and placed it in the drawer where her pistol was.

'Okay if I leave this here until we get back?'

His tone was as detached as an investigating policeman.

'Yes.'

'Where is your car?'

'In the park. Close to the main entrance.'

That would mean they would have to pass Ledoux's hut on the way out. They were probably asleep, judging from the fact that he had entered Corbel Camp unmolested. But Rencha would only have to stop and give a blast on the car's hooter to bring them running . . .

'We'll go out the top way, round the back of the new huts,' he said tightly.

'Top way?'

'That's what I said.'

For a moment she seemed about to say something, then went silent. Kepler was talking to the enemy, she realized.

'Start as quietly as you can, and don't use your lights until we are well clear of the camp.'

Rencha took her own cue from his cold tone.

'I want to leave a note for Mrs Bonsma the housekeeper because I won't be here when she arrives.' She found a pencil and a scrap of paper. 'What time shall I say we'll be back?'

Was it a ploy of some kind? He went to her and checked that the note was genuine. There was no reaction from her at all.

'Afternoon – I guess the drive and the hospital itself will take time.'

She finished the note, turned to go.

'I'll come too,' he said.

The implication was unmistakable, and she saw it. She had only to make a dash for it, for Ledoux and Maurette . . .

She bit her lips, nodded.

Together they went to the kitchen. 'No lights,' warned Kepler. He used his flashlight instead. Rencha put the note in the middle of the big table, with a couple of dishes and cups to draw attention to it. Was her apparent passivity and acquiescence part of the act?

Kepler carried Bossiere to the car; Rencha led the way, with blankets and cushions. Because it was so cold, they took the precaution of wrapping him in a blanket beforehand. Bossiere's colour was awful, but he still breathed. Rencha had roughly bandaged the head wound with a small towel: they could only hope for the best on the long, rough journey.

The whirr of the car's self-starter sounded to Kepler like machine-gun fire in the still night. Rencha might almost have been on his side, the cautious way she eased the car up the slope towards the top exit.

Kepler spotted his own car. 'Stop!'

He jumped out, opened the trunk, and disgorged the two guns, his own Colt and Bossiere's Walther, plus the spare magazines. He intended to take both for the face-out with the

Bakunins on their return. He relocked the trunk and joined Rencha. She offered no comment. The car jolted over the uneven basalt surface until Rencha found the track leading out of Corbel Camp.

'Headlights?'

The great Southern Cross, whirling towards its nightly grave in the sky above their route south to the Gougo–Carnarvon road, was closer to him than she was.

He hesitated, considering pursuit.

'If I lose the road, the jolt could damage him further,' she added.

'Okay. Make your best time.'

She did. Had the driver been anyone else – Kepler himself, for example – they would have thrashed out the insupportable build-up of inner tensions on the machine. With Rencha, transference took a different form. It gave her a supersensitivity in handling the vehicle, a rapport between it, herself and the road surface, like piloting a prize show-jumper. The stretch from Corbel Camp beyond the Bonsma homestead was (as others had found) bad and twisty; Rencha got the maximum out of it, a splendid balance between acceleration, braking and speed.

But two hundred and twenty kilometres is as long as the Golden Journey to Samarkand when there is ice in the heart and frost on the face of the countryside. Nor was their journey to Carnarvon golden: the landscape was the washed-out colour of a corpse, and as barren of life.

Their route took them due south for about fifty kilometres to the junction of the main road to Gougo. They had travelled this way before together on the way to Sak River – that journey had been golden. At the top of Hartogskloof, the first suggestion of dawn reached out for their faces from the east, a light so pale that it seemed fearful to throw the sun against the bleak landscape for yet another day of torment.

They passed the flatbeds' road which led to the repository itself, then they reached a small irrigation settlement, hidden by night and Sunday morning lethargy, called Vanwyksvlei.

Here they turned almost due south for the last run-in of eighty kilometres towards the little town of Carnarvon.

It was the sight of the Gougo turn-off earlier which had crystallized Kepler's plans. He could have ordered her to turn off to the repository: there was a round-the-clock at the gate and Captain Fourie, as a security man, was born to be wakened at any hour . . .

But he let it pass, and Rencha drove on, fast and skilfully. They exchanged no conversation beyond an occasional question from Rencha – once, after the heavily corrugated surface of Hartogskloof, legacy of the heavy SYNROC-R transporters, as to Bossiere's condition.

Kepler knew he would have to bring in South African Security. Time was running out: the day following, Monday, was the IAEA delegates' last, and it would be devoted to the inspection of the Gougo repository itself. He could not go to Captain Fourie with a series of half-baked allegations, and no concrete proof. Fourie might not regard the Bossiere assault in itself as watertight proof of terrorist activity. Kepler left the nagging, unanswered question of why Ledoux and Maurette had not killed Bossiere outright at the grave and went for his onward strategy. His mind reiterated that South African Security must be involved, and yet had felt unhappy about it. By some strange transference of Bossiere's own revenge-lust against Ledoux, his own overriding desire was to go it alone and bring Ledoux to book without outside assistance. Ledoux was now his own special target; he would get him.

That meant – proof. The proof lay in the grave. He decided that on their return from Carnarvon he would collect his own car and pistols from Corbel Camp and try to find out what Bossiere had not discovered at the graveyard. The thought satisfied and pleased him.

First, he would unearth one of the demolition charges and a detonator or two as proof positive for Captain Fourie. More than that, though, he would make a thorough search of the whole graveyard (it would be daylight) in a way which neither he nor Bossiere had had the opportunity of doing.

What were the terrorists going to be up to in the long day ahead? They could come and go as they wished; Corbel Camp was empty; they could plant the bomb where they intended in complete security.

Kepler glanced at Rencha, remoter than the nearest galaxy. Inside that beautiful head, perhaps, lay the secret of the Bakunin masterplan. Maybe that was why she had so readily agreed to come along. It might be giving Ledoux and Maurette just the opportunity of free movement they desired. Had he made a fool of himself by coming at all? Had he been completely outwitted again by this woman?

The bitterness of the thought ignited his anger. He demanded harshly, 'How far still?'

She indicated the loom of a hill on her right, dun as a dead dinosaur against the fading stars.

'That's a landmark. Another twenty-five or thirty kilometres.'

'Can't you go faster?'

It was unfair, and they both knew it. She didn't answer.

Sunrise was the colour of the dirty sheep which stood in small groups on the outskirts of the bleak little town as they drove in. The town's time-switch cut the street lights with a dramatic gesture as they entered the main street, almost as if it had been expecting them.

'Know your way?' Kepler's question was impersonal.

'I told you. I was here with pneumonia. The hospital's right over there.'

On their way, a single blue light burned at a building.

Rencha indicated it. 'Police. We'll have to report the accident after we've got him to hospital.'

'Accident?' Kepler repeated. 'Accident?'

She went on, 'Have you thought what you will say?'

Local police were a complication which had never entered his mind.

To buy time, he asked rhetorically, 'Have you?'

'As the official owner of Corbel Camp, I am obliged to report it.'

Checkmate.

'I see.'

They drove on another block and she repeated, 'Have you?'

'You called it an accident.' If he revealed what he intended to say, she would pass it all back to Ledoux and Maurette and they then would know how to play their cards.

'It's up to you.'

Their war of opposite wavelengths came to a stop, the hospital showed ahead. An ambulance stood in its forecourt.

To get a doctor in a small town is difficult enough; to prise a duty practitioner out of his bed by telephone on a Sunday morning at six o'clock is a virtual impossibility. The casualty attendant was as comatose as the patients in the wards. It required time and patience – and Rencha's limited knowledge of Afrikaans – to get her firing on sufficient cylinders to summon the doctor. The doctor insisted on knowing details of the casualty before he would even consent to come. Finally, he dressed with the alacrity of a prima donna going on stage for a gala performance.

The paleness in the sky turned to sun, and the day arrived. Kepler commandeered a stretcher and with Rencha's help carried Bossiere into the warmth of the hospital building. The attendant maintained that it wasn't her function to be a stretcher-bearer.

Kepler sat in the cheerless, clinical casualty room with Bossiere. Even the electric light shining directly into his eyes failed to evoke a single turn of the head or groan. They themselves had nothing to say to one another – what was there to say?

Nor had the doctor anything to say, when he arrived. He was a middle-aged man with an unshaven woolliness on his chin which looked as if he had wasted precious time on his way to the hospital rubbing his face against a sheep. He drew the towel aside from Bossiere's wound, sucked his breath through his teeth in a muted whistle, and asked Kepler and Rencha to leave.

As they reached the door, the doctor asked, 'Car smash?'

Kepler knew the extent of the strain he was under when he was tempted to retort, 'No, shovel.' Instead, he replied without inflection, 'Assault. Blunt instrument.'

'Then it's a police matter.' The way he said it, spelled more trouble.

Rencha intervened. 'We'll report to the police as soon as we know how he is.'

'He's bad. I can say that right away.'

'Will he live?'

'Lady, I haven't a crystal ball.'

A crystal ball would have been quicker than the next hour and a half the doctor spent on consulting his prognosis oracle. Rencha and Kepler ate a hospital breakfast, which helped pass the time.

When finally the doctor emerged, Rencha asked anxiously, 'Yes?'

'I have to consult my senior colleague.'

'Is that all you have to say?' Kepler demanded.

The doctor regarded him coldly. 'I have taken the Hippocratic Oath to sacrifice my sleep and my breakfast in service to my fellow-man. This I have done. You cannot ask me more.'

From all dedicated do-gooders, good Lord deliver us.

Kepler absorbed this. 'Your senior colleague?'

'He makes his round of the hospital on Sundays after church.'

'After church?' Kepler tried not to show, for Rencha's benefit, the impatience which was burning him up. *What were Ledoux and Maurette getting up to?* 'When will that be?'

'After eleven.'

'Eleven!' That meant they could not reach Corbel Camp before early afternoon, at the earliest!

'Is he alive?' Rencha broke in.

'If he weren't, I wouldn't be asking my senior colleague to examine him.'

Stumps drawn.

Kepler said, 'We will go and report to the police meanwhile.'

The prospect of sitting around for still another couple of

hours with his inner tensions tearing him to pieces was intolerable.

'You may not. Not until the district surgeon has examined the casualty.'

'May not?'

'That is the administrative process.' The doctor shrugged it off.

'Can't we call the district surgeon?'

The doctor eyed him from a height as lofty as the hillock Rencha had pointed out on their way in.

'My senior colleague *is* the district surgeon. Only when he has been may you report to the police. Now, if you will excuse me, I will go. You can see, I haven't even shaved yet.'

Testimony of dedication in that unshorn beard. Hippocratic Oath.

He went.

Kepler couldn't bear to sit in the cheerless waiting-room with Rencha. Their wrecked emotions were like a ship caught by her keel on a reef, irrevocably holed and sinking, but on the surface apparently still afloat. Under pressure of the hours, the vessel's back would break.

'I'm going for a walk,' he said briefly.

To kill time in Carnarvon is counter-reactive. It slays you. In ten minutes, Kepler had covered everything he ever wanted to see. He noticed a couple of curious glances directed at him. He realized the state of his hands and neck with dried blood. He went into one of the two hotels and washed them in the public toilet. The place stank of urine and Saturday night.

The church bells started to ring as he came out. Still an interminable church service to follow!

What was Ledoux up to?

It was 12.30 p.m. before the two doctors came up with their answer to Bossiere.

'The assault victim needs further examination. We have stitched the wound and made him comfortable. You may now inform the police.'

Except the police in Carnarvon did not take kindly to

unpleasant information just before Sunday lunch, especially when they established that an international scientist (so they were told) and member of the IAEA was involved. Officers had to be contacted, the district commandant of the area (stationed one hundred and thirty kilometres away at another town named Williston) had to be consulted by phone, and he, also, resented being dragged away from his Sunday mutton joint. The constable on duty, mindful of Sunday dinners on every hand, ordered a meal from the nearest hotel for Rencha and Kepler. Again, it served to pass the time.

Finally, it was 3 p.m. when they left Carnarvon for Corbel Camp. All day, they had spoken over each other's heads to others; now, together, there was nothing to say. The ground-swell of treachery and mistrust was grinding away at the keel of the ship which had set sail so splendidly. Reconciliation was impossible.

The sun was low when they reached Corbel Camp, but light enough still, Kepler decided, to get out to the graveyard and see what he could discover.

'Take the roundabout way in again,' he told Rencha briefly. 'I want Bossiere's accreditation card from your hut.'

He had thought of this during the long and painful drive home. There was no knowing what Ledoux and Maurette would get up to with a kosher DST card in their hands. Their backdoor approach to the car park would mask their arrival long enough for him to obtain the card and slip back and remove his car, even if Ledoux and Maurette were on the look-out.

They were.

Rencha and Kepler walked into the muzzles of two Bakunin pistols as she opened her door.

Chapter 35

Rencha kept going – straight to the drawer which held her small pistol. She had already palmed it into a firing position before Maurette – who had been assigned to take care of her while Ledoux marked Kepler – hurled himself forward and lashed out savagely at her trigger-hand with the barrel of his own gun. The force of the blow contained the counterpunch of fear and complete surprise at Rencha's daring move. His reply could so easily have been a shot to the head. But Maurette was under orders from Ledoux. She and Kepler were to be put through the hoop of interrogation – before they were disposed of.

Rencha gave a cry of agony, grabbed her hand, doubling over with pain as she did so.

'Stand!' Ledoux's gun was full on Kepler's face.

Maurette fell back, his pistol tracking Rencha as she writhed.

'One move and you're both dead!' There was no mistaking the menace in the barked command. Maurette had been relieved when Ledoux had ordered him to take Rencha instead of Kepler – the Bakunin remembered all too freshly those lethal blows from the Australian. Now it seemed he had been mistaken. The woman had shown incredible guts in going for the bright little weapon which now lay between them. Maurette whipped forward, snatched it away, as if he feared a kamikaze repetition of her earlier break. He resumed a firing position.

Kepler was too stunned by Rencha's lightning move – she had summed up the situation in a split second and acted within that split second.

'Don't shoot your own side!' All the bitterness of the long day, all her numbing treachery revealed in his discovery of Bossiere, was behind Kepler's sarcastic thrust.

'Shut up! In there – against the door! Both of you!'

Kepler moved towards the inner door leading to Rencha's bedroom; Rencha hung on to her injured hand, not moving. Maurette edged behind her, once he was sure Kepler could not jump him, and gave her a savage push which sent her staggering in the direction the Bakunin leader had indicated. Kepler instinctively steadied her; she threw him a glance of appreciation. Her eyes were full of tears, not of pain but anger. Maurette would have been dead if he had missed the few seconds before disarming her.

'Own side?' Ledoux's question was rhetorical, delayed-action, now that he and Maurette had shepherded their victims to safety. The terrorist guns were unwavering.

'She summoned you back from Vaalputs, didn't she? The three of you engineered what happened to Bossiere – he would be dead now if I hadn't . . .'

Ledoux seemed genuinely amused. 'Did she tell you that?'

'No. It's quite clear what you are up to.'

'Quite clear, Dr Kepler bloody West? Quite clear, you say? How clear – eh?'

They always said it took Ledoux a long time to warm up. Perhaps the long hours of tense waiting for their return from Carnarvon had speeded up the process.

'You tried to kill Bossiere because . . . because . . .' Suddenly Kepler found he couldn't say it. He had meant to mouth a string of accusations against Rencha and her double-crossing. Yet, her action in going for her gun inhibited him. Now she herself stood under the sights of her Bakunin bosses.

'You can't say it, eh, Dr West? Let me say it for you, then. This woman is Anna-Kai Cerny, a Bakunin courier.'

'I know that already.'

'You got it from Bossiere.'

'What if I did?'

'In the Bakunin, we have a code of conduct. If a member fails on an assignment, or is identified, there is only one way out – death.'

Kepler shrugged. Rencha concentrated on massaging her fingers.

'There is no such thing as a Bakunin defector. No such thing, I tell you! No one ever defected, except one.' He gestured at Rencha by a slight movement of the gun barrel. 'Anna-Kai Cerny.'

What Kepler replied was to keep up his own spirits. He didn't like the rising glare in Ledoux's pale eyes, and the gravelly note taking over in his voice. Either could be the hallmark of a madman or a killer.

'From my own experience, she probably realized what a shower of bastards you are.'

Maurette started forward at the taunt, but Ledoux restrained him. 'All right, Louis, he'll talk on the other side of his mouth soon.'

'I've got a score to settle with him, apart from anything else,' he said thickly.

Kepler asked levelly, 'Where'd you learn your fighting trade, Maurette – in the gutter?'

'Shut up!' snapped Ledoux. 'I said, there has never been a Bakunin defector: the penalty is death. In this case, her crime has been compounded. Not only did she defect, she became a collaborator of the DST.'

Rencha spoke for the first time. 'You've got it wrong!'

Ledoux said menacingly, 'I'll deal with you in a moment. I am telling Dr West what the situation is. There could be no greater crime than for a Bakunin to sell out to the DST. The DST!'

'DST?' Kepler pretended innocence.

'Don't play dumb with me!' Ledoux's voice became more gravelly, more sinister. 'You know perfectly well that Bossiere was a DST operative. How else would you have known to have gone to the graveyard, eh?'

His right thumb reached for the hammer of his gun; it seemed to have a life of its own. It palpated empty air in a tiny reflex arc, longing for the butterfly-kiss of the firing pin against the shell's percussion-cap. Ledoux himself was unaware of his action.

'You also know what Bossiere found in the grave.'

It was a flat statement of fact. Kepler did not reply.

Ledoux went on, mustering his words carefully. 'You are in it, the woman is in it – up to the neck. She was Bossiere's assistant; she called on you; you removed Bossiere from the graveyard . . .'

'To hospital in Carnarvon, where he will recover.'

It was an assertion calculated to needle Ledoux; it had the desired effect on Maurette.

'Aw, hell!' he burst out. 'Jeez! Jaw, jaw, jaw! Let's get it over and done with, Jean, instead of listening to this crap!'

Ledoux answered, surprisingly, 'Patience is bitter but its fruits are sweet, my friend. They will be sweet for you – when the time comes.'

He addressed Rencha. 'If Bossiere lives, that is his good luck. All that matters is that he is out of the way for the time we need him out of the way.'

It all sounded so reasonable, so reasoned – had it not been for that impatient thumb clamouring to get at the pistol hammer.

At Ledoux's words, a double revelation hit Kepler with the force of a Maurette mule-kick.

Rencha was in the clear! What a fool he had been!

That do-or-die rush of hers to get her gun plus his own deduction of the time factor of her original arrival at Corbel Camp – which he had allowed to get lost sight of in the avalanche of events – proved beyond all doubt that she was not associated with the Bakunin or Ledoux any longer. Ledoux had practically said so himself.

Kepler cursed himself inwardly. He should have trusted his own reasoning, trusted Rencha, trusted her love. She was none of the things Bossiere had accused her of, none that Ledoux was accusing her – she was his. And now he meant to get her out of this!

Kepler moved a fraction closer to Rencha, as if he also wanted her to feel the uprush of trust within himself. His flash of insight regarding her also threw a dissecting, assessing spotlight at Ledoux – if he were going to outwit him, he must know what made him tick. And he reckoned he knew now!

Ledoux was a pervert who fed on sadism. Maurette by contrast was an uncomplicated killer-thug: he lived by thuggery, and he would die by thuggery. Ledoux gained sastisfaction from – *needed* – his cat-and-mouse game with his victims. Fundamentally, he craved human intimacy; his corrupt nature used, instead of kisses, the torturer's mouth-probe; instead of the accoutrements of love, he resorted to the crab's electrodes. The feedback of screams and groans at some hideous stage of his proceedings gave him the naked contact with the victim's self he desired. That would satisfy him – perhaps for years – until the next time. Ledoux was as irrevocably hooked on sadism as a mainliner on hard drugs.

Ledoux's gun elevated so that its blue mouth was in a position to spit between Kepler's eyes.

He said, 'You – even the woman – can still get off the hook. Write down the formula for SYNROC-R and we'll talk . . .'

'Stuff it!'

Ledoux seemed pleased, rather than disappointed. Now he would not be denied the revolting inner cartharsis which torture brought.

'Very well. This is not the place to interrogate you. Someone might pass by chance while we are busy.'

Rencha broke in. 'The staff won't be here until morning, and Mrs Bonsma will have gone home by now.'

Ledoux pulled her note to the housekeeper from his pocket. 'We sent her home.' He waved the slip of paper at her. 'We knew where you were, when you were returning. Now you will write her another note, just in case we are late back tomorrow morning.'

Kepler felt a cold stab of apprehension. 'Tomorrow morning?'

Ledoux indicated the growing dusk outside. 'It depends on you. What we have to discuss may take up quite a bit of the night, eh?'

'I have to be back. The delegates will come from Gougo in the afternoon . . .' interjected Rencha.

'That is just the reason why we have to inform your housekeeper,' sneered Ledoux. 'You will say, you and Dr West will be back – by lunch-time.'

'But . . .'

'Do it, blast you!' he snarled. 'Get her paper and pencil, Louis! Close up, you two!'

Maurette went to the drawer where Rencha's pistol had been. He gave a low whistle.

'Look at this!'

He handed Bossiere's DST accreditation card to Ledoux.

Ledoux gave it a glance. 'I didn't expect to see this again. The situation now is very different from when we left this previously – no question of compromising ourselves at this stage by taking it as we might have before. With a little suitable doctoring, the card will come in very handy when we get back to France. Fancy a Bakunin passing himself off as a DST operative!'

Maurette found paper and pencil. Ledoux dictated, and Rencha wrote. 'Say, "I will be back in good time tomorrow for the IAEA delegates. Carry on with the arrangements we discussed."'

He addressed Rencha. 'I want a candle.'

There was a curious overtone in his voice which Kepler didn't like.

'In the cupboard near the kitchen sink. They're our standbys – the power's always failing.'

'Bring one, no two – and a bottle to hold it,' Ledoux ordered Maurette. 'You never know, we might need both.' Again, that off-beat note in his voice.

Ledoux passed Maurette Rencha's note. 'Put that where we found the other. It will fill the housekeeper with romantic thoughts about lovers' meetings.'

The spot for the assignation Ledoux had chosen was the same as the dead lovers'.

When Maurette returned with two candles and a bottle, the two Bakunins frisked their captives for weapons, found none, and bundled them into the station wagon.

They headed for the Haunted Graveyard.

Chapter 36

'Up, up! Get up those steps! Both of you!'

Ledoux traced the way up the stone ladder of the lying-in hut with his flashlight beam.

The terrorists parked alongside Bossiere's locked, deserted car at the graveyard gate, cut the headlights, and marched Rencha and Kepler inside at gunpoint. The rough ladder seemed to curve away up the white sloping roof to the stars. Neither Rencha nor Kepler knew that the summit of the egg-shaped structure had been foreshortened to form the hatchway which gave access to the upper chamber. All they could make out in the darkness was the stone roof and the shadow of the angled slits in the upper section, whose original purpose had been to deflect Bushman arrows. The fact that the top was open to the sky was not discernible from the ground.

'I'll go first,' interrupted Maurette. 'I can keep 'em covered as they come up, in case of any funny business.'

'Okay – away you go,' responded Ledoux.

Maurette sprang on to the lowermost step by the door, and swung himself up, torch in one hand, pistol in the other. He turned and checked the trio below – Ledoux standing a little back from Rencha and Kepler, armed likewise with a gun and flashlight.

He went up a couple of steps. 'Send West up first.'

'You heard,' snapped Ledoux. 'Any monkey business, and you'll get a bullet in the face from Maurette and one in the arse from me.'

Kepler realized that his chances of escape would evaporate with every step he took, especially (as the Bakunins' conversation seemed to indicate) there was a room of some kind above.

Maurette sat on the hatchway lip and tracked Kepler as he ascended. He needed only a fag in the corner of his mouth and a sub-machine-gun in his hand to make him resemble the pictures one sees of Nazi thugs on the edge of mass graves ready to mow down victims. His poise, enjoyment, nerve-strung readiness – all were the same. Kepler knew it would be suicide to attempt anything – yet.

Maurette deliberately blinded him with the flashlight beam to hinder any attempt at escape. The ruse was effective. Kepler reached the top of the ladder without realizing it. Maurette's hand clamped on his shoulder.

'In! Down! There's a ladder – it's not far! Then stand still where you arrive – see? If you duck away, I'll come after you!'

Kepler made out little through his blinded eyes except a dark pit as he went through the hatchway. His feet encountered what seemed to be the rough rungs of a ladder. In the room itself he could make out nothing; there was an elusive smell of what appeared to be paraffin.

He heard Maurette up above order Rencha up, and Ledoux's voice as well. Rencha came down the ladder. Then Maurette's torch was directed into his eyes again, and he turned aside to avoid it.

'Stand still!' Maurette was taking no chances. Kepler's chance would be as Maurette came through the hatchway. His body would practically fill the aperture. He wouldn't be able to aim his gun. Grab him round the legs, pull him in . . .

However, Maurette was too clever. He squirmed in, head first, shining the flashlight, quartering the pistol. He couldn't have missed, had Kepler tried to jump him.

'Back – back against the wall – behind the drum!'

The torchlight held a strange sight: in the middle of the small chamber was a flat wooden slatted 'bed' and on it stood a two hundred litre drum – the sort used to transport petrol or power paraffin. The slatted structure had once been used for grain storage. A star ricocheted off the angle of a firing slit, and showed as a point of light. These slits had been converted

267

from war to peace. They had served subsequently as ventilation slits for the grain to prevent spontaneous combustion.

Kepler recognized the drum set-up immediately for what it was by virtue of a thin plastic pipe leading from its bung through one of the firing slits to the outside. It was simple and effective siphon arrangement which supplied the living flame in the lovers' headstone with a continuous source of fuel. It needed no tending, and renewal only at long intervals.

Ledoux dropped in last like a god-in-the-box. His torch illuminated the far side of the chamber. Its beam fell on another drum, a green drum.

Kepler grasped Rencha involuntarily by the shoulder.

'In heaven's name . . .'

KO-RAD-003.

The beam revealed the lettering clearly.

Its wire strop set it apart from an ordinary drum.

Two objects at its base were not ordinary either.

They were the two SZ demolition charges Bossiere had pulled from the grave.

A Koeberg drum! A drum filled with lethal radio-active waste! Its place was safely lodged in the repository . . .!

Kepler rounded on Ledoux and Maurette, lunging toward them as if there had been no guns in their hands.

'*Where did you get this?*'

'Sit down! Shut up!' was Ledoux's response. 'Get yourself on to that wooden frame – don't move!'

Maurette reinforced Ledoux's words and compelled Kepler and Rencha to sit on the edge of the wooden frame, their backs to the power paraffin barrel.

'You don't know what you're doing! That drum is deadly!' burst out Kepler.

'I know what I am doing,' retorted Ledoux coldly. 'Louis, candle! You'll learn that pretty soon!'

Maurette passed Ledoux his gun, clambered up the crude pole ladder out of the hatchway, and returned with a candle and bottle he had brought from Rencha's kitchen. Ledoux squatted on his hunkers, his eyes fixed unwaveringly on the two captives.

Maurette thrust the candle into the neck of the bottle and produced matches to light it.

Rencha exclaimed, 'What about the barrel of fuel?'

'It's not petrol, it's paraffin – no danger,' replied Ledoux.

Kepler rapped out, 'Ledoux, I don't know what the hell you are playing at, but that green drum is deadly! It's filled with radio-active cast-offs and if you are going to blow it up with those charges . . .'

Ledoux was genuinely amused. 'You'd have to do better than that to be admitted to the Bakunin! Blow it up? Who said I was intending to blow it up?'

'Those demolition charges there . . .'

'Shut up, d'ye hear? I don't want any more from either of you – clear? Now . . .'

He walked far enough under the overhang to be able to stand upright; elsewhere he had to stoop. Both flashlights snapped out. The solitary candle evoked disturbed shadows against the sloping walls.

Ledoux held his pistol full on Rencha's head. The thumb which had waited so long that evening found its outlet. It pulled back the hammer, tested its tension, easing it back slightly. How much tension would it need to fall harmlessly, how much to blow out her brains?

Rencha had been through it all before, lived through it. Would she live again?

Ledoux's eyes fixed on hers, mesmerized her, pale reflectors which reached inward and found no mercy, no compassion.

'Ah!'

The tiny click and his sigh were instantaneous. He had got it right!

The release of tension jerked Rencha involuntarily, white-faced, to her feet.

Maurette knew his part in the act. He was at her with his gun and heavy hand before she could do anything; he shoved her back into a sitting position next to Kepler.

'You sadistic swine!' breathed Kepler.

'It requires a lot of practice,' replied Ledoux. 'It cost a few people their lives in experiments till I got it right. Anna-Kai Cerny should be grateful to me.'

Kepler felt the backlash drain his nerves and muscles. Would Ledoux try it again? He leaned sideways to Rencha, took her hand – a firm grip which said everything. Surprise flooded into her face.

But there was no time for anything. Ledoux swivelled the pistol on him and was busy cocking it. He hadn't yet started the hellish hammer routine.

'There is one way you can save yourself – and the woman,' he said.

'The hell with that!' growled Maurette. 'Kill 'em!'

Ledoux's pale eyes turned on him. They were more telling than a blow to the mouth. Maurette went silent.

'I'm listening,' Kepler said.

'The woman is a traitor,' Ledoux replied obliquely. 'There is no such thing as a defector in the Bakunin. She is under sentence of death.'

'By whom – a kangaroo court?' retorted Kepler.

'I am the leader of the Bakunin Movement, and it is my privilege to execute traitors. I intend to do my duty.'

The calm, off-beat announcement was more chilling than any process of a summary terrorist court.

'That's not the way it was – not that way at all!' broke in Rencha. 'You devils killed Charles my doctor whom I loved, after he had helped one of you out of the goodness of his heart, a Bakunin that came to the door after he had been shot by the police. Your reward that you battened on him, put pressure on him, until he wouldn't go along with you any more! Then – you killed him. I know – I was there!'

'You lie, Anna-Kai Cerny! You were our courier, the best terrorist courier in Europe. I wasn't the leader then . . .'

'Detroyat was.'

'. . . I have heard how good you were. You were one of us.'

'I wasn't! I was dragged in because of Charles! I lived with him, shared his secrets, his bed, everything! Won't you understand? I was a courier only because of him, because I spoke so many languages! I only carried your messages, nothing more . . .'

'Once a Bakunin, always a Bakunin.' The cliché echoed from the shadowed walls. Bossiere, Kepler recalled, had used the same words to justify a fact which changed his entire picture of Rencha. Kepler reproached himself briefly now; he would never forgive himself for misjudging her. Every word the Bakunin leader was uttering now made her innocent of involvement in whatever the terrorists were up to at Corbel Camp.

'Couriers don't only carry messages,' retorted Ledoux. 'They carry guns, money, orders. That is what you did. You are a traitor!'

'I passed on verbal messages, that is all. I never ferried guns or bombs!'

'The Bakunin never write down anything and a reliable courier is worth her weight in fine gold,' went on Ledoux. 'You conveyed orders from the leaders to our members. You were part of the set-up. A Bakunin through and through.'

'Never! The moment you shot Charles I fled from France! Escaped – here!'

'I wasn't in the Bakunin then, so I don't know the other side of the story,' replied Ledoux. 'But you have admitted your crime. You fled, you defected. That in itself is enough. You thought by hiding yourself away in this god-forsaken corner of Africa we would never find you. But we have. And the penalty is . . .'

He raised the gun at her head and let go the hammer, all in one swift movement. His expertise was incredible.

There was no crash. Only a click of steel on copper.

Rencha cringed aside. Tension drummed off the walls.

Ledoux swung the gun on Kepler. He said tightly, 'You can still save yourself, and the woman. Write down the SYNROC-R formula – now! It will indemnify her from

Bakunin justice. That I guarantee. Take your choice.'

The foresight aimed on Kepler's forehead was the alternative.

Kepler remained silent. Rencha moved against him. It might be the last time they felt each other's bodies.

Ledoux was a slow starter. Kepler's contemptuous silence was the trigger which fired the torture motor, a lust for brutality which was like the smell of strong drink to an alcoholic. In the half-dark his eyes, striking and wide normally, closed to mere slits; the upwelling of incipient cruelty seemed to sharpen the structure of his face.

'Get her clothes off!' he ordered Maurette.

Ledoux snapped the pistol on full cock; there was to be no toying with percussion caps any more. The hammer would strike, and the bullet would be on its way.

Maurette got behind Rencha, ripped off her sweater upwards over her long hair. Her arms remained in the sleeves. She was pinned in a woolly strait-jacket.

Ledoux's lips were wet; his breath came in quick pants.

Rencha fought Maurette as he tried to tear the sweater completely free. Maurette rammed his gun into her stomach. It knocked the breath out of her. She keeled over sideways in agony.

Ledoux's eyes strayed. In that split second, Kepler was up, switch-stepped, got Maurette between himself and Ledoux's gun, and went for the back of Maurette's neck.

Ledoux's gun came up. The crash and flash of the shot in the confined space drowned sight and hearing. It froze everyone. The bullet whanged off the wall.

Kepler knew that he had not been hit. He went on with his attack on Maurette. But he hadn't bargained for Ledoux or his lightning reaction. The terrorist's boot tripped the legs from under him. The assault became a staggering lunge which ended on his elbows and knees and his head against the concrete floor. Ledoux's boot went into his ribs, and then against his head. The candle's single flame burst into fragments of exploding light like a multiple warhead. Something else took

im amidships as he plunged down a long tunnel into blackness.

Kepler was uncertain as to what woke him. It was to a
consciousness he would rather not have had.

Rencha was naked. The clothes they had ripped from her
lay about the floor. She was crushed against Ledoux's body.
The Bakunin leader had one arm round her neck. It could
have been an embrace or a stranglehold. Maurette stood close
with a gun.

Kepler thought he was being forced to watch a gang rape.

Ledoux's gun was missing. Instead, he held in his free hand
what looked like a tiny phial. Rencha whooped for breath
under the forearm clamped round her. Ledoux was forcing
Rencha's neck back, trying to get at her eyes.

Maurette must have heard the tiny sound Kepler made on
stirring. His pistol swivelled at him.

Ledoux noted, too, that he was conscious.

'Stop! For God's sake, stop! What are you doing . . .!'

Ledoux indicated the object in his fingers. It wasn't a phial
but a small tube.

'Instant-setting superglue,' he said. 'It will take a surgeon
to get her eyelids open again – if the stuff doesn't blind her
anyway.'

Rencha's fight for breath was appalling. Ledoux had to raise
his voice for Kepler to hear. 'That SYNROC-R formula! Now!
Or she gets it!'

Kepler dragged himself to his knees. 'Give me a paper and
pencil . . .' he got out.

An incoherent burp of dissent burst from Rencha's mouth.
Ledoux tightened his arm. Her face went purple; her head fell
forward. Her lovely eyes were twice their size, distorted, no
sense left in them. Ledoux let her go; she sprawled untidily to
the floor.

Ledoux didn't have eyes for her. His gun was back in his
hand. 'Hand him the paper – don't get too close,' he ordered
Maurette.

Maurette found a slip of paper and pencil in his pocket –

perhaps he was expecting to be asked for them during the interrogation – and passed them to Kepler. Kepler's vision blurred, cleared, blurred into wateriness as he tried to focus.

'Get on with it!'

'Light – I need more light.'

That helped. Kepler mustered a series of cryptic symbols on to paper. No one but Dr Waldegg would realize that the essentials were missing. And Waldegg would not be back before tomorrow. The ruse would buy time, at least.

Ledoux took the paper contemptuously. The lack of climax to the proceedings had left him frustrated, in a dangerous mood. He had not expected that Kepler would buckle.

'They were tougher than you, those Argentines were,' he said, as if the reminiscence would offset his disappointment. 'True, we had to use rougher methods to make 'em come clean – the electricity, the crabs, the mouth probe, the "submarine" . . .'

'You bastard, Ledoux, you bastard!'

Ledoux went forward and jerked Kepler's face upwards by the hair. 'Don't tempt me, see? Don't tempt me! We've got what we came for, and I suppose that's what matters. Dr Waldegg will know whether this is kosher when he returns tomorrow.' The brittle sound he emitted was meant to be a laugh. 'It doesn't matter. We've hedged our bets. We've got this – and a more spectacular bonus as well. *That's* more to my liking . . .'

Rencha started to move on the floor, fumbling to find her clothes.

'For Pete's sake give them to her!' snapped Ledoux to Maurette. 'I can't stand tit all over the place.'

The floor had stabilized for Kepler. He was able to hold his head up.

'You won't get away with this, Ledoux, even if you kill us.'

Ledoux ignored him, addressed Maurette. 'Tie 'em up, get the cord from the station wagon.'

'You'll be okay?'

'Leave me your gun. Go! Quick!'

Maurette passed his leader his pistol, went up the ladder through the hatchway. Kepler got himself into a seating position on the wooden 'bed' next to the drum. Rencha, her back turned, was dressing herself. Ledoux stood clear, the candle between him and his captives, a gun in either hand.

He allowed silence to scrape their nerves. It was so still that they heard Maurette's jump to the ground from the lowermost stone step.

If Ledoux had not been alone, he probably would not have said what he did. But his craving for intimacy – that pathological intimacy through pain – had not been satisfied by the earlier proceedings. Kepler's note of the formula had cut him off in full flight, so to speak. Normal stimulus . . . the sight of Rencha's naked body – left him cold. His needs were more perverted.

He said abruptly, 'I am not going to kill you. You are going to kill yourselves.'

Kepler did not respond: what was to follow? His mind jumped to the demolition charges, within hand's reach.

'A pair of lovers.'

Silence.

'There's a pair of names on the headstone down there,' he went on. 'Two bodies in one grave. The light burning all the time means something. What is it?'

Rencha had regained her clothes and some of her composure. She sat hard against Kepler.

'They were lovers. He died of thirst. She shot herself over his body.'

Kepler had forgotten that the terrorists were ignorant of the Bonsma family tragedy.

Ledoux smiled. As before, Kepler didn't care for it. 'Ah, but how romantic – just what we want! This time a new pair of lovers are found dead – a suicide pact, eh? You would like that? It touches my romantic French blood. However, Maurette and I will spare you the personal trauma – we will do the job for you.'

Rencha put her hand in Kepler's. His reply to Ledoux was

derisive. He wanted to keep him talking, just in case . . .

'A staged suicide! That won't convince anyone, Ledoux! The calibre of the bullet alone will give you away.'

Ledoux began to enjoy twisting the arm of his victims.

'Anna-Kai Cerny very obligingly provided us with the suicide weapon – her little Bakunin pistol,' he sneered. 'I wouldn't be such a fool as to use my own or Maurette's gun.'

Kepler kept a bold face. Ledoux seemed to have relaxed; his eyes were almost their normal size again – and just as fathomless. A wave of nausea passed over Kepler. How long could he go on bandying words with a psychopath?

He said, with great effort, 'You've forgotten post-mortem techniques and the time factor, Ledoux. The police will be able to tell right away . . .'

There was something horrifyingly normal about discussing their own corpses.

'I am not going to shoot you tonight,' he broke in with a detachment which made it sound as if he were discussing someone else. 'In all the uproar of tomorrow's happening, I am sure the police will not find time to bother about sorting out the finer points of a suicide. They'll have too much hay on their forks for that.'

Kepler hung on to his senses. 'Meaning?'

Maurette spoilt it. He returned with the length of thin, strong nylon cord the terrorists had used to lash the marker drum to the roof-rack.

Ledoux clammed up. 'Wait until tomorrow.'

Tomorrow? What hellishness was in store – tomorrow?

Kepler's tottering senses were in no shape to sort out the connections between Ledoux's innuendoes and half-revelations. They were meant to be just that, in order to needle him. Perhaps Bossiere had found out everything – but why then hadn't he paid the full price for that knowledge?

Ledoux snapped, 'Tie 'em up, Louis. Tight as hell.'

'You bet.'

Kepler couldn't have resisted even if he had wanted to. Maurette first went to Rencha's wrists and ankles, then his own. The constriction of circulation probably helped topple his senses. Through a gathering haze he saw the two Bakunins blow out the candle, take it away, and make their way through the hatchway, watchful with their guns to the last moment. Which was true darkness or his own oblivion, he had no way of telling. Even the star vanished from the firing slit.

Chapter 37

KO-RAD-003.

The Radwaste drum code sputtered through Kepler's mind like a fuse and prickled him back to consciousness.

KO-RAD-003!

He forced his eyes open. The fog in his brain matched the darkness in the loft; for a moment he wasn't sure which was which. A cluster of stars above the hatchway could have been real – or stars reeling in his brain.

Kepler hauled his shoulder clear of the drum, against which he had fallen after passing out. The nausea rose in his throat. He retched drily.

'Kepler!' It was Rencha. 'Kepler! Are you . . .?' There was something like a sob from the darkness near him. 'I've waited . . . I thought . . . thought you were dead . . . waited, but you didn't answer . . . Kepler! Can you hear me? Can you hear me? Answer me!'

He said, 'Rencha, darling.'

'Dear God, I thought they had killed you.'

Kepler tried to move; he became aware of the cords on his wrists and ankles. 'I'm okay. How long have I been out?'

'I can't see my watch. I don't know when they left.'

'They've gone – you're sure?'

'I heard the sound of their engine. It went away. It could have been hours ago. I've lost count of time.'

Kepler swivelled to try and see his watch; the stars and the darkness danced together, merged, separated. For the first time, he was aware of the pain on the right side of his head, high up above the ear.

'Kepler! Kepler! What . . .!'

'I'll be all right in a moment,' he answered thickly. 'Anything for some water!'

There was a silence. When he had pulled himself together, he said, 'I managed to catch a glimpse of my watch – a little after midnight.'

'Can you feel anything in your hands?' she asked.

He experimented. 'Very little.'

'Try flexing your fingers – I've been trying to keep my circulation going. Talking to you, too, to keep my spirits going . . .'

'Rencha . . .'

'I know what you are attempting to say, Kepler. I want to hear it more than anything in the world. But now is not the time. Tell me when we get out of here. We have got to escape! We owe it to ourselves!'

KO-RAD-003.

The symbols which had jerked him back to consciousness were before him again; at his back, somewhere in the blackness, was the physical reality, a green drum with a wire strop, chalked with that lettering.

'We owe it to others, too.' He went on urgently, 'Rencha, listen, we're sitting here with a drum of radio-active waste which somehow Ledoux and Maurette must have stolen . . .'

'Why?' she broke in. 'Why, Kepler? What possible use can they have for it? We don't even know whether it is genuine.'

'It's genuine, all right,' replied Kepler grimly. 'I saw the first load as it was being made up. I recognize the writing – you see, we hadn't the time for the proper stencilling, so the codes were written on with packaging pencil. I'd put my head on a block that that drum is genuine.'

'While I've been lying here, I've been thinking,' said Rencha quietly. 'To me, the demolition charges are the main thing. I

278

understand the way Bakunins' minds function. My interpretation is that there will be a bomb explosion at Corbel Camp when the delegates return from their inspection of the repository.'

'What would that achieve?' demanded Kepler. 'True, it would kill some important people, but in turn what would that prove?'

'You have to do mental handsprings to keep up with terrorists' reasoning processes,' she replied. 'What we must try and do is project ourselves into their way of thinking. The sixty-four-dollar question is, what do Ledoux and Maurette hope to achieve or demonstrate by a bomb? One of their objectives is now out . . . Ledoux got from you what he was after, the formula for SYNROC-R.'

Kepler managed a thin laugh. 'Of course I didn't write down the correct formula. The moment Dr Waldegg sees it, he'll realize that it's phoney.'

'Then if it's a bomb, why did they leave behind here two charges, detonators, and the radwaste drum?'

Her juxtaposition of words sparked the answer which the code had thrown to the forefront of his mind when it had prised him out of semi-consciousness.

'Rencha. That's it! That's it! Drum – charges!' he exclaimed excitedly. 'Bossiere maintained that what remained in the grave were left-overs – the weight of the two suitcases was anything up to forty kilograms. These two charges weigh only a fraction of that! Ledoux and Maurette had to find a *container* for the main body of the demolition charges – a drum would fit the bill! A radwaste drum – a green drum!'

'Not even fanatics like Ledoux and Maurette would risk opening a drum of radio-active material.'

'No, no!' Kepler went on excitedly. 'Not *this* drum! What if they used *another* drum like it. What if somehow they smuggled that drum into Gougo . . .'

'A fake drum would never have passed the security checks,' Rencha answered.

'I don't know how they managed it, but it's my guess they did, by some hellishly ingenious method, and that a drumful of high explosive is now waiting for the delegates when they visit Gougo tomorrow . . .'

'Today,' corrected Rencha. 'It's after midnight. We're into the last day.'

'The main inspection will be this afternoon, for several hours after lunch,' Kepler resumed. 'That is when the blast must take place. That is also what Ledoux hinted at with his remark that the police would have too much hay on their forks to worry about a lovers' suicide – us! Dear heavens! An explosion in the repository! It would finish Gougo for good, sanitize the whole surrounding countryside for years!'

'You're trying to talk yourself into a solution,' argued Rencha. 'How could the drum have got in, in the first place?'

'If it didn't emit radio-activity and had the same code, looked the same, had the same colour and same weight, it would!'

'It's ingenious, but there are too many soft spots in the argument, Kepler.'

'We've got to get out of here!' Kepler was imperative. 'One phone call to Gougo will be enough! If their records show that a drum bearing the code KO-RAD-003 has been admitted to the repository – and all drums are carefully logged – then that is it? We'll have the place cleared, the delegates moved to safety, try and establish where the first transporter-load of drums was stacked in the final disposal trench . . .'

'Couldn't we intercept the delegates before they leave Vaalputs even?' asked Rencha.

'If we can get out in time, we will,' responded Kepler. 'They are, as you know, due to fly direct from Vaalputs to Gougo in the Hercules and land at the Gougo airfield at 11.30. There is a short pre-lunch inspection of the reception facility where drums are off-loaded on arrival. They then have lunch at the repository and spend the afternoon until 3.30 inspecting the repository itself. Finally, they fly back to Cheating Pan . . .'

Rencha added sombrely, 'If we assume that there is to be a bomb blast at Gougo this afternoon, it means that Ledoux and Maurette will come on here afterwards and kill us. That is what he meant when he spoke about a lovers' suicide – staged.'

'It all fits, Rencha!' went on Kepler. 'Our only hope is to get out of here!'

'I have thought about that until my mind reels – all the time you were out,' she replied. 'The only possible means of rescue seems to be by being snatched out of the hatchway by helicopter.'

The fantasy was so way-out that it killed their exchanges. There was a long silence.

Finally, Rencha said, 'I'm frightened, Kepler. I've never been so scared in my life.'

'We have each other – even if we don't get away.'

'That's all that keeps me going.'

She said again after a while, 'I'm cold, Kepler. I can't feel anything in my hands any more.'

The cold came with the wind. It paralysed further their immobilized muscles. It threw sand against the beehive's sloping surface with a muted susurrus like a ghost fumbling its way through curtains. The friendly stars vanished from the hatchway in the rising murk. Icy grit filtered in from above into their eyes. It was better to keep them closed. There was nothing to be seen, anyway.

Rencha tried rolling about to keep her circulation moving; Kepler tried it too, but the effort of hoisting himself upright again into a sitting position sent the blood wheeling through his mind and left him nauseated.

They gave up trying to speak. Their desolation was colder than Cheating Pan outside.

Somewhere, somehow, reasoned Kepler, must lie a way of escape! Less than twelve hours from now, if his assumptions and deductions were correct, there would be an explosion which would tear life and limb apart and all hope of SYNROC-R's international acceptance . . .

Slowly, painfully, Kepler eased himself into a position to try and check the luminous dial of his watch. He could make it out! There was light!

'Rencha! Rencha! It's dawn!'

It was. As Campbell had found for *Bluebird*'s speed runs,

281

the wind always fell off with the approach of day. The wind died; the curtain of murk over the hatchway disappeared; the aperture became grey with incipient light. It might have been better if it had stayed dark. It revealed Rencha lying half-on, half-off the wooden frame which supported the fuel drum. Her face was grey with pain and strain. Kepler hadn't bled much from Ledoux's kick to the head: he needed to test the bruising with his fingers. They were a dirty purple from lack of blood caused by the restricting nylon cords. They felt as if they would never move again.

Rencha managed a wan smile. 'Does it help us, Kepler?'

'We can see – there must be something we can do!'

She talked like a sleepwalker. 'They even took the candle, Kepler. They could have left us one small bit of warmth and cheer for the night.'

Candle. Light. Flame.

'What is it, Kepler?'

Kepler jerked upright so forcefully that he had to bite back the pain from his bonds.

He indicated by inclining his head in the direction of the thin plastic tube leading from the drum on its way to its ultimate destination in the headstone.

'We don't need a candle – we've got our own flame.'

'What are you saying?'

'That pipe! This drum at our backs! Rencha!'

'They're about as useful in getting free as the radwaste drum against the wall . . .'

'We can burn ourselves loose! Use a piece of the pipe and the paraffin! Burn these cords loose!'

'I don't get it – the flame isn't here, it's down in the graveyard . . .'

'Remember when they frisked me before we left Corbel Camp?' went on Kepler, his voice vibrating with excitement. 'My lighter – it's still in my top pocket! Maurette was only after guns! He left the lighter alone!'

'Can you get at it with your hands tied, Kepler?'

'No. You'll have to try.'

'Why not simply use it by itself – it'll do the trick without resorting to the fuel pipe . . .'

'It doesn't have the endurance for a long operation like burning the cords,' replied Kepler. 'We need a flame that will go on for some time. Here is my plan . . .'

When he had finished, Rencha said, 'Aren't you inviting disaster? The drum could explode.'

'It won't, it's paraffin, not petrol,' replied Kepler. 'It's a small risk we have got to take anyway. It's our only hope. Ready?'

'Yes.'

Kepler's plan was simple, its logistics were tough. It got off to a tough start. The simple act of closing the gap between Rencha and himself was an agonizing, muscle-cracking, painful exercise which left his head wound throbbing and his forehead sweating. When he was alongside her, she couldn't reach his top pocket without dropping on her knees – the agony lanced through her calves and ankles as she did so – and extending her hand in a kind of prayerful attitude. Had the pocket button been closed, she would never have opened it. Her fingers were like fumbling unguided automatons. Finally, she extracted the tiny gold-plated sliver of metal. Would she ever be able to spin the wheel to spark it alight?

The only place the plastic pipe became accessible to anyone unable to get to their feet was low down near the floor where it led through the firing slit exit.

'We do this together,' said Kepler. 'I go first.'

'Wait a few minutes – the blood is starting to ooze out of your hair.'

'No. Every minute counts. Here goes.'

His attempt to roll to the firing slit misfired. At less than a quarter of the distance, the blood pounded so fast through his head that he was in danger of passing out. It wasn't a roll of the body: it was an angular exercise which tore at the arms, the shoulders, the neck muscles, everything.

He reached the pipe. It was impossible to judge how long he had taken. He lay on his back because it was more comfortable than his shoulder. He saw a gleam of sunlight through the hatchway.

They must hurry!

Rencha's passage to him seemed slower and more awkward even than his own. In fact, it wasn't, but her face was white when she reached him. He had to give her time to recover before they could proceed with the next step of the plan.

Kepler went for the plastic pipe with his teeth. It was as unyielding as a Bakunin's mind. His teeth clamped hard; the pipe, now slippery from saliva, eluded him. He could not grip it manually to obtain a firm bite.

He manœuvred it across his lower jaw, then bit as hard as he could.

All night he had craved for water; now, instead, he got a mouthful of acrid paraffin. The reflex of nausea was instantaneous. He ejected the paraffin like vomit.

The pipe dripped paraffin at the chewed section. It was only half severed.

Kepler knew he couldn't stand another mouthful of the pungent stuff.

'I'm going to pin down this section by sitting on it – can you try and pull it apart at the break?'

Rencha's portion was wet with the slippery fuel. Laboriously, she managed to loop it round both her hands to give herself purchase. The procedure occupied a quarter of an hour.

Then she jerked. The pipe snapped.

Next, she rolled back to where she had dropped the lighter. She held it extended while Kepler presented the length of plastic pipe. However, she could not open the lighter's top.

She put it down, banged her right hand savagely against the concrete floor to obtain enough circulation to make a finger work.

Her fingers became operative.

8.30 a.m.

From the direction of the airfield came the rumble of heavy aircraft engines.

Rencha looked questioningly at Kepler. 'It's the Hercules.

It's on its way to collect the delegates,' he said. 'Then comes the last lap of their tour.'

Last lap – to death?

'In three hours they'll begin their inspection of Gougo,' Rencha added.

'At any cost, we have to get out and warn them,' Kepler jerked out. '*Now!*'

The pipe gave a sputter or two, died, flared, then it picked up steadily. They had a tiny living flame of their own!

Kepler held out his wrists and she inserted the flame beneath the lashings.

He had expected heat like a blowtorch, instant severing of the tough nylon fibres. Instead, the flame was disappointingly cool and weak. It seemed hours before the cords fell away. In fact, it was not more than fifteen minutes.

8.45.

The agony of his circulation returning was worse than the bite of the bonds themselves. The blood pulsed through his fingers like liquid fire. It also set his head throbbing again.

Another twenty minutes was lost before he could muster enough flexibility in his hands to use the flame on Rencha's wrists and free her.

9.05.

Both of them were still roped by their ankles.

They repeated the process, Kepler freeing himself first while Rencha regained the use of her fingers. Hers were still not mobile enough to function by the time the cords had fallen from his ankles; he helped her with massage, stopping for long intervals while the pain of returning circulation lanced through his limbs.

Then – they were both free!

Chapter 38

10 a.m.

Countdown to catastrophe.

'Let's get out of here – quick!' said Kepler tersely. 'Do you think you can manage?'

Rencha tried a step or two. 'It's like trying out a pair of shoes that's too tight.'

The sun was up; a square of light formed by the hatchway streamed down on to the fuel drum in the centre of the chamber; it also showed Kepler the radwaste drum with its giveaway code standing against the wall, as well as the spare demolition charges and detonators.

The rough ladder made of round poles led out into the open air – and freedom.

Kepler started towards it, then went back to the plastic pipe, at the end of which their flame of deliverance still burned. He doused it between his thumb and forefinger and hooked the pipe up to stop any further siphon effect.

Next, he put his weight on his right foot on the ladder's bottom rung, but doubled over from the agony of it. His back still ached from the final terrorist kick which had put him under. Finally, it took him five minutes to ascend the handful of steps. With each rung, however, his feet recovered as his circulation returned to normal. Then, his head and shoulders rose out of the hatchway.

He made a quick check. There was no sign of anyone, no movement. Bossiere's car, shrouded grey from the night's dust storm, still stood by the gate. In the direction of the airfield the air seemed thick, amorphous still with fine dust. It was warm outside, too, by contrast with the built-in chill of the upper chamber.

'All clear – come!' he called down to Rencha.

Rencha emerged into the sunlight. Grime and near-death competed for pole position in the shadows round her eyes. But neither of them could dull the brightness in them when she regarded Kepler.

'I don't believe it! I don't believe it!' She held on to his shoulder. 'Kiss me, Kepler!'

He looked deep into her green eyes. 'My mouth is like a flame-thrower – full of paraffin.'

'I'll remember it the better for that.'

They kissed. 'Paraffin or no paraffin, I don't want this ever to end.'

'We must hurry, Rencha – every moment is precious.'

They climbed cautiously down the stone ladder, their grip becoming surer as they progressed. The door of the hut below was shut. Kepler checked it warily. Nothing.

'Things are going our way,' said Rencha. 'We'll use Bossiere's car to get to Corbel Camp.'

She was mistaken. The doors were locked, the ignition keys removed.

Kepler peered through the driver's window. 'It's got one of those sophisticated anti-thief locks on the steering column. I'd try smashing a window and connecting the ignition wires if it hadn't. But I wouldn't know how to get past a gadget like this.'

The elation which had buoyed them up dimmed.

'What is the alternative?' asked Rencha.

'Walk.'

As if to emphasize his response, Rencha pulled off her sweater and held it over his head for improvised shade against the sun.

'Not before I've done something for that place on your head. It's oozing again.'

'Forget it,' he said. 'Look, we've got to get to a phone – some point of civilization where I can contact Gougo and set the wheels in motion.' He glanced at his watch. 'It's already 10.30. In an hour, the Hercules will be at the repository with the delegates.'

Now he, like Rencha, pulled off his windcheater and held it over his head.

'The nearest place is the airfield,' said Rencha. She indicated the tracks. 'That way. Three kilometres.'

'Is there a phone there?'

'I doubt it. I expect all their contact is by radio.'

'That's fine,' replied Kepler. 'I can have them signal Gougo airfield . . .'

'You've forgotten something,' answered Rencha. 'They didn't have enough ground crew or maintenance staff to man Cheating Pan, Vaalputs and Gougo airfields at the same time. So they loaded all ground grew in the Hercules for Vaalputs. From there, they'll take them to Gougo. Only by late afternoon will they be back here.'

'How do you know this?'

'When Ledoux and Maurette returned so unexpectedly, I also asked about the flying personnel – I wanted to know in order to feed and accommodate them. Ledoux said that only the pilot, co-pilot and flight engineer had come aboard the Hercules. The three of them went on to Gougo, where they are normally housed, and gave Corbel Camp a miss because they knew nobody would be expecting them. Cheating Pan will be unmanned until this afternoon.'

'That's that, then. How far is it from the airfield to Corbel Camp?'

'Another four kilometres. Listen, Kepler, to go to the airfield on the off-chance is taking an enormous unnecessary risk. The road makes a dog-leg – the total distance to Corbel Camp via the airfield is seven kilometres. If we cut directly across the Pan – I'm sure I can find the way – it's a mere five kilometres.'

Kepler ran his tongue over his lips and eyed the sky. The sun appeared to be using every particle of dust filtering down as a minute reflecting mirror. The total effect was unnerving.

'If we don't have water, we'll go blooey,' he said bluntly.

'I also need to fix your head.'

They walked in silence to the shade of the lying-in hut.

'If we simply stay here, we're sitting ducks for Ledoux and Maurette when they return after the blast,' said Rencha.

'I've got it!' exclaimed Kepler excitedly. 'Bossiere's car – water!'

Rencha was smiling, too. 'I never thought of the radiator.'

'It isn't the radiator I'm thinking about – if you drink water with anti-freeze in, you'll poison yourself, and I'm sure it contains it because of the cold. No, the windscreen washer reservoir!'

'If the doors are locked, how will you open the bonnet?'

'Here!' Kepler grabbed a spade and together they made for the abandoned car. 'This won't take a moment!'

He lifted the spade to thrust the blade under the bonnet catch but paused.

He indicated the blade. 'Look at that!'

Rencha recoiled. 'Blood.'

'They must have used this on Bossiere.'

Kepler thrust the steel into place, threw his weight on the shaft. The catch gave way with a snap.

'There!'

The plastic reservoir for the washers contained more than a litre of water. Kepler ripped loose the plastic pipes and electric pump fittings and handed the bottle to Rencha.

She shook her head. 'You first. My mouth's not full of paraffin.'

The water tasted stale and flat, but it was water. When they had both swallowed some, Rencha bathed Kepler's head cut as best she could and tied his handkerchief round it as an improvised bandage.

'How long will it take us to Corbel Camp?' he asked.

'I reckon we should get there by midday,' replied Rencha. 'The last stretch is off the Pan proper – it's among the anti-erosion works on the fringe and the ground's hard and even there. That should speed us up.'

'Midday – time enough, but it's cutting things fine,' answered Kepler. 'The IAEA delegates will just have arrived and Fourie can evacuate them before any damage is done.'

Rencha took her bearings from the airfield track; she headed off half-left from it, to the south-west. This was to short-circuit the roundabout dog-leg route which they had discussed.

Cheating Pan.

They should have remembered the reason which gave the place its name; they should have thought about one of the dead lovers beneath the headstone who had lived all his life there and knew it so well, yet had lost his way in the mirages en route to his tryst; they should not have allowed their one firm landmark, the fifteen-metre hill named Deelkop which backed the graveyard, to be swallowed up before they started to walk blind.

11 a.m.

'Kepler – we're lost!'

Kepler wondered whether his delirium of the night had returned: the blank haze was interspersed with creeks of shining water, great whirlpools of light and reflections – grotesque, other-world figures seemed to form and dissolve in thin air about them. Their sense of direction was not helped by the improvised burnouses they had made of sweater and wind-cheater round their heads to keep off the blazing sun. Their directionless progress was slow; purple weals and swellings now showed round their wrists and ankles from their cords as blood pounded through their veins in their effort to move fast.

'Stop! Water!'

Rencha nodded. Kepler added, 'As little as we both can. There is no knowing how much we'll need before we're through.'

'I haven't a clue where we're heading,' she said desperately.

'We can try steering by the sun.'

It was she again who evoked the goad which was making him drive his body remorselessly. In one hour's time, she reminded him, with the same note of desperation in her voice, the IAEA delegates would begin their pre-lunch inspection of Gougo . . .

'After that, anything can happen!' added Kepler. 'Rencha, somehow we have to get a warning through to Gougo!'

The sun was a shakier compass than their own guesses. Its disc seemed to be all over the sky from the distortion of the mirages and its winter inclination to the south left them further bewildered.

All it seemed to do was to generate more sickening heat, more fantastic mirages – on one occasion, they thought they had homed in on the airfield when they saw *Bluebird*'s track. But the track did not lie flat – one end of it pointed like a launching-ramp to heaven. In reality, it was kilometres away.

The water was down to less than half a litre. The full horror of Cheating Pan threw itself at the two staggering figures, stunned by heat, directionless, as they passed into successive stage-curtains of mirage-light, wheeling, sliding light, like elusive fiends of hell dancing them on to death. It was a nightmare ballet of blinding brilliance and spontaneous movement.

11.45.

The pre-lunch inspection of the repository was due to start in fifteen minutes. By now the Hercules must have landed and disgorged its victims for Ledoux's bomb.

When?

'Keep going – we may hit something.' That was the best that Kepler could do. The paraffin taste had recurred in his mouth. Sips of water had not been enough to exorcize it.

They shielded their eyes with their hands, they shielded their senses against the rising panic in both their hearts.

The eye-and-mind contorting light ballet came at them as soon as they moved on again from a water-halt – a bodiless, intangible nightmare which would take on tangible form as death the moment they dropped down from exhaustion.

Then – they felt new ground under their feet before they saw it – their heads were down, their eyes blanked out.

They were off the hideous surface of Cheating Pan!

They were on the hard ground among the scrubby flats and anti-erosion works on the Pan's edge!

This new surface robbed the atmosphere of Cheating Pan's death-dealing mirages. Like a dream, the air cleared to their left; Cheating Pan lay on their right.

Far away, about two and a half kilometres, Kepler guessed, rode a posse of white corbelled roofs on a dun surface – Corbel Camp!

The domes beckoned like some mystic city of Arabia to the pilgrim out of desert sands.

There was a hysterical edge to Rencha's voice. 'We must have circled and backtracked quite close to the edge of the Pan, Kepler! Half a kilometre, maybe, and we didn't know – couldn't see –'

Kepler passed her the water bottle. 'We'll finish this, get on. Ledoux must have passed on my phoney formula to Dr Waldegg by now. That in itself would have been the go-ahead for the bomb.'

They walked – tried unsuccessfully to run – on the flattest sections.

12.45.

They reached the first signpost at the camp's entrance and Kepler said, 'We can't be seen like this – we'll go to my hut first.'

Rencha tried to smile. 'Water! That's all I want.'

Kepler's hut was protected from view from the main farmhouse block by the new lounge complex. Preparations and activities for the IAEA delegates' scheduled arrival late that afternoon would be proceeding there under Mrs Bonsma.

They threw themselves at Kepler's bathroom water. Drink, wash, drink. Kepler threw off his dust-stained clothes, she worked on his wound with sticking plaster as he spruced up. She, too, tidied up hastily; they both rushed to the main block where the phone was.

Mrs Bonsma eyed them curiously. 'Car trouble,' said Rencha. 'Skid. Kepler got a bang on the head.'

His anxiety to get to the phone left Mrs Bonsma staring after them as he rushed for the telephone cubicle.

'Exchange – get me the Gougo nuclear waste repository – quick! *What!*'

'*Kepler – has it happened?*'

He blanked out the mouthpiece with a hand. 'Lines down!'

Rencha took the instrument, spoke in Afrikaans to the operator. 'The lines are down – last night's windstorm!' She spoke rapid-fire. 'Exchange – I must get through to Gougo! It's a matter of life and death!'

'I'm sorry, we're doing all we can,' came the reply. 'It's Monday, so the technicians began late. Their first job was to locate the fault . . .'

'Where is it?' Rencha cut in. 'Where can I phone from to get through to Gougo?'

'It's between Hartogskloof and Gougo. The repair teams are still trying to pinpoint the spot.'

Rencha didn't reply. She had translated the operator's words for Kepler as she spoke.

'There's only one thing for it!' snapped Kepler. 'We must get to Gougo by car! It's about one and a half hours' drive – you know the route. We can still make it by 3.30 – that's the time of the final inspection of the disposal area.'

'If the bomb hasn't gone up by then.'

'We're still in with a chance. Come! You drive!'

Rencha hung back for a moment. 'We can't go on without something to eat and drink – we're half dead on our feet anyway.'

'Quick! For pity's sake, quick, Rencha! We'll eat as we drive.'

'Whose car – yours or mine?'

'Mine. Yours must be pretty low on fuel. In the car park – hurry!'

Kepler sprinted for the park. He knew first of all what he wanted. He took his Colt from the boot and checked the long ten-round magazine, and thrust the spare shells he had with the weapon into his pocket. Next, he checked Bossiere's gun. One magazine was in place; there was a spare with eight more. He might need every shot.

1.15 p.m.

Rencha accelerated out of Corbel Camp.

'How did you explain to Mrs Bonsma?' asked Kepler.

'The less said, the better. Just that I hoped to be back in the late afternoon.'

'Hoped.'

'That's the whole story, isn't it?'

The first, twistiest section of about ten kilometres out of Corbel Camp was the worst of the entire one hundred and ten-kilometre route. Rencha seemed to know every depression, every soft patch. But at a bad corner she lost control and the car spun off the road into the thick sand. It stayed on its wheels, however. They lost ten minutes getting it back on the road.

Then they were on the harder, straighter section of road running due south from Corbel Camp towards the junction of the main road which would take them on to Hartogskloof and Gougo. Rencha began to make time.

Kepler spotted it first – a high plume of dust coming towards them. At speed.

The road surface was slightly below the general level of the surrounding countryside because traffic had cut into the soft ground.

Orange and blue flashing lights therefore showed first before the approaching vehicle's body became fully visible.

'Rencha – look! Flashers . . .!'

The white body emerged as the vehicle raced towards them.

'It's an ambulance! What is an ambulance doing in these parts – an ambulance . . .!'

Rencha's eyes left the road and locked with his for a split second. 'Only an emergency would have brought it here. The worst could have happened, Kepler!'

'Stop it – find out –'

There was no need. The ambulance's siren whooped and ululated as it caught sight of them. It swung into the centre of the road to block their path and halted, still yelling, in a cloud of dust.

Rencha braked and also slid to a standstill.

From the white bandage round his head, it seemed that the ambulance was being driven by a casualty.

Kepler threw open his door.

'*Bossiere!*'

294

Chapter 39

Bossiere leapt out, hurried across to the car as unselfconsciously as if a pyjama top tucked into ordinary trousers, untied shoes with no socks, and a white turban were standard ambulance driver uniform. No cap. Just that mound of hospital dressing. His pallor matched it: off-white grey.

'Where are they?'

The flung question short-circuited explanation of everything that had gone on since Kepler had carried his unconscious body from the graveyard. It was superfluous to ask who 'they' were.

'We're after them – get in!' Kepler was equally cryptic.

Rencha broke in. Her gesture embraced his rig, the ambulance, everything. 'What on earth . . .! Are you all right? – That wound . . . What are you doing in an *ambulance* . . .!'

The grimness on the DST man's face lightened a fraction. He patted his bandage. 'They didn't know that Henri Bossiere had the reputation of having the thickest skull in French rugby. Whatever hit me . . .'

'A terrorist. A spade.'

Kepler's monosyllables made Bossiere equally brief. 'I bluffed the doctor. I asked for a priest – he was in Carnarvon for his monthly visit. He went to him to give me the last rites.' He grinned. 'I stole his ambulance in reply. Here I am.'

'Didn't they come after you?' asked Rencha incredulously.

'You can drive an ambulance like a bat out of hell and nobody dreams of stopping you,' Bossiere responded. 'They actually help – get out of your way. Plus lights, plus flashers.'

'We're wasting time,' snapped Kepler. 'Get in, Bossiere.'

'Tell us while we drive.'

'*Where are they?*'

'At the repository.'

'A bomb?'

'For sure. A big green drum stuffed full of explosive. You were right.'

'How'd you know?'

'I found the drum's counterpart – real radwaste. Top of the lying-in hut.'

Bossiere glanced at the plaster on Kepler's head. 'Trouble?'

'Yeah. It'll keep.' His voice went into rapid-fire. 'Get in, for Pete's sake, and let's go! Ledoux and Maurette substituted a drum of explosive for one of radwaste – God knows how, but they did. Somehow – again, I don't know how – they insinuated it into the repository. It will go up before 3.30 – it may have gone up already! Get in.'

'No,' retorted Bossiere incisively. 'Dump the car, take my ambulance. It's a passport in itself. If Ledoux and Maurette spot us, they won't realize who it is until the last minute. It's the perfect cover. I'll explain more along the way. I'm sure of the facts now.'

'What were you doing heading for Corbel Camp?' demanded Rencha.

'I didn't know then what I know now. I wanted to nail them. I needed my gun . . .'

Kepler snapped open the car's cubby-hole. He pulled out the short-barrelled Walther and its spare magazine.

'Here it is.'

The sight of the weapon was like a restorative hypodermic shot in the arm for Bossiere. Even his colour looked better.

He said, 'Ledoux is mine when we find them.'

Kepler snatched his own gun and spare ammunition from the cubby-hole also.

'Rencha – can you drive that thing?'

'I'll drive anything.'

She proved she could. She wheeled the big vehicle round, cut the flashers and siren (Bossiere showed her how) and picked up speed. Bossiere and Kepler were with her on the big front seat. The ambulance's soft springing was a help on the poor road: soon she was driving on the limit. At her suggestion, they consumed the coffee and snacks she had brought.

Bossiere asked Kepler, 'Where do you hope to find them?'

'I don't know. We'll have to play it by ear. The first thing to do at the gate will be to get Security to clear the whole area . . .'

'It's too late for that already,' answered Bossiere. 'Let me tell you my reading of the situation. Your deduction about the drum was masterly – even if we don't know at this stage how they smuggled it in. Where do you reckon the drum of explosive is – right now?'

'Either buried, or about to be buried, in the disposal trench in the final excavation area.'

'How far is that from the gate?'

'For crying out, Bossiere, what in hell has the distance of the trench got to do with what we're discussing? It's a bomb, man, one hell of a bomb . . .'

'I told you that myself,' retorted Bossiere. 'Thirty to forty kilograms of Russian demolition charges.'

'Then what . . .'

'Ledoux and Maurette have to detonate that drum. They had a whole range of detonators to choose from – we saw them at the graveyard – but they threw them out. Why? Because Ledoux will be using his own – a superdetonator.'

'What are you driving at?'

'That so-called radio he carried everywhere with him – I explained to you what it was all about . . .'

'Main road!' remarked Rencha. She swung the ambulance westwards, towards Hartogskloof, towards Gougo. 'Sixty kilometres to go!'

'It's got an effective range of only about two or three kilometres, and my guess is that they will fire it from *outside* the repository gate and not risk their skins by being too close to the heart of the explosion.'

'At 3.30 all the delegates are scheduled to be at the disposal area,' said Kepler.

'That's the critical time, for sure,' responded Bossiere. 'Our

Bakunins will find some excuse not to be there with the other delegates. That doesn't matter. They'll also have to keep well clear of the contamination hazard which is going to follow immediately after the bomb goes up.'

Kepler said quietly, 'God help Gougo, if that happens. God help us all!'

The ambulance was up the steep bends of Hartogskloof now. The road surface was corrugated and loose from the heavy radwaste transporters. Rencha went round in a series of controlled slides; the ambulance heeled down on its soft suspension.

'Ledoux and Maurette will keep well clear of the radiation hazard as well as the blast itself,' repeated Bossiere. 'If there's a small hill anywhere close to the gate, that's the place they'll choose – it will give the radio signal clear passage.' He fiddled with the Walther. 'We can start looking for them within five kilometres of the repository gate.'

'And then?'

'There are too many contingencies for us to make a plan at this stage. We'll play it off the cuff when we see the set-up.'

'That doesn't give us much time, Bossiere.'

'Less than even you think. It takes only a second to throw the radio detonator switch. Now – how'd you find out about the drum?'

'After Rencha and I had taken you off to hospital, we walked into Ledoux and Maurette's guns at Corbel Camp on our return . . .'

When he had finished, Bossiere said, 'The living flame pipe, eh? I wish I'd been there. As it was, I lay in bed . . .'

'Fuming,' smiled Rencha. She braked, slowed. 'Here we are. Turn-off to Gougo. Twenty kilometres to the gate.'

'Stop!' ordered Bossiere.

2.30 p.m.

'Kepler, you and I are getting in the back at this point,' he said. 'Rencha, it's over to you now. You've got to get us within pistol range without Ledoux and Maurette suspecting.'

'Will this help?'

298

Rencha had found the ambulance driver's cap. She put it on.

'Good girl – they won't spot your hair now until the last minute. Tuck it well in, will you?'

'When you sight Ledoux and Maurette, start sounding the siren and using the flashers – distract them as long as you can. Rush 'em. Surprise is vital – there will be no preliminary warnings.' He addressed Kepler. 'Go for Ledoux's radio with your gun. That, above everything. One second! It must be smashed before we even account for the terrorists themselves.' He smiled grimly, a long-dead rugby allusion rising in his mind from excitement. 'Go for the ball and not the man, Kepler! The ball's the thing! Wreck it!'

Rencha asked in a small voice, 'What if the bomb has already gone up?'

'Then keep well clear,' replied Kepler. 'The place will be sick with radiation.'

'We could detach the ambulance for casualties.'

'We will, if we have to.'

'One last thing,' said Kepler, rechecking his Colt. 'It worries me. There's a road from the Gougo airfield – it's south-west of the repository – which skirts the fenced-off area and joins the road we're now on about five kilometres from the gate . . .'

'We can't take everything into account,' retorted Bossiere. 'From what you've just said, it seems in any event that to be within detonation range Ledoux and Maurette must position themselves between that five-kilometre turn-off and the repository gate – right?'

'Right.'

'Into the back, then.'

Rencha waited until she heard the rear doors shut, then accelerated away.

The vital airfield road junction was upon her before she realized it. Five kilometres to go!

She slowed a little, in order to watch either flank of the road.

One of the five kilometres disappeared into the dust.

Then two . . .

3.15.

Any moment the ambulance would be at the gate.

A flash of reflected light off a windscreen lanced like a laser beam from her right into Rencha's eyes.

Her reactions were lightning-quick.

She snapped on the siren's switch and flashers: that was the signal to Kepler and Bossiere in the back that she had sighted the target.

She hauled the big wheel round, flung the ambulance, lights flashing, siren screaming like a suicide's soul, at a rough track running up a small hillock on her driving side.

Less than half a kilometre away, Ledoux and Maurette were poised at the side of their station wagon.

The radio detonator stood on the bonnet. Its antenna was up, in position to transmit the firing impulse.

Rencha switched into a lower gear, gunned the engine hard. The heavy vehicle bumped and bounced like an off-balance steeple-chaser. The siren whooped; the lights flashed. Would the Bakunins be deceived long enough?

They made a mistake: they hesitated.

Rencha braked, slewed side-on to present the back doors as near as possible to the target. The ambulance's nose ducked like an out-of-control carrier plane.

Bossiere and Kepler's shots seemed to equate with the crash of the rear doors flung wide.

It was impossible to see whose bullet – it could have been both Kepler and Bossiere's – pumped into the detonator. It spun away into pieces.

Ledoux's reflexes were superb. Nor did surprise deaden them. As the radio went flying, he flung himself out of the line of fire behind the station wagon. His intervening snapshot at Bossiere was too hurried for reliable aim.

Now Maurette was down also, crawling on to the far side of the station wagon to join Ledoux for cover.

A shower of glass from the windscreen spurted over Rencha. She never heard the sound of the shot. She threw herself on to the floor where the bulkhead and engine would serve as armour-plate against further bullets.

The close-range exchange of fire was rapid, vicious, deafening. Then – the terrorists' fire cut suddenly. The fusillade continued from Bossiere and Kepler.

Ledoux knew what he was doing; he had been under fire before.

In a moment or two, both Kepler and Bossiere's guns were empty. Ledoux had noted the way their fire had been simultaneous. There had been no pause to let one man do the work while the other would give covering fire when the first magazine ran out.

Now both magazines were empty together.

Ledoux used that desperate intermission while Kepler and Bossiere rammed new shells into their pistols. In a flash, he leapt behind the steering-wheel. Maurette, with him, screwed down the passenger's window as the engine took and Ledoux gunned it brutally. Maurette ignored Rencha in the ambulance as they whipped past: he was after the men with the guns.

The bounce and cant of the accelerating vehicle was too much for accurate aim: his parting snapshots at Kepler and Bossiere went anywhere.

Then the two men were on their feet, magazines replenished. But it was too late.

The dust which the fleeing vehicle kicked up blanketed their aim. A couple of shots whanged away hopelessly.

Rencha anticipated the chase. In the seconds the last volleys went after the Bakunins she hauled herself from the floor on to the driver's seat – full of glass fragments – and fired the engine. She moved round to pursue Ledoux and Maurette. A hole in the windscreen, the size of a cricket ball with long accompanying tails of opaque splintering, was slightly to the left of where her face had been.

She barely came to a full halt to pick up Kepler and Bossiere. They dived in next to her. There was no need for Bossiere's order, 'After them!'

Chapter 40

The ambulance bucketed down the rough track, into the wake of the Bakunins, into the wall of dust thrown up by the fleeing station wagon. Dust spurted through the hole in the windscreen. Its dry harshness blended with the acrid reek of spent cordite and hot gun oil in the cab.

Rencha had difficulty in seeing the way; the ambulance smacked into and crashed over a big rock on the blindside verge, the side obscured by the shattered, clouded glass.

It was only a short run to the main road at the hillock's foot. A plume of dust was already building up in the still air to show the way Ledoux and Maurette had taken – left, away from the repository gate, left, towards the main road, left towards Hartogskloof – and then?

Rencha jammed her shoulder against the driver's door in an attempt to find a spot to focus on the turn. The murk seemed thicker where the station wagon had wheeled round. She slowed prematurely.

'It's only a couple of kilometres to the gate,' she said quickly. 'We could get help – Security – perhaps intercept them along the main road . . .'

Bossiere's reply was as short and ugly as the short, ugly Walther in his hand.

'Never! Get on! After them!' He brandished the pistol. 'There are seven slugs left. One of them is for Ledoux. This is my show, no one else's!'

Kepler broke in, 'I also have a private score to settle with Ledoux and Maurette.'

Bossiere jerked out, 'It was the most agonizing decision of my life, back there. To have the man under my sights, and to fire at something else – ten years – Ledoux! Turn left, after him, for Chrissake! He hasn't escaped me yet!'

Rencha swung into the main road, put on speed. Visibility was worse here. Down the hillock track the ambulance had been moving relatively slowly, now speed made it a high-risk projectile, blind except for a section of the right side of the screen.

'I can't see!' she burst out. 'I'll kill us all if I go on like this!'

'Stop!' snapped Kepler. 'Bossiere, help me knock out the glass – it's the only way.'

Bossiere acquiesced reluctantly. 'Use the barrel! Kick it out – anything! Only for God's sake, don't let 'em get away!'

They lost more than five valuable minutes while the two men punched out the glass. Any fragments which fell on to the bonnet they left; they had, however, to get rid of the shards on the seat before they could get on.

Now they could only travel as fast as they could stand the wind whistling in. The dust thinned; they were losing ground all the time on the Bakunins. Rencha drove faster than her streaming eyes justified. By the time they reached the junction of the Gougo road with the main artery leading to Hartogskloof and beyond, the ambulance had lost sight of the terrorists' giveaway dust trail. The chase had been on for a mere twenty kilometres; they were lagging badly.

Rencha slowed for the major turn ahead. She had to raise her voice to be heard above the wind's din.

'Which way?'

'Corbel Camp, of course,' retorted Bossiere. 'Then on to the graveyard.'

Kepler, who was sitting next to Rencha, said, 'You seem damn sure – for all we know, they could be heading in the opposite direction.'

'There is explosive at the graveyard, and where there is explosive, there Ledoux will be. Those two SZ charges are still enough to do immense damage. That's where we'll find them.'

'They've missed their main trick at the repository – what can they get up to with the rest of the explosive?' demanded Kepler.

'I don't know – it is impossible to project oneself into

the warped mind of a Bakunin.' Bossiere's chin thrust out aggressively. 'Motives, targets – at this stage, I couldn't care less about them. All I want is Ledoux in my sights.'

As the main road came up, Rencha exclaimed, 'Look – skid marks! That's the way they went.'

Hartogskloof! Corbel Camp!

She made the turn, gunned the engine afresh.

Kepler took the opportunity to speak before his voice was drowned out by the wind. In any event, he had to yell at Bossiere.

'Maybe you're right – for a different reason. Ledoux and Maurette could grab the SZ charges and hijack the Hercules later this afternoon when it comes in to land with all the delegates on board. It's a long-range aircraft. They could still save their skins.'

'It all points to the graveyard, or the airfield, and the SZ charges!' retorted Bossiere. 'Faster! Faster!'

But Rencha couldn't go faster. The wind in their faces and eyes was more effective than a speed control monitor. They simply couldn't face into it. The smoother road surface offered better going; Rencha couldn't take advantage of it.

It was now 4.15 p.m. They were approaching the head of Hartogskloof pass, where the road dropped down from the Gougo plateau on to the lower-lying ground ahead.

They had come about forty-five kilometres.

Now the sun threw its weight on the side of the pursued, making vision difficult as it sank low ahead. Soon it would be sunset.

Rencha tried to squint round the sun visor. It provided some relief from the wind, but at the same time inhibited her view still further.

Perhaps if the windscreen had still been intact they would have been able – from the high ground at the top of the pass – to track the tell-tale dust plume now streaking for the Corbel Camp turn-off. As it was, they had to go by guess and by God. That guess brought a further loss of time at the top of Hartogskloof.

Rencha slowed. Bossiere swore. Kepler couldn't understand the French, but the tone was enough.

'What now?'

'What if they're waiting for us in the pass – ambush?' she asked. 'Any one of these slow bends could be a trap.'

Kepler threw in his weight behind Rencha. 'She could be right, Bossiere! There's no sign of the station wagon ahead – they could have stopped. They know we're on their heels.'

'We are three sitting ducks here together in the front seat,' added Rencha. 'They couldn't miss from the roadside. I can't take the bends fast, they're too tight.'

'Must everything slow us down!' Bossiere exploded, gesturing with the Walther. 'I *know* they're heading for the graveyard! I feel it in my water!'

'You know, we know,' answered Kepler. 'But if they kill us in the pass, who else will know? I back Rencha.'

'What do you intend to do – walk down with a red flag in front of you to see if the way ahead is clear?' Bossiere lashed out.

'Stop!' Kepler told Rencha.

'No!' protested Bossiere.

'Get in the back again with me,' Kepler told him rapidly. 'We'll ride shotgun, one on either side. Knock out the small side windows, hang out. We'll see 'em just as they see us, that way.'

Bossiere had already flung open his door as Kepler said to Rencha, 'If they're there, you know they'll go for the driver first, don't you?'

'Yes, Kepler.'

He held her wrist for a fraction of time. 'Good luck. I'll try for the first shot.'

Then he was gone. She heard the crash of the side windows being smashed.

Rencha felt totally exposed and alone. She headed into the first bend as gingerly as a novice sweeper into an unmarked minefield.

Nothing.

She tried the next – faster. The rocks and trees looked twice their proper size. She could have reached out and touched them. She could still smell a faint smell of dust.

Nothing.

She lost count of the number of bends to the bottom of the pass. When eventually she spotted the causeway ahead, she tramped on the accelerator and raced to the open patch on the far side.

She paused, engine running.

The red fuel level danger light came on.

Kepler and Bossiere piled in alongside her.

'Look!' She stubbed a finger at the gauge. 'Almost empty.'

Bossiere went pale. The mottled colour which excitement of the shoot-out had brought to his face, plus windburn, disappeared.

'No!' he burst out. 'It cannot be! I cannot lose Ledoux like this! Not because of a piddling empty petrol tank!'

'The ambulance has been driven hard – first from Carnarvon, that's two hundred and twenty kilometres,' Rencha pointed out. 'Then half that distance back again from Corbel Camp to the repository. Now we've added another fifty kilometres . . .'

Bossiere snapped the safety catch of his gun on and off, as if that would help.

'We'll never make it home to Corbel Camp,' continued Rencha. 'If I thought we had enough even to get by, I'd make for the Bonsma homestead. But it's also too far, it's close to Corbel Camp itself.'

'You can't – can't – let Ledoux get away!' mouthed Bossiere.

'There's only one thing to do, to overshoot the Corbel Camp turn-off on the main road –'

'No!' Bossiere's agony was exquisite.

'. . . and carry on to Brospan, where Ledoux rendezvouses with the helicopter, remember?'

'How far?' The question was torn from Bossiere.

'About five kilometres . . . There's a filling station at the trading store there . . .'

The coloured attendant was goggle-eyed at the sight of the

ambulance with its smashed screen and windows. Rencha dismissed his curiosity by saying the vehicle had been in an accident.

'Fill it up – quick!' Rencha said.

'No electricity, power failure,' said the man. 'I have to pump by hand.'

Bossiere went round the far side of the ambulance to hide his face. The sun seemed to be taking as long to go down the sky as the fuel did into the tank.

Kepler checked the time when they finally moved off. 4.45 p.m. It would be dusk by the time they reached the graveyard. Rencha drove.

The Brospan–Corbel Camp road was never meant to be traversed in half an hour: it was only 5.15 when they sighted the beehives of Corbel Camp. None of the trio had eyes for their rosy luminosity in the fading light.

'Ready?' Bossiere had his Walther ready.

'Try their hut first – at any sign of the station wagon, hold everything!' Kepler said.

'I have only six rounds . . .' Bossiere said.

'You said seven earlier.'

'I told you, one is reserved. How many have you got?'

'Plenty,' answered Kepler. 'A whole lot in my pocket, plus a full magazine.'

'Ledoux is mine – understand?'

'I understand.'

The uprush of adrenalin to their veins was wasted. The parking space at Ledoux's hut was vacant. So was the car park.

Rencha pulled in to the kitchen door. Bossiere and Kepler remained behind. Mrs Bonsma spotted them in the ambulance. But Mrs Bonsma was discreet. If Kepler's second irruption into Corbel Camp that day with Rencha was love, it was a manifestation of it which had not yet hit the outback at Cheating Pan. She asked no questions. Nor about the bandaged man whom she recognized as one of the French delegates. When pressed by Rencha, Mrs Bonsma said she had not seen either Herr Lentz or Herr Fichte, although she was expecting the IAEA delegates at any minute.

So was the air controller at the airfield: there had been a technical delay at Gougo airfield; he hoped the Hercules would be in soon because poor light was a risk and there was no flarepath.

The man regarded the battered ambulance. 'What's cooking?'

Kepler countered with a question of his own. 'You're sure everything's okay at Gougo?'

'Why shouldn't it be?'

He had never heard of Ledoux and Maurette. But he had heard, in response to Kepler's question, the sound of a vehicle – he hadn't actually seen it because he had been busy in his caravan – passing about an hour previously. It had seemed to follow *Bluebird*'s track deep into the Pan . . .

The ambulance shot off parallel with *Bluebird*'s track. The graveyard turn-off would still be visible. Perhaps the air controller's anxieties about flying conditions were justified. A fine pall of dust was beginning to form under the impact of what was known as a 'berg wind'. It stirred up the surface of the Pan. The air was thick, the hot wind seared their already seared faces.

Kepler murmured, half to himself, 'They couldn't have doubled back and given us the slip and hijacked the Hercules at Gougo.'

'They're at the graveyard.' Bossiere trusted his water.

They were.

From a distance of about a kilometre, they sighted the station wagon at the gate.

Chapter 41

'Stand off! Keep out of range!'

Bossiere held up his hand like a cavalry officer restraining his troop from the charge.

'Pistol or rifle range?' Kepler had laid out spare shells along the dashboard.

'Pistol. They're not likely to have a rifle.'

Rencha halted. The long light from the sun at their backs reached out and coloured the lying-in hut, the stone wall encircling the graveyard, and, behind, the skull-bare hill called Deelkop. She found it hard to reconcile the peaceful, almost elegaic scene with that light-drunk morning when the sun had powered its way across the same stretch with the intent of killing both Kepler and herself. Hard, too, to credit that inside the white dome lurked one of the most dangerous terrorists in the world.

That he and Maurette were there, there was no doubt. The lingering sun showed Bossiere's car still, next to the terrorists'.

Bossiere indicated his own car. 'I don't like it! Why didn't they take my car? It could have provided them with the perfect get-away vehicle if they felt the station wagon was too easily identifiable. Keep moving – a little closer, but not too close.'

'Maybe they're lying in wait for the Hercules to return,' suggested Kepler. 'They could have the explosive charges all ready and high tail across to the airfield when they hear it coming in to land.'

'I don't see men of their experience resorting to such last-minute hit-or-miss tactics,' replied Bossiere. 'I don't like it, I say! The pattern is all wrong! It isn't the way Bakunins operate!'

Rencha made a wide sweep, at a distance, of three sides of

the graveyard wall. The fourth, at the rear, was blocked by Deelkop.

'See anybody?' Bossiere's was a nervous, redundant question.

'They could be holed up behind the wall – perfect cover,' said Kepler. The sun threw long shadows on the far side of the wall fronting them; a company of men could have found shelter behind it.

'I can try and draw their fire,' Rencha said.

'Go in closer,' Bossiere agreed.

Rencha accelerated suddenly towards the gate where the two vehicles stood, then swerved in a fast circle.

A single shot rang out from one of the firing/ventilation slits at the top of the hut.

'Now we know! Good for you, Rencha!'

'That's where they are!' exclaimed Kepler.

Bossiere threw cold water on his enthusiasm. 'More than ever, I don't like it! Until a moment ago, Ledoux and Maurette held all the trumps – of surprise, concealment – then they give away their position with a useless shot. Even with a rifle, the ambulance would have been a tricky moving target in this light and at the range.'

'It's white,' Rencha pointed out. 'That makes it easier to spot.'

'Ledoux and Maurette knew from the moment they saw the ambulance it was us, and that we'd come after them,' answered Bossiere. 'All they've done in reply is to sit on their backsides and pass us the initiative on a plate. We've got to go in closer and find out what they're up to!'

'What's the plan?' asked Kepler. Rencha smelt his sweat of excitement close next to her. It blended with the hospital odour of Bossiere's turban. Both men's fighting blood was up. 'Try and rush them? In *there*? It's as safe as a blockhouse. Shoot it out at long range? Keep them nailed until help arrives . . .?'

'There is going to be no outside help on this job!' Bossiere reiterated. 'I told you, Ledoux is mine. I have him . . .' he pointed with the Walther's short barrel '. . . right there.'

Rencha said in a small voice, 'Nothing is more dangerous than a cornered Bakunin.'

Bossiere gave a half-smile. 'I know that also. Try again, Rencha. Trail your coat.'

Again, one shot. It was lost somewhere in the half-light.

'We could go on doing this all night,' observed Rencha. 'Once it's dark, they will have the advantage.'

'While it was light, don't forget, they threw away their biggest asset – mobility, freedom of movement,' answered Bossiere. 'I must know *why*!' He addressed Rencha. 'Drive round the back of the graveyard and stop behind the hill. You'll be perfectly safe there. Kepler and I will try the wall at the back and make an approach to the hut from there . . .'

Rencha took her hands from the wheel. 'I'm not staying behind! What do you take me for? A Victorian Dresden-china lady who has to be cosseted . . .'

'You're not coming with us!' Bossiere retorted hotly. 'You haven't even got a gun!'

'Is that my fault?'

'No, but . . .'

'There are no buts.' Rencha threw in the gear, faced the ambulance the way they had come, back towards the airfield.

'Either you take me with you, or I drive back to the airfield! Take your choice!'

'Saints above!' exclaimed Bossiere. 'Here we have one of the world's worst terrorists penned down and you want to defect!'

'Not defect – participate.'

Bossiere leaned round Kepler and eyed her speculatively. Then he shrugged, tried to grin, but it failed. 'Once a Bakunin, always a Bakunin,' he said. 'Okay.'

Rencha reversed direction towards Deelkop. As she did so, there was the sound of aircraft engines from over the airfield. The big Hercules came in low, its downward-pointing landing spotlight blazing like a noisy falling star.

Rencha parked behind the hill. Kepler stuffed spare shells into his pockets – Bossiere had only the one magazine for the Walther.

'You'll have to do the rapid-fire work,' he told Kepler. 'I'll save mine for selected targets.'

Until the three emerged round the shoulder of Deelkop, they did not realize how comforting its bulky cover had been. Between the hill and itself and the graveyard wall was a small open space, within range of the hut.

'Run!'

They sprinted for the wall, across the open ground.

One shot.

They flung themselves down, unharmed, behind the stone wall.

'Listen to that!' exclaimed Bossiere. 'It wasn't even a heavy-calibre bullet!'

'They took my gun – it's only a .22,' said Rencha.

'Something's wrong here!' repeated Bossiere. 'Bastards like that don't use a .22 when they're fighting for their lives.'

'I'll take a crack at them,' said Kepler.

'Be careful . . .'

Rencha's warning was lost in his quick action and the crash of his shot. It was meant for one of the firing slits. The old-time defence was still effective. The bullet whanged away, deflected by the angled slit which had once done the same thing to Bushman arrows.

The shot seemed to provoke the holed-up Bakunins to open up in reply. Chips of stone flew off the wall above their heads as Bossiere, Kepler and Rencha crouched hard against it. The sound effects were dramatic: they were in no real danger so long as they kept their heads down.

When the racket had died down – the echoes seemed to leap from headstone to headstone – Bossiere said, 'What in hell are they doing blowing off all that ammunition? It's not a terrorist technique to allow yourself to be cornered and then shoot it out. They know it is only a matter of time till they are smoked out! We ourselves can keep 'em penned there all night. If they make a break through the hatchway, they're done for. They're playing a deep game. There's something going on here that doesn't meet the eye.'

'Perhaps they're preparing a bomb from those two charges and just keeping us at bay while they do so,' suggested Rencha.

'They've still got to come out finally,' Kepler pointed out.

Bossiere said, 'They've got enough high explosive there to do a hell of a lot of damage. Nine kilograms of SZ charge can bring down a fair-sized building.'

'Or blow the hut to kingdom come. Plus the drum of radwaste,' added Kepler.

'What for?' demanded Bossiere. 'It's only a matter of time before they're finished. We could pin them down all night, summon a helicopter in daylight, lob a grenade or a tear gas canister through the hatchway, and they're done for. They *know* all this!'

Then he said to Kepler, 'It's my turn. I'm going to waste one of my shells. We've got to keep 'em on the hop!'

Bossiere carefully raised his head above the level of the wall. This exposure in itself should have provoked any terrorist worth his salt. There was no reaction. Bossiere took careful aim. It was good shooting. The bullet made a completely different sound from Kepler's earlier ricochet. It went in through a firing slit.

Retaliation was instantaneous. A whole fusillade from two heavy pistols tore chips off the wall above their heads.

Bossiere grinned for the first time that day. 'That's better!'

Rencha's station – at a crouch – was at the corner of the Deelkop wall with another demarcating the side boundary of the graveyard. By peering round the latter she had a half-view of the hut, and at the same time was tolerably safe.

Her urgent hiss stopped Kepler's response to the volley.
'*Look! Look! They're surrendering!*'

'Watch out – it could be a bluff . . .'

Bossiere's warning was lost as the trio got their heads high enough to see what was going on.

A hand waved a white handkerchief above the hatchway.

The hand and signal were an easy shot, silhouetted against the last remnants of the sunset.

'Hold your fire!' snapped Bossiere. 'But give it to him if there's any funny business!'

Kepler almost did, a second later.

The white flag jerked convulsively upward, as if its owner had torn himself free of some restraint inside.

Simultaneously, Maurette's head and shoulders shot into view. His face was contorted with fear.

'Don't shoot . . .!'

He threw himself over the lip of the hatchway at the topmost step of the stone ladder. His violent movement tipped him off-balance. He slid, grabbed, held. His body was spreadeagled between the hatchway and the ladder proper leading down the egg-shaped roof. His feet scrabbled for their next downward foothold.

They never found it.

Ledoux's head and shoulders materialized in the hatchway. He had a pistol in his hand. He doubled over from the waist close to Maurette's squirming body. He wasn't more than a metre away. He took deliberate aim at the head.

'I'll get him!' rasped Bossiere. This was the moment he had saved for the Walther.

Bossiere wasn't fast enough.

Ledoux needed only one shot at that point-blank, skin-singeing range. The heavy slug ripped through Maurette's brain. His body rolled, as if in slow motion, bumping and thumping from stone step to stone step, and landed on the ground with a sickening sound. Its reflexes twitched.

Ledoux's lightning reaction outpaced Bossiere's volley. He was already safe before the first bullets plucked and splintered at the hatchway. Kepler joined in.

Bossiere and Kepler were out in the open now.

'Get down! For pity's sake, get down! You're in full view!' Rencha's shriek penetrated their kill-lust. Both slumped down beside her.

Silence.

There was no retaliation from Ledoux. The only evidence of the past few hectic minutes was Maurette's body at the foot of the hut, grotesquely slumped in a growing pool of blood.

Bossiere licked his dry lips. 'Ledoux must have gone mad! He's cut his chances of survival by fifty per cent by killing Maurette!'

'Why did he do it?' asked Rencha.

Neither man seemed to hear her.

Kepler said, 'I can work round to the other side of the hut by the gate while you stay here,' he suggested to Bossiere. 'Ledoux will then have to face enemy fire on two fronts.'

'No.' Bossiere vetoed the idea. 'It also divides our firepower. There's only one place Ledoux can come out – through the hatchway. We'll get him next time he does.'

They waited.

Five minutes.

Ten minutes.

The hut was as quiet as the graves it overlooked.

The last light struck through the gathering dust pall over-hanging Cheating Pan and died in eerie, macabre gloom among the headstones. There was no living flame any more from the lovers' grave as a point of light in a hopeless world.

Crash!

A single shot rang out from the hut. It sounded different to the three nerve-strung besiegers.

'Inside! It came from *inside*!' Bossiere exclaimed.

That is what made it sound different. The previous shots projected their racket outward from the firing slits; this one was muffled, dampened in addition by the roof cover.

Kepler raised his head above the wall.

'Keep down!' ordered Bossiere. 'More than ever, I don't like it! Ledoux is as cunning as a snake. It could be a trap.'

They waited.

The growing darkness seemed to brake the minutes. Kepler found his gun-hand trembling from nerves – the first time that day.

He said abruptly, 'We can't go on like this – nor can he. I'm going to make a dash. The living flame headstone is the biggest in the graveyard. Plenty of cover. That should draw his fire.'

Before either Rencha or Bossiere could prevent him, Kepler was on his feet, vaulted the wall, sprinted through the gravestones and flung himself behind the lovers' headstone.

There was no response from the hut.

They waited.

Nothing.

It was darker now, but still enough afterglow for Bossiere and Rencha to make out Kepler's hand signal. He was going for the lower section of the hut itself!

His break from headstone to hut should have given Ledoux the chance to gun him down, although he would have paid the price from Bossiere, who now waited in full view with his Walther aimed on the hatchway.

Nothing happened.

Kepler found himself standing amongst the spades and graveside rubbish. There appeared to be nothing else there – except that immediately above his head lurked a diabolical killer with nine kilograms of high explosive to hand.

He stood in the doorway – he was out of sight from above in that position by virtue of the sloping roof – and tried to hand-signal his intentions to Bossiere and Rencha. Should he take the ultimate risk and scramble up the stone ladder to the hatchway itself?

'Wait – we're joining you!' Bossiere's return signal was imperative.

First the DST man, then Rencha, made their way across the graveyard at a running crouch to join Kepler.

Bossiere's voice was a whisper. 'Maybe we're a trio of suckers. Maybe he *wants* us here before blowing us all to hell! This place could be a death-trap. Rencha – out to the station wagon – quick!'

He gave her a shove, and she raced through the gate to the vehicle outside and took cover behind it.

Kepler checked the Colt's long magazine. 'There's no future in this, Bossiere! We've got to find out what Ledoux is up to! I'm going up top! Cover me – from the big headstone . . .'

'You're crazy . . .'

But Kepler had already projected himself at the stone steps. Bossiere spurned the headstone's cover. He stood in the open, pistol aimed at the hatchway above Kepler's head. He was so rapt that he did not realize that Rencha had rejoined him.

Kepler went up the stone steps at the double. Immediately below the hatchway's lip, he flung himself flat on his stomach. The Colt preceded his last footholds to the top. Then he froze, hands outstretched like a mountaineer going for an impossible fingerhold. The similarity of his spreadeagled stance with Maurette's crashed home on Rencha. The Bakunin had died like that; his blood wasn't yet dry below the steps . . . What had Kepler heard?

Kepler had heard nothing from inside. He had paused to quieten his own breathing so that Ledoux, in turn, would hear nothing.

He inched upwards. Now, if Ledoux emerged, they would fire straight into one another's faces.

His eyes and upper face edged over the hatchway's lip.

The watchers below saw Kepler's body give a convulsive spasm, like electric shock treatment. His muscles pulled his limbs tighter than his nerves had done.

'What . . .!' Rencha didn't recognize her own whisper.

Then Kepler's body and head pulled back into an upright position; he eased on to his hunkers on the topmost step.

'You'd better come up,' he called tightly.

They went.

So you eluded Bossiere's revenge at the end, Ledoux.

He lay on the wooden stretcher which had carried the fuel drum for the living flame. The drum itself had been shoved to one side. The top of his head was blown away. He had put the barrel in his mouth and pulled the trigger. That single shot.

That would have been suicide: this was Bakunin death ritual.

It was the ultimate for the Bakunin who has failed and has been identified. The French terrorists inherited the iron code from their soul-mates, the Japanese Red Army, whose roots go back into medieval assassination.

Ledoux had intended it differently.

At his feet was the candle, still stuck in its bottle, and a pair of crossed pistols (one of them Rencha's) at the head. Like chain-mail links of brass, the body was surrounded by scores of rounds of pistol bullets, all nose-up, carefully positioned. It was a twentieth-century death-shroud.

The bizarre ritual was completed by something more sinister.

Encircling the body was a train of SZ powder granules. They had been prised from the smaller SZ-3, whose casing lay discarded in the background. The fuse led to the big SZ-6 at the head.

The intention was clear: in falling after the shot, the body would have convulsively knocked over the candle. It would have toppled into the granules, and fired the train to the high explosive.

Not only high explosive. The hijacked drum of radwaste would have been ruptured by the explosion. The contamination would have lasted for years.

Kepler stood with Rencha, his pistol hanging at his side, his other arm through hers.

Bossiere went forward. Kepler believed he intended to remove the candle. It still guttered menacingly within reach of the fuse.

Instead, Bossiere raised his gun so that it traversed the dead face, empty of everything now except a vicious twist of the lips. Kepler thought he meant to smash it in with a heavy-calibre volley. Rencha came hard against him.

The sigh that came from Bossiere was deeper than his lungs.

'The only thing you were faithful to, Ledoux, was death,' he said.

Fontana Paperbacks: Fiction

Fontana is a leading paperback publisher of both non-fiction, popular and academic, and fiction. Below are some recent fiction titles.

- ☐ THE ROSE STONE Teresa Crane £2.95
- ☐ THE DANCING MEN Duncan Kyle £2.50
- ☐ AN EXCESS OF LOVE Cathy Cash Spellman £3.50
- ☐ THE ANVIL CHORUS Shane Stevens £2.95
- ☐ A SONG TWICE OVER Brenda Jagger £3.50
- ☐ SHELL GAME Douglas Terman £2.95
- ☐ FAMILY TRUTHS Syrell Leahy £2.95
- ☐ ROUGH JUSTICE Jerry Oster £2.50
- ☐ ANOTHER DOOR OPENS Lee Mackenzie £2.25
- ☐ THE MONEY STONES Ian St James £2.95
- ☐ THE BAD AND THE BEAUTIFUL Vera Cowie £2.95
- ☐ RAMAGE'S CHALLENGE Dudley Pope £2.95
- ☐ THE ROAD TO UNDERFALL Mike Jefferies £2.95

You can buy Fontana paperbacks at your local bookshop or newsagent. Or you can order them from Fontana Paperbacks, Cash Sales Department, Box 29, Douglas, Isle of Man. Please send a cheque, postal or money order (not currency) worth the purchase price plus 22p per book for postage (maximum postage required is £3.00 for orders within the UK).

NAME (Block letters) _____

ADDRESS _____

_____

_____